Praise for Joanne Kennedy

"A delightful read full of heart and passion."

—**Jodi Thomas**, *New York Times* and *USA Today* bestselling author, for *Cowboy Fever*

"HOT, HOT, HOT…with more twists and turns than a buckin' bull at a world-class rodeo, lots of sizzlin' sex, and characters so real, you'll swear they live down the road!"

—**Carolyn Brown**, *New York Times* bestselling author, for *Cowboy Fever*

"A refreshing and fun story from the first page to the last. Beautifully done!"

—*Fresh Fiction* for *One Fine Cowboy*

"Realistic and romantic… Kennedy's forte is in making relationships genuine and heartfelt."

—*Booklist* Starred Review for *How to Handle a Cowboy*

"A sassy and sexy wild ride that is more fun than a wild hootenanny! Don't miss it!"

—*The Romance Reviews* for *Tall, Dark and Cowboy*

"Joanne Kennedy creates the kind of cowboys we wish existed. Her heroes are strong, honest, down to earth, and sexy as all get out."

—*New York Journal of Books* for *Cowboy Crazy*

"Kennedy's love of the West shines."

—*Publishers Weekly* for *Cowboy Tough*

Also by Joanne Kennedy

AUTHOR'S NOTE

Dear Reader:

If I dropped you in the middle of nowhere with nothing but fifty dollars, a beat-up muscle car, and an ugly stray dog, would you able to build yourself a new life?

That's what former trophy wife Lacey Bradford has to do when her ex-husband is exposed as a con man. Swearing off his ill-gotten gains, she hits the road, running from the wreckage of her reputation. Hundreds of miles and one hunky cowboy later, she tries to rebuild her life in a world that's as foreign to her as another planet.

I love "fresh start" stories. On long road trips through the vast plains of Wyoming, I study every small town, wondering what I'd do if I had to live there. Could I get a job at that little café? How hard would it be to tend bar at that tumbledown saloon on the edge of town?

But while a house and a job are essential, what really makes a place home is the people. Stopping at diners or coffee shops, I shamelessly eavesdrop on the locals to see where I might fit in and what I'd have to offer.

Of course, it would help to have just one friend to ease the way. That's why Lacey chooses Grady, Wyoming, for her fresh start. She figures her old friend Chase Caldwell will be her safety net—but Chase turns out to be anything but safe. The gangling farm boy who mooned over her in high school is now a smokin' hot cowboy who's not about to let the woman who broke his heart back into his life.

Depending on a man never worked out for Lacey anyway, so she goes to work building a life of her own. She learns a lot along the way, and finds happiness in her new independence—until her past catches up to her. She's in real danger, and has to turn to Chase—but can he forgive her for breaking his heart? And can she trust a man who pushed her away when she needed him most?

I'm always happy with a book when I find myself missing the characters after it's done, and I sometimes catch myself wondering what Chase and Lacey are doing now. Hopefully they'll become your friends, too.

I love to hear from readers! Please stop by my lively Facebook page at Joanne Kennedy Books, or drop by my website, joannekennedybooks.com, to tell me about your own life and share in my adventures on the wild edge of Wyoming.

Joanne Kennedy
Stillwater
December 2019

Tall, Dark and Cowboy

JOANNE KENNEDY

sourcebooks
casablanca

Published by Sourcebooks, Casablanca, an imprint of Sourcebooks
P.O. Box 4410, Naperville, Illinois 60567-4410
(630) 961-3900
sourcebooks.com

Originally published as *Tall, Dark and Cowboy* in 2011 in The United States
of America by Sourcebooks Casablanca, an imprint of Sourcebooks.

Printed and bound in Canada.
MBP 10 9 8 7 6 5 4 3 2 1

To my sister
Carolyn Smyth,
who taught me how to read, how to write,
and how to live a life filled with books
and art and beauty.
Thanks, Kezia!

CHAPTER 1

THE HIGHER YOU FLY, THE HARDER YOU FALL—AND THE harder reality smacks you in the butt when you land. Lacey Bradford learned that lesson for the first time in high school, when the cheer team fumbled the catch after flinging her in the air. Hair flying, pom-poms aflutter, she'd struck the grassy sidelines with a bone-rattling thump.

This time her fall was figurative, but it hurt just as much. Standing on the cracked macadam of a gas station in Nebraska, fishing in her purse for the last remnants of her gas money, it was hard to believe she'd gone from trophy wife to transient in one short month.

"Hey. That your dog?"

She turned to see a teenager lounging beside the minimart's smudged glass door with a cigarette dangling from one hand. His hair was overlong and greasy, his jeans streaked with what appeared to be automotive grease and Cheez Doodle dust.

"Better take it if it is." He flicked his butt into a puddle on the asphalt that was so glossy with oil, Lacey half expected it to burst into flames. "Boss said I should get rid of it."

He nodded toward a dog standing next to the dumpster. It looked like a rat or maybe a badger. Did they have those in Wyoming? They had all kinds of weird animals. Lacey had seen a pronghorn antelope a few miles back that looked like a cross between a deer and a prehistoric donkey.

"What do you mean, get rid of it?"

The boy shrugged and looked away as the dog collapsed and rested its whiskered chin in the dirt, sighing as if resigned to its fate. Its body was small, not much bigger than a cat's, and its head was far too big for its body. A massively plumed tail flailed above its scrawny hind end.

Hell, if she looked like that, she'd crawl behind the dumpster and die.

Wait a minute. She *did* look kind of like that. Her formerly silky hair was frizzed by the heat, and her once-creamy complexion was spattered with freckles. But she was proud of the way she looked. She was a real person now—not somebody's china doll. She'd earned her freckles, and she'd wear them with pride.

"Can't you just call the shelter?" she asked.

The kid looked at her blankly.

"You know. Animal Control?"

"Yeah, right." He jutted his thumb toward the west. "Closest town's Grady, and they ain't even got people control." He kicked the butt out of the puddle and ground it under his heel, eyeing the dog speculatively. "I'll just, you know, get rid of it."

He bent his knees and pointed at her. For a second she thought he was going to do some weird John Travolta disco move, but then he swiveled toward the dog, sighted down his finger, and twitched his thumb.

"Bang," he said.

Dang. She was headed to Grady, but it was almost an hour away. If the animal rode in the car for that long, it would probably infest the upholstery with mites or fleas or something.

The kid blew on the tip of his finger and shoved his hand

in his pocket. She stared at him a moment, then patted her thigh and started toward her car.

"Come on, pup-dog. We're going to Grady."

A half hour later, she heard a disgruntled rumble from the backseat and checked the rearview mirror. The dog appeared to be sleeping. Or maybe he was dead—but judging from the sounds emanating from his belly, his innards were still very much alive. He sounded even worse than the car, which had frequent fits of automotive rheumatism that made it putt-putt along with all the speed and power of a Toro lawn mower. Taking the old Mustang she'd driven in high school on her road trip had seemed like a good idea—after all, it was *her* car, her own, not her ex-husband's—but maybe doing a little maintenance on it over the years would have been smart. A trip down memory lane should have been a smooth ride, but I-80 was an automotive ordeal pitted with potholes and scattered with stones, and the car's lurching and coughing didn't help.

The dog's stomach rumbled again. *Better pull over. Don't want to take any chances.*

Yeah, right. She steered the car to the shoulder and slid to a stop, kicking up gravel with a barely controlled skid. She was taking one heck of a chance with this whole trip. Her resolution to swear off the ill-gotten gains her husband had reaped from his real estate scams had seemed noble at first. She'd told herself she was turning over a new leaf, turning her back on the past.

But the past kept popping up like a persistent Whack-A-Mole. When she'd hit the job-hunting trail back in Conway, she discovered she'd become an overnight pariah. Nobody would hire the ex-wife of the man who'd cheated half the town. Then Wade Simpson had turned up, looking for her husband, making vague threats that made her uncomfortably aware that she was alone and unprotected.

Her gut had told her to leave, and for once in her life, she'd listened.

As her hometown had fallen behind her, a spirit of adventure had taken over and she'd felt footloose—free, like a kid running away from home. Running felt as good as it did back when she was a little girl on the playground playing kick the can or tag.

Unfortunately, she was "it" this time. But at least she wasn't the can, and she wasn't going to let anyone kick her around.

She was just going to keep on running.

Letting the dog out of the car, she watched him lift his leg on a tuft of grass that had pushed its way through the gravel by the side of the road. The pup angled his hind leg impossibly high, almost tipping over in his determination to mark his newfound territory.

"Don't get too excited," she said. "It's not yours just because you peed on it."

His brown eyes regarded her with an accusatory, bitter gaze, as if it was her fault someone had dumped him at a gas station in the middle of nowhere. His sparse, spiky hair and bushy eyebrows gave him the air of an angry and slightly insane senior citizen, but she was glad she'd taken him with her. He made her laugh, and laughing made her feel like something inside her had given way and released the real Lacey from the stiff little Stepford wife she'd been.

"Come on, Sinclair." Sinclair was the name of the gas station where she'd found him. The symbol for the place was a dinosaur—a friendly, green brontosaurus. Even if it had been a Tyrannosaurus Rex, it would have exuded more warm fuzzies than the dog.

Naming the dog was a mistake. Naming him made him hers. But why shouldn't she have a dog? She didn't have anything else. She gripped the steering wheel and jutted her chin, glancing up in the rearview mirror to see if she'd nailed her I'll-never-be-hungry-again Scarlett O'Hara impression. With her dark hair and pale skin, her green eyes and sharp, determined little chin, she'd always identified with the feisty heroine of *Gone with the Wind*, and she'd lived her life by the philosophy of WWSD: What Would Scarlett Do?

Scarlett wouldn't worry. She wouldn't torture herself thinking up worst-case scenarios. She'd say "fiddle-dee-dee" and think about it tomorrow.

But the freckles weren't helping the impersonation any. Neither was the trembling of her chin.

Scarlett had never been this scared.

Finally, the cornfields petered out and the town of Grady appeared in the twilit distance, a glittering oasis on the endless plains. Somewhere in that lonely nest of lights was Chase Caldwell: old friend and admirer and hopefully her new knight in shining armor. She hated to ask a man for help so soon after she'd set out to be self-reliant, but there was a good chance she wouldn't have to ask Chase for anything. Back in high school, he'd do anything just for a smile and a wink. Hopefully, he still would—because a smile and a wink were about all she had to offer. A smile, a wink, and a really ugly dog.

She slowed to the posted thirty miles per hour and poked down a shoddy small-town main street lined with tortured trees and crumbling brick storefronts. It looked like a town from a creepy movie—maybe the one about that serial killer with the weird haircut, or the one where Angelina Jolie's little boy was abducted. But it was exactly what she was looking for: a remote outpost where no one would ever look for her.

And actually, the old brick-fronted buildings had promise. The town could be quaint, if some energetic real estate agent marketed it right. She pictured the street lined with gift shops, maybe a sporting goods store, and a good breakfast place. There seemed to be lots of pickups with gun racks on the highway, and every town needed a breakfast mecca. That was the kind of thing that made a hometown into a home—a place people cared about.

That's what she'd wanted to do back home. She'd planned to get her license and partner with her ex in his real estate office, but she hadn't planned to join him in chopping up the surrounding farmland into cookie-cutter developments. She wanted to match homes with families, find spaces for small businesses that could help the town grow. But somehow the years had passed, and she'd never gotten past the receptionist's desk where she'd worked since high school.

Trent had always agreed she should get her license, but then he needed her in the office, he needed a special dinner for a client, he needed her home. That's why it had been so hard to walk away from the marriage: he'd ended up being the only person in the world who needed her.

The buildings dropped off at the end of town, giving way to a more modest structure that crouched below a lighted yellow sign that spun slowly above a dirt parking lot.

Chase Caldwell Used Cars: Guaranteed Dependable.

Used cars? Lacey slapped on her turn signal and swung into the lot.

She hadn't expected Chase to be a used car dealer, and she knew better than to depend on anyone other than herself, but after the last few disastrous days, a guarantee—on a car, a man, or life in general—sounded like a sanctuary.

Navigating a motley row of pickups interspersed with rusting farm equipment, she pulled to a stop in front of a lopsided trailer with a battered cardboard "open" sign baking in the sunlit window.

"We're going to stop here and talk to somebody," she told the dog. He lifted his head, and the glow from the revolving sign highlighted the snaggletooth that jutted from his undershot jaw. He peered down his nose at her like an old man with bifocals.

"Don't give me that look. I didn't know he sold used cars."

She'd expected to find Chase Caldwell tilling fields, not hawking cars. Back in high school, her friends had fallen into four classes: jocks, geeks, stoners, and hicks. Chase was the head of the hicks—two-term president of the Future Farmers of America and a champion breeder of goats, sheep, and every other breed of livestock sanctioned by the 4-H Club. He'd looked like a budding Mr. Green Jeans in his button-down shirts and string ties.

She smiled, remembering his unabashed enthusiasm

for his chosen career. He'd been immune to the total lack of cool connected with the farming profession, and when his nanny goat won grand champion at the Tennessee State Fair, he'd distributed wallet-size photos of the slit-eyed, pink-nosed Princess to all his friends in sixth grade. She winced, remembering how mercilessly the kids had teased him about his new girlfriend. She hadn't joined in, but she hadn't done anything to stop it either.

That sin of omission hadn't done a thing to kill his crush on her, though. His devotion had never wavered, surviving from sixth grade all through high school. The kid had been like a golden retriever—sweet, faithful, and eager to please.

Golden retrievers never changed. Hopefully boys like Chase didn't either.

CHAPTER 2

A WOMAN APPROACHED THE MUSTANG, TEETERING ON heels that rivaled Lacey's own for sheer impracticality. They looked reasonably professional, though—black pumps, simple and classic. The matching suit seemed almost prim until you noticed how the nipped-in waist emphasized the woman's figure and the lapels plunged an inch or two too low, exposing a shiny bauble hanging from her neck on a thin gold chain. Judging from the way the fabric clung to her tiny heinie, it had to be some kind of cheap polyester blend.

Quit being a snob. Lacey cranked down her window. *Without Trent's money, you can't afford anything better. You've got hand-crank windows, for God's sake.*

She looked down at her sporty Steve Maddens, scuffed almost beyond recognition. She wasn't sorry to leave her old life behind, but she was going to miss high-end footwear almost as much as she missed automatic windows.

The woman smiled with a practiced air Lacey recognized—the same trying-too-hard, aren't-I-pretty smile she'd learned as a cheerleader. She felt an instant stab of sympathy. She knew just what the car-lot lady was up against. She probably wanted to use her brains to get ahead too, but it was her body everybody noticed—her body and her smile. If a less attractive woman had worn that suit, it would have looked sleek instead of slutty.

"Are you here to trade this in?" The woman patted the side of the Mustang.

Lacey tightened her lips and shook her head. "Not today."

She wished she could trade it in, because the car was clearly going to die on her. It looked like death, with paint chipping from the hood and a jagged crack that had spread from a rock chip on the windshield, but its appearance wouldn't matter if the alternator hadn't failed in Missouri and the starter in Kansas. The Mustang wasn't just a gas-guzzler; it was a cash-guzzler too. Thanks to the repair bills and the Tennessee attorney general who'd frozen her assets along with her ex-husband's, she barely had enough cash left to pay for a few nights in a motel.

She really *was* depending on Chase Caldwell.

"I'm here to see Chase."

The woman's friendly veneer cracked for a moment, but she pasted the smile back on and nodded toward the trailer.

"He's in there."

The woman spun on one heel and sashayed off across the lot with her tightly clad butt twitching, but the grating sound of high heels on the dirt lot halted as Lacey stepped out of the car. Lacey could feel the woman's hostility burning a hole in her back as she mounted the worn wooden steps that led up to the door of the aluminum-clad trailer that served as the car lot's office.

But there was no way this woman could have a hold on Chase. She was too flashy. If Chase had a girlfriend, she'd be the farm-girl type. And hopefully, she'd be a nice person who wouldn't mind if her guy helped an old friend.

Pausing at the top of the steps, Lacey glanced back at the crumbling brick buildings lining the street. Ancient glass shop windows reflected wavering fun-house renditions of their neighbors across the street, so only the signs that hung over Grady's pitted sidewalk offered clues to their contents. *Pookie's Candles and More*, read a fading oval. *Dollar Mart*, said a cracked white plastic sign in bold red letters. The only places that looked reasonably prosperous were the Quick Lube next door and the café across the street.

She took one last look at the Mustang to make sure the windows were cracked open so Sinclair wouldn't get heat stroke. Opening the door to the trailer, she dug her best cheerleader smile out from under all the baggage she'd accumulated in eight years as a trophy wife.

She aimed the smile at the man behind the counter and faltered, one foot twisting slightly on its high heel.

This couldn't be Chase Caldwell. It must be his partner or something. Chase had big brown eyes and a love-struck, goofy grin. This guy had a beard—along with a simmering, sexy, scorch-your-clothes-off stare that made her feel suddenly naked.

She glanced down to make sure she hadn't forgotten to put her pants on that morning. Nope. She was still wearing her white capris—her favorite pair, tight enough to showcase her gym-toned derriere but still classy. She adjusted the collar of her silk T-shirt, wishing she'd chosen something that showed a little less cleavage.

His eyes dipped to the cleavage in question, and the smile widened. Lacey cleared her throat, feeling her lips tremble along with her knees, and glanced down again to make sure her nipples didn't show through the shirt.

Because her nipples were definitely happy to see this guy.

Who was definitely not Chase Caldwell.

Because this was no farmer. This was a cowboy, tan

and muscular, with sinewy arms exposed by the carelessly rolled-up sleeves of a snap-button shirt and slim-hipped Wranglers suggestively worn white at the thighs and fly. Lacey had never felt the effects of airborne testosterone before, but this guy made her wobble like a Weeble.

His gaze traveled from her cleavage over to one happy nipple, then the other, lingering a moment before it drifted downward on a long, leisurely journey that took in her hips, her thighs, and the tips of her French-manicured toes. His gaze would have been insulting if it hadn't been so appreciative—and so very much appreciated on her end too. Overheated and exhausted from the long road trip, she couldn't help doing a self-congratulatory mental fist pump at the guy's obvious interest.

She let him finish the once-over and met his eyes just in time to see his appreciative assessment harden into shock, then pass through something that looked almost like fear before it froze into a cold, hard glare.

"Lacey Bradford," he said. "Holy…" He pressed his lips together, as if suppressing a curse.

Lacey squeaked. She couldn't help it—it was that much of a jolt to hear Chase's husky Southern drawl coming from this paragon of masculinity. She knew boys matured later than girls, but he hadn't just improved with age; he'd transformed. It was like watching Clark Kent step out of a phone booth in a cape and tights.

"Chase," she said. "Um, hi."

"What the hell are you doing in Wyoming?" he asked.

It was a question that should have been accompanied by a smile, or at least a curious tilt of the head. Instead, Chase scowled when he said it.

Scowls always made Lacey babble. She could feel the urge coming on and was helpless to stop it.

"I need—I need help. Things went—well, *wrong* in Conway. Very wrong."

"Join the crowd," Chase said dryly.

"I got a divorce," Lacey continued. The words were spilling out, and she had the sudden sensation of tumbling down a steep hill, limbs flailing, completely out of control. "Trent was…" She sucked in a deep breath. Trent had told her not to tell anyone anything, but it was all going to come out eventually anyway. Besides, Trent wasn't the boss of her. Not anymore. "He was a liar and a cheat. I couldn't stay married to him once I knew what he'd done, and now everybody hates me and nobody can find him and they're after me."

"They?"

"My ex-husband's business associates."

"What, you've got a bunch of vicious real estate agents on your tail?" Chase's lip quirked up on one side in the first indication Lacey had seen that he might have a sense of humor.

"No. I've got Wade Simpson on my tail."

That got his attention.

"Wade Simpson? The guy who…"

"The guy who cornered me at that party and practically raped me. The guy you rescued me from."

"I always figured Wade would be in jail by now." He turned his attention to a sheaf of papers on the counter, picking them up and straightening the edges.

"He's a cop," she said.

Chase looked surprised, and she couldn't blame him. Wade Simpson had been Conway High's resident juvenile delinquent. His beleaguered parents had been as surprised as anyone when he'd channeled his penchant for violence and bullying into a stint at the police academy and a job patrolling the normally placid streets of Conway.

And she'd been surprised when she discovered Trent was doing business with the guy. She wasn't sure how a small-town cop had amassed enough money to invest in real estate, but Wade had evidently become a player.

"Or at least he's a cop now, but he won't be once Trent testifies," she said. "He was one of Trent's investors, and I guess he was kind of an enforcer, threatening people. He's good at that kind of thing." She looked down at the floor, tracing the edge of a linoleum tile with the toe of her shoe. "You saved me from him once."

"That was a long time ago."

"It was."

"I was a different person then."

She scanned him from his broad shoulders down to the big square belt buckle that guarded his fly. "Yeah. You sure were."

Had she just licked her lips? She couldn't believe she'd licked her lips. She was normally more dignified than that. More subtle.

But the blatant come-on didn't seem to have any effect. He was still eyeing her with undisguised disdain. "So you've been living on dirty money all this time?"

She set her fists on her hips and glared at him. In response, he gave her another once-over, and this time it was downright insulting. When had that sweet boy who'd followed her around like a lost puppy all through school become this bitter, caustic man?

"I've been trying to find a job. Nobody would hire me. It's not fair. I didn't know Trent was a crook."

"You should have."

He was right. Lacey sucked in a deep breath and blew it out, wishing her guilt would go with it. She wasn't responsible for what her husband had done. She hadn't had any idea how he managed to buy so much land cheap from the government. But it was hard to admit that she hadn't known she was living on ill-gotten gains for the past eight years. She might not be evil like Trent, but she'd been stupid. Stupid and naive.

"It was complicated. Trent was bribing people. Getting them to condemn land, so he could buy it cheap. There's a law in Tennessee—it's called eminent domain—where the state can take people's land if they want to build a highway or something."

"I know."

She resisted the urge to scowl back at Chase. He wasn't just mean and sarcastic; he was a know-it-all too. "But then the highway project would get canceled, and Trent would buy the land cheap from the state, and…"

Chase's brown golden retriever eyes looked more like a Rottweiler's now. A mean Rottweiler. She half expected a growl to rise from his throat.

This was not going well.

"He was a crook," she admitted.

"I know," Chase said again. "So that makes you Mrs. Crook, right?"

"Not anymore." She splayed her hands. "Look, I made a mistake. I never loved him. He wasn't—wasn't what I thought he was."

"I could have told you that."

"Well, you should have."

"How could I? You kept the whole thing a secret."

He was right. Her relationship with Trent had been hushed up almost until the day they married. She'd been seventeen when she'd started working weekends in his office, and the twelve-year age difference between them had been more than a challenge; it had been a legal obstacle. Trent could have gone to jail for their relationship. The day they could go public as a couple was only a week before her wedding.

Her eighteenth birthday.

"Look, I married way too young, and I married the wrong guy. He told me he'd do anything for me, told me I could go to school, get my real estate license, study marketing—everything I wanted. And then he turned out to be a liar. A liar and a crook." She looked down at her hands twisting in front of her and remembered how the realization had crept up on her, darkening her future like vines covering a bright window. "But lots of girls make bad decisions. It's not like I did drugs or anything."

She angled her gaze up to his face, biting her lip. Chase had probably never made a bad decision in his life. He'd pursued his chosen future so single-mindedly that he probably didn't have a clue what it was like to be young and foolish.

"No, but you drank."

"Just that one night."

He would have to bring that up. It had been a week before her wedding, and she'd realized at some point during a graduation celebration that this might be her last carefree high school party. She'd had a few too many drinks—way too many, really—and ended up alone in an empty bedroom with a drunk and determined Wade Simpson. Chase, straight-arrow Chase, had hauled Simpson off her and taken her home. It was a good thing too. She'd been so loopy on sloe gin fizzes she couldn't even remember the drive or how she'd gotten in the house.

She'd relied on him then, and surely she could rely on him now. She just had to make him understand the danger she was in.

"Once Trent testifies, a lot of important people will go to jail," she said.

"Good."

"So they're desperate. And dangerous. Wade came to my house. He...he threatened me."

"What did he say?"

"It's not what he said. It's how he said it."

CHAPTER 3

ON HER LAST NIGHT IN CONWAY, SHE'D WANDERED around the house locking doors and windows and daydreaming about a future without Trent. She'd find a job eventually, she'd told herself. Maybe she'd move to some other town, someplace where nobody knew about her past. And the first thing she'd do, after she found a little apartment somewhere, was buy some comfortable furniture. The house she'd shared with her husband looked like a photo from a decorating magazine, but it had never felt like home. The sofa cushions were hard as military cots, and the wing chairs flanking the fireplace were as straitlaced and erect as the colonial Puritans who'd designed them.

It was too bad her ex hadn't had that kind of backbone.

With his neatly trimmed hair tipped gray at the temples, Trent Bradford had looked the part of an upright elder statesman when they'd first met. Of course, she'd been seventeen and pretty much everybody was "elder." But after her father died, she'd been all alone in the world. And there was her boss, so willing to step in and help. So handsome. So distinguished. So very, very rich.

Sadly, she'd mistaken money for class and a slick salesman for a savior.

She perched on one of the chairs, drained her Sleepytime tea, and set the cup carefully on its matching saucer. The wafer-thin, flowered teacups were one of the few formal features of her leftover life that she still enjoyed. Drinking her bedtime tea felt special when she used them. Ceremonial. Maybe she'd take one along—a souvenir to link the past to her new, independent life.

Maybe she'd make nighttime tea-drinking a ritual—a time to reflect on the day gone by and plan her next adventure. Her old bedtime routines had always centered on her husband. Now she could create new ones of her own. She reached up and flicked off the lamp.

Click.

The formal furniture, the gilt-framed paintings, the oriental carpets—all the trappings of Trent's nouveau wealth—faded into darkness with the flick of the switch.

Tap.

What was that? An echo? She sat up straight and listened.

Tap. Tap.

It must be a branch hitting a window.

Tap.

No, wait. It couldn't be a branch. There were no trees near the house. Actually, there were no trees in their entire suburban development—just a few spindly but hopeful seedlings sprouting from the neat gravel.

So it wasn't a branch. It was somebody at the door.

At midnight? That couldn't be good news. Maybe something had happened to Trent.

Tap.

Maybe it was Trent himself. She'd been trying to get in touch with him for a week, and he wasn't answering his phone. She knew he was probably avoiding people now that he was out on bail. The folks he'd cheated might be out for revenge since his schemes had come to light.

Maybe one of them was at the door. Trent had put on

a pretty convincing show when they were married, making like she was the light of his life. Somebody might think hurting her would hurt him. She'd seen the sideways glances and heard the whispers. Even though she'd divorced him the minute she found out what he'd done, people still blamed her. Hated her. Shunned her.

But no one had ever tried to hurt her. She tamped down the rising panic in her chest.

Tap.

The slow, stealthy tapping was somehow more threatening than a knock. She stood, brushing imaginary crumbs from her thighs, and walked to the front door, her heels clicking sharply on the hardwood floor.

She opened the door to find Wade Simpson on the doorstep, dressed in his policeman's uniform.

Oh, God, something had happened to Trent. Maybe he'd hurt himself, even killed himself. He'd been so upset when the lawyer told him three families were going to prosecute. He hadn't been ashamed or contrite; he'd been afraid of losing his social standing.

He'd been worried about losing his wife too, but she was pretty sure that was just part of the status and power thing. Trent had never loved her; he'd just wanted her for decoration, like the wing chairs and china teacups. He'd seen the way his clients looked at his eager young receptionist, and he was the kind of man who had to have what other people wanted. She was just another gilt-edged treasure for his collection.

Wade stretched his lips in a grin that was as convincing as a cheap Halloween clown mask. "Hello, Lacey."

This wasn't how it was supposed to happen. There

were supposed to be two cops, and they were supposed to take off their hats and look grave and sorrowful. Wade just looked pissed.

"Where is he?" He took her arm as if he wanted to steer her inside. He was a bodybuilder, and she'd always suspected he popped steroids like potato chips. His muscles were pumped up to the point where his head looked absurdly small on his massive body. Veins stood out in his arms, and now there was one pulsing at his temple.

She flinched at his touch and jerked away, but the movement gave him an opening and he stepped further into the foyer, kicking the door closed behind him with a click that echoed like a gunshot. Despite the wide curving staircase and cathedral ceiling, the foyer suddenly felt small and hot.

"Whatsa matter, Lacey?" He stepped closer. "What are you scared of?" He wasn't much taller than her, but he still seemed to loom over her. His arms were bowed at his side, as if the cords of muscle were strung so tight he couldn't straighten them.

"Nothing. I just—when you see a cop at your door…"

"I'm just here to talk to Trent. He moved out of his apartment. I figured he'd come back here."

Her mind raced, trying to figure out where Trent might have gone. He'd been arraigned for fraud and corruption just days ago and released on his own recognizance.

Holy crap. He was probably in Mexico by now.

"He's not here."

Wade's eyes narrowed, his massive forehead creasing. "He must have called you. You must know where he is."

"Honestly," Lacey said. "I have no idea."

Wade began to pace the tiled floor. She could almost smell the barely suppressed rage coursing through him.

"He'd better not have made a deal."

With sudden certainty, Lacey knew that was exactly what Trent had done: turned state's evidence, like some mobster in a bad movie. He'd do anything to save himself, just as he'd done anything to keep the money coming in.

"If he talks, he's going to ruin a lot of lives. It's my job to serve and protect this town. I need to find him before he ruins everything."

Lacey would have laughed if she could have caught a breath, but her heart was fluttering in her chest like a trapped sparrow. Wade didn't care about the town. He cared about himself. If he was worried about Trent talking, it was because he'd been involved in the scheme himself.

"He can't hide from the law," he mumbled, as if he were talking to himself. "I'm the law. Me. I'm the law in this town."

"That's right." She pasted on a perky cheerleader smile to encourage him. It had worked on big, dumb football players, so it ought to work on Wade. She knew he wasn't dumb, but the steroids had probably fried a few synapses and slowed down his thinking. "You'll be able to find him."

"I'm not wasting time looking for him. I'm setting a trap." He stopped his pacing and stood with his arms crossed over his chest, his feet spaced wide apart. "You know, Belle's been worried about you. You oughta come over to see her."

The sudden change of topic threw her off balance. Belle? His wife? Why were they talking about her all of a sudden?

Wade reached over and grabbed Lacey's upper arm before she could dodge away.

"What?" Panic rose in her chest. "Now?"

"Sure. Your divorce and all, you probably need somebody to talk to."

Belle was the one who needed to talk to someone about divorce. Wade's wife was a hesitant, birdlike woman with a tentative manner, and Lacey suspected she spent most of her time fending off her husband's fists. Besides, Lacey knew Belle wasn't home right now. Her sister was sick, and she'd gone to Memphis to take care of her.

"Come on," Wade said. "She'll be real glad to see you."

"No." The refusal came out louder than Lacey intended, but her tone actually made Wade take a step back. "It's *midnight*, Wade. Why would I visit now?"

"Because I told you to."

"Maybe tomorrow…"

"Look, I been hunting for your no-good ex all day, all night. You need to tell me where he is *now*. Otherwise you're coming with me." He grabbed her arm and tugged her toward him. She tried not to breathe in the man's scent. It was a sickening mix of animal and chemical, as if one of the dead frogs they'd dissected in biology class had come to life and started hanging out in the boy's locker room.

"Wade, I don't know where he is."

"Well, once he finds out you're not home, he'll come looking for you. And he'll have to come straight to me."

He leaned over to open the door, and she managed to shrug herself out of his grasp.

"Wait." Her mind scrambled for excuses. "I think I know where he is, but it'll take me a couple days to get hold of him."

She had no idea where Trent was. None. But somehow, she had to get rid of Wade. He looked her in the eyes as if scanning her for lies, and she did her best to hold a steady gaze.

He blinked expressionless, reptilian eyes. "Okay. But I like to clear my to-do list as fast as I can, so if you don't get this done, I'll be back on Saturday."

Saturday. Lacey's stomach clenched again. That was two days away.

"I'm not the only one looking for him, Lacey. I had a meeting with Bart Cross." Bart was a lawyer and a legislator—Conway, Tennessee's version of the powers that be. "Sue Parker and Dominic Huntley were there, too, and Steve Carpenter."

Wade had just listed half the Conway City Council and the chief of police. The implication was clear: she had no one to turn to.

"They all have a lot to lose," he said. "We need to find him."

"Sure." She nodded and pasted on a smile. "Me too. I'll call you when I get hold of him."

"You'd better."

He grabbed her biceps, his hands trembling as he pulled her close. She could smell his breath, a mixture of bad teeth, whiskey, and nacho cheese.

"Don't you try to fool me, Lacey. You run, I'll find you. I have the law on my side." He shook her, making her teeth rattle and her head bobble on her neck. "I'll find you. I'll use all the resources of the police department. I'll report you missing, and I'll track you down." He shoved her away, flashing one last threatening look over his shoulder as she stumbled to catch her balance. "I'm not giving you until Saturday. I'll be back tomorrow."

"Wh—what time?"

"Bright and early." He looked her up and down, and the way he smiled made her skin crawl. "Maybe I oughta just stay."

"No."

He narrowed his eyes and took a step toward her.

"I have to, um, call some people. They'll know if there's someone else here." She glanced from one window to another and lowered her voice to a whisper. "*They might be watching now.*"

"They?" Wade looked a little uncertain.

"*Witness Protection.*"

Wade's face flushed purple and his hands closed into fists. "That bastard. That son of a bitch. He's going to ruin everything."

"I won't let him, Wade." She tried to sound soothing as she opened the door. "I'll take care of it."

He pointed at her, then shook his finger in her face. "You'd better. Because if he talks, you pay. *You pay.* Be sure and tell him that. I'm not the only one involved in this."

As she shut the door behind him, she told herself she didn't care who was involved—the city council, or the entire House of Representatives. Hell, she didn't care if the president of the United States was involved.

All she knew was that she didn't want to spend one moment in a confined space with Wade.

———————————

"Hello?"

Lacey jerked out of her memories to see a very pissed-off cowboy watching her from behind the counter. When Trent was mad at her, he went cold. Chase's anger was hot.

Pretty much everything about him was hot. She could feel his gaze burning through her clothes. Maybe if she flirted more...

Darn it, she always fell back on flirting. She wasn't proud of that skill, but it was all she had. She'd hadn't worked outside the confines of his real estate office a day in her life, unless you called party planning for charity fund-raisers a job. At the office, all she did was answer the phone. Trent never let her handle paperwork—and now she knew why.

So her only experience was as prom queen, head cheerleader, and trophy wife. She could flirt, she could do splits, and she could sparkle.

Doing splits didn't seem appropriate right now, so flirting and sparkling would have to do. She tilted her chin down and her eyes up, giving Chase her best Scarlett smile. "I need a place to stay where nobody can find me. Just until I can get my feet under me, find a job. Just for a while."

His gaze met hers for a moment, then flicked away. "Why me?"

"You're the only person I know who doesn't live in Conway."

"So you don't want me. You want Grady." His eyes were hard again—hard and cold.

"No, it's not just that." Her voice rose in pitch along with her desperation. "We were close, kind of, you know? And you were always a nice guy, and I need..."

"A favor?" He thumped his palms on the counter and leaned forward.

She'd forgotten what a big guy he was. He'd...filled out, and the muscles looked real—lean, not swollen like Wade's. He must work out. He was resting on his hands, making the ropy muscles between his shoulders and neck stand out and his biceps bulge. His pecs were nice too, she could tell, even under that loose cotton shirt, because it didn't just hang there, it...

He scowled, and she snapped out of her lust-induced trance.

"You came here to ask *me* for a favor?"

This was not going well. She might as well go for broke and get it over with.

"Well, not exactly. Not really." She sucked in a bracing breath of air conditioning and set the babble machine loose again. "I just need a little help." She glanced around the trailer. "I could work for you, maybe. Help out. And—and the car's about to die on me, so please don't say no."

He shot her a hard, cold look that hit her like a blow to the gut. Her breath stalled in her throat, and she put her fist to her suddenly constricted chest, pulling in a hard-won breath. She'd always been an expert at sugarcoating reality, but in the past month she'd had to face a lot of uncomfortable truths.

And now she had to face the fact that the one man she'd figured she could count on obviously didn't give a damn.

Panic attack. She stared down at the spinning floor, trying to urge some oxygen to her brain, trying to control the fear that bound her chest like a boa constrictor, squeezing out breath and life and logic. She put one hand on the counter and concentrated on inhaling and exhaling, one breath at a time.

You're okay, she told herself. *You're going to be fine. Just fine.*

CHAPTER 4

CHASE SCOWLED, STOKING HIS ANGER AND STIFLING ALL his other responses to Lacey Bradford. His first reaction had been the same as any man's would have been. When a woman like Lacey walked into your office and presented you with a smile that knocked your socks off and damn near took your trousers too, you enjoyed the experience. Savored it, even. He'd spent a very stimulating thirty seconds taking in every detail of the new arrival's appearance, from the sassy flip of her chestnut hair to the sweet pink piggies in her peep-toe shoes.

Then he'd noticed those odd, distinctive eyes—eyes that were almost eerie in their intensity, with pale flecks like floating shards of ice breaking a clear sea of green. The cool hue warred with the warmth of her smile, her long black lashes intensifying the effect. Only one person in the world had eyes like that.

Lacey. A quick surge of joy had lifted in his heart, sudden and erratic as a meadowlark flitting up from a fence post, but he'd downed it with one quick shot of realism, reminding himself just who this woman was. Who she'd *chosen* to be.

She wasn't the girl next door anymore. She wasn't the kind, sweet girl who never let her beauty go to her head, who acted like she was just another teenaged girl and not a goddess who had fallen to earth to boost the testosterone levels of teenaged boys.

She was Mrs. Trent Bradford, country club wife of Conway's most successful—and dishonest—real estate developer.

No, she isn't. She got a divorce. And then she came to you for help.

But what the hell could he do for her that her ex-husband couldn't? Trent Bradford had the power to make and break lives, and he was more than willing to wield that power. His ex couldn't possibly need help from a scruffy Tennessee farm boy turned cowboy who had to sell used trucks and tractors to supplement the income from his struggling ranch. A Tennessee farm boy without a Tennessee farm— thanks to Trent Bradford.

Chase knew all about the scheme Lacey had described. It was the reason his father had lost his land.

He remembered the day he left for basic training in Texas. His dad had told him some developer was after him to sell the place. The guy wanted to chop it into little bitty pieces and put in a trailer court.

No way, his father had said. *This place belonged to my grandfather, and when I'm gone, it'll belong to you.* He'd laughed and slapped Chase on the shoulder. *Don't worry, son, it'll be here waiting for you when you get back.*

But Trent's scheme was dizzyingly effective. While Chase was off serving his country, the government claimed eminent domain. They said they'd paid a fair price for the land, but there was no price that could pay for what Chase had lost. The farm had been his birthright. More importantly, it had been his father's life.

After the sale, his dad had tried to start over. He'd taken a job at the John Deere dealership in Conway, selling everything from combines to lawn tractors. But the shift from long, orderly days tilling crops and raising livestock to the frantic day-to-day desperation of commission sales took its toll. According to his sister, his dad had slowly faded, lapsing into a depression so gradually that she didn't realize how bad it had gotten until it was too late.

The supposedly essential turnpike that was going to cut through their old farm was canceled days before he died in the newly abandoned barn that was once the center of his life. One gunshot to the head. The cops said it was self-inflicted.

Two weeks later, Trent Bradford bought the land for a song. Chase called the cops and begged them to look into his father's death. They refused.

He called one lawyer, then another. Both declared Trent's machinations entirely legal. One told him it was the third time Trent had profited from eminent domain.

Chase had never felt so powerless. Trent Bradford had taken his father's life and his own future, and he couldn't do a damn thing about it.

Glancing outside, he expected to see a Mercedes or maybe a Beemer parked by the trailer. Instead, he saw a familiar red 1985 Mustang with chipped paint on the hood and a crooked headlight that made the car look like it had a headache.

"That's your old car."

Lacey nodded.

"Why are you driving that? Didn't you have a Mercedes or something?"

"A Beemer."

She licked her lips and the quick flick of her tongue sent

another spasm of desire into the danger zone. He stepped closer to the counter to hide the sudden effect it had on his Wranglers.

"But I figured Wade might be looking for it, and the Mustang has been in the garage for years. So I thought it would be safer."

He felt sorry for her for a second, but then she tucked a strand of hair behind her ear. As she lifted her hand, a gold ring bearing a stone the size of a quail egg flashed, sending shards of reflected light dancing over the cheap paneling behind the lobby's white resin chairs. That ring must have cost dang near as much as his father's funeral. And she probably had three more just like it.

If she'd asked for less, he might have helped her. If she'd wanted her car fixed, for example, he'd have been glad to crawl under her chassis and twist a few screws.

He swallowed. How could the notion of fixing her car so quickly turn his thoughts to sex? That first moment when she'd walked in the door had sent pleasure rippling through him like wind through a field of wheat. He hadn't been able to take his eyes off that lush body, still toned and athletic as it had been in high school. She'd led the cheers at every football game, leaping high, spinning and twirling, her compact, athletic body so taut and strong, he couldn't take his eyes off her. He wondered if she could still do a split.

He looked her up and down, his eyes chasing the curves that led from her breasts to her buttocks. She needed a place to stay, right? Maybe he should take her home. Help her out. Help himself.

Then he looked at that ring and remembered all he'd lost—and all she'd gained.

For the past—what was it? Seven years? Eight?—she'd been living off the profits of the wheeling and dealing that had cost his family so much. Eating bonbons, probably, and lunching at the club. Had the theft of his father's land paid to get those pretty, perfect toes painted? Had it helped her keep her hair perfectly cut, her body toned and firm?

"Sorry," he said. "You came to the wrong guy."

She looked wounded. "But Chase, we were friends. I thought…"

"Well, you thought wrong."

She blinked up at him, and he felt something inside him soften. Damn. He needed to end this. Scare her away so she'd never come back. One more blink of those sea-green eyes and he'd tumble into the same bottomless abyss of heartbreak he'd fallen into when she got married. He'd do something stupid, like help her. Or fall in love with her.

He'd done both a long time ago. Graduation night, she'd celebrated a little too hard by having a lot too much to drink. He'd found her backed against the wall in an empty bedroom with Wade breathing hot whiskey breath in her face and pawing at her skirt.

Chase had rescued her and taken her home, but that had been the end of his heroics. He wasn't sure any man could have fought the temptation of having her alone in the car in the dark, her eyes bright with promise, her breath sweet with the scent of sloe gin.

Still, he never would have kissed her if she hadn't seemed to want it as much as he did. She'd hesitated when he pulled the car to a stop outside her father's house, glanced at him from under her eyelashes, and smiled that smile. He was pretty sure they'd shared equal responsibility for their one heart-stopping, smoldering kiss.

But they obviously hadn't shared an equal assessment of what the kiss meant.

For him, it was a turning point. He'd graduated from high school just three days earlier, and with that kiss he thought he'd graduated from dreams to reality. Lacey was his. He was stunned, surprised, gobsmacked to hell and back, but he was certain that kiss had sealed them together forever. He'd driven home planning their next date. Their engagement. Their wedding.

She'd gone inside, fallen into bed, and apparently forgotten all about it. He wondered if she remembered even now.

Probably not. The next day, the announcement of her engagement to Trent Bradford had appeared in the paper. She hadn't just been saying good-bye to high school that night; she'd been kissing her old life good-bye. That's what she'd been doing with him too—kissing him good-bye.

To her, that kiss had been the end of something—but to him, it was a new beginning, an introduction to adulthood's inevitable cycle of hope and heartbreak. Years later, when he lost the farm, he'd been better able to deal with the pain because he'd already had to deal with the kind of loss that changed your life.

"Please, Chase."

Please. How could he say no to that?

Easy. He chased away the memory of that kiss and called up an image that had haunted him for years: the image of his father's face, gray and sightless in his coffin.

He knew he should be over his family tragedy. It had

been six years. How long could you hang on to that kind of anger before it turned you bitter?

But how could you get over the discovery that everything you had was gone? The realization that the future you'd taken for granted had disappeared? And even if you could recover from that, how could you forget the day your father died? Or the way he died, so despondent he took his own life?

You couldn't get over that. And even if you could, you shouldn't. Not unless you were heartless.

Despite the grim memories, he couldn't stop his eyes from flicking involuntarily from her pleading eyes to her tempting breasts. Why was it so hard to say no to her? If she flashed him that come-hither look one more time, he was going to break down and give her anything she wanted.

He focused carefully on her left ear—though even that made him want to put his finger out and trace the perfect pink spiral that reminded him of the curved heart of a seashell.

"Forget it, Lacey." He barely recognized his own voice, bitter and hard. "I'm not some tenth grade loser, panting after your perky little cheerleader ass anymore." He shifted his gaze to meet her eyes. "Go sell yourself to somebody else."

Lurching out from behind the counter, he strode into his office and slammed the door. Throwing himself into his rolling desk chair, he let it slide backward and bang the wall. His heart was thumping like a Memphis blues band, and all the blood in his body seemed to have flowed south. What he'd said was true. He wasn't a tenth grader panting after her perky little ass anymore.

He was a grown man panting after her ass.

He couldn't believe he'd been so cruel. It had been a reflex—pure self-defense, because seeing Lacey had brought back the fantasy that had haunted him since high school. He'd had a sudden urge to step up to her and cup his hands under that firm, rounded ass, lift her up onto the counter, and flip up her little cheerleader skirt to reveal the panties that flashed the crowd every time she did a high kick. Then he'd…

Then he'd get back to reality and finish his paperwork. Lacey wasn't wearing her cheerleader uniform; she was dressed like a typical lady who lunched in those stupid pants women wore that didn't even reach their ankles. And she was what—almost thirty now? She probably couldn't even do a high kick any more.

Hey, he should check.

No, he shouldn't. He should hide in the office until she left. If he saw her again, he'd break down and help her. If he helped her, he'd be involved with her—and by extension, he'd be involved with Trent Bradford. He'd lost to the guy twice now—once when Lacey had married the guy, and once when he'd lost the farm. He wasn't about to let it happen again. Slumping forward, he rested his elbows on his knees and raked his fingers through his hair.

He almost had his life in order. He'd recovered financially and found himself again, buying a played-out piece of land out here in Wyoming and using his ag know-how to bring the range grasses back to life. Now he grazed almost a hundred cattle on the place—not ordinary cattle, but purebred Black Angus that produced more double-A prime steaks per pound than any other breed.

He was making a new start, getting back on his feet. He didn't need Lacey Bradford to come along and knock them out from under him again.

CHAPTER 5

LACEY STARED AT THE DOOR TO CHASE'S OFFICE, TRYING to figure out what had just happened. It was hard to believe that the nicest guy she'd ever known had just called her a prostitute.

She'd always thought Chase liked her, maybe even loved her, though he'd never said anything. She'd just felt it in the way he'd looked at her. She used to catch him watching her back in high school. If he hadn't been such a nice guy, it would have been creepy.

Well, he wasn't a nice guy anymore. He was a total stranger. The change in his appearance underlined just how long it had been since they'd seen each other, and the change in his personality clinched it. There was no reason for him to remember her—though he obviously did.

Too bad those memories weren't a little fonder.

Had she somehow led him on all those years ago? Had he thought they'd wind up together? She'd always tried to include him in conversations when he'd hovered around her like a fruit fly at the banana bowl. She'd always tried to be nice, even though she hadn't been the least bit interested in harnessing him up with the string of aspiring boyfriends she herded through the halls of her high school every day.

Maybe she should have been.

She caught a quick glimpse of an alternate universe where she'd ended up with Chase instead of Trent. Looking at him now, it wasn't hard to imagine. Trent hadn't exactly made her hormones stand up and salute back when she'd said yes to his proposal or anytime after that. But he'd just about overwhelmed her with declarations of passion and with gifts. Lavish, expensive gifts that shut down the little voice inside her that told her he wasn't what she wanted. Jewelry, clothes—even a car to replace the aging Mustang. When she'd said yes to his proposal, he'd presented her with an engagement ring that sported a diamond almost as big as the cubic zirconia she was wearing now.

And the promises: He'd send her to school. Help her get her license. Use his influence to get her some clients, give her a chance to prove she was more than a pretty face and a bright smile.

She'd always been the town sweetheart, pretty and rich and perky and bright. Everyone had assumed she'd go on to college, be a success. She'd assumed it too—but when her father died, there was nothing left of her family but a mountain of debt.

Trent had stepped in and saved her. Or so she'd thought.

Maybe Chase was right.

Maybe she really had sold herself.

She scanned the office. The place didn't look very prosperous, but it was tidy and clean. The floor was cracked brown linoleum, but it was buffed to a shine, and six white plastic patio chairs flanked each side of a low table in the corner. The table held an assortment of manly magazines—*Field & Stream*, *Guns & Ammo*, and an issue of *Men's Fitness* featuring a shot of a buff, bearded model with a sexy toothpaste smile that reminded her of the man who'd just left the room. She wondered if he looked that good with his shirt off.

Well, she obviously wasn't going to find out.

She stepped back out in the hot sun and surveyed the town from the trailer's warped top step. A huge dog with a shaggy yellow coat slept in the dust of Main Street just outside Pookie's Candles. He looked like he hadn't moved for days. As Lacey watched, a panel van eased around the corner and carefully steered around him, tooting its horn. The dog lifted its head and watched the van disappear down the street, then sighed and settled its chin back onto its paws and closed its eyes. This town had all the energy of a nursing home on an off-night for bingo.

Climbing back into the car, she pulled a haphazardly folded map from the center console. Spreading it on the steering wheel, she scanned her options.

If she drove south, she'd hit Cheyenne in about two hundred miles. But that was a cowboy town, and she'd just had all the cowboy she ever wanted to deal with. Denver would be a hundred miles further on, but it would be worth the extra travel to return to civilization.

Besides, Denver was a big city. She'd find a job in Denver.

She hauled her seat belt over her shoulder like she was strapping on a gun for battle, shoved the key in the ignition, and gave it a twist.

Pop. Bang!

The car had backfired before, but this time it sent up an impressive cloud of black oily smoke from the tailpipe. The engine died, and she cranked it again.

Bang!

The car gasped, coughed, and shuddered to life for one quaking, shivering instant before it died again.

"Shoot." She unstrapped herself and pulled the hood release. Walking to the front of the car, she lifted the hood and propped it open. Then she stared into the engine and willed it to miraculously heal itself.

Chase lifted his head at the sound of a sharp report from the front of the trailer. Good. Krystal must have found somebody to test-drive that old Chevy pickup. The thing always started up like it was on its last legs, but once you got it going, it was a monster. Some people were leery of the fireworks, but Chase figured some amateur mechanic would want it for a project.

And if Krystal got somebody into the truck, they'd probably buy it. The woman could sell snow to Eskimos. He didn't know how she did it.

The explosion sounded again, and he waited for the distinctive growl of the Chevy's engine—but there was nothing. Hoisting himself out of his chair, he left the office, stepped outside and was immediately confronted with Lacey's shapely backside protruding from beneath the hood of her Mustang.

He'd already begun to regret his harsh words, and now he was really sorry. He'd completely underestimated her. It must have been the Mustang that backfired, and now she was going to fix it. He felt a strange stirring at the sight of her bending over the car. There was something about a confident, capable woman taking on a task like that that really turned him on.

It had nothing to do with the way her pants stretched over her ass.

He started to dodge back inside, but she turned and

fixed her wide eyes on his face. She didn't look confident and capable. She looked like she was going to cry.

"It won't start," she said. "It blew up, and now it won't start."

He walked slowly down the steps and peered under the Mustang's lifted hood.

What a mess. A grimy, oily, burned-up, steaming mess. The engine was black and greasy where it should have been clean, and it sported a coat of baked-on, crumbling soot where the grease should have been.

"Somebody didn't take very good care of this thing," he said.

She nodded, her lips pressed together as if she didn't dare speak for fear she'd cry.

"That was me, I guess," she finally said. "I didn't think I'd ever need it."

Yeah, well, he was sensing a pattern here. She hadn't thought she'd ever need him either. The Mustang's neglected engine looked like his heart: a black hole caked with soot and burned beyond recognition.

He glanced under the car and saw just what he'd expected: a spreading pool of oil glossing the hard-packed dirt of the lot.

"It doesn't look good, but Jeb might be able to fix it." He pointed toward the Quick Lube. "He's got a couple of decent mechanics over there."

"Okay." She looked from the car to the garage across the alley, then back at Chase. "Could you help me push it?"

"Just leave it." He shrugged. "Maybe they can get it started long enough to move it."

"Okay. Sorry it's—here. I mean, right in front of your

place." She looked at the beat-up muscle car as if she was seeing it for the first time. "I guess it doesn't look too good."

He had to smile at the understatement, and she smiled back and met his eyes.

Damn. That was just what he'd sworn he wouldn't do. Those green eyes hit his like high beams, and he was sure she could see the lingering traces of the long-running fantasies she'd starred in all these years. She stepped toward him, and for half a second, he thought about touching her, maybe kissing her, making all those fantasies come true. She'd let him, he was sure of it. She needed him.

"How long do you think it'll take them to fix it?" she asked.

"Overnight," he said. "At least overnight."

He was inches away now, and incredibly, she was still smiling, those eyes inviting him closer. She'd have to stay, then. Stay the night in Grady. And from the way she was looking at him, she wouldn't mind staying the night with him.

But it wouldn't mean a thing to her, not like it would to him. She'd walk away when it was over, just like she had before. He took a quick step back, almost falling in his haste to break the tension simmering between them. He had a good life here—a regular, orderly life. Every day went just like he'd planned it. Nobody could take anything away from him—not his land, not his life, and definitely not his heart. He'd learned about loss from Lacey, and he was never going to go through that again.

"Look, Lacey, you have to go." He licked his lips. "My— my fiancée will be back any minute."

"Fiancée?" She looked startled.

He was startled too. He hadn't meant to say that, but now that he'd ventured into a life of lies, he might as well go for it. He leaned on the railing and lied his heart out. "Yeah. She's terrific, but she's the jealous type. So you'd better go."

"Chase, I'm already here," said a high, breathy voice. He watched Krystal appear behind the Mustang like a prairie dog popping from its hole.

He almost smacked a hand to his forehead. Krystal must have been watching him, no doubt seeing Lacey as an attractive interloper and guarding her investment. Ever since he'd hired her, Krystal had spent all her time flaunting her curves and flashing him suggestive smiles. It was obvious that while he was interviewing her for the position of sales associate, she'd been interviewing him for the position of sugar daddy.

He'd apparently passed with flying colors. She'd quit her job at the Quick Lube, broken her engagement to the owner, and set her sights on Chase as clearly as if she'd closed one eye, swiveled, and pointed.

He wondered why the notion of a relationship with Krystal made him want to crawl under the counter and hide until she went away. The girl had the body of a Vegas showgirl and the libido of a lioness, licking her lips every time she looked at him. Sure, any relationship between them would be shallow and meaningless, and the woman was clearly only after him for his money, what little he had—but all his relationships were shallow and meaningless. At least she understood money was all he had to give. He couldn't have given her his heart if he'd wanted to. He'd never gotten it back from Lacey Bradford.

"He's not kidding. I *am* the jealous type." Krystal

narrowed her eyes at Lacey. "If you're after Chase's money, you'd better get out of here. It's mine." She widened her eyes as she realized what she'd said and had the decency to blush. "I mean, *he's* mine. I'm his fiancée." Her voice took on a wondering tone. "He *said* so."

She turned and gave Chase a luminous smile and a perky Sarah Palin wink. "So what do you want for dinner tonight, honey pie?"

CHAPTER 6

LACEY WATCHED KRYSTAL HOOK ONE SLENDER ARM around Chase's waist and rest her headful of big hair on his shoulder. Why hadn't he told her in the first place that he was engaged? She'd have understood. Instead, he'd heaped scorn on her marriage and called her a slut.

Krystal gave Chase a squeeze and looked disappointed when he didn't respond. "He has a little trouble expressing his emotions," she said, simpering.

"Really?" Lacey felt her inner bitch rise. "He doesn't have much trouble with anger, or jealousy, or sheer ornery meanness. I guess it's just the complicated emotions he has trouble with. You know, like caring. Friendship. Charity. That kind of thing."

Krystal looked at her like she didn't know what those words meant either. It was a match made in heaven.

Lacey tossed her keys in the air and caught them. She didn't know where she was going to go or how she was going to get there, but she'd figure it out. One thing was for sure: she wasn't going to waste another ounce of energy on Chase Caldwell.

She opened the Mustang's back door and Sinclair jumped out. Krystal let out a little scream and hopped backward, falling against Chase and making a production out of clinging to him to keep her balance.

"Oh! What *is* that?" She clutched at his arm.

"It's a dog," Lacey said. How would this woman react to

Chase's fixation with animals? Cowboy or not, she had no doubt he still kept a goat or two around the place. She was surprised he didn't have one on a leash at the lot.

Opening the trunk, she hauled out her suitcase. There was a motel across the street. She could stay the night on the money she had left. Get the car fixed somehow. Move on.

Chase made a quick motion toward her as if to help, but Krystal kept a firm grip on his arm.

"I'll be fine." Lacey let the suitcase thump to the ground. "I don't need your help."

She hauled the suitcase across the street, bumping over the pitted blacktop. Like Chase's trailer, the Ranch House Motel was a remnant of the sixties, with a structural simplicity that had probably once passed for clean, modern lines. Now, the peeling turquoise trim and dirt-brown siding just looked cheap. The place wouldn't have rated so much as half a star on TripAdvisor—but then, the town of Grady didn't even rate a dot on the map. Lacey looked up at the marquee sign with its crooked letters. Some of the words had blanks in them, like missing teeth.

"Look, Sinclair. *PETS WE_COME,*" she said. "That's you. And they have a *H_ATED POOL*. Sounds about right."

Sinclair cocked his head and studied her, his eyes serious beneath his beetled brows as they headed for the motel office. She wondered if Chase was watching from across the street and caught herself putting a little extra oomph in her walk. She carefully moderated the swing of her hips. She wasn't here to seduce anybody. Especially not Mr. Cowboy Congeniality at the car lot.

The motel office was small and not terribly clean. A window-mounted air conditioner rattled in one corner, struggling to pump some air into the room but failing to dispel the odor of ancient indoor-outdoor carpeting and stale cigarette smoke. At a counter across from the door, an older man was reading a tattered Louis L'Amour paperback.

"King or two queens?" he asked without looking up.

For a minute she thought he was talking about a poker hand, but then she realized he was asking her what kind of bed she wanted.

"What's cheaper?"

He glanced up at her, and she almost laughed at how much he looked like Sinclair. Unkempt eyebrows almost obscured sharp dark eyes in an angular face, and his black hair looked like a Ronald Reagan toupee. His expression was skeptical and disapproving.

Dang, did this guy think she was a prostitute too?

"It's just me and the dog," she explained, gesturing toward the car. "Either kind of bed will do, but I guess two queens would be nice. We haven't been together long, so I don't want to sleep with him."

He slid a sheet of paper across the counter and slashed an X next to each of three blank lines.

"Sign here and here. Make and model of car here. Credit card?"

She hesitated. She had a credit card—the first one she'd ever had in her own name. But the bills would go to the house, and someone might intercept the mail. Until she had time to change the billing address, she'd have to use her rapidly-dwindling store of cash.

"Cash."

His eyes narrowed and his lips thinned. Yep. He thought she was a prostitute.

"Works for me." He watched silently as she scrawled her signature on the indicated spaces. The rate, $29.99, was noted at the top of the sheet, and she fished the requisite amount of cash out of her purse and slapped it on top of the signed paper.

The old man tossed down a key with an oversized plastic tag.

"Checkout's at eleven," he said. "No exceptions."

"No kidding," Lacey muttered as she turned away. So far, Grady had been less than welcoming. She wondered if all the men in town were grumpy or if it was something she alone inspired.

Cruising home, Chase willed himself to stop replaying the afternoon in his mind. Krystal had spent the entire day batting her lashes and performing an elaborate pantomime that was evidently intended to let him know how excited she was to be his phony fiancée. He'd taken pains to explain slowly and clearly that he'd only pretended they were engaged to get rid of Lacey and that he didn't want a relationship any more than she did. Unfortunately, she took him at his word, and she apparently wanted a relationship badly enough for both of them.

At least he'd managed to evade the "what do you want for dinner" question. What he wanted for dinner was a Hungry-Man meal and a beer. One dinner. One beer. He and Krystal didn't have enough in common to carry on a conversation at the office. He couldn't imagine staring her down across the dinner table.

Besides, he had work to do.

The drive home was blessedly peaceful, and he looked forward to the sanctuary of the ranch. He'd take a little time to enjoy what he'd created out beyond the Grady city limits, do a little landscape appreciation. He'd grown up in Tennessee's rich green grass, but he'd come to love the rugged, rocky landscape of his adopted home. He'd sit out on the back step and sip a beer, savoring the whisper of the wind in the grass and the distant lowing of his cattle.

But as he spun the wheel to turn into the dirt road that led home, the lowing was anything but distant. He slammed on the brakes and fishtailed the pickup's back end to avoid a heifer that stood in the middle of the road, staring at the skidding pickup with mild, curious eyes as if wondering what kind of critter slid sideways like that. Beyond her, about a tenth of his herd was milling around in the road; a few had even crossed it and were yanking up what little grass grew on his neighbor's parched and overgrazed land.

So much for his life of leisure. Fletcher Galt didn't take kindly to having his grass cropped by cattle other than his own. Fletcher Galt didn't take kindly to anything.

He wasn't a kind man.

Chase eased through the herd, jerking the pickup to a stop five hundred feet from the ranch gate where a tangle of downed barbed wire and a path beaten in the grass marked the spot where the herd had breached the fence. A calf lay on her side nearby, moaning more than mooing, her mother watching over her with wary, frightened eyes. Chase was on the ground in seconds, struggling to keep his motions slow and easy.

"It's okay, Lulabelle."

All the heifers were Lulabelle to him, and all the steers were Ernie. He didn't know why; he just had to call them something, and those names seemed to fit.

He talked softly to Lulabelle the umpteenth as he gently examined her wounds. He'd expected to find jagged gashes from the barbed wire; instead, she was pockmarked with wounds clearly inflicted by birdshot.

"Fletcher Galt." The name was satisfyingly explosive, like a swear word—a perfect fit for the man himself. Chase had put up with Galt's insults—the ones the man said to his face and the ones he delivered behind his back in town. He dealt with the man's hostility when they encountered each other at meetings and functions. But there was no need for Galt to take out his resentment on an innocent animal.

Biting back a curse, Chase tilted his face to the sky, taking a ten-count. He clenched his fists once, then released the tension and stroked the calf, soothing her in slow, easy tones.

"S'okay, Lula." He patted her neck. "S'okay, girl."

He wrapped the wire around the post and smacked his hat on his thigh, but the cattle simply turned and stared at him, wearing their usual mournful, uncomprehending expressions. The mother stayed by her baby. She hadn't escaped unscathed herself; a few pellets had grazed her haunch, leaving a bald trail in her thick hide.

Climbing back in the pickup, he headed for the house. He had Jimbo saddled in seconds, and he spun the fresh, feisty quarter horse gelding twice before goading him down the road. The barely contained energy of the horse beneath him and the sound of hooves thudding out an irregular beat was better than that beer he'd been looking forward to anyway.

This was the real Chase Caldwell—the man he was

meant to be. It was like he hung up his life every time he went to town, as surely as he hung his Stetson on the hook by the door. Then he slipped his true self back on when he got home.

He remembered his father's farm—the one cooperative but ancient mutt of a horse he'd had, the few goats and sheep his father had let him keep on an acre of pasture, and the miles and miles of hay and corn he'd had to till and plant and harvest. Losing the farm had led him here, and now he was working from horseback instead of suffocating in a tractor cab. He was better off now, even if he did have to sell cars all day to make it work.

Quashing the thought, he concentrated on the horse. He'd loved his dad. Loved the farm. It had been his life, and thoughts like that were disloyal and wrong.

Once they reached the cattle, Jimbo didn't need much direction. The horse was cow-savvy and quick, dodging from side to side, plunging forward and spinning back to urge the cattle through the break in the fence and steer them back to pasture.

But little Lulabelle still lay on the far side of the road, her mama watching him with wild, white-rimmed eyes. Giving the horse an appreciative pat, Chase swung down from the saddle and knelt beside her. Some of the shot had raked her skin, leaving long scratches he'd need to stitch up; others had lodged in her side and would need to be eased out, the wounds cleaned. He stood up and rifled through his saddlebags, pulling out a vet kit rolled in a strip of canvas and some sterile wipes. He'd learned long ago to do his own veterinary work. Otherwise he'd have gone broke before he'd even gotten started.

He was quick with a syringe, and the calf lay still as he worked, only her rolling eye showing she was still conscious and scared. He tried to make quick work of the sutures, numbing the area with lidocaine and stitching quickly and neatly. He'd just knotted the last thread when she started to wake and struggle to her feet.

She stood a moment, swaying and staring blankly at him, then the road. Her mother let out a mildly hysterical moo that broke into a weird falsetto at the end and the calf swung her head to look at Chase and backed away, almost falling. He stepped toward her and shoved at her shoulder to point her in the right direction, then slapped her flank and watched her trot off with her mother to join the herd.

He watched a while, stroking Jimbo's neck absentmindedly while he made sure the calf was steady on her feet. He hadn't made any money at the car lot today, and an innocent animal had paid for his absence in pain and suffering. If he could find a trustworthy salesperson, he could spend more time at the ranch and keep these things from happening. Krystal sold a lot of cars, but the woman had no moral compass whatsoever. Just the other day, he'd caught her telling one of his neighbors that the battered Oldsmobile Cutlass at the back of the lot was a one-of-a-kind collector car, when really it was a sad survivor of the local demolition derby. And she'd told a local teenager that a Datsun B210 had an eight-cylinder engine. He had a reputation to maintain, and she wasn't helping any.

Swinging up into the saddle, he headed for home as the herd moved away. The heifer seemed to have forgotten all about her ordeal, but the picture of her lying in the grass suffering would stay with Chase a long time.

CHAPTER 7

ONCE JIMBO WAS MUNCHING ON HIS EVENING RATION of hay, Chase climbed back in the pickup and headed down the drive. He turned right onto the county road, drove a few hundred feet, and took a left toward Galt's. He could see the tumbledown barn looming at the end of the drive and an ancient trailer tilting beside it. The two buildings both listed toward the west from a century of prairie wind. Even an old cottonwood in the yard leaned left, its branches reaching toward the hills like a beseeching bride beckoning her groom.

He pulled the truck to a stop at the edge of a turnout that scarred the scant grass of the yard. The old man hadn't bothered to skirt the trailer; it was perched on stacks of cinder blocks, and Chase wondered how long it would be before the prevailing winds pushed it off its makeshift foundation.

He stepped up onto a front porch sloppily hammered together with mismatched two-by-fours and rapped on the door.

"Go home," said a surly voice from within. "Leave me alone."

"No," Chase said to the door. "We need to talk."

"Don't have anything to talk about."

"You're right. We don't." Chase turned the knob and let the door swing open to reveal the tawdry interior of the trailer. The tweedy brown carpet had been designed to hide dirt but still looked hopelessly soiled, and there was hardly any furniture—just an ancient TV set furnished with rabbit ears in one corner and a rocker/recliner upholstered in garish blue velvet positioned with its back to the door. All Chase could see of the occupant was a bald head cresting the back of the chair, with two or three strands of gray hair spanning an expanse of pale, mottled skin.

"We don't have a damn thing to talk about," Chase said. "I'm just here to tell you that if you hurt one of my animals again, I'll come over here and do the same to you."

The bald head turned, revealing a pair of beady eyes set deep over a hawklike nose. "You threatening me?"

"Mr. Galt, you shot my heifer."

"Wasn't trying to. Damn animals broke through the fence, were eating my grass. All I did was shoot in their general direction to scare 'em off. It's my right. Says so in the Constitution."

Chase gritted his teeth. It was all he could do not to lunge into the house and drag the old man out of his chair. He reminded himself that Galt had suffered, that he was barely lucid since the death of his son. That he'd lost everything that mattered to him and let the rest go downhill until he was left with a parched patch of overgrazed, mismanaged rangeland and a bunch of mutt cattle he'd had to sell for pennies on the dollar. He'd been forced to sell half his ranch to Chase, and apparently he lived on social security and dedicated his once robust life to watching game shows and drinking.

But he was lucid enough to go out and take potshots at Chase's cattle when they breached the fence. Chase scanned the kitchen, noting the streaked, stained counters. A dog food dish on the floor overflowed with kibble, but there was no sign of human food. A grubby plastic trash bin was filled with empty beer bottles. Not even Fletcher Galt should have to live like this. Somebody ought to check on him.

Chase would talk to his sister about it. She'd see to it.

"Goddamn out-of-towner," Galt bit his words off hard. Talking to him always made Chase uncomfortably aware of his own slow speech, the drawl that exposed his Southern roots. He *was* an out-of-towner, it was true, but that didn't give the man a right to shoot his livestock. He'd bought half of Galt's ranch fair and square.

The old man eased the chair a quarter-turn toward the door.

"Didn't kill it, did I?"

"Not quite."

Galt was quiet for a while, and Chase thought he'd lost him to Bob Barker's rhapsody over a washer-dryer combo, but then the chair swiveled another quarter turn toward him. The normally hard planes of the old man's face seemed to droop, and the look in his eyes bore a hint of worry behind the hate.

"Was it hurt bad?"

"Pretty bad. You do it again, and I'll call the cops."

"Cops won't arrest me."

"No, but they'll take the gun away."

The creases deepened, and the hard glint came back to the old man's eyes. "I'll shoot 'em first."

Chase drove home, frustration simmering in his gut. He'd headed out angry and he was going home the same way, with nothing resolved and nothing changed. Galt would take any opportunity to avenge what he saw as Chase's unforgivable crime of nurturing the land the old man had planned to pass on to his boy. It wasn't Chase's fault the kid had killed himself in a car wreck, but Fletcher had to blame somebody, and Chase was right next door.

He was just pulling off his boots in the mudroom when he heard the slam of the front door. Padding out to the kitchen, he caught Krystal draping her purse over the back of a kitchen chair and setting a plastic grocery sack on the table.

Shit.

"Hi." She tossed him a perky smile and headed for the sink to wash her hands, making herself right at home. "You didn't say what you wanted for dinner, so I got rib eyes." She narrowed her eyes and smiled like a cat eyeing a hapless sparrow. "I figure real men eat steaks, and you are definitely a real man."

"Krystal, go home," he said. "We're not getting married."

"Oh, I know." She swatted his arm like a teasing kid sister. "But you really ought to think about it." She spread her hands and spun in a sweeping circle to indicate his kitchen, reminding him of the game show hostess on Fletcher Galt's TV. "This place needs a woman."

He didn't see why. The kitchen was tidy and stocked with everything he needed. There weren't a lot of froufrou decorations or anything, but that was the way he liked it.

"I don't need a woman," he said. "Especially not a high-maintenance one that wants to come out here and change everything."

She set her fists on her shapely hips and gazed around the room like she owned it. "I wouldn't change much. I'd put up some curtains, those real cute ones with the ruffles, and maybe paint the walls yellow. Like sunshine." She grabbed two beers out of the fridge, heading for the sliding door off the dining room. "I thought we'd eat on the deck."

The deck. Right. What Krystal called the deck was his back step, a crumbling concrete pad at the back door. Chase had fitted it out with a gas grill and a cheap redwood picnic table so he could cook steak and drink beer out there in the evenings, and ponder the future of the ranch while he watched the herd grazing in the distance.

Krystal set to work covering the perfectly adequate table with a tacky vinyl tablecloth decorated with garish flowers. At least she'd brought him a beer. She didn't seem to notice his abstraction while she settled onto the bench across from him and gabbed, skewering various townspeople and promoting her ideas for his future, which included a glass-walled showroom and a Toyota dealership. He ignored her campaign to turn him from a rancher into a deskbound businessman, and he managed to ignore the way she wiggled to make her breasts bobble while she shifted her butt on the bench. He'd never been to a so called gentleman's club, but he had a feeling Krystal's lap-dancing skills rivaled those of any stripper in the business.

There was apparently no point in telling her he didn't want her there. She'd just pout and ignore him. When she went in to get the steaks, he fired up the grill, then slouched back down against the far side of the picnic table with his back to the house so he could watch dusk settle over the land.

She pranced out of the kitchen bearing a plate of steaks and that same perky smile.

"What's the matter, Chase?"

He took a long draught of his beer and surprised himself by telling her.

"Galt shot one of my cows."

"What?" She seemed appropriately outraged.

"They got through the fence somehow, and he took a shot. Hit a calf. I found her on the way home." He took another gulp of beer and set the bottle down, resting his elbows on the table behind him and stretching out his legs.

"That's *terrible*," she said.

He nodded.

"How much was it worth?"

He ignored the question, staring off across the pasture. "Poor thing suffered all day before I got home and found her."

"And now the meat's probably gone bad. Really, you should make him pay for it."

"The meat?" He stared at her. It took him a minute to realize what she was saying. She wasn't upset that the animal had suffered; she was worried about the money.

"Krystal, the cow's not dead. She's going to be all right."

"Oh. Well, no big deal then, right?"

"I said she suffered all day."

She nodded sagely. "Pain and suffering. He should pay for that, then."

He stared off across the pasture, resisting the urge to argue. Nobody ever got anywhere arguing with Krystal. She was immune to sarcasm, logic, and clear-cut facts. He might as well change the subject. "We didn't sell a single car today."

"I like the way you say 'we.'"

He suddenly had a notion of how the cows felt, hemmed in by barbed wire. No wonder they'd stormed the fence. "Krystal, I told you…"

"I was thinking we might get more business if we stayed open later," she said. "People get off work at five."

"I have to be here." He nodded toward the pasture. "I'm gone too long as it is. I told you, that heifer…"

"I know," she interrupted. "This place is a lot of work for you." She came over and sat beside him. He edged aside to give her space, but she scooted right along with him. "I could work late the next couple of nights. See if I could sell anything to people in the evenings."

He turned to look at her, surprised. Krystal had never done more than the bare minimum of work around the dealership. She'd never volunteered for anything.

"Thanks," he said. "That would really help."

"We're a team."

He shifted away. "Krystal, we're not…"

She didn't give him a chance to finish. "Don't worry. One of these days, it'll get a lot easier." She gave a perky nod. "I figure once we get that Toyota dealership, you won't have to raise cows anymore and you can get a place in town." She hopped up and headed over to the grill to flip the steaks. "Then all you'll have to do is mow the lawn, 'cause I never mind cooking."

If he hadn't already known the two of them didn't have a future, he'd know it now. Giving up his dream would be *moving up* to her. She wasn't the least bit interested in sharing anything but his checkbook. He looked at her spiky manicured fingernails and remembered Lacey's pink-painted toenails.

She was probably the same way.

CHAPTER 8

LACEY PICKED HER WAY OVER THE PITTED SIDEWALK in her high-heeled sandals, lagging behind the suddenly energetic Sinclair as the sky beyond the brick buildings on Main Street blushed pink with morning light. The dog checked out every post and parking meter, sniffing delicately as a wine connoisseur and cocking his leg to mark his progress. She had no idea how a creature so small could hold such a seemingly inexhaustible supply of pee.

"Good boy, Sinclair," she said. "Keep it up. You're going to own this town."

As she passed a dark shop window, Lacey glanced at her reflection. She still looked like the woman who'd left Tennessee five days ago—poised and perfectly coiffed, with fashionable clothes and the mincing walk demanded by her pretty but totally impractical shoes. No one would ever guess the woman in the window had fallen on hard times.

She knew she ought to feel discouraged. Hell, she ought to feel suicidal. She was stuck in the middle of Wyoming with no money, no transportation, and the ugliest dog in the universe. The town was a backwater, with half a dozen boarded-up buildings interspersed with a few mom-and-pop businesses—a discount clothing store, a gift shop, and a Quick Lube oil change garage.

Hopefully she wouldn't be stuck here more than a day. Once the car was fixed, she'd stock up on supplies with the credit card, get a nice cash advance, and move on to a place in Denver she could rent by the week. There would be a lot more job opportunities there, and the whole hiding-in-a-small-town plan was stupid anyway. It would be a lot easier to disappear in a city.

She hummed a few bars of "Footloose" while Sinclair watered a wall, then headed back to the motel, moving a little more efficiently now that the dog had laid claim to most of Main Street.

"You're going to have to stay in the room," she said, unlocking the door. "No barking, okay?" Dumping a cup of kibble onto a paper plate on the floor and hooking the "Do Not Disturb" sign on the doorknob, she trotted down the steps and across the street to the café.

Judging from the homespun ambience and the heavenly scent of bacon, she'd found the town's breakfast mecca. The long, narrow space was simply decorated and very clean, with old-fashioned vinyl booths lined up against the windows and a long, Formica-topped counter. It was empty except for a heavyset waitress in a salmon-colored dress and crisp white apron who greeted Lacey with a smile that lit up her ordinary features into glowing, homespun prettiness.

"Oh my *God*. Lacey *Bradford*." The smile widened, and the woman's eyes gleamed with something that looked suspiciously like tears.

Happy tears.

How did this woman know who she was? And why would anyone be that glad to see her? Lacey did a quick double take, covering her confusion with the all-purpose mask she'd worn at Trent's cocktail parties. The woman swiped at her eyes, and suddenly recognition dawned.

"Pam," Lacey said. "You're Pam Caldwell. Did you come out here with your brother?"

"I came out here a few years earlier," Pam said, still smiling. "After—you know."

Lacey did know. She remembered Pam hunching over her pregnant belly, making her way through the halls of Conway High amid the whispers and sneers of the other students. Lacey had never joined in the general condemnation, but true to form, she'd never done anything to stop it either—and when Pam disappeared from classes a few weeks later, she'd never given the girl a second thought.

"This was my uncle's place. I came out here to work for him and raise Annie. After he died, his wife wanted to move to Florida, so I took over. Then Chase came out and bought the ranch after the farm—after Dad—you know."

A brief flicker of pain crossed Pam's face so quickly Lacey might have imagined it, and then the smile returned.

"You've come to see Chase! That's *so great*. The best thing that could have happened."

"I—no, I'm sorry. I didn't come to see Chase. Not really. I…"

"Sure you didn't." Pam slapped her arm playfully with her stack of menus. "What the heck else would bring you to Grady?"

Lacey opened her mouth and closed it again. She didn't have an answer for that.

Pam rested one hip against the table and pulled an order pad out of the apron pocket. "So have you seen him?"

"Yeah. He's…grown."

Pam laughed. "Yeah, I guess he has. Hasn't changed much, though. Not since—you know."

"Since what?"

"Since the whole thing with you, and your husband, and losing the farm."

"Me? My husband?" Lacey slid into a vinyl-covered booth, glad there was a place right handy to sit before she fell down. "Oh."

No wonder Chase seemed so bitter and angry. She hadn't made the connection before, but it should have been obvious there was a link between her husband's nefarious dealings and the fact that Chase wasn't living out his destiny on the Caldwell farm.

She swallowed, her throat suddenly as dry as the dusty street outside. "I didn't know what Trent was doing. Honestly. I didn't."

"Oh, don't worry about that. Water under the bridge. For me, anyway. Chase might be another story. You talk to him?"

"Sort of."

"Yeah, he's not the forgive-and-forget type." She tightened her lips in disapproval. "He has to blame somebody. Can't just face the fact that shit happens."

"But it shouldn't have happened. My husband was a crook." Something about Pam's frank assessment of the situation loosened Lacey's tongue and made her feel like getting the whole thing off her chest. "I didn't know. Didn't realize..."

"Well, it wasn't you, was it? You were just married to the guy."

"I divorced him."

"Good for you." Pam lifted her fist in a girl-power salute. "Hope you took him to the cleaners."

"I-I guess I did. But I was living in the house, living off his money. I shouldn't. It's dirty money."

"I suspect you earned it."

Lacey thought back to her life with Trent—the long, empty afternoons behind the desk, greeting people, answering the phone. When she was in high school, she'd felt so smart, so official, answering the phone in a clipped, professional tone on weekday evenings and all day Saturday, scheduling appointments and describing properties to potential buyers. She loved real estate. It was a way to help people, find them homes, make their lives complete.

But when she'd wanted to do more, Trent had said no. He wouldn't even let her file papers. She suspected he'd married her because she was so young—and so foolishly dazzled by his wealth that she never asked where it came from. Never asked any questions at all.

"I guess I did earn it. But I still feel guilty about what he did."

"Well, I know how you could pay it back." Pam grinned. "Try and snap my brother out of his funk. All he thinks about is getting back what he lost. Building that ranch of his. The guy needs a life." She gave Lacey a wink. "And a woman."

"He's got a woman."

"Really? That's news to me." She widened her eyes and smacked her forehead with one hand. "Don't tell me it's Krystal."

"Yeah, I guess they're engaged."

Pam gave her an incredulous stare. "Is that what she told you?"

"Nope. *He* told me."

"No way." Pam tapped her pencil on the order pad and

frowned. Lacey could swear there was steam coming out of her ears, and her face was turning red. "It must have been self-defense."

"Self-defense?"

"Against you. He's probably scared to death you'll break his heart again." The smile disappeared. "You won't, will you?"

"I..." Lacey felt color flooding her face. "No. I wouldn't do that. What do you mean, *again*? We were just friends, Pam."

"Not to Chase, you weren't. Are you telling me you didn't know how he felt about you?" Pam set her fists on her hips. "No way."

Lacey scrambled through her repertoire of polite responses for an answer, but Pam wagged the pencil at her like an angry schoolmarm.

"My brother's been in love with you since sixth grade. You didn't know that? He was just waiting to make his move—the dummy. When you got married, he realized maybe he'd waited a little too long."

Lacey opened her mouth, then closed it.

"Okay, you didn't know that."

"No," Lacey said. "I didn't."

A male voice called from the pass-through window behind the counter.

"She want anything, Pam? 'Cause I'm thinking 'bout a break." A man peered through, his face flushed from the heat, his head wrapped in a red bandanna.

Pam flashed an annoyed scowl toward the pass-through.

"I'll have eggs," Lacey said. "Scrambled. And do I smell bacon?"

Pam nodded. "Toast or pancakes?"

"Whole wheat toast. Dry, please."

"Our pancakes are better." Pam winked. "And if you're worried about eating right, just remember—maple syrup comes from a plant. That makes it a vegetable."

"You're right." Pam's good cheer was contagious, and Lacey had no reason to stay model skinny anymore. Trent had liked her that way, but now she didn't have anyone to please but herself.

"So how long are you staying?" Pam asked.

"Just long enough to get my car fixed. Chase said the Quick Lube could do it."

"Good luck with that." Pam grinned. "If you need anything more than an oil change, Jeb'll probably have to order the manual. He's not the brightest bulb, and I don't think he's got much of a mechanic over there since Don Morris graduated and left for college."

"Oh."

"So if you didn't come for Chase, what brought you here?"

Lacey cursed her pale skin, knowing the flush rising up her neck was clearly visible.

"You *did* come for Chase. I knew it."

"No. I mean—I knew he was here, and I thought it would be nice to go somewhere where I knew someone. Do you remember Wade Simpson?"

"Do I ever. That kid was psycho."

"Well, now he's a cop. And he had something to do with Trent's deals, somehow. He was—he was making my life pretty difficult, and then Trent disappeared, and I couldn't get a job because everybody hates me because of what he did. I figured it would be best to just go. Start over some-place fresh."

"God, Lacey, that's awful."

"Not really. It's been kind of—well, fun."

Pam arched a disbelieving eyebrow.

"The traveling, I mean. I feel free."

"Well, feel free to spend some time with my brother."

"That's really not what I came here for."

She was telling the truth. She hadn't planned on starting anything with Chase—she just wanted to know she had a friend wherever she ended up. So why was her face so hot all of a sudden?

"Well, do me a favor," Pam said. "Stick around and save him from Krystal, would you? Sounds like he's made things even worse with that woman. It was bad enough he hired her. She used to work over at the Quick Lube, but Jeb wasn't rich enough for her, so she ditched him and went to work for Chase."

"Chase is rich?" Lacey couldn't hide her skepticism.

"He owns a ranch." Pam snorted. "'Course, that pretty much keeps him poor, since he spends every dime he makes on livestock and improvements." She slid into the opposite side of the booth, sticking her feet under the table and prop-ping them up beside Lacey. They were a working woman's feet, clad in old-fashioned white nursing shoes and slightly swollen around the ankles. "Krystal'll put a stop to that if she can, though. She thinks he should tear down that trailer and build one of those glass-front showrooms. She'll get him to do it too. Just give her time. That girl gets 'em roped and hog-tied in a heartbeat."

"Really?"

"You seen her?" The woman made a gesture indicating big breasts, then gave Lacey a slow smile. "Although you could give her a run for her money."

Lacey looked down at her own fairly modest endowment. She knew she had a good body, but she was hardly as top-heavy as the bodacious Krystal. "What do you mean?"

"You're every bit as pretty as she is, and you've got a lot more class. *And* he's already in love with you." She shoved the pencil behind her ear. "I'd say you've got this game won before you even start."

"Well, thanks. I'm not looking to date him, though. I didn't realize he—we were friends, that's all, and I thought…" She flushed again.

Pam tilted her head like a curious bird. "You telling me nothing ever happened between you two?"

"No. Honest." Lacey had wondered if Chase's rudeness stemmed from something she'd done in high school. Now that she knew he'd had a crush on her and then wound up on the losing end of her husband's high-stakes real estate game, she realized his resentment didn't come from some minor teenaged snub.

No, he flat-out hated her, and he had a good reason. Pam's scheme was doomed before it even started.

Maybe changing the subject would steer the woman's sisterly determination in some other direction.

"So when did your brother turn into a cowboy?" she asked.

"Oh, he's always been into that."

"I thought he was into goats."

Pam waved a dismissive hand. "Goats are a lot cheaper to raise than horses, and frankly, that farm of Dad's wasn't big enough to do what Chase wanted. Land back East is too expensive." She looked thoughtful. "My hardheaded brother never would have sold the damn place and moved out here on his own. What happened gave him a boot in the butt—and he needed that. He's living his dream, but all he can think about is what happened to Dad."

"Losing the farm?"

"That, and Dad—he, um, died right after." She looked down at her lap, momentarily sobered. "Chase blames your husband for that too." She raised a hand to halt Lacey's response. "He shouldn't, I know, but he does. It's easier than blaming himself for not being there to stop the sale. He was in Iraq when it happened. It happened so fast, he probably couldn't have done a thing about it—but Chase sees himself as being responsible for everything, and the guilt's eating him up inside."

"He was in Iraq?" Lacey had no idea Chase had ever deviated from his single-minded ambition to raise quality goats.

"Yeah. You know my brother. Gotta save the world."

"No wonder he seems so different. Did something happen over there?"

"Something happened over *here*. I think his heart's broken. And I think you're the one person who can help him."

Lacey shook her head and slumped her shoulders. "Yeah, right. I've never helped anybody in my life. I wouldn't even know how to start. I'm a trophy wife. The Tennessee version of Paris Hilton." She sighed and waved one hand in a languid Blanche DuBois gesture. "'I have always depended on the kindness of strangers.'"

"Maybe you just haven't had a chance to help anyone." Pam leaned forward, her expression earnest. "This is it— your chance to do good. You ought to go talk to Chase again." The smile returned, dimpling her cheeks. "Plus, you and I could be friends. I always thought you were so pretty and cool."

Lacey looked down at the table. "I wasn't a very nice person. If I was, we would have been friends back then."

"You *were* nice, though." Pam sounded downright defensive, as if Lacey had insulted her best friend. "You were nice to everybody. Half of us girls wanted to hate you, because you were so pretty, but you were sweet." She cocked her head and met Lacey's eyes. "You still are. I can tell."

"Thanks." A rush of gratitude relaxed Lacey's shoulders and cleared her head. It felt good to talk to someone real about real things. Most of her friends back in Tennessee had been "ladies who lunched," and their conversations were endless rounds of one-upmanship revolving around topics like who had dropped the most money at the boutiques in Memphis, whose kid had made the lacrosse team at the local private school, and who had paid the most for a haircut, color, and highlights. Lacey bought most of her clothes online because Trent didn't like her to drive into the city, and for some reason they hadn't had any kids, so those discussions were actually kind of painful. And she was perfectly happy with the reddish glints in her natural brown hair, so hair color was out as a topic of conversation.

But she felt like she could talk to Pam about anything.

"Stick around," Pam said. "You might like it here. And besides, Chase needs you."

Lacey gave her a rueful smile. "He doesn't need me. Not anymore. I needed him."

"And he let you down, didn't he?"

Lacey shrugged. "He's mad. I don't blame him."

"Good." Pam rocked to her feet and shoved the order pad in her pocket as if sheathing her sword. "Then give him another chance."

CHAPTER 9

LACEY TURNED TO THE WINDOW AS PAM HEADED BACK to the kitchen. She watched Chase pace the rows of pickups, polishing a fender here, wiping a windshield there. He was wearing cowboy boots and a pair of beat-up Wranglers that stretched taut over his behind as he shoved the rag in his back pocket and climbed the steps to the trailer. Instead of yesterday's snap-button shirt, he was wearing a light blue T-shirt with a bucking horse kicking up its heels on the back. She squinted. *District Ten Rodeo* read the lettering under the picture.

She'd never been to the rodeo back in Conway. It just wasn't something the cool kids did. Except for confirmed hicks like Chase, everybody she knew back home wanted to shed Tennessee's redneck image and be cosmopolitan. A few people wore cowboy hats, but it was a Nashville thing—an act. She'd always preferred the guys who wore football helmets.

But looking at Chase now, she decided being a cowboy wasn't such a bad thing. She couldn't remember his shoulders being that broad, and the muscles that flexed under his shirt as he opened the trailer door were definitely a new development. She wondered again what he'd look like without that shirt.

I think you could help him, Pam had said.

Yeah, right. She could help him. Help him right out of his clothes.

Oh, Lord. What was happening to her? She'd never been this sex-crazed when she was married. Bedding Trent had been a duty, not a pleasure. He was a good-looking man, but he grunted and closed his eyes once things got underway, absorbed in his own pleasure. He took what he wanted and was so intent on getting it, she suspected it didn't really matter who was naked in his bed so long as she was female and cooperative. The only time he paid attention to Lacey was when he could show her off to someone else.

"Hon?"

Lacey flicked her gaze to Pam, who stood over her with a plate bearing breakfast.

"Sorry. Daydreaming."

Pam gave her a knowing smile as she set the food on the table. "Sure you are. Krystal has that daydream too, but you just might have what it takes to make it come true."

"Not me." Lacey felt hot again, and it wasn't from the steam wafting from the heaping plate of food. She needed to be careful. If just watching the guy from across the street heated her up like this, what would another close encounter do? And what if he made another comment like yesterday's? She'd lose all her self-respect if she let him talk to her that way again.

Not that she had much to lose. Once she'd unhitched herself from Trent, she'd realized her self-respect was in short supply. She'd never done anything important in her life. She was still the same girl she'd always been, too pretty and too precious. The total implosion of her life really hadn't changed her much; she was just a little less naive and a lot less sure of herself.

"Go ahead," Pam urged. "Give him one more chance.

Just go over there and talk to him. Tell him you want to buy a truck or something." She slid into the booth, clasped her hands, and leaned forward, obviously caught up in her plan. "Yeah, that's it. Make him take you for a test-drive."

Lacey scooped up a forkful of eggs. "I don't have money for a truck."

"He doesn't know that. He probably thinks you're rich."

"He thinks I'm living off the money my husband made from your farm."

"Well, you were, right? For a while."

Lacey nodded reluctantly, and Pam's smile turned sly.

"So like I was saying, you owe him one more chance." She shifted forward, the vinyl squeaking under her ample backside. "You came all this way to see him. You can't just leave."

Lacey almost laughed. Pam didn't know how true that was. With the Mustang in the shop, no money, and no prospects, she was stuck in Grady anyway. Heck, her car hadn't even made it to the shop yet. It was still parked in front of Chase's trailer. And she had no idea how she'd pay for repairs.

"All right. I'll talk to him. But if he's rude again…"

"If he's rude again, come see me. I'll set him straight."

Lacey had to smile at the thought of plump little Pam setting her broad-shouldered brother straight. "I'll bet you will."

"Hey, Mom." A pigtailed tween girl skipped up to the table and slid into the booth, eying Lacey curiously. "Who are you?"

"Manners." Pam's voice was low and stern, a don't-mess-with-Mom voice. The kid had to be the product of that long-ago pregnancy. She had her mother's dimples and the same thick russet hair.

"Oh." The kid straightened and put out a small hand. "Hi. I'm Annie. Nice to meet you. I have a cat that lets me dress him up in doll clothes. Do you want to see him?"

"Maybe sometime." Lacey took the child's hand and received a surprisingly firm handshake.

"Okay." Annie turned to her mother. "Can I go to Tracy's?"

Pam nodded, and the child jumped up from the table and skedaddled, her sneakered feet sliding on the gleaming linoleum. She rounded the corner and dashed through the door to the yard on long, coltish legs that promised there was one heck of a high school basketball player in Grady's future.

Pam watched her go. "I'm raising a hooligan."

Lacey grinned. "She's adorable."

"My cat doesn't think so. Annie's done with dolls, but that animal takes the brunt of whatever maternal impulse I passed on and ends up dressed in baby clothes all the time. You ought to come up after you eat. I think she crammed the poor thing into a onesie today."

Lacey smiled. "Maybe I will."

She watched Pam head back to the kitchen and felt a stab of envy. Who would have thought Prentiss High's head cheerleader would end up being jealous of an unwed mother?

But she was. Pam had a real life. Not only did she take care of herself; she took care of Annie too. And Chase, by the sound of it.

But it sounded like she needed some help taking care of

her brother. And helping each other—that was what friends were for.

Lacey opened her purse and fished out her wallet, staring down at her dwindling hoard of dollar bills. Pam's freckled face appeared in the pass-through.

"Don't you dare pay me," she said. "We're friends, right? Just do me that favor and go see my brother." She waved toward the door. "Hey. Here he comes. Tell him you want to go for a test-drive." She dropped her voice to a stage whisper. "You don't have to sleep with him or anything. Just show him there's something to life besides cattle, cars, and sulking about stuff."

Chase swung open the door to the café, setting off the copper cowbell Pam had tied to the door. He tipped off his hat and ran the fingers of one hand through his hair as he scanned the room. The café was empty except for the one person he least wanted to see: Lacey. She glanced up as he walked in, then turned quickly toward the window as if she was embarrassed.

He was sure as hell embarrassed. The harsh words he'd said came back to him, along with the lie about Krystal. They echoed in his ears, clanging louder than the cowbell. He resisted the urge to turn and run as Pam stepped out of the kitchen and a cat-got-the-canary smile spread across her face.

"Chase. Hey." She gestured toward Lacey like a game show hostess revealing the answer to a million-dollar puzzle. "Look who's here. It's like a high school reunion! Come on and sit down."

She placed a menu on the table across from Lacey and stepped back expectantly. When he didn't move, her smile was replaced by a stern big-sister stare.

"Come on, Chase. You remember Lacey."

Did he ever. Despite his determination to push her away for good, he'd reverted back to his high school self since she'd arrived in Grady, thinking about her every minute of the night, every hour of the day. He was like a hormone-addled adolescent again, unable to stop the fantasies flickering behind his eyelids.

He remembered her topping the cheerleader's pyramid in her short skirt. Puzzling over a math problem with her perfectly arched brows. Best of all, he remembered the warmth of her lips when he'd finally, finally kissed her.

Unfortunately, that memory was always accompanied by a recollection of the day after, like cheap wine followed by a headache. He'd never forget the stab of disbelief when he'd seen her picture in the paper, smiling proudly beside Trent Bradford in the announcement of her engagement.

He hadn't been one of the school's big winners. He hadn't been a football star or a singing sensation. But he'd always gotten what he'd gone after. Lacey was his first and worst failure—his welcome to the real world.

"Come on, Chase," Pam urged. "Have a seat. I'll make you something to eat."

"No thanks." He turned his hat in his hands, first clockwise, then counter-clockwise, but neither succeeded in making the world pause on its axis long enough for him to dodge out the door. "I can't stay. I just came to see you about Galt."

"Galt."

He nodded and swallowed, his tongue thick in his mouth. "I'm worried he's not eating right."

"Well, feed him, then."

"It's not that easy." He leaned one hip against the built-in planter that divided the entryway from the booths in an effort to look casual.

"Sure it is. I'll box up some meatloaf, and you can take it to him."

"I thought maybe you'd take it."

Pam frowned—not the reaction he'd hoped for. Maybe flattery would help.

"You're the one who takes care of people. You could check on him once in a while, bring him something nutritious for dinner or something."

"Tell you what. I'll make him a meal a couple times a week, and you can take it to him."

"Ah, no. I'd rather not."

"Chase, you pass his place on the way home every day. There's no point in me going out there."

"He and I aren't getting along too well."

"Wow. News flash." Pam turned to Lacey. "Chase bought half of Galt's land after the guy's son died. Galt hates him." She turned back to Chase. "Seems to me this is the perfect chance to mend fences."

"There's nothing wrong with my fences." He remembered the loose cattle the day before. "At least, not anymore. I'm just surprised Galt hasn't strung razor wire on his."

"I know he's difficult, but it's a chance for you to be the bigger man."

"I don't want to be bigger."

It was true. He already felt huge and awkward standing

there. Lacey was making like Martha Stewart with the flatware, trying to line it up in a perfect row, but her gaze flicked up to his face once in a while when she thought he wasn't looking. Of course, he *was* looking. That's what was so awkward.

He needed to get Galt taken care of and get out. He couldn't understand why Pam was being so difficult. Normally she was Grady's angel, a willing helper to the sick, the lame, and the needy.

"Dammit, Pam, I don't want to make friends with the guy. I just want to make sure he doesn't die over there."

"Then go see him."

"No."

"Okay. Then help Lacey."

"What?" He looked around the diner as if he didn't know who she was talking about. "I—Lacey and I already talked."

"I know you did. And I know you were a total jerk." Pam set her fists on her hips, and Chase could swear he felt a wind whipping up. His sister was the nicest person he knew, but her anger was not pretty.

"Look, Chase, no man is an island. Not in a town this size. Take your pick: Fletcher or Lacey. You've got to help somebody sometime or you'll wither up and die."

When he didn't respond, she whisked the menu off Lacey's table and nodded toward the car lot. "I'll do my job, you do yours. I'll take dinner to Galt. You take Lacey out to test-drive that Dodge. She's shopping for a truck." She nodded sharply at Lacey. "Right?"

Lacey didn't look very enthusiastic, and Chase didn't blame her—but nobody crossed Pam when she got like this. "Um, yeah. Right."

Pam spun on her heel, heading for the diner kitchen without a backward glance.

Lacey looked up at Chase, then back down at her silverware. "We don't have to," she said.

"Yeah, we do." Chase stuck his hat on his head and straightened. "Trust me, it's a lot easier to just do what she says. And if I have to pick between you and Galt, I'll take you."

"Gee," Lacey said. "Thanks."

Krystal turned from the shelf she was dusting and gave Chase a wink as he stepped into the trailer. He offered a tight smile, wondering when she'd get the message and give up trying to seduce him. No matter how gruff and standoffish his behavior, she seemed to assume it was only a matter of time before he'd succumb to her charms and she'd own him—body, soul, and dealership.

Most men wouldn't have minded. The girl was gorgeous, and anyone with a testosterone quotient higher than their IQ would have just hauled her off to bed. But he'd learned his lesson with Lacey. Sex without strings—or even kisses without commitment—only led to heartache.

Besides, he needed Krystal. She manned the lot with a combination of bold-faced lies and blatant seduction that seemed to short men's circuits and rewire them to spend money on stuff they didn't need. Just a few days ago she'd gotten a hundred bucks for a rusty harrow he'd hauled to the lot just to clear up space in the barn. God knew what she'd told somebody about it.

Her eyes narrowed when Lacey followed him inside. She practically shoved Chase aside to enter into her receptionist duties with a gusto he'd never seen before.

"How can we help you?" she asked.

Anyone else would have thought she was smiling, but Chase knew better. She was baring her teeth.

"Chase is taking care of it." Lacey smiled back, and Chase was stunned by the difference in the two women. He always felt like Krystal practiced her poses and pouts in the mirror before trying them on him, but Lacey smiled with her whole being. The trailer, the town, the colored pennants fluttering from the trailer's eaves, all faded like a black-and-white movie background behind a Technicolor star. The woman lit up the room.

"I'm going to test-drive a Dodge, I guess."

Chase pictured himself in the pickup with Lacey a mere foot away on the slippery vinyl bench seat. His blood hummed in his veins at the thought of getting that close to her again, but Krystal rose and grabbed the keys from the corkboard behind the counter and stuffed them in her pocket.

"I'll take you."

Lacey smiled sweetly. "Thanks, but if you don't mind, I wanted Chase to do it."

Krystal glowered. She might not have Lacey's firepower when she smiled, but her scowl dimmed the lights.

"I figure he probably knows more about engines and stuff like that," Lacey said.

"Good point." Chase held out his hand for the keys. "The truck has a lot of four-wheeling features, Krystal. Remember, I was going to explain those to you, but you didn't have time?"

He stifled a smile. Krystal had evaded his attempts at on-the-job training over and over, changing the subject every time he tried to talk about trucks or farm machinery. It was almost like she didn't want to know any actual facts so she could lie her little heart out to the customers and fake innocence later on.

She dangled the keys at arm's length, forcing him to step up and grab them, then held onto them a moment too long, meeting his eyes with an obvious threat glinting in her own. He tugged them away, and she plopped down behind the counter and crossed her legs, pulling out the latest issue of *People*.

"I'll be *waiting*."

That was all she'd be doing, he knew, unless some poor stooge came to buy a truck. She never did a lick of work cleaning the place when he wasn't around.

CHAPTER 10

CHASE'S SALES BANTER DRIED UP LIKE USUAL AS HE AND Lacey approached the Dodge. He should be pointing out the truck's virtues—the add-on cast-steel bumpers and fog lights, the almost-new Goodyear tires—but he had to stifle the urge to tell her all its faults instead. It had an awful lot of miles on it, and it pulled to the right a little when you braked.

He was the worst salesman in the world. He hated to see someone buy something that wasn't right for them. But this was a nice truck. Reliable, as far as he could tell, and the body was in great shape.

The body.

He resisted the urge to help Lacey hike herself into the driver's seat and handed her the keys, watching her brows arch in concentration as she fitted them in the ignition and scanned the controls, biting her lower lip. It was all he could do not to lean over and nibble it himself. He'd pictured Lacey naked so many times, he felt like he could see through her clothes—although he had no way of knowing if his vision of her body was accurate.

Maybe that was the problem. Maybe he just needed to confirm the picture in his mind. He needed resolution. Closure.

Sex.

Hell, he needed to get a grip on his runaway imagination. That's what he needed. Nothing was going to happen between them. Nothing. This was business. Strictly business.

"It's an older model," he said. "A '99, but cherry."

Cherry. Shit. Why did everything he say around Lacey turn sexual? Hell, everything he thought around her turned sexual. He needed to get ahold of himself.

Either that, or he needed to get ahold of Lacey.

She cranked the key and pressed the accelerator to the floor, nodding in appreciation of the pickup's throaty roar. "What kind of engine is it?"

"V-6." He cleared his throat. "You going to trade in that Mustang? 'Cause I gotta tell you, I can't give you much for a car that doesn't run. You'd be better off getting it fixed first." He swallowed again, wishing he could get his voice to cooperate. Tension was making it sound strangled and weirdly high-pitched, and judging from Lacey's smile, she'd noticed.

"She's definitely made for rocky terrain," Chase blurted out. Lacey couldn't figure out who he was talking about at first. Certainly not her. She was made for smooth sailing. Things had been a little choppy lately, though, and she was hoping to find a safe harbor in Grady. But maybe not.

"The previous owner really knew what he was doing when it came to four-wheeling," he continued.

Oh. The truck. "I'm not really into that stuff. What I wanted to ask was…"

"He put on a Skyjacker suspension and Magnaflow exhaust. Super Swamper tires—top-of-the-line. He switched out the transmission too."

Couldn't he tell she didn't care? She didn't even know what he was talking about.

"And he took good care of it." He pointed to a sticker on the windshield. "You can see the last oil change was only a thousand miles ago. Brakes are almost new, and you'll notice when you look under the hood that he gave this baby a lot of tender loving care."

Maybe she should ask him who had owned the truck and track that guy down instead. She could use some TLC herself, and it was becoming painfully obvious she wasn't going to get it from Chase.

"Baby's got a Duratec power train. Tons of towing capacity."

Lacey nodded, despite the fact that she had no idea what any of this meant.

"Chase, listen. I really need to talk to you."

"What's unusual is the power. The acceleration feels like a sports car on the highway, but what you really need that kind of torque for is mud. Between those tires and the extra horsepower, you should be able to drive this baby through quicksand. It'll handle just about anything."

Dang. Maybe business was a little slow. Chase seemed awfully anxious to make a sale. Either that, or he was avoiding a real conversation on purpose.

"Chase, I don't want to buy a truck."

"Then why are we going for a test-drive?"

The minute he asked the question, he wanted to take it back. The answer was obvious: she wanted to be alone with him. Probably just to talk, but maybe…

Maybe something more.

But nothing was liable to happen if he made her say it out loud.

"Never mind." He faked absorption in the process of fastening his seat belt. "I don't need to know."

"Yeah, you do. We're going for a test-drive because your sister wants us to talk. She's worried about you. She says all you do is sulk about stuff."

"I don't sulk. I-I brood a little, that's all."

"What, like a chicken? A broody hen?" She laughed. "That means you want to have babies, right?" She slid her gaze toward him, and suddenly his breath was stolen by a whiff of the perfume that curled through the truck cab like a twining vine on a current of steamy summer air. He wanted to *make* babies, that was for sure.

He opened his mouth but nothing came out. When he tried again, he realized he was sitting in the passenger seat gasping like a fish. He needed to change the subject. Fast.

Fortunately, Lacey did it for him. "Never mind. I wish I could buy a big ol' truck like this, though. I thought driving a muscle car would make me feel tough, but I don't know."

"You're not tough?"

"Oh, I'm tough." She smiled that secret smile again. "But I'm not sure it was the car. I think I'm just toughening up from being on my own. I'm so used to people looking after me—Daddy, and then Trent. Now I don't have anyone to rely on but myself." Her head toss was casual, but her knuckles whitened on the wheel. "I'm never letting a man tell me what to do again."

He gave her a sharp glance. *Never? Did she really mean that?*

One way to find out.

"Go ahead and put it in reverse."

She took her hands off the steering wheel and crossed her arms over her chest, flashing him a hard look.

Yup. She meant it.

"Uh, whenever you're ready," he said.

She considered him a moment longer before turning her attention back to the truck and shoving the gear shift over and back. She turned her head and backed out of the space at warp speed, missing the rear fender of the truck to their right by fractions of an inch. He tried not to react. He'd been on test-drives with worse drivers.

Maybe.

Pushing the shifter into first, she popped the clutch and launched them toward the lot's exit. Chase tried not to crush the door handle in his panicked grip as she rounded the curb and hit the empty expanse of Main Street, the engine growling into a powerful crescendo.

"Sorry." She pressed the brakes. "I didn't expect it to go like that."

"It's geared low for off-road driving. You ever handle a stick before?"

There it was again. Everything he said sounded sexual. He needed to think before he spoke—think about cars, engines, transmissions. Anything but sex.

"I had a Beemer at home." Lacey seemed oblivious to the innuendo. He didn't know if that was a good thing or not.

He cleared his throat. "Must have been nice, driving a Beemer."

She shook her head. "Not really. Nothing back home is nice. Not anymore."

How could it not be nice? Bradford had made a fortune by dividing up the Caldwell land into dozens of suburban lots. He'd done it with a score of other farms too. The guy was rolling in misbegotten gains.

"BMWs are nice cars," he said. "Expensive."

"Yeah, well, I paid a pretty high price." She stared ahead and downshifted, then accelerated into a curve. "So did a lot of other people."

Lacey lost herself in the rumble of the truck's engine and the smooth glide of the gears, downshifting to skim the curves as she sped along the blacktop road out of town.

She wished Chase hadn't brought up Trent, or Trent's money, or the car Trent had bought her. She hated to admit she'd been a party to preying on her hometown, even unintentionally. But she needed to clear her conscience, and maybe talking about it would help Chase get on with his life, like Pam said.

"Chase, I didn't know what Trent was doing. I really didn't. And when I came here, I didn't realize you were one of the—the victims."

"I'm not a victim." He kept his eyes averted and stared moodily out the windshield. She wondered if the grim set of his mouth had anything to do with her or if he was always like that.

"I didn't know until I talked to Pam that he'd taken your land. I came here because I thought we were friends— friends forever. You know, like you wrote in my yearbook." She smiled tentatively. "I thought I could depend on you, like the sign says."

Chase's eye twitched just the slightest bit, telling her

she'd hit a nerve, but he covered his reaction in an instant and shot her a cold stare. Then he looked away quickly, as if he was embarrassed by what he'd seen. She wanted to smooth her hair or run a finger over the delicate skin under her eyes to make sure her makeup hadn't caked into her brand-new wrinkles. But she kept both hands resolutely on the wheel.

Chase cleared his throat. "How did you find me?"

"Facebook."

"Facebook?" He looked confused.

"I needed to go somewhere new, start over. And wherever I went, I wanted to make sure I knew someone there, in case something happened. I saw you lived in Wyoming, so..." She concentrated on a curve, accelerating gradually as the arc tightened. "I didn't friend you because I didn't plan to ask you for help. I just needed to know I had someone around, just in case. Like a security blanket."

She pictured Chase wrapping himself around her, holding her tightly to the solid plane of his chest. She wasn't sure "security" really defined the way that would make her feel.

"God, I didn't even remember I was on Facebook."

"I know. It said you only had two friends. I figure one of them was Pam, and the other one was Mark Zuckerberg."

"Yeah," he said. "I'm still Mr. Popular. So how come you hunted me down?"

"What are you, a rabbit? I didn't hunt you down; you were impossible to miss once I got here. You've practically got your name in lights with that sign and everything." She sighed. "Besides, everything went wrong back home. I really didn't know what to do, and when I thought of you, I remembered—I don't know. I remembered you were always there for me. I guess I was hoping you still were."

The grim set of his mouth softened slightly. He'd always been a sucker for a pity party. "I'm sorry about the divorce."

"Oh, don't be sorry about that. That was the one part that went right." She tried to laugh, but it came out flat and insincere. "The day I signed those papers was the first time I had a say in my life since the time I had a temper tantrum in the Safeway when I was five."

"Oh, come on," he said. "You were head cheerleader. Prom queen. You ran the whole school."

"By doing everything everybody wanted me to do," she said. "It was nice, Chase, I admit it. I thought it was what I wanted. But when I walked out of that lawyer's office, I wanted to fling my hat in the air like Mary Tyler Moore. I was finally free to be my own self."

"So did you?"

"Fling my hat? Nope." She shook her head regretfully. "Didn't have one. All I could do was stand on that sidewalk and grin. Somebody walking by asked me if I was okay. I must have looked like an idiot."

"No, I meant did you get to be yourself?"

"Not for long. Reality set in pretty quick. I didn't want to live on Trent's money, so I started looking for work. I was looking forward to it. I was going to go to school at night and get my real estate license." She glanced over at him, biting her lip. "Not to do what Trent did. I wanted to find people homes. Maybe help revitalize Conway—you know, spruce up the downtown. Stuff like that." She blinked a couple times, fast, as if fighting back tears. "I figured I'd finally get started on being *me*. My own self."

"Which is who?" Chase asked.

Lacey pressed the accelerator hard, veering into a turn,

fixing her eyes on the road. "I have no freaking idea. I've depended on other people all my life, Chase. I never realized it until I had to depend on myself. And I hate to admit this, but there's not much there to depend on. Nobody in Conway would hire me. Everybody hates me."

"Nobody could hate you."

"*You* do."

"No, I don't." He sighed. "I tried to. But I don't." He looked down at his lap, then up at her. "I can't."

She blew out a long breath. "Well, anyway, they froze Trent's assets, which is fine with me. Like I said, I didn't want to live on that money anyway. But the Mustang and the motel have just about eaten up all my cash. I have a credit card, but the limit's two thousand dollars. It's going to cost me more than that to fix the car. And meanwhile, Wade's probably looking for me. Like I told you, he came to my house. He was always a problem, Chase. Remember back in high school?"

Chase nodded. Of course he remembered. He'd helped her out that night when Wade came on to her. She'd been drunk, and Wade had been persistent, and Chase had come along just in time. He'd been there for her, just like she said. The fact that he'd kissed her in the car didn't change that. Unfortunately, it hadn't changed anything.

"Well, he kept that up. He was always hanging around, always sucking up to Trent and then looking at me like— well, you know."

He nodded.

"And once Trent got in trouble, it got even worse. It was like Wade knew there was nobody to stop him. He'd park across the street, watching me. And then he came over in the middle of the night, and I just…" She looked down at her hands. "I'd rather drive off the face of the earth than be alone with him again." She scanned the barren landscape through the windshield. "I guess I did drive off the face of the earth. But as long as he doesn't find me, this is right where I want to be."

CHAPTER 11

THE TRUCK HIT A BUMP, JARRING LACEY OUT OF HER memories. She realized she'd been staring unseeing at the road ahead while she slid down the slippery slope of memory lane. It was a wonder they hadn't ended up in a ditch.

Maybe that's what they needed, though. The air in the cab shimmered with tension from all they'd left unsaid. Maybe she needed to shake things up a little.

Cranking the wheel to the right, she bounced onto the rocky shoulder and pitched the truck down onto the weedy strip bordering the road. Chase slapped one hand on the dashboard and held on, turning to her with a wide-eyed stare.

"Hey, you're so hot on this four-wheeling thing, I figured I'd try it." She steered along a barbed wire fence, then fishtailed around a corner, letting the rear wheels slide until they gripped the dirt and heaved the truck forward. "This is kind of fun."

"Get back on the road," he said through clenched teeth.

"Oh, come on. You said she was made for rocky terrain, right?"

"Not this rocky terrain. You need to get out of this hayfield."

"Hayfield?" She laughed. There wasn't a scrap of hay where she was driving—just an occasional tangle of thistles and clumps of spiky yucca sticking up from the bare, cracked dirt. "This isn't a hayfield. This is a desert."

"Fletcher Galt thinks it's a hayfield," Chase said. "And since he owns it and he'll shoot anybody who trespasses, you'd better turn left."

"He'll shoot us? You're kidding."

"He shot one of my cattle."

"Holy crap. You're not too civilized out here in Wyoming, are you?"

"Fletcher wouldn't be civilized if he lived in Buckingham Palace. He'd probably shoot the queen if she crossed him."

He grunted as she veered left onto a dirt two-track that was almost invisible under a cloak of weeds. The truck lurched over a washout and plunged into a wooded area scattered with boulders.

"That better?" Lacey shot him a grin. Back when she was a kid she'd loved to have outdoor adventures—swimming at the quarry, building bonfires, creating all those teenage memories—but she hadn't done anything like that in years. She'd been hovering like a ghost in the air-conditioned confines of Trent's big house for so long, she'd forgotten what it was like to be real, to *do* things. Cranking down the driver's-side window, she propped her arm on the track and enjoyed the heat of the sun on her skin.

The truck took every obstacle in stride, heaving over the rocks like a lumbering beast. Stray limbs from the trees bordering the long-abandoned road thwapped the doors as they passed, and the sound reminded her of running onto the field at the Lions games with the cheer squad, the team in their pads and helmets high-fiving them as they bounded onto the field. She could almost hear the cheers of the crowd. It made her feel like the old Lacey again—her perky, confident self.

The pickup humped over another washout, and she returned her attention to the road and downshifted. The front end heaved upward and crashed down, then repeated the motion as the rear tires topped a massive rock. Easing out the clutch, she pressed the accelerator, frowning when their forward motion failed to resume.

"What the…" She pressed the accelerator again, harder this time. The truck roared, tires spinning uselessly as mud spattered the rock behind them.

"Ease up," Chase shouted over the racket. "Ease up!"

She let up on the pedal and felt the truck inch forward, then dip. There was a harsh grating noise as the rock scraped the truck's undercarriage, and the tires spun again. Looking left and right, she realized they weren't in a washout; she'd driven into a creek. Ahead was a muddy bank; beyond that, a swampy morass of mud and tufted grass. She turned and looked behind her.

"Oops."

The rock she'd driven over loomed surprisingly large in the rearview mirror.

Chase lifted himself out of the seat to lean out the window, gazing ahead. The move put his butt right at eye level, so she couldn't help looking—especially since his jeans were worn white at the seat in testament to the hard work that had built those flexing muscles. He shifted to look behind them, his biceps swelling to lift the weight of his broad shoulders. It was incredible to think that her geeky, gangly friend had turned into this—this *stud*. She could barely believe it was the same guy.

She eyed his slim hips and smiled. Yup, it was Chase. It said so on the back of his belt, in fancy letters tooled into the leather. He'd worn a belt like that all through school, apparently unaware that having his name emblazoned on his backside was hardly a fashion statement. Apparently, his sense of style hadn't grown with the rest of him.

So maybe he really hadn't changed that much. Maybe the old Chase was still in there somewhere.

He pitched back into the seat, then opened the door and climbed down from the high cab.

Lacey set her hand on the gear shift, ready for action. "You going to push?"

"I'm going to drive." He edged around the front of the truck, balancing on the rocks that jutted out of the flowing water. In moments he was at her window, gesturing for her to open the door. She opened the window instead.

"I think I can make it if you push," she said.

He gave her a deadpan look, then headed for the back of the truck. She watched in the rearview as he set both hands on the tailgate and braced himself against the boulder. Focusing on the rocky path ahead, she set both hands on the wheel and bit her lower lip until it hurt. *Don't gun it. Take it easy.*

"Don't gun it," he said.

"I *know*."

She gripped the wheel and eased up on the clutch, watching Chase in the rearview mirror. His face was set in concentration, his jaw jutting forward. As their eyes met in the mirror, she finally recognized the Chase Caldwell she'd known—the old friend she'd come here to find. The jolt of recognition brought all her old feelings for him back—friendship, caring, and most of all, trust. She had always trusted him.

And looking into those brown eyes, she knew she still could. He might be angry, he might be difficult, he might have changed in a million ways. But the sign at the dealership hadn't lied.

You could depend on Chase Caldwell.

She smiled, and he looked away, his sharp nod cutting the moment off as abruptly as an ax splitting wood. She eased up on the clutch a little more, simultaneously pressing the accelerator, then jammed on the brake as the truck lurched backward.

Chase disappeared from the mirror, and all she could see was trees and rocks.

Damn. Just when she'd figured out she could trust him, she'd gone and killed the guy.

His face suddenly popped back into view in the mirror. She didn't want to meet his eyes now. He looked furious.

"Go forward! *Forward!* You're in reverse, Lacey!"

"Sorry." She shoved the stick into first and tried again, but she caught his eyes and the anger in his gaze made her panic. She gunned it. The tires spun and mud flew, spattering his face and chest. He put his head down and pushed anyway, his arms straightening as the truck inched forward. She held her breath and gave it a little gas.

The engine died. The truck lurched backward again, and she looked in the mirror to catch a look of horror on Chase's face before he dropped from sight again.

When he reappeared at her window, she thought maybe she should run over him in self-defense, because he looked mad enough to kill her. Maybe she should make a preemptive strike.

Or maybe it was time to get the peace process under way.

"Sorry." She smiled hesitantly. "I think we're stuck."

"*You're* stuck," he said. "*I'll* get us out of here. Move over."

She started to protest, then sighed and did as he said. She'd made two stupid mistakes, first leaving the truck in reverse, then letting it stall. She couldn't blame him for losing faith in her driving abilities.

"You want me to push?" she asked.

He shook his head, his lips pressed into a thin line. "I think a decent driver can handle this without a push."

"I'm a decent driver," she said. "I just forgot I had it in reverse. And then it stalled. Guess this jalopy isn't the gem you made it out to be."

"There's nothing wrong with the truck." He cranked the engine to life. She was almost disappointed when it inched forward.

"I set it up for you," she said. "If it hadn't stalled, I'd have gotten us out of here."

He ignored her. She wasn't sure if the noise in the cab was the engine growling or Chase, but the end result was another spin of the tires.

Without a word, he yanked open his door and slid out of the cab. Stomping and cursing, he circled the truck, then stood in front of it and scratched his head as he regarded their predicament.

Lacey opened her door and slid from the cab, setting her high-heeled foot carefully on a rock, only to slip and end up ankle-deep in the stream.

"Shoot." She picked her way through the rocks, ignoring the cold water. If it hadn't been ruining her shoes, it would have felt good.

Joining him in front of the truck, she eyed their situation

and sighed, blowing a stubborn strand of hair out of her face. The truck was stuck, all right. The left front tire was wedged between two rocks, and the right one had spun a deep trench into the streambed. The rock behind the rear wheels seemed to have grown since she'd driven over it.

"I'm going to have to call Cody," he said.

"Who's Cody?"

"Guy with a winch." He waded back to the truck, sloshing water onto her capris. "Damn," he said. "I'll never hear the end of this."

"You can tell him it was my fault," she said.

"I sure will." He glowered down at the phone he'd taken from his pocket and stabbed at the keypad.

She gave him a wink. "I won't tell him how it was your stupid truck that got us stuck."

CHAPTER 12

THAT SPUNKY RESPONSE WAS VINTAGE LACEY, AND suddenly Chase felt their old friendship reasserting itself. They hadn't spent a lot of time together, and except for that one night, they'd never been close, but they'd always joked around like Burns and Allen, her playing zany Gracie to his George.

He couldn't help smiling. "You're not going to give an inch, are you?"

"Why should I?" Her voice wavered a little, and he knew he'd win this one.

"You can't drive for shit," he said. "And you'll never admit it."

"Well, you'll never admit this truck's a piece of crap. Made for off-road driving, my…patootie."

She hadn't sworn in high school either. She played tough, but she had more euphemisms in her vocabulary than an old maid aunt.

"You still don't curse, do you?"

She looked away. "No. Only when I'm really mad. And I guess this was kind of my fault." She looked back at the rock, her green eyes tearful. "You're the one who's probably mad."

She looked away, blinking fast. Damn. He hadn't meant to make her cry. And the truck probably wasn't the gem he'd made it out to be. But at least it had been clean. Now it was spattered with mud from its white sidewalls to the fog lights on top.

So was he. His ass felt damp where he'd landed on it when she'd backed into him, and the front of his shirt was speckled with goop. He put a hand up to brush his hair back from his forehead and felt a glob of mud matting the hank that fell over his face.

He keyed a text message into the phone. Cody would come and pull them out. He was the fry cook at the diner, and he spent every penny of his limited income on a Jeep that looked like something out of a cartoon and could probably haul an elephant up the mud-slicked banks of the Ganges. The Dodge would be no problem.

The phone beeped back immediately, and he scanned the reply.

"Cody's on his way." He looked at Lacey, who quickly dashed away a tear that was dangling from her lower lashes. "It's okay, Lacey."

She looked up at him, eyes wide and hopeful. Her reluctance to curse wasn't the only thing that hadn't changed since high school. She still had that knockout combination of indomitable spirit and sweet vulnerability that had captivated him since sixth grade. A moment ago, she'd been barreling down the fence line like a seasoned four-wheeler; now she was hesitant and scared. She'd gone from trucker chick to delicate flower in six seconds, shifting gears faster than a Grand Prix racer.

It was those eyes. Looking into Lacey's eyes was like looking into the jagged, icebound heart of a glacier, but instead of chilling him, her gaze warmed him from the inside out. And right now, there was a question there he couldn't quite interpret. Was she asking if he'd forgive her for getting them stuck? Or was she asking him to kiss her?

He sure as hell wanted to kiss her. A warning bell chimed in the back of his mind, reminding him he'd never gotten over their last kiss, urging him to back off, but most of him was on autopilot, overwhelmed by the way her closeness set his blood humming in his veins and the way she smelled, all peaches and soap and sex.

She looked expectant, with her pink lips parted as if she couldn't quite catch her breath, and suddenly kissing her seemed like an easier choice than pulling away. He lowered his head to hers and brought one hand up to cup the back of her head while he wrapped the other arm around her shoulders. He almost pulled her off her feet in his rush to draw her close.

She felt just as soft and giving and sweet as he remembered, her curves round but firm. Kissing her didn't feel like the start of something new; it felt like a continuation of the long-running fantasy he'd been enmeshed in half his life. In the years since he'd known her, he'd bedded a dozen women, but every one of them had been Lacey when the lights went out. And if they wanted to do it with the lights on, that had been okay. All he had to do was close his eyes.

Thinking of Lacey had worked for years, putting distance between his heart and the women he slept with and keeping it safe. After all, you couldn't lose what you'd never had. And the idea of Lacey ever being in his arms for real had been laughably unlikely, especially once he'd moved to Wyoming.

Or so he'd believed.

Her body molded to his, her breasts pressing into his chest. He dipped to taste her lips, and she parted them easily, letting him trace the soft skin inside her lower lip, letting him lick the slight fullness below her cupid's bow with the tip of his tongue before he rededicated himself to living this moment as completely as he could.

Because it was too much of a miracle to ever be repeated. He needed to memorize every detail. The brush of her breath on his cheek, the faint scent of warm skin and sunshine, the teasing tickle of her hair on his arm. He moved his hand down to cup her breast, savoring the warmth of her skin, hoarding every sensation like ammunition that would protect him from all the other women who might share his bed. Women like Krystal, who didn't care whether he gave them his heart as long as he gave them a good time and paid for dinner.

He pulled away and watched her tilt her face to the sun. There was Lacey as he'd always pictured her, eyes closed, lips parted, her thick, dark lashes lying on her pale cheeks. She looked like a woman in ecstasy, a woman in love, and for a heartfelt half-second, his heart swelled at the possibility she could be his.

Take that, Trent Bradford.

He slapped that thought away. Getting back at Trent Bradford had been part of the fantasy—but that wasn't what this moment was about. It was about revisiting old times. Rekindling old flames.

Revitalizing an unhealthy obsession.

A harsh, grating noise suddenly swelled from the trees beyond the truck. Lacey snapped back to reality as the sound grew louder, the snapping of tree limbs accompanying it like a percussion backbeat.

"It's Cody," Chase said. "We're saved."

He didn't look like a man who wanted to be saved. He looked like a man who wanted something else—something more than a kiss.

"Saved," she echoed faintly.

But the vehicle that crashed into sight in a copse of trees didn't look like any kind of savior. It reminded her of the Jabberwock in *Through the Looking-Glass*, which "came whiffling through the tulgey wood, and burbled as it came." The headlights, set high on the hood, looked like wide googly eyes, and the cast-steel bumper created a sneering mouth.

The thing was terrifying.

It slid to a stop five feet away, spattering muck every which way. A wiry man in a stained white T-shirt jumped from the driver's seat. Lacey couldn't tell if he was tanned or dirty, but his teeth flashed white and his loose-limbed grace indicated he was in his element crashing through the woods. His sunlit brown hair looked like it had been hacked off at random intervals with a pair of dull scissors, and he clearly hadn't shaved for days.

"Man, you are stuck," he announced. "Stuck good. What the hell you doing out here, buddy?"

Lacey picked her way around the front of the pickup, watching her step in the rocky terrain. When she looked up, both men were staring at her.

"Oh," the Jeep driver said. A knowing smile split his lean face. "Got it. You sure you're ready to leave? I can give you two a minute."

"There's nothing to stay for," Chase said.

"You sure?" Cody gave her a long head-to-toe look. It wasn't sexy like Chase's; it was amused.

She was probably a muddy mess.

"I fell in the mud," she said.

Cody grinned. "Sure you did."

He shot a knowing glance at Chase, and she looked down to see that a muddy five-fingered handprint marked her tank top, right over her left breast. She remembered Chase's hand there, and as the memory flooded her mind, her body reacted, her nipples tightening against the cold, wet fabric.

The men probably knew exactly what she was thinking. She blushed, her chest and neck suffused with heat, and realized flushed pink skin probably made the situation even worse. Crossing her arms to cover herself, she looked Cody straight in the eye.

"I fell in the mud. That's my story, and I'm sticking to it."

"Well, all right." He scratched his head and pondered the stuck truck. "Let's get started, then." He turned to face her. "Since Doofus here isn't going to introduce us, I'll do it myself. I'm Cody. Work at the diner, but I'm a knight in shining armor the rest of the time." He gestured toward the Jeep. "Me and Sal. Lot of people get stuck on these country roads."

"The diner? Oh, you work with Pam." Lacey realized now that she'd seen him before, behind the pass-through at the diner. He'd been clean then, but it was the same guy.

"Sure do." He grew suddenly serious. "You know her?"

Lacey nodded.

"Put in a good word for me, would you? Tell her I rescued you and all that."

"Sure." Lacey tried to picture Pam with this wild man and failed. "I'll tell her."

Cody strolled around the pickup in a slow circle, taking in its awkward position. Shaking his head, he shifted his grin toward Chase.

"How the hell did you do this?"

"I didn't. She did."

"You let her drive?"

"It was a test-drive," Lacey said.

"You going to buy it?"

"Nope." She hiked herself up on a boulder and crossed her legs. "Gets stuck too easy."

Cody laughed. "I'll get Sal past you here and pull you over the creek. There's a clearing a ways up there where you can turn around. If you're careful, you can get through this area just fine."

"Yeah," Chase said, shooting Lacey a glare. "If you're careful."

Cody started the Jeep and roared to the front of the truck, the huge tires clearing rocks like they were pebbles. Unwinding a thick steel cable from a pulley on the back, Chase headed for the pickup. He bent over the bumper, struggling to fasten a huge hook onto the vehicle's frame. Lacey couldn't help enjoying the view as his shirt hiked up to reveal the muscles flexing in his back.

"Got it?" Cody yelled when Chase rose and headed back to the driver's seat.

"Got it."

Lacey hastily jumped from her rock as Chase started the truck and the two vehicles began moving, Cody's Jeep rolling steadily through the stream while the winch tightened. The pickup's tires spun briefly, flinging mud, then gripped the ground. The truck tilted and creaked as Chase negotiated the stream and drove up the bank, following Cody off into the woods.

Lacey leaned against a tree, listening to the engines fading in the distance. She wondered briefly if they'd left her behind, but soon the noise increased and the pickup roared into sight, splashing through the stream and heaving up the bank to stop just beyond the rock where they'd gotten stuck.

Lacey looked across the stream.

"Where's Cody?"

"He took off. There's another way through the woods to the county road."

She glanced warily at Chase. Had he sent his friend off so they could be alone? So they could finish what they'd started? He was looking at her like he could see her naked.

She looked down at her shirt and realized she might as well be. The handprint still stood out clearly over her breast, and everything under her shirt stood out clearly too. Her thin cotton bra was no help at all.

"Oh, God." She tried to flick off the mud but it only made things worse. "I hope I can get back to the motel and change before anyone sees me like this."

"There's no way you'd get in without everybody seeing you. Maybe you could rinse off in the stream. Kind of smear that around." He looked away, embarrassed, and she was suddenly embarrassed herself. What had she been thinking? That kiss had been a mistake—for both of them. She could spend all her life trying to make up for what her ex-husband had done to Chase. He'd resent her forever, and she didn't blame him.

She sighed. "I guess."

Mincing down the muddy bank, she bent over the water and cupped it in her hands, splashing it over her chest. It was cold enough to make the bones of her hand ache, but it felt good on her hot skin. Besides, it was the closest thing she could find to a cold shower.

She looked down at her shirt. Instead of being marked with a handprint, it was now a uniform shade of brown, and the fabric, wet through, clung even more tightly to her breasts.

Turning, she caught Chase staring at her and straightened, suddenly self-conscious. Judging from his expression, he needed a cold shower too.

"Here." He extended a hand and helped her up the bank. When she reached the truck, she teetered a little and put out one hand to steady herself against his chest.

To heck with cold showers. She splayed her fingers and ran her hand up his chest and over his shoulder. When she slid her fingers into his hair, he bent his head and brushed her lips with his, reviving the kiss and all the feelings that went with it.

CHAPTER 13

LACEY LOVED TO KISS. SHE WAS GOOD AT IT TOO, having spent her entire high school career at first base. She hadn't given herself to any of the groping, gasping boys who'd tried to steal second in the backseats of their cars, and she'd become expert at parrying their stealth moves— the slow hand creeping under her shirt, the subtle tug that signaled an attack on her bra strap.

But Chase wasn't trying to steal anything. Unlike those high school boys, he didn't seem to be thinking about the usual male goals and aspirations like seeing her naked or working toward his own satisfaction. More than any man she'd ever kissed, he was in the moment, making the most of every touch, every stunned intake of breath, every whisper of sensation. She laced her fingers around his neck and gave herself up to the sheer pleasure of it.

Pressing her breasts into his chest, she tried to smother the sharp ache of longing for more, harder, *now*, but he was so tall, she couldn't plaster her body to his quite the way she wanted. She let out a mew of frustration. Twisting against him, she hiked herself up on her toes, then felt his arms wrap around her as he hoisted her onto the truck's open tailgate. She wrapped one leg around his waist and deepened the kiss with an aggression that surprised her.

She'd always played submissive with Trent, letting him take what he wanted. There hadn't been anything he could give her she'd needed enough to work for, but now, for the first time, she wanted a man for herself. Chase seemed to sense her need as he cupped the back of her head and lowered her onto the hot black plastic of the truck's bed liner in one swift move.

Now their bodies were aligned and his weight pressed down on her, finally giving her some relief from the ache of need that was pulsing in her breasts and between her legs. She brought one foot up to stroke his calf and wondered when she'd lost her shoes, but she'd never cared less about fashion than she did now. In fact, all she wanted from her designer duds at this moment was easy removal.

Chase had known exactly how Lacey's body would feel. He'd fantasized about it for years—how soft her skin would be under his work-hardened hands, how quickly her nipples would rise under his touch—but he hadn't realized how strongly his own body would react. He'd been uncomfortably erect ever since Cody had left them alone, and now he ached so fiercely it was hard to take things slow.

He took a deep breath, feeling every muscle in his body, every nerve, every fiber reaching toward her and aching for the culmination of all those years of desire. He felt like his accelerator was pressed to the floor, his engine roaring, but his wheels were spinning and he was heating up and going nowhere.

He had to have her—had to. And if he couldn't have her honestly, he'd gladly pay for the privilege. She needed money? Sure. How much? A job? Hired. A place to stay?

How about his bed? Tonight and every night. He'd give her anything. Everything.

"What do you want, Lacey?" He could barely speak for the ache in his throat. "Just tell me what you want. I'll help you. Just tell me."

He brushed her nipple with his thumb while he kissed her, tormenting her gently but with a firm touch to tell her he wanted to take charge. She sucked in a quick breath and squirmed against him, and for a minute, he thought he'd gone too far, that she was going to cover herself, that he'd lost his chance—but then she tugged the wet shirt up over her breast and pressed herself into his hand.

She moaned, and his brain shut down completely except for a flash of memory that reminded him how much he'd wanted this, how many years he'd longed to touch this woman.

He looked down at her and gentled his touch, moving his finger in a slow circle around the smooth, dark aureole before he palmed her breast and squeezed. Her bra was made of some kind of thin, stretchy fabric that was almost transparent. Drawing away from the kiss, he slid it aside and took her nipple between his lips, flicking his tongue over the tip, before sucking it into his mouth and moving his hand down to her waist. Her hand flew to her waistband before he could get there, and again he thought she was going to stop him, but she was pulling at the hem of her shirt, then yanking it over her head. He watched it fly upward from her hand in slow-motion, catching on a tree branch and hanging there like a flag of surrender.

He looked back down at Lacey. She'd lifted her hands back over her head when she'd thrown the shirt, and now she'd crossed her wrists as though she wore invisible shackles. There couldn't be a clearer signal that she was his.

She closed her eyes and he kissed her again, resisting the urge to move too fast, to unsnap those silly short pants and slip his hand down to the heart of her. He had to wait, to make her want him with an ache as strong as his own. His fantasy wasn't about taking Lacey, or having Lacey; it was about the two of them being truly together, wanting each other. He gentled his touch to a whisper, stroking her as gently as the breeze cooled his face. She moved her hips, asking for more, but he kept the pressure light while he bent his head and kissed the tender skin on the underside of her smooth upper arms.

He worked his way down all the softest parts of her, the side of her breast, the thin skin over her ribs, the slight depression where her hip bone dipped and disappeared under her belt. She tensed, lifting her hips, pressing herself against his hand, and he worked his way back up again, up over the landscape of her body, across the gentle swells of creamy flesh and the pink tips of her breasts to kiss her neck and rest his cheek against hers.

Chase's breath brushed Lacey's ear, and she shivered in spite of the heat. It felt so good to be wanted. To be with a man who didn't take you for granted.

She'd never, ever felt like this with Trent. When she'd married him, she'd discovered that her determination to save herself for marriage had left her unskilled and unsure of herself. But Trent hadn't seemed to care. He'd scaled her like Everest, because she was there, and she'd let him, even when she hadn't wanted to.

With Chase, she wanted to.

She had ever since she'd laid eyes on him behind the counter at the dealership. She'd wanted those strong square hands on her breasts and those lips on her mouth. As if reading her mind, he palmed her breast and ran his thumb over the peak. She hadn't thought the ache inside her could get any stronger, but her nipple hardened until it hurt. God, she wanted him. Even when he'd insulted her that first day, she'd wanted to...

She froze. What was it he'd said?

Go sell yourself to someone else.

And that's probably what he thought she was doing now.

What do you want? he'd asked *Tell me what you want.*

She was doing it again. She was selling herself. She'd sleep with Chase, he'd help her out, and then he'd own her, body and soul, just like Trent had.

He'd sweet-talk her into a relationship, get her to walk away from her former life, and then slowly his love would turn to disapproval, his advice and assistance to rigid control. He'd mock everything she wanted to do, put down all her accomplishments, and criticize her until she felt utterly helpless, all because she'd sold herself to him. She'd be absorbed into his world, and her own would become smaller and smaller until it didn't exist at all. Until she became nothing but his.

She felt herself shrinking as if she was turning into a plastic Barbie doll whose only purpose was to pose for Ken. The world around her—the trees, the sunshine, the breeze tickling her skin—seemed to recede like an outgoing tide, and all she could see was Chase, so big, so strong, so possessive.

She jerked out from under him and scrambled to a sitting position, tugging the strap of her bra back onto her shoulder and reaching up to snatch her tank top out of the tree. Sliding down from the tailgate, she stubbed a toe on a rock and stumbled away from the truck, struggling to put her shirt back on.

She'd been an idiot. She'd been telling herself this meant something—to Chase as well as her. But as soon as he'd offered to help her, he'd moved from kisses to more intimate touches. As if he'd earned the right. As if she really was for sale.

Clutching a branch for balance, she took another step backward, then stumbled as something slithered through the mud and slid into the water.

Snake.

She shrieked, jerking away and tripping over a rock before she landed on her butt in what she now assumed was a snake-infested stream.

"Lacey, for God's sake." Strong hands lifted her from behind, and she kicked out and slapped him away, spinning around and stepping backward onto the bank. She couldn't let him touch her. Couldn't let him own her.

She was never going to let that happen again. She'd flip burgers. She'd clean motel rooms. She'd pump gas. She'd do anything but take money from a man and become his plaything.

She backed away. Chase stood calf-deep in the stream, his shoulders hunched and knees bent as if he was about to clap a wrestling hold on her. His shirt was soaked through and stuck to his skin, the damp glossing his muscles and confirming that yes, he did look strikingly like the man on the cover of the *Men's Fitness* magazine in his waiting room.

Only that man had been smiling.

Chase stared at the drenched, muddy female in front of him and wondered how she could possibly be the same person as the sweet, fragrant, willing woman who'd been lying beneath him moments before.

He should have known better. Lacey wanted something, and she'd worked him up into a frenzy so he'd do anything she asked. He could have sworn she was enjoying herself dang near as much as he was—but she'd been playing him, well aware that giving him everything she had wasn't the way to get what she wanted.

She was picking her way over the gravel scattered between the boulders, mincing along like a cat in wet grass.

"What happened to your shoes?" he asked.

She nodded toward the truck's front tire, where one gold sandal glittered just beneath the surface of the water between two rocks. Plucking it from the stream with one finger, he tossed it her way.

Cheering on other players had apparently been the limit of her athletic prowess. She didn't just catch like a girl; she didn't catch at all. Flailing at the sandal, she knocked it back into the water and nearly fell as she bent to pick it up. She wavered precariously on one foot while she shoved her toes in it and struggled with the delicate straps.

Straightening, she tossed her head. Her hair had

somehow escaped the mud that had splattered them both, but the rest of her was wet, muddy, flushed, or all three.

While she fished another shoe out of the water and fumbled it onto her foot, she teetered and almost lost her balance. He stepped forward and caught her, but she pushed him away.

"Leave me alone, Chase. I'm not for sale."

"What?"

"You told me to go sell myself to someone else, but then you decided you were buying after all, didn't you?"

Chase looked as if she'd slapped him.

"Lacey, I didn't mean that. I'm sorry, okay? I didn't…"

"I'm not. It made me realize I *had* sold myself to Trent. I always sell myself, because I don't have anything else to offer."

"You have a lot more to offer."

"I have nothing, Chase. No skills, no talents. Not even a car that runs. Hell, I can't even live in the damn thing because it's parked right in front of your office."

He widened his eyes at the curse words, but she wasn't about to take them back. She meant every damn word.

"So let me help you."

"No." She tilted her chin up and gave him her best *I'll never be hungry again* look. "I'll get a job."

His eyes scanned her body, fixing on her lips, her breasts, and then her hand.

"What about that ring? Couldn't you sell it?"

Lacey looked down at the ring gracing her finger.

She'd forgotten about the cubic zirconia she'd bought in a Walmart after a trucker had tried to pick her up at a gas station. Men had mostly left her alone once she'd marked herself married. They respected another man's ownership more than they ever respected a woman.

Plucking it off her finger, she tossed it downstream and felt suddenly buoyant. The fake diamond hadn't weighed a thing, but tossing it away had felt symbolic, somehow, especially since she'd decided in that moment that she didn't need Chase's help.

"Walmart. $2.99. Maybe there's a muskrat out there that wants it." She waved her now-naked hand in the air. "I bought it to keep truckers from trying to pick me up."

She held her hand out, splaying her fingers, tilting it left and right like a newlywed admiring her diamond— but what she was admiring was the pale ring of flesh where her wedding ring had been. She'd thrown off her shackles, and no way was she putting on a ring, ever again. If another trucker tried to pick her up, she'd kick him in the shins and spit.

"I need to get back to the motel," she told Chase. "I told you, I don't want to buy your damn truck."

They drove into town in silence. When he pulled up to the motel, he dared to look at her for the first time.

"I didn't mean what I said the other day, Lacey."

"It doesn't matter. It was true, in a way. I've always had some man paying my way. I'm not letting that happen anymore." She grabbed her purse and slid down from the truck. "I'm sorry about my language. Sorry about—well, everything."

He watched her slide down to the ground and walk up the concrete steps to the second floor of the motel, where she let herself into one of the dozen identical turquoise doors. Number seventeen. When the door closed behind her, he got out of the truck and headed for the motel office. Lacey might not want to rely on a man, but somebody had to help her.

"I want to pay for a room in advance," he told Floyd Ledger. Floyd had been the owner of the Ranch Motel for as long as Chase could remember. The guy spent all day, every day in the tiny, cluttered rooms that could be seen from the counter. There was always a laugh track blaring from an unseen television, and Floyd's flesh was as pale and hairless as the underbelly of a frog from living in the dim recesses of the motel.

"Number seventeen," Chase told him.

Floyd squinted, his slack lips twisting into a scowl. "Won't have that kind of thing going on here. That girl…"

"That girl might as well be my sister," Chase said. "There's nothing going on."

Chase could feel the doubt radiating from Floyd's blank stare like some kind of psychic wave.

"There's nothing going on, and there probably never will be," Chase said. "I blew it. Don't tell her I paid for the room either. She'll move if she finds out."

Floyd grumbled something incomprehensible that sounded distinctly vulgar, but he lifted the credit card imprinter from under the counter and set Chase's card in place willingly enough. Setting an old-fashioned carbon form into the machine, he grunted as he pulled the slide slowly over the card. "How many nights?"

"Give her a week," Chase said. "Maybe that'll be long enough for her to get over the dumb things I said."

CHAPTER 14

"GUESS YOU LIKED THE PANCAKES."

Lacey hadn't been sure of her reception from Pam this morning. She didn't know how often Chase and his sister talked, but she knew she hadn't exactly helped him the day before. Not the way Pam had wanted her to, and not the way Chase wanted her to either. But judging from Pam's welcoming smile, she didn't know a thing about the way the test-drive had turned out.

"They were great." Lacey swung her purse into a booth and slid in behind it. "But I think I'll just have coffee today."

"Oh, come on. I've got the batter made, so it's on the house. I know you've got to get that car fixed, and that'll run you a pretty penny even if Jeb gives you his special hot chick discount."

Lacey flushed. "Actually, that's why I came in." She rushed to cover her gaffe. "I mean, I would have come to see you anyway, but I wondered if you were hiring."

"I wish." Pam slid into the booth across from her, propping herself against the windowsill with her legs thrust straight out on the vinyl bench. She eyed her white-shod feet with her face creased in mock pain. "I could use the help, but as you can see, business isn't exactly booming."

It was the answer Lacey had expected, but she still felt a dull thud of disappointment as her heart sank to the bottom of her rib cage. "Do you know anybody in town who's got a job opening?"

Pam swiveled to face the table and leaned forward on her elbows. "Wish you'd come to town a week ago, before Chase hired Krystal. That would have been perfect." Her plain face lit up with sudden curiosity. "Hey, how did that test-drive go?"

Lacey fooled with the bundle of flatware in front of her, carefully unsticking the glued paper strip that encircled it. "I didn't buy the truck."

"That's not what I'm asking."

"It went—not so good."

"That's not what I heard." Pam gave her a knowing smile. "Cody said you two had a pretty good time."

"It started out okay." Lacey felt like she was teetering on the slippery rocks in the stream again. "But your brother—he was really rude that first day, Pam. I'm not sure I can get over it."

"Oh." Pam sighed. "You can't just forget about it?"

"I wish I could." As she said the words, Lacey realized they were true. She'd give anything to be able to forget what Chase had said—to start fresh and finish what had begun in the bed of the pickup.

"Maybe if you give it a couple days, you'll feel better."

Pam was definitely an optimist. A very determined, matchmaking optimist. Lacey knew she should tell her the truth—that she'd never get over what Chase had said to her—but she didn't want to disappoint her new friend. The woman's good cheer and sunny outlook were like a shot of oxygen, making Lacey feel lighter and stronger. Her optimism was contagious.

"Maybe I will, somehow. Meanwhile, I need to find a job."

Chase watched Lacey sashay down the sidewalk. Couldn't the girl ever just walk? She seemed to sashay everywhere, or strut, or worse yet, trot. Trotting made her jiggle—not a lot, because she wore a decent bra. He knew that because he'd had to get past it when he'd…

Stop thinking about it. She shut you down. It's done.

He leaned sideways, almost tipping the high stool behind the counter so he could watch her cross the street. It looked like she'd gotten her outfit dirty somehow. Or maybe that was some kind of pattern on the fabric. He hadn't noticed it this morning, though, when she'd come out of the motel room.

Not that he'd been watching for her or anything. He'd just happened to be looking up at the balcony for the seventeenth time in five minutes when she stepped out of the room. He wondered if she'd found out he'd paid for it. If so, she'd chosen to ignore it.

That was okay with him. He didn't need her thanks. Hell, he didn't deserve it. Paying for the room was small potatoes compared to the way he'd insulted her.

The trailer door banged against the wall with a report like a rifle.

"Chase." Krystal's voice was sharp as she slapped a set of keys on their hook behind the counter with a thump and a jangle. "What are you doing?"

"Nothing." He frowned at the computer screen. "You sell anything?"

"Do you see customers with me?" she asked. "No. But I'm staying tonight, remember? I'll sell something then."

She pouted. "If we had brand new Toyotas, I bet I'd have sold something."

"Krystal, that was Link Masters and his wife. They have twenty acres outside of town and raise chickens and foster kids. They're not going to buy a new car."

She plopped down on the stool as he got up and stepped around the counter. "Maybe we'd get a better class of customers if we had better cars."

"From where? Nobody in this town can afford a new car."

"Maybe people would come up from Cheyenne."

He didn't bother to answer. Cheyenne had their own dealerships, so nobody was going to come to Grady for a Camry. He headed for his office, which was starting to feel more and more like a sanctuary from Krystal's pipe dreams and nagging.

"You were watching that woman, weren't you?"

He didn't answer that either.

"She's over at Jeb's. I bet she's applying for my old job."

Chase paused with his handle on the doorknob. "You think?"

"Yeah. But she won't get it. He's holding it for me. Hoping I'll come back." She gave Chase a flirtatious smile. "I told him I wouldn't. I told him you were going to start selling new cars, and I'd probably get to drive a Tundra."

"Krystal, no car company's giving us a dealership. Not in Grady."

"Go ahead." She tossed her hair and her sunny mood turned stormy as fast as a Texas tornado. "Kill my dreams."

Chase slammed the door of his pickup and slouched over the steering wheel, gripping it in both hands and banging his head twice on his knuckles. He'd left Krystal behind the counter, going on and on about the relative merits of the Toyota Camry versus the Honda Accord. She didn't know a damned thing about any of the cars on the lot, but she'd boned up on all the stuff they didn't have.

He'd been looking forward to spending a quiet evening at home, but Pam had run over with a bag of takeout for Fletcher Galt just before he left.

"The dinner rush is about to start," she said. "I don't have time to take this to him. You can do it, right?"

It wasn't really a question. Chase had taken the fragrant sack without a word and shrugged into his jacket.

"I put some in there for you too. Thought maybe you could stay, make sure he really eats it."

Chase rolled his eyes. He wasn't about to spend any more time with Galt than he had to. The guy hated his guts.

He was still stewing when he turned off the graded road onto the rutted two-track that had once been Galt's driveway. As he jounced his way to the ramshackle trailer, he could see his neighbor sitting on a tattered old sofa on his porch, a shotgun cradled in his lap. As he stepped out of the truck, the old man lifted it to his shoulder and closed one eye to aim.

"Don't shoot." Chase lifted one hand in the air and hoisted Pam's package in the other while he prayed that the last thing he'd see in this world wouldn't be Galt in his holey, sagging union suit. "I come bearing meatloaf."

Galt lowered the gun slightly and opened his left eye. "From your sister? She make those biscuits today?"

Chase opened the bag and peered inside. "Yep."

"Then I guess you can bring it on up." He used the shot-gun as a cane, hobbling into the house.

Chase followed him inside, noticing a distinct scent of lemon Pledge and bleach as the door opened. Someone had vacuumed the carpet, and the counters were clean. Even the picture on the TV had improved; shreds of aluminum foil topped the lopsided rabbit ears. His sister really was an angel.

Galt snatched the bag and unearthed its contents with the suppressed glee of a kid too cool for Santa opening gifts on Christmas day. He opened a Styrofoam coffee cup, releasing a torrent of rich-scented steam, then pulled out two lidded to-go plates, a bakery bag stuffed with bis-cuits, and a couple of smaller containers that looked like they contained some kind of dessert. Knowing Pam, it was probably pie.

Galt shoved one of the lidded containers across the counter that divided the kitchen from the living room. "Guess that one's yours," he said.

"Mine?"

Galt nodded, picking up a plastic fork and tucking into the meatloaf and gravy like he'd just returned from an excur-sion with the Donner party. "Your sister said she was going to pack for both of us. She stays to make sure I eat, said you would too, but I don't give a shit. And don't be thinking you're getting the biscuits. Those are mine."

So Pam's excuse about the dinner rush was bullshit. She'd planned this.

Chase watched the old man wipe his chin with the back of his hand as gravy dripped from a misplaced mouthful. It was hardly an appetizing sight. The guy finally looked up from the food when he was about three-quarters finished.

"Eat," he said, churning his free hand in a get-going gesture. "It's getting cold." His eyes narrowed as his gaze shifted to the smaller containers. "You going to want that pie?"

"No." Chase shoved the container toward the old man. "You can have it." He opened up his meatloaf and started eating. "Don't know why I'm staying. I don't think there's any doubt you're going to eat."

He watched the old man crouch over his dinner, downing the meatloaf like a wild dog. The guy had been alone too long, and it had turned him into an ornery old cuss with no manners. Chase was probably on his way to becoming just like him.

Maybe Pam was right that he needed to help somebody to be whole. Maybe Lacey's arrival was a second chance at life, a new purpose. Helping Lacey, protecting her, loving her, had been his mission back in high school—a mission that had ended with that smoldering kiss the night he'd rescued her from Wade. He'd told himself that night that he'd always watch out for her. It had been a boyish, foolish promise—but hadn't that foolish boy been a better person than the bitter, cynical man he'd become?

CHAPTER 15

LACEY WOKE THE NEXT MORNING WITH A HEADACHE that felt like the world's worst hangover, even though she hadn't had a thing to drink. In fact, she hadn't had any fun at all. She'd spent the night staring at the ceiling of the motel room, listening to Sinclair snore like a chain saw cutting through steel and wondering how she'd managed to mess up her life so badly.

Back when she'd left Tennessee, she'd thought she was stepping into a new life. And when she'd thrown away her Walmart ring, she'd had a clear vision of what that life was all about.

Realizing her dreams. Being on her own. She'd get a job, and then she'd get her real estate license, maybe even that marketing degree. Grady needed revitalizing even worse than Conway did. She could sell those boarded-up businesses on Main Street. The town was quaint. Adorable, really. There was an old Victorian that could be a bed-and-breakfast. They already had a great café.

But Trent had been right. Her dreams were stupid. What did she know about real estate? About business? Here she was, thinking she could make a home in Grady, and she couldn't even find a job.

She squinted out the motel window, seeing the town through Trent's eyes. He'd buy up a block or two of buildings and tear them down. Put up a trailer park. *That's all these yahoos can afford*—that's what Trent would say. There weren't even any jobs here; she'd figured that out yesterday. Every business on Main Street seemed to be on its last shaky legs, and there was nothing but prairie dogs and bug-eyed antelope outside town for fifty miles in either direction.

Suddenly the world beyond the Grady city limits seemed like another planet, unknown, unexplored, and unwelcoming. There wasn't a soul she knew from here to California. Here at least she had Pam—and Chase. He might not be what she'd hoped for or expected, but at least he knew who she was, and he knew she was here. Otherwise, she was about as substantial as a speck of dandelion fluff on the wind. She could disappear, and no one would even notice.

Grady might be the losingest town in the world, but right now, it was the closest thing she had to a home.

Not for long, though. She had no doubt the old guy in the lobby would eventually stick a bill under her door, or accost her in the parking lot. She'd managed to avoid making eye contact with him since the day before, but if he caught up to her tonight, she'd have to pay for her stay somehow.

Dropping into a scarred captain's chair by the room's only window, she opened her purse and pulled out a credit card. It was silver, with sparkles like mica, and bore her name in raised letters under the account number. Her name, not Trent's.

He'd kept her on all his accounts after the divorce. He'd pretended he was being generous, but it had actually allowed him to keep on controlling her, to question her about every expense, and chide her about shopping trips and eating out.

She'd hated that, and she hated the fact that the bribes he'd taken were paying her bills. So when she'd received a junk mailing that offered her a credit card in her own name, she'd filled it out and sent it in. Now she angled the card in the sunlight, watching the silver flecks shine. She hadn't planned on using it. She'd parceled out her money carefully and made it to her destination with a few dollars left, but the car breaking down had ruined everything.

She'd just pray that Wade wouldn't have some way to trace it. As long as the bill didn't go to the house or her old email account, she'd be safe. She just needed to change her address with the company. Then she'd have a month before the bill came due. A month to find a job.

Picking up the receiver on the old-fashioned phone, she dialed nine for an outside line, then poked in the customer service number on the back of the card.

"Welcome to MagiCard. Press one for English, two for Spanish," said a smooth, canned voice.

She ran through six or eight menus, keying in the account number and listening to her choices until she finally came to an address change option. The smooth-talking virtual operator asked her to press, or say, her new address. She glanced around. The motel was on Main Street, but what the heck was the number? She flopped across the bed and opened the nightstand drawer.

Nothing. Places like this didn't give out stationery with their address on it. She doubted anyone stayed long enough to write a letter. Hell, she doubted anyone stayed a whole night. It seemed like a by-the-hour kind of motel.

"To try again, press one," the canned voice urged her. "To return to main menu, press two."

She pressed one to buy more time and glanced across the street, searching for an address. There was nothing on the Quick Lube or the candle shop, but there were three shining gold numerals affixed to Chase's trailer.

"Four-twenty-three Main Street, Grady, Wyoming," she said clearly into the phone.

As soon as she found a place to live, she'd change it. It was the tenth of the month now, so the bill probably wouldn't come for two weeks. She'd find a place by then— but only if she found a job.

She hung up the phone and tucked her hands under Sinclair's furry armpits, turning him from side to side. "Looking good, bud. Keep putting weight on and you'll be cuddly soon, like a real dog." Sinclair huffed out a half-bark—or maybe it was a belch—and she shrugged. "Or not. Real dogs are friendly and love their owners."

He might have put on weight, but his attitude hadn't changed. His facial expression was still a comical blend of ennui and malice, with his eyes focused on the television and his lip curled into a snarl over his jutting underbite.

"All right. Finish watching your show, and I'll go get something to eat." She glanced at the TV, where Dr. Phil was lecturing a heavyset man on treating his wife better. "Who knows? Maybe you'll learn something. You and Dr. Phil even look alike." She scrubbed her fist over his head, earning a dagger-like stare. "You have more hair, though."

Food would help, she told herself on the way to the café. Food, and some female company. She needed some girl time.

Lacey smiled when Pam slid into the booth across from her. "So how's your brother doing?"

"Oh, he's the same as ever. Wish I could get Krystal away from him."

Annie popped up from behind her mother. She must have been in the next booth, quietly taking in their conversation. "Krystal's a hooker," she said.

Lacey didn't know if she should act shocked or laugh. Either way, it was all she could do to keep from spewing her sandwich all over the table.

"Annie!" Pam had decided on the shock option.

"Well, she dresses like a hooker," Annie continued. "I think the car lot's a front."

"I'm cutting off your *Law & Order* reruns," Pam said.

"No, really. Think about it," Annie urged. "They never sell much, and that lady just sits around all day. Uncle Chase must be making money somehow."

"He has a ranch," Lacey said.

"That's boring." Annie sat sideways at the edge of the booth, kicking her heels. "Nothing ever happens here. I want to move to New York."

Pam gave her a stern look, and Annie slouched upstairs, grumbling under her breath.

"Kid watches too much TV," Pam said. "Wish there was more for her to do."

Lacey glanced up the stairs. "She still dressing up the cat?"

"Yeah, but the cat just sits around. Wish I could afford to get her a dog."

Lacey thought of Sinclair back in the room and smiled. If only all her problems could solve themselves this easily.

"Maybe she could take care of mine."

"You have a dog?"

"He's not really mine. I found him at a gas station. He's kind of ugly, but he might look good in a onesie." Her smile widened, thinking of the dog's glum expression peering out from under a baby bonnet. "She could take him while I work. Heck, she could take him, period." She ignored the spasm of regret that pressed her chest when she thought of giving up the dog. What was that all about? She didn't even like the animal, and she'd never planned to keep him.

"You think he'd put up with the whole dress-up thing?"

Lacey thought a moment. "He's kind of grumpy, but I think he might like the attention. We could give it a try."

"I couldn't afford the vet bills."

"Chase would pay them," Lacey said.

"You know, he probably would. You want to bring him over later?" She hesitated. "Actually, I wondered if you could come over anyway. I know it's short notice, but Cody's going to a truck meet. I'd really like to go along, but there are a lot of rough redneck guys there, and I don't want to bring Annie."

"You want me to watch her?" Lacey felt a sudden heat behind her eyes.

"Would you mind? Do you have any plans?"

"No, I'd love to. And it would be a good time to bring Sinclair. What time?"

"Eight. It's a beer and nachos kind of thing in the parking lot at Herbie's Bar."

"Sounds fun." Lacey stood and carried her dishes to the pass-through. "I'll go walk the dog, and then I'll be over."

"You could come to the next one." Pam waggled her eyebrows. "We could double date."

"If I had a date."

"Chase," Pam said hopefully. "I really think…"

"Pam, I'm not going to date your brother."

"We'll see," Pam said. "He's a good guy, and he needs you. You guys should have been together from the start."

CHAPTER 16

KRYSTAL WAS LEANING AGAINST THE COUNTER WHEN Chase returned to the trailer, her long legs crossed at the ankles while she carefully considered the state of her fingernails. She was wearing a suit that should have been irreproachably professional, but something about the cut made it look like a sexy librarian stripper costume.

That wasn't fair. The girl couldn't help the way she was built. He just had a dirty mind. He pictured Lacey in the suit. The skirt was pretty short. If Lacey was wearing it, he'd hike it up and…

What the hell was wrong with him? Why was he panting after the girl the Conway High yearbook should have named *Most Likely to Break Chase Caldwell's Heart* when he had a hot number like Krystal panting after him every day at work?

She looked up at him and smiled, obviously mistaking his appraisal of the suit for approval of its contents.

"Tell you what. I'll make a yummy dinner tonight, and then I'll give you a nice back rub," she said. "And then we'll do something *else* yummy."

"Krystal, that's not going to happen. I'm your boss."

"So?"

"So you can't come to my house, and you can't give me a back rub or anything else. Besides, I thought you were going to work late tonight."

She pouted. "Wouldn't you rather I come home with you?"

Did the girl ever give up? It took two to tango, and he wasn't even stepping onto the dance floor.

"I'd rather sell something. We haven't made a sale in two days."

"'We.' I like that."

Damn. Everything he said brought him a giant step closer to trouble with this girl.

"There is no 'we.'"

Her eyes narrowed. "Well, I'll bet I can bring the guys in. I'll sell something for you." She shimmied her shoulders. "If you're not buying, I'm sure someone else will."

"Krystal, cut it out." He sniffed the air and caught an acidic tang. "Have you been drinking?"

"It's none of your business what I do on my time off."

"It is if you're drunk at work."

"I am not drunk." She straightened with a suspiciously exaggerated dignity that emphasized the low cut of her suit.

"You'd better not be. And we need to have a conversation about appropriate attire. You look like you're ready for a night on the town, not a work shift." He smiled, trying to lessen the sting. "We want the customers to focus on the cars, right?"

She gave him a little-girl frowny face. "Jeb liked it when I dressed like this."

"Jeb's customers were spending $19.99," he said.

Her face reddened. "Are you calling me low-rent?"

"No." He almost shouted the word, then clutched his forehead, trying to regain control. "Look, if you don't want to work tonight, it's okay. But I'm going home alone."

She narrowed her eyes. "You sure you don't have a dinner date?"

"Actually, I do. I'm having dinner with Fletcher Galt."

Krystal's eyes widened. "Isn't that the guy who shot your cow?"

"Yeah. It was a misunderstanding."

Actually, it was impossible to misunderstand Fletcher Galt. The guy was nothing if not direct. The night before, he'd told Chase he'd bypass the cattle and shoot him if the fence failed again.

"So why are you hanging out with him? Are you trying to get the rest of his land or something?"

"No. Not everyone has an ulterior motive, you know."

"Well, I just want to make money. If that's *unterior,* I'm sorry." She jutted out her chin and stiffened her shoulders. "I'll stay, and I'll show you who can sell stuff. I can sell a lot more than oil changes. I could sell new Toyotas if you'd let me."

"Okay," he said, ignoring her mention of new cars. "Good."

She edged closer. "You sure you're not seeing that bimbo tonight?"

"She's not a bimbo, and that's none of your business. But no, I'm not," Chase said.

She pouted. "I know you want to."

She was right. He hadn't been thinking Lacey would ever come to the ranch, but now that the subject had come up, his mind was rifling through images of Lacey in every room of his house. Lacey in the kitchen. Lacey in the den. Lacey in the bedroom.

Naked.

He hated himself for it, but he really did wish he was having Lacey over.

Cody was cleaning the grill when Chase walked into the café to pick up Galt's dinner. The cook glanced through the pass-through and grinned. "You coming to the truck rally?"

"No." Chase headed straight for the staircase. "I'm not obsessed with that stuff like you are."

"There'll be a lot of potential customers there. You could maybe talk up that Dodge."

"You do it for me. My sister here?"

"She's upstairs. She left this for you, though." He shoved a brown paper bag through the pass-through. Judging from the scent, Chase and Galt were having hot turkey sand-wiches tonight. "Hey, you oughta go to the meet, though. I think that trucker girl's coming."

"Trucker girl?"

"The one who's staying in the motel." Cody jabbed a thumb in the direction of the Ranch Motel as if Chase hadn't been staring at it all day. "You know, the pretty one."

Chase turned, surprised, and almost clocked himself on the side of the doorway. He sat down on one of the stools at the counter, hoping Cody would think he'd meant to stop and talk all along.

"She's going to the rally?" Chase pulled a napkin out of the chrome holder and began wiping down the salt and pepper shaker as if smudge-free condiments held the key to world peace.

"I guess." Cody scraped a metal spatula across the grill, sliding the burned bits from the day's business into the waste channel. "Pam said something about her coming over."

"When?"

Cody shrugged. "A half hour or so, I guess. That's when we're leaving."

"So is Pam upstairs?"

"Yeah. She's getting ready. Like anybody cares what she looks like at a truck rally." Cody wiped his hands on his smudged apron and untied the back, slipping the loop over his head and hanging it on a hood. Underneath it, he was wearing a Jeremiah Weed T-shirt that was almost worn through at the shoulders. He shook his head. "Girls."

"Well, I better run up and talk to her. I wanted Annie to come out Saturday."

"Works for me." Cody waggled his eyebrows suggestively. "Give us a little one-on-one time."

"That's my sister you're talking about," Chase said.

"I know. Your fine, fine sister."

Chase tossed off an eye roll that would have done Annie proud and headed up the stairs. His sister was in the kitchen with her back to him, rummaging through the freezer, intent on finding something. He tiptoed up behind her and was just about to poke her in the side when she spun around and hollered into his face.

"*Macaroni and cheese okay, Annie?*"

He clutched his heart and stumbled backward into one of the chairs at the old-fashioned dinette table. "Holy mother of God," he said. "You about gave me a heart attack."

"Which is what you were trying to do to me." Pam dusted off her hands with satisfaction. "That's what you get for sneaking up on your big sister." She swatted his arm as she strode past, heading down the hallway to Annie's room. "*Annie? Mac and cheese?*" She turned as she opened her daughter's bedroom door. "Kid's turning into a teenager. Got earbuds in 24/7. I'll be right out."

Chase glanced around the kitchen. The afternoon sun slanted through the small window over the sink, reflecting off the gleaming faucet and casting a grid of bright light onto the shiny linoleum floor. His sister was such a good housekeeper, such a good mom. She'd built a great life out here in Wyoming.

He was always a step behind his older sister. He'd built a life, but great? Not so much. While her tiny apartment felt homey and warm, his own home didn't feel much more than functional—someplace to eat and sleep and run the ranch. It was more a headquarters than a home. If he didn't watch out, he really would end up like Galt.

Borrowing Annie for the weekend would help, but watching the old man made him realize he spent way too much time alone. Once again, pictures of Lacey at the ranch danced through his consciousness. He set his elbows on the table and rested his forehead on his fists, squeezing his eyes shut in an effort to erase the fantasies. He didn't even bother to sit up when he heard steps on the staircase—no doubt Cody coming up to see if Pam was ready.

"Hello?" said a voice from the stairs.

That wasn't Cody. He spun to see Lacey standing uncertainly in the doorway.

"You okay?" she asked.

"Yeah." He rose awkwardly, shoving his hands in his pockets. "Cody said you wouldn't be here for half an hour. I was just going to talk to Pam a minute."

"Well, sorry I didn't suit your schedule. I thought I'd come a little early, make sure I knew the drill for Annie.

You know, bedtime and stuff." Her ugly dog galloped up the stairs and trotted past her as if he owned the joint, heading for Annie's bedroom.

"Bedtime?" That was the only word in the whole sentence that had registered.

"Yeah. And I wasn't sure what to do for dinner."

"Macaroni and cheese."

"Oh." She looked disappointed. "You're watching her?"

"No. I thought she was going with—*you're* watching her?"

"Yes." She set her fists on her hips. "Why? Is that a problem?"

CHAPTER 17

"No." Chase hadn't meant to sound so incredulous. There was really no reason Lacey shouldn't watch Annie. It just surprised him. "I think it's great you're watching her. It's just…"

"What? Just that I'm not competent?"

A childish shriek of joy emanated from the hallway. "A dog! Look, Mom. He's so *cute*!"

Chase couldn't help laughing. The dog was anything but cute. Lacey evidently agreed, because she dimpled up and for just a second they shared something that felt like a moment. Or at least they were in agreement on something.

Shoot, they hadn't agreed on anything since yesterday in the bed of the pickup, when they'd agreed—well, when they'd agreed on pretty much everything that mattered.

"'Cute' isn't how I'd describe that animal," he said.

"No, but he's healthy. Which is a good thing, because you're paying the vet bills."

"What, he needs shots?" He smiled tentatively, like he was trying to ease the fears of a timid child. She'd finally decided to let him help her—for the dog's sake, but still… "Sure. I'll pay for 'em."

Lacey looked startled. "You will?"

"Sure." He slowly raised his hands to shoulder level, palms out. "And look. No hands."

The dimples were back. "Well, thanks. But I wasn't asking for me. I'm going to give the dog to Annie."

Annie blasted out of her room, followed by a very disgruntled Sinclair dressed in a plaid sundress. "You *what*? You're going to *give* him to me?" She threw herself at Lacey, who caught the child in her arms and almost staggered back onto the stairs. "Oh, Lacey. Oh my gosh. Can I really? Mom? Lacey wants to give me the dog. Can I have him? Please? *Please*?"

Pam was beaming, her arms folded over her chest. "Yes, honey. Lacey and I talked about it."

"Oh, *thank* you. Thank you, thank you, thank you!" Annie gave Lacey one more squeeze and released her hold to jump up and down in front of her. "This is the best thing that ever happened to me. I will *never* forget you, Aunt Lacey. Never never *never*. Not *ever*." She paused, sliding her eyes toward her mother. "Is it all right if I call her Aunt Lacey, Mom?"

"Sure." Pam passed the same questioning glance toward Chase. "I'd like it if you called her that."

Chase sputtered, feeling hot and supremely embarrassed. Pam was always a matchmaker, especially where he was concerned, but she usually didn't do it right in front of the woman in question. And judging from Lacey's reaction, she was embarrassed too. Annie had squeezed her into an enormous hug again, and the woman looked like she was going to cry.

Was he that bad?

"Never never *ever*," Annie repeated like a prayer. "Never."

"Not ever?" Lacey wrapped her arms around Annie and rested her cheek on the child's head, closing her eyes. The tears weren't about Chase. Not at all. She hadn't even noticed the "Aunt Lacey" thing. Was she so lonely that a declaration of love from an eight-year-old meant that much?

He thought of what Annie meant to him and knew the answer to his question. Suddenly, he was blinking back tears too.

"I—well…" He backed out of the room. "I have to go home. Chores to do."

"I think Sinclair needs a break," Lacey said. It was eight o'clock, and the dog had modeled two sundresses, a baby-doll nightgown, a one-piece ruffled romper, and an assortment of bonnets. He'd apparently drawn the line at the romper—maybe it was the ruffles—because he skulked away as soon as Annie removed it, tossing a look over his shoulder that reminded Lacey of a Victoria's Secret angel gone diva.

"Okay. Come on, Sinclair." Annie patted the sofa and the dog hopped up beside her, but he kept his head down, ready to dodge any attempt at dressing him again.

"You want to watch TV? Your mom said you watch *Law & Order*." Considering the kid's theory about Krystal's moonlighting as a hooker, Lacey wasn't sure that was wise, but Annie wasn't her kid, and Pam had said she didn't want to fight the TV battle that night.

"No. I want to do a stakeout," Annie said, as if that was a perfectly normal option for an eight-year-old. She plopped into a threadbare rocker-recliner and spun it toward the window, grabbing a pair of binoculars and a well-used note-book from the sill. "I'm staking out the car lot."

"You're watching Chase?"

"I'm watching his girlfriend." Annie levered the Venetian

blinds shut, then poked the binoculars between two slats. "I'm telling you, she's suspicious. Look." She handed the binoculars to Lacey.

Lacey hesitated, but she couldn't resist taking a peek. She told herself she just wanted to know what was getting Annie so riled up. Squinting through the lenses, she watched Krystal walk the length of the car lot. In her skimpy suit and high heels, she really did look oddly out-of-place in the small-town car lot. She paraded through the rows with a hip-swinging gait that looked to Lacey like a clear invitation to any passing man—and possibly the result of a couple drinks with dinner.

Pausing next to a Pontiac, Krystal bent at the waist to check her lipstick in the side mirror, her rump turned toward the street for all to see and appreciate.

"Geez," Lacey said.

"What? Lemme see." Annie reached for the glasses, but Lacey shrugged her off.

"I'm not sure you're old enough to watch this."

"What? Did she get a customer? Are they doing it?"

"No! And you shouldn't even think about stuff like that!"

"I watch TV, Aunt Lacey."

Krystal straightened, changing the view back to a PG rating, and Lacey handed the binoculars back. "Well, you need to switch to the Disney Channel."

"Oh, come on. That *High School Musical* stuff is lame." Annie poked the binoculars through the blinds and resumed her stakeout while Lacey leaned back on the sofa and closed her eyes, then opened them. She could feel every bone, tendon, and muscle in her body, and every one of them ached and throbbed. She'd covered a lot of concrete in her job search today. She got up to get some Tylenol from her purse.

"She went back inside," Annie murmured. "Still didn't sell anything. I *told* you."

Lacey popped two tablets and lay down again.

"Uh-oh." Annie sounded genuinely concerned.

"What?"

The little girl turned around, her eyes wide. "Some guy just snuck up to the back of the trailer. I think he's one of her customers." She turned back around, jamming the lenses through the blinds. "I told you, it's a front," Annie said. "He's one of her johns."

"That's it," Lacey said. "Your mom needs to cut off the HBO."

Lacey heard a loud "bang" from across the street and a high, harsh scream broke the night stillness. Sinclair let out a sharp volley of barks, and Annie gasped, spinning around and shoving the binoculars at Lacey. "Oh my gosh. They came out from behind the counter and she slapped him and he grabbed her wrists and pulled her back there with him! He's probably going to—you know."

Lacey had a feeling Annie did know but wasn't about to lose her cable TV privileges.

"We have to go over there!" Annie said.

"I don't think so." Lacey grabbed the kid's arm as she jumped up from the chair. "Are you sure it wasn't just the guy from the Quick Lube?"

"It might have been." Annie looked troubled. "But so what? He looks like a bad guy. He has tattoos and every-thing. And he was being real sneaky, like..." She put her hands up like bunny paws and did a dramatization that reminded Lacey of the Pink Panther cartoon.

It sounded like Jeb from the Quick Lube, all right. And judging from the hungry way he'd looked at Lacey that afternoon while she filled out a job application, he wouldn't be able to resist Krystal's sexy swagger.

Sinclair growled low in his throat, and Lacey felt her stomach clench. Dogs were supposed to have instincts that told them when something was wrong.

"Oh my God," she murmured. Annie had a point. All those tattoos and the muscles bulging from his tight T-shirt indicated the guy fancied himself as some sort of badass, and he and Krystal had a history. If he drank or did drugs, who knew what he'd do? Krystal had frustrated him and hurt him. For some men, that was a clear call to use their fists.

Annie turned to her, tears standing in her eyes. "We have to stop him." Her forehead was creased with worry lines. "I don't like that lady, but..."

"I guess we should call the police," Lacey said.

"I'm on it." Annie raced out of the room. Lacey chased after her but was too late to stop her from grabbing a cell phone from the kitchen counter and poking the three magic emergency numbers into the keypad. Realizing what an eight-year-old's panicked account would sound like, Lacey grabbed the phone as the operator picked up.

"Highway patrol," the operator intoned. "State your emergency."

"I'm calling about Caldwell's Used Cars in Grady," Lacey began, wishing she'd caught Annie before she hit the number. The nonemergency line would have been fine, probably, but she was stuck now. "I'm at the café across the street, and we—well, my friend saw a man go in the back door. When he approached the saleswoman, they had an altercation. My friend says he grabbed the girl's wrists and pulled her into the back." She strode over to the window with the handset. "I heard a scream, and now there's no sign of life over there."

Now that she'd put the scene into words, maybe it was a good thing they *had* called the emergency line.

"A car is on the way. Can you describe the assailant?"

"Hold on. Let me put my—my niece on." She handed the phone to Annie. "*Describe him,*" she whispered.

"I'd say about six-four, two-fifty," Annie said in a smooth, professional tone. "Dark hair, long in the back. Wearing a dark T-shirt with some kind of logo on the front and blue jeans." She finally took a breath. "I couldn't see any tattoos or identifying marks from this distance."

Lacey wondered if it was bad to be proud of a child when a woman could be under attack right across the street. She couldn't help it, though. She knew Annie was scared, but the kid was cool, professional, and observant.

"I'm eight," Annie said into the phone, obviously answering a question from the operator. She listened a moment. "Thank you. Okay."

She handed the handset back to Lacey.

"*She said I did a good job,*" she whispered.

Lacey smiled and nodded enthusiastically, trying to telegraph her own praise before she got back on the phone. The woman grilled her for more information, then asked her name.

Lacey hesitated. She couldn't give her name to the police. Trent's partners were both devious and desperate. There was no telling how they might try to trace her, or what kind of stories they might tell. For all she knew, they'd played family friend and declared her missing. There could be an APB out on her at that very moment.

While she struggled to make a decision, sirens screamed in the distance.

"Ma'am?" the operator said.

"They're here. Thanks," Lacey blurted out and hung up the phone.

CHAPTER 18

RED LIGHTS CHASED BLUE ACROSS THE CAR LOT, CAST from the spinning cherry-tops of no less than three police cruisers. Evidently, the cops who served the tiny outpost of Grady didn't have much to do on a Monday night.

Lacey eased open Annie's bedroom window and a burst of radio babble broke the silence. The transmission was garbled and impossible to understand.

A crackle of radio static cut through the night air, and Jeb appeared in the store's lighted window. He was shirtless and staggering slightly, and in a moment Lacey understood why. A policeman was close behind him, shoving him through the door from the back room. Jeb's hands were evidently cuffed behind him. The awkward pose made his belly pooch out and highlighted the fact that his belt was undone.

"You probably shouldn't be watching this," she told Annie.

The kid stared at her a moment with wide, horrified eyes before turning back to the live-action drama across the street.

"You're kidding, right? This is better than *Law & Order.* It's *real.*"

They both watched Krystal appear in the lighted doorway of the trailer. She was smoothing her hair and adjusting the neckline of her jacket.

She wasn't acting much like a victim. Following behind

the policeman, she waved her arms. As they pushed Jeb out the front door and down the steps, she followed, her shrill voice carrying across the street.

"You can't arrest him! He's my boyfriend! We were just…talking."

The policeman, grim-faced, didn't respond as he marched Jeb across the lot to one of the waiting cruisers.

"He wasn't raping me!" Krystal ran alongside the officer, then put on a burst of speed and beat them to the car where another cop waited at the opened door. "I *wanted* to do it!" Throwing herself across the opening to the cage-enclosed backseat, she spread her arms over the roof and rear window and thrust her hips forward while she tossed her head back. It was a drama queen gesture that would have played well on a low-budget police drama, but it was a little over-the-top for real life.

"I won't let you take him!" she cried in the tragic, heart-felt tones of a soap opera queen. "I *love* him!"

"Lady, get out of the way. You come on over here and we'll talk, but he's cooling his heels in the car for now. After the call we got, he's got some explaining to do."

"Who called?" Krystal demanded.

"We should go tell them it was us," Annie whispered. "That lady said I did a good job."

Lacey shook her head.

"We're not sure." The officer pointed toward another pair of cops, who were leaning against the trunk of another cruiser, arms folded, ankles crossed, casually watching Krystal's antics. "But those guys are about to go find out. Check out that motel across the street, guys. Call probably came from there."

Lacey jerked away from the window. Good. If they checked the motel, they'd find her room empty. Once they figured out the call came from the café, they'd probably assume Pam had called. She was off the hook.

But not with Annie. "Look, they're going inside. I want to tell them I was the one who gave the description, okay?"

"We'd better wait," Lacey said weakly. "It might be a dangerous situation."

She didn't want to tell Annie they weren't going over there at all. Introducing herself as the reporting caller would only lead to questions.

Questions Lacey simply couldn't answer.

"The police have a job to do, honey."

"I know. And I want to watch them do it."

Annie jumped off the chair and ran out of the room. Lacey followed her, pausing at the top of the steps.

"Annie, no. Come back here."

The only answer was the swish of slippered feet rushing down the stairs.

Lacey swore under her breath. Pam had trusted her with Annie, so she had to follow. But going outside would put her square in the glare from the police cars' whirling lights.

If Wade had declared her missing, she was about to get found.

Chase's phone buzzed just as he pulled up to the ranch house. He and Fletcher Galt had shared a silent but surprisingly companionable dinner. He'd even started to think about bringing Annie over to see the guy on Saturday.

"Dude." It was Cody. "We just got back from the rally, and something's going on at the lot."

"It's about time," Chase said. "Nothing's gone on there for days. We haven't had so much as a nibble since Krystal sold that harrow."

"Is that what that was? Guy who bought it said it was an antique."

"It was junk. So what did she sell?"

"Nothing."

Chase swallowed. Judging from the repressed excitement in Cody's voice, something bad was happening.

"It's that girlfriend of yours."

Chase pressed the phone to his ear. He could barely hear Cody over the static and noise in the background.

"Where are you? Pam's?"

"Nope. I'm out front. We didn't even go in yet. Well, I didn't. Pam ran up to check on Annie. I hung out here when I saw the cop cars pull up. Three of 'em."

"What?"

"I told you, that girlfriend of yours finally went batshit crazy. I think she got herself arrested."

"*What?*"

Chase tossed the phone on the passenger seat and peeled out of the driveway. He could hear Cody's voice squawking from the speaker as he took the corner at the end of the driveway, and the phone slid sideways and fell to the floor.

"Chase, what the hell?" shouted Cody.

Chase ducked down and picked up the phone as he straightened out the truck.

"Sorry," he said. "Dropped the phone. So *what* happened?"

"Your girlfriend almost got herself arrested. I think they actually did arrest Jeb. It was like an episode of *Bad Boys: Redneck Edition* around here. She was throwing herself all over the place, screeching, and Jeb looked like the last of the red-hot losers. No shirt, no shoes, no smarts."

"She's not my girlfriend," Chase said. Because he needed to make that clear—to Cody, and to himself. No matter how viscerally he responded to Lacey, she wasn't likely to forgive him for what he'd said.

"Good thing, 'cause she was yelling about how much she loves Jeb," Cody said.

Okay, this was just bizarre.

"Sounds like she's changed her mind about chasing you and gone back to her old fiancé." Cody pronounced the word "fee-ancy." Four-wheeling, gum-smacking Cody calling anybody a redneck was definitely a case of the pot calling the kettle names.

"Her...oh." Chase slumped with relief, and the knot in his belly loosened up. "You're talking about Krystal."

"Yeah. You thought I was talking about that little piece of action from the truck, didn't you? Pam said there was something going on there."

"No, I..."

"Sly dog. No wonder you don't care if Krystal goes back to Jeb."

"Krystal and I were never anything," Chase protested. "She just kept kind of following me around."

"Man, you're a player, you know that?" Cody chuckled. "Hey, something's happening. I'll call you back."

Chase tossed the phone aside and pressed the accelerator, then wondered why he was in such a hurry. Lacey was at Pam's, so he knew she was safe. This was some kind of shenanigans on Krystal's part. For all he knew, she was just trying to get his attention. He slowed the truck to a safer speed as the phone rang again.

"Got the scoop," Cody said. "I guess old Jeb snuck in the back of the trailer to make up with Krystal, and somebody saw him and thought he was a crook. Cops came and arrested him and Krystal both. Or maybe she just went along to explain. Judging from how she's carrying on, she's not about to let anybody mess up her booty call."

"Please," Chase said. The image of Krystal and Jeb together wasn't pretty. "You say he went in the back?"

"Yep. And I hate to be the one to tell you, but they had to be getting down to business in there. He was barely dressed when he came out, and Krystal looked like she'd stuck her finger in an electric socket."

Chase blanched. There was nowhere in the trailer Krystal could have taken Jeb but his office. He'd never look at his desk the same way again. He made a mental note to grab some disinfectant from the cupboard under the kitchen sink and take it to work the next morning.

"Well, I guess now you're free to take up with the trucker girl," Cody said.

"I'm not taking up with anybody. Especially not Lacey. And she's not a trucker girl. That lady's fresh from the trophy-wife circuit."

"Really? She sure looked at home in that mud bath to me."

Chase rocked with the truck as the tires lurched off the dirt road onto the blacktop two-lane into town. "She's having some hard times."

"Well, if I didn't have Pam, I'd try and rescue her." Cody laughed again. "Have at it, man. You don't have to marry her."

Chase felt an involuntary tug at his vitals at Cody's phraseology. If only "having at it" was as simple as it sounded.

"Meanwhile, the trailer's standing open," Cody said. "I'm out in the lot, but I need to get back to Pam. Unlike you, I'm a man with a happy, healthy relationship with the opposite sex, if you know what I mean."

"I'll be right there."

"Good. And you might want to talk to the cops after all, because they just marched Trucker Girl out to their car."

CHAPTER 19

THE MINUTE LACEY STEPPED OUT THE DOOR OF THE café, a policeman turned and pinned her to the wall with the beam of a flashlight. She tried not to look guilty.

"My—my daughter." She pointed at Annie, who was watching wide-eyed from the sidewalk. "I mean, my friend's daughter. I just came to get her."

The cop's eyes met hers, then moved down her body to her feet before flicking back up again guiltily. "We had a call from 911 about an incident here, ma'am. The little girl informed us that she made the call. Are you the woman who spoke to the operator?"

Lacey swallowed and nodded. She flicked her tongue out to lick her dry lips.

"And me," said Annie, coming up beside her. "I was the one who gave the description."

"Well, thank you, miss." He turned back to Lacey. "I'm sorry to trouble you, ma'am, but the dispatcher informed us you neglected to identify yourself."

She blinked again, doing her best imitation of a woman roused from a deep sleep. "What?"

A blast of static blared from his radio. "*I talked to a witness over here in the motel office. There's a transient woman staying at the motel. 'Round thirty, dark hair.*"

Transient woman? That certainly wasn't a compliment, but for some unaccountable reason, Lacey felt a swell of pride at the description. She turned the word over in her head. Transient. Loner. Desperado. Any way you looked at it, she'd come a long way from being a kept woman.

"*Guy at the desk says he saw her go over to the café earlier, and she never returned to her room. Hold on.*" The radio hushed a moment, then crackled back to life. "*Yeah, he says that's her you're talking to. Room's registered to the owner of the car lot. Caldwell. Guess she's his girlfriend or something. He paid for a week, guy says.*"

Lacey felt the bottom drop out of her stomach. Chase paid for the room? Damn. She was a kept woman after all. No wonder the desk clerk hadn't bothered her. The room had been paid for the whole time.

The thought should make her angry, or at least nervous. If Chase had paid for the room, chances were he had a key. But her visceral response to that thought was a not-unpleasant twist in her belly and a mental picture of Chase in her bed.

He looked good there.

She rubbed her eyes, trying to erase the picture. She'd told him she didn't want his money, and he'd gone and paid for the room anyway, behind her back. She couldn't trust him. Men were always trying to own women so they could control them.

Of course, she'd probably be a real transient by now if he hadn't paid her bill.

"Miss," the cop said.

"Sorry." She struggled to return to the here and now. She needed to be alert and aware.

He narrowed his eyes. "I need some ID."

"Is she under arrest?" Annie asked.

The cop looked startled. "No."

Annie stepped up to Lacey, her fists on her hips. "Then she doesn't have to tell you anything."

The cop's lips tipped up into a grin. "This your lawyer?"

"Um, no." Lacey felt a dull thud in the pit of her stomach. Her friend had trusted her with her daughter for one night, and now they were being questioned by the police. Hopefully Pam would see it as healthy civic involvement.

"What's your name, honey?" The cop bent his knees so he was eye level with Annie, who crossed her arms over her chest and jutted out her chin.

"I refuse to answer any questions except in the presence of my attorney."

The cop flashed Lacey a questioning glance. "You had trouble with the police before?"

Lacey waved her hand, dismissing the notion. "She watches a lot of TV."

"*Law & Order*," Annie said. "So I know better than to get railroaded by the good cop, bad cop thing." She peered through the doorway past him. "Where's the good cop, anyway?"

"That's me," he said indignantly, then flinched as if he'd just noticed he was arguing with a kid and turned back to Lacey. "Ma'am, you're not under arrest, but it turns out the call was unsubstantiated. We just need to establish whether you have any kind of personal relationship with the parties involved."

"I can assure you, I don't." Lacey backed toward the café, but the cop stopped her with an upraised hand.

"We just need to see some identification so we can confirm that," he said kindly.

"I-I don't have anything."

He arched his brows, looking pointedly at the purse slung over her shoulder.

"I think you'd better come with me, ma'am," he said. "I'm starting to think the parties involved may be able to identify you."

Chase pulled into the car lot just in time to witness a stand-off. Krystal stood a few feet from a police car, feet planted wide apart, fists on her hips, torso tilted forward so that she could more effectively berate Lacey, who was sitting on the edge of the cruiser's backseat. He rolled down his window to hear his employee's shrill voice raised above the noise of the radio and the faint murmur rising from the small crowd that had gathered. He could see Cody standing on the edge of the knot of spectators, along with Pam and Annie.

"You *bitch*," Krystal was saying. "You did this on purpose. You saw Jeb come over here, and you called the cops so Chase would find out. You want him all to yourself, but I've got news for you. He's not interested. He told me. He said he wasn't interested in high-maintenance women." She paused for a breath, then started in again an octave higher. "You know what that means? He's not interested in a woman who wants to dress nice, or go out to dinner once in a while. He wants some dumb bitch he can keep down on the farm."

"I'm not interested in Chase," Lacey said. "We're old friends. I thought we still were, but we're not. End of story."

Ouch. Once again, Chase's insides balled up in a knot. He'd handled everything wrong that first day Lacey had come to town. He should have just helped her. Then he'd gone and made matters worse with those shenanigans on the test-drive. What kind of used car dealer made out with his customers in the vehicles? He'd lectured Krystal about being professional, but he wasn't any better.

"You came out here thinking you'd start something. I'll bet you two dated in high school."

"No," Lacey said, still sounding cool and detached. "We never did. We should have—he was the nicest guy in the whole school—but we didn't."

"*See?*" Krystal straightened in triumph. "I knew it."

Chase felt like standing up a little straighter himself. He'd never known Lacey thought so highly of him. He thought she'd seen him as another loser adoring her from afar—just one of the crowd.

"But he's changed. He's not the nice guy I used to know," Lacey continued. "He's—hardened. Bitter."

Chase winced. He *was* bitter and hard—but he had good reason. Couldn't Lacey see that? He'd lost everything when his dad had lost the farm. His future. His family.

Then again, he still had Pam. And Annie. He remembered Lacey's expression when Annie had hugged her hours before. She'd obviously had a lot less love in her life than he did. Maybe he should quit feeling sorry for himself.

"You ladies can discuss your gentleman friend some other time," a second policeman said, stepping between the two women. "Right now I need to talk to this one." He gestured toward Lacey, then turned to Krystal. "You can go."

Krystal turned on her high heel, stumbled a little, and flounced off with her nose in the air. The blue and white strobes flicked off as she departed, but Lacey's eyes glinted in the mercury lights of the car lot as she looked up at the policeman.

"Are you going to arrest me? I swear, I never meant to call in a false report. I just saw something, and I thought she was in danger. I wasn't sure what was happening, but I was honestly worried about Krystal."

"Was that your little girl that called Officer Nelson the bad cop?" He could barely suppress a smile, and Lacey grinned back, meeting his eyes. Chase felt a stab of envy. He'd never wished for a career in law enforcement before, but he'd ace the police academy to have Lacey look at him like that.

"My friend's daughter. She watches a lot of *Law & Order*," she said.

"Well, I guess if I let you off with a warning, you'll know I'm the good cop, right?"

Lacey nodded. "I sure will." Her smile lit up a little brighter. "I knew that anyway."

Chase could swear the cop was melting in front of his eyes. He knew the guy—Rick Platt. He lived in Wynott and had a wife and two little boys, so he had no business flirting with Lacey—but that smile had made him forget his family and probably his own name.

"How'd you know I was the good one?" Rick asked.

Lacey shrugged, lifting one shoulder gracefully and tossing a smile over her shoulder while she turned to walk away. "You *look* good," she said.

The guy grinned. "Thanks. But I'll still need identification to complete the report."

Lacey slumped, and Chase realized her flirtation was a ploy to get the cop to move on. He stepped up beside her.

"I know her, Rick," he said. "I'll vouch for her."

"Caldwell? What have you got going on here?"

"A mess." Chase stepped away and tilted his head to one side. Officer Platt got the signal and walked around to the back of the car with him, leaving Lacey in the shaft of light from the cruiser's open door. She stood poised to flee, glancing nervously at the knots of people on the sidewalk.

"Look," Chase said to the cop. "I know this lady. She's got issues, but she hasn't done anything wrong."

"Then what's the problem? All I need is her name and some ID."

"She can't do that. She's left an abusive relationship, and she's terrified her husband will find her."

"We're not going to put her on the news, for God's sake. And if her husband's abusing her, she needs law enforcement. There are things we can…"

"He *is* law enforcement," Chase said. He wasn't a liar, and he doubted he was good at it, but the story came easily enough that he might persuade the cop to believe him. "He's the chief of police in her hometown in…" He paused. "In Virginia."

Rick turned, and Chase wondered if he noticed Lacey looking at Chase as if he'd sprouted antennae and turned green. Staring at her, the cop staggered back and nearly tripped over Chase's boot. Chase doubted he'd been stunned by Lacey's wide-eyed look. More likely, he'd simply been stunned by Lacey.

Finally, the officer steadied himself on the trunk of his car and scowled at both of them. "All right. You can go. But there'd better not be any more trouble."

Lacey backed away, nodding, until she stood by the

still-open driver's side of Chase's truck. She was backlit by
the dome light so he couldn't see her expression as she spoke.

"There won't be," she said. "I swear. No trouble."

The cop, back in control, nodded briskly as he slid into
the cruiser. "Good. And if you're truly on the run, miss, I'd
move on. We'll drive by here a little more often, but that's
all we can do. We may not have the resources to protect you
if your husband finds you."

Chase looked down at Lacey as the cop car left the lot.

"Listen." She looked a little shell-shocked so he took her
arm, steadying her. "Can we start over? We got off on the
wrong foot the other day."

"Which day was that?" She seemed roused from her
stupor. "The day you insulted me, or the day you attacked
me?"

"The day I insulted you." He scowled. "I didn't attack you."

"I know." She shrugged. "We were both to blame for that
mess."

He winced. It hadn't been a mess by his standards. It
had been one of the finest moments of his life—until she
changed her mind and put a stop to it. Which was the right
thing to do. He'd had to remind himself of that fact every
five minutes ever since.

"Look, let's forget it happened," he said. He'd never
forget, but until Lacey did, she wouldn't forgive him. And
until she forgave him, she wouldn't let him help her.

"All right. We'll start over," she said. "Nothing ever
happened."

That was what he wanted, right? So why did he feel so
miserable?

CHAPTER 20

LACEY LOOKED UP AT CHASE, BITING HER LOWER LIP. He was standing close, gripping her elbow with one strong hand. The other held the open door, so she was trapped between him and the truck. She could feel the warmth of his body and was suddenly overwhelmed with the scent of him—hints of leather and hay mixed with the more civilized fragrances of fabric softener and toothpaste.

But they had important issues to talk about, so why was she *smelling* him?

"Let's talk about my motel room," she said. "I just found out you paid for it."

He shrugged. "I didn't mean for you to know. I just wanted to help. I don't have a key or anything."

"Okay," she said, softening her tone. "I should thank you, I guess. I didn't want to ask for help, but I don't know how I would have survived. I'll pay you back as soon as I get a job, okay?"

He nodded.

"I thought the guy that runs the place was getting senile and forgot about me." She smiled. "I kept sneaking past him so he wouldn't remember I was there and make me pay."

"I was glad to help."

"Well, thanks. I'll be okay next week, though. I have a credit card."

He looked alarmed. "They'll trace it."

She looked away. "That's a risk I'll have to take." She set

her palm on his chest to push him back, but she couldn't help pausing as their eyes met. She could feel his heart thumping as he reached up, took her hand, and pulled her close.

Lacey meant to wriggle away, or push him off, but they were trapped between the truck and the door—so it wasn't her fault she let him kiss her. Then, once his lips touched hers, warm and giving, it wasn't her fault she responded.

Any woman would respond to Chase's kiss. His lips were soft and questioning, gliding gently over hers until he upped the pressure and tugged her hard against his chest. Suddenly she was back in the glade by the stream, only now it was night and kissing him seemed safer, more secret, and she knew this was the sanctuary she'd run all those miles to find. Nobody could hurt her as long as she was here in his arms, in this circle of safety.

A flurry of footsteps interrupted her thoughts, and something streaked through her peripheral vision. Something large, headed right for Chase's head.

Whap!

Whatever it was hit him hard, shoving his face against hers and slamming the back of her head into the roof of the truck. She tasted the sharp, metallic flavor of blood and wondered if she'd bitten his lip or her own. Stunned by the impact, her vision clouded, and all she saw was light, bright light all around her.

Oh God, he found me. Somehow, some way, Wade found me.

She put a hand to the back of her head and felt the sticky warmth of fresh blood coat her fingers. Blinking away the pain, she sat down hard in the truck, her hands clutching the door frame, her legs dangling. Chase was gone. She was a sitting duck, and she had about the same IQ as a duck, too, staying there in full view of whoever had attacked them.

Slamming the truck door, she slid off the seat and knelt on the floor, rummaging around for some kind of weapon. A tire iron would have been nice, but all she could find was a plastic flashlight and a wrench. Well, if anybody opened the door, she could blind them with the light and then bash them over the head with the wrench. Pushing down the lock, she put her hands over her head in crash position, the weapons clenched in her fists, and waited for disaster to strike.

Chase spun away from Lacey and lunged for his attacker. He hadn't really been hurt—whatever had struck him was heavy, but soft—but he was worried about Lacey. He heard the truck door slam behind him and prayed she was okay as he hauled ass after the shadowy figure scampering across the lot. His attacker was long-legged but ran with a mincing, tender-footed gait, as if his feet hurt. It was almost like he was wearing high heels. In fact, he *was* wearing high heels. It wasn't a man. It was...

"Krystal!" He caught up to her and grabbed the strap of her purse—the one she'd slung into his head. She tried to tug it away and keep running, but he held fast and jerked her to a stop. The two of them planted their feet for an impromptu game of tug-of-war.

"Give it, you bastard! Give it!" Her face was contorted with fury. "I'll scratch your eyes out! I'll scratch 'em out, and then I'll kill that slut, you lying bastard!"

He let the purse go and grabbed her arms, wincing as she kicked at his shins with her sharp-toed pumps. Her breath bore the distinctive scent of whiskey. She and Jeb had evidently had quite a party.

"Krystal, stop."

"You said you weren't seeing her! You told me..."

He shoved her away and she stumbled backward, dropping her purse and coming at him again, all scarlet nails and rage. Ducking his head, he shoved her away again. Theatrically, she stumbled and lowered herself to the ground in what was supposed to be a fall but was far too slow and cautious to be painful.

"You knocked me down!" she shrieked. "You brute! I can't believe you'd hit a woman! I'm going to call the cops!"

She crawled over and snagged her purse, fishing out her cell phone and squinting at the screen.

"Go ahead," Chase said. "I'll have them arrest you for assault."

"You hit me! I didn't do anything!"

"You clubbed me over the head with that purse, and I have a witness." He pointed toward the truck. Fortunately Krystal didn't notice there was no head and shoulders silhouette behind the windshield. He wondered where Lacey had run off to. Pam's, hopefully.

Stumbling to her feet, Krystal faced him, her breasts heaving, her hair hanging in lank tendrils around her face.

"I will get you for this, Chase Caldwell. I'll get you for this, and I'll make you pay. I'll..."

"Tell you what," he said. "I'll pay. I'll pay you your last paycheck. You're fired."

"You can't fire me. You just want to hire your new

girlfriend, that's all. You have no reason to fire me. I'll sue. I'll…"

"Krystal, I have every reason to fire you. You got drunk and screwed your boyfriend on my desk and then you hit me in the head."

"We didn't do it on your desk. We were going to, but then the cops came and…oh."

She looked left, then right, panicked as a weasel in a wolf trap. "Never mind," she said in a small voice. Gathering up her purse and what was left of her dignity, she sniffed, turned away, and minced across the parking lot toward home.

Chase sighed and rubbed his mouth. He'd bitten his lip when she hit him, and a streak of scarlet slashed the back of his hand. He needed to check on Lacey. There was a figure at the diner across the street, but it was Pam peering over at him.

"Pam?" he called. "Lacey over there?"

She shook her head. "Nope. She's in your truck."

"Shh." That probably wasn't information they wanted to broadcast as long as Krystal was nearby.

"I'm here, Chase." The truck door opened and Lacey climbed out of the cab. Her hair was tousled, her face pale and drawn.

Relieved, he stepped up to take her in his arms, but she shook her head.

He sighed, silently cursing Krystal. "Can I walk you back to the motel?"

She took a step back. "I'll be okay." She called to Pam. "Is Annie okay?"

Pam grinned. "Never better. She says you're her favorite sitter."

The ghost of a smile crossed Lacey's face, but she still looked wiped out.

"I'll—I'll see you both later, okay?" she said. "Maybe tomorrow, or maybe—I don't know." She forked her fingers through her hair and blew out a shaky breath. "I need to think."

Chase watched her walk away and wondered why it was that every time he kissed Lacey Bradford, it ended up being a kiss goodbye.

CHAPTER 21

LACEY STARED AT HER SHABBY MOTEL ROOM AND TRIED to dredge up the anger she'd felt when she'd first found out Chase had paid for it. He should have told her. He should have asked. She didn't need a knight in shining armor who saved her on the sly.

But his silence about paying the bill meant he didn't expect anything in return. He'd helped her. She remembered what he'd said when he'd agreed to pay Sinclair's vet bills.

No hands.

He'd lied to the cop for her too, and that was an even bigger favor than paying for the room. Chase had always taken pride in his honesty, which was a good thing, because his lying was nothing to brag about. He'd told the story with a halting, fumbling hesitation Lacey was sure the cop saw straight through.

The fact that the officer let her go was a testament to how much people instinctively trusted Chase. She didn't know how long he'd been living out here, but either people here were gullible enough to believe the "Guaranteed Dependable" sign on the store or he'd earned their respect.

Of course he had.

People had always respected Chase. Even when he was a geeky kid, he'd been straightforward and reliable. Someone you could count on. Evidently, he'd earned that reputation in Grady too—and he'd put it on the line for her.

She really ought to thank him.

She went to the window and stared across the street. The town was quiet now, the only sign of life a light glowing in the trailer's office window and Chase's truck parked outside. He was still there. All alone.

A transient woman, the cop had said. She'd taken that to mean she was a loner—but it also meant she was temporary. Just passing through.

It was probably an accurate description. She didn't see her way to a future in Grady. There were no opportunities for a woman making her way in the world alone. Sooner or later, she'd either go back to Tennessee or move on—alone.

She'd told herself she'd never marry or rely on a man again, but she'd seen the faces of old people who'd ended up on their own. They were scarred with regret, their wrinkles like the dry land outside Grady, parched earth furrowed with sorrow.

That could be her in fifty years. She needed to take her chances where she could. Live life to the fullest.

She needed to thank Chase *now*.

He was standing against the counter right across from the door when she walked into the trailer, his thumbs hooked in his belt loops, legs crossed at the ankles. His posture was so perfectly casual, she wondered if he'd been waiting for her.

Looking at him, she realized she was the one who'd been waiting all these years—waiting for him. She never would have guessed what kind of man he'd become, but somehow the image of him, just the way he was now, had been branded in her mind from before she knew him, from the first time she'd sprawled on her lace-bedecked canopy bed and stared up at the ceiling and pretended there was a man pressing down on her, touching her, pushing against her. She hadn't known a thing about sex, but she'd somehow known how he would look at her, how his eyes would consume her and hold her with a mixture of love and hopeless, helpless adoration.

She'd looked into the deep well of his eyes in her fantasies and imagined his touch and clenched her legs together, feeling the dizzying sensation of orgasm for the first time. She'd been overwhelmed not by love but by need and by the dizzying thought that he might need her too, whoever this man was, rugged and soft all at once, with his hard, stony face and his tender, lovelorn eyes. That was what she wanted—not a man who took her and overpowered her, but a man who bent her to his will because he wanted her so badly he couldn't help himself.

She stared at Chase until his gaze turned questioning and she remembered why she'd come. "Thank you," she said. "I know you don't like to lie."

He shoved his hands in his pockets and shrugged, looking away.

She smiled. "You weren't any good at it in high school either."

"I never lied in high school."

Her grin widened. "Three words. Mr. Huber's Volkswagen."

Chase groaned, but the memory brought a reluctant smile. Mr. Huber's Volkswagen Beetle had ended up in the school's gymnasium, right on the foul line of the basketball

court. It had been decorated with feathers and construc-
tion paper to look like a bird, a rough representation of the
mascot of the school's greatest nemesis, the Lathrop Eagles.
The prank amused most of the faculty, including Mr. Huber,
but the assistant principal had taken it upon himself to find
and punish the perpetrators. Questioning every boy in turn,
he failed to uncover the truth: that the cheerleading squad
had been behind the operation.

A bunch of girls in pleated skirts and bobby socks
couldn't move a car on their own, but they could definitely
harness the manpower to get it done. And not one boy would
jeopardize his chances with the prettiest girls in school by
squealing on the ringleaders or their helpers.

"I'd forgotten about that."

"You've forgotten a lot of things," Lacey said.

He gave her a questioning look.

"Like the fact that we used to be friends."

"I didn't forget that." His voice was low and husky, and
she suddenly realized he was standing very close to her. Had
he just stepped in, or had he been inches away from her all
along? "It's just that I always wanted to be something more,
and you never did."

"I want it now."

He'd kept his eyes averted until then, and she'd felt a bar-
rier between them, as if he was holding up a shield, but now
his gaze locked on hers like a weapon fixing on a target. He
stepped forward, tilting her off-balance, and she hiked herself up on her toes as he wrapped his arms around her and
bent his head to hers.

His lips were firm, almost hard, but they softened when
she accidentally let out a little mew and hooked her arms

around his neck. She interlaced her fingers and pulled him down so she could reach him and have him her way. Waltzing her through the doorway, he kissed her with a new intensity, tasting and testing as he pushed her backward. She tried to take over the lead, but he kept her just slightly off-kilter so that she was forced to move with him, steering through the office door, across the small room, and behind the desk. When he fell back into the chair, it spun slightly and careened backward on its rolling base, slamming into the wall.

The kiss never broke.

He pushed his fingers into the thick fall of hair at the back of her neck and tucked his thumbs into the hollow just behind her jawbone, pulling her toward him and deepening the kiss. She'd pitched into his lap when he fell, straddling him, her knees bending so her hips slid into his and she ended up with her pelvis slung forward like a rodeo rider on the upswing. He was already hard.

"You came to me this time," he whispered. "I'm not attacking you, right?"

She nodded and his hands slid down her neck and swept under the collar of her shirt, sweeping down the smooth, seldom-touched skin in the hollow below her shoulders, savoring the swell of her flesh and slipping under the lace of her bra. She pushed herself into his rough palms as he cupped her breasts, the backs of his hands pushing her bra away as the buttons on her shirt strained and popped open, one, two, three.

He squeezed her breasts together, and his thumbs moved up to stroke her nipples. The kiss wasn't conscious anymore; it was what she wanted, what both of them needed. For a moment she stepped outside herself and almost recoiled, seeing them like a stranger through the window with their mouths open, their tongues slicking wet against each other. There was no film-star romance in this kiss; it was as unthinking and intimate as anything she'd ever imagined. Then his tongue swept over her bottom lip and she was lost again.

She skidded her butt back on his thighs and put her fingers to work, fumbling at his belt buckle, tugging at the leather and the metal, grabbing the snap of his jeans between two fingers and pulling so hard his fly was halfway down before she grabbed the zipper tag. He flexed his hips once and she tucked her hand into the opening, pushing her palm against the hardness of him and feeling his warmth through the stretched-thin fabric of whatever he was wearing. She slid her fingers over the bulge from one side to the other and ran the pad of her thumb over the top to feel the bead of moisture blossom at her touch. He tipped his head back, sucking in a breath, and suddenly he was helpless, rocked back in the chair, his long-muscled body entirely at her mercy.

She was in charge. Suddenly shy, she watched his face while she moved her hand against him, watching his eyelids flutter as his jaw tightened and relaxed. She could read him, find the exact touch that made him hers, the touch that made his breath catch and his heart quicken. Bending down, she licked the hollow at the base of his throat with a quick, scooping tongue. He was salty and hot. She licked him again.

He groaned, pulling her against him with one arm while the other scooped under her bottom and lifted her off the chair. She wrapped her legs around his waist, pressing herself against his arousal while he set her down on the desk, tilting her backward so her hair fanned out over the gleaming wood. Her legs were still wrapped around his waist, but he stood over her now, quickly unfastening the rest of the buttons on her shirt and popping the front clasp on her bra.

He peeled the cups away from her breasts so he could bend down and take one tight nipple in his mouth while his fingers toyed with the other, pinching and pulling while she pushed herself into his hand. Tilting her head back, she closed her eyes. His lips on her breast, his tongue flicking the aching, hot bead of her nipple—she had to grit her teeth to keep herself from letting out a cry of need and urgency.

His hand left her breast to work at her pants, unsnapping, unzipping, stripping them down her hips, dragging her thin panties with them while he kept licking and sucking at her nipple. Suddenly she was laid out naked on his desk, her legs dangling over the edge. She felt like the sexy secretary in some hot romance novel, letting the boss have his way with her on lunch break.

But he wasn't the boss. She didn't have a boss, not when it came to this. She reached up and tugged at his shirt, undoing the buttons and sliding the fabric off his shoulders so she could run her palms over his skin. He bent down and kissed her, his beard rough against her face, his hand skimming down her belly until his fingers touched the warm, wet heart of her and he dipped one inside. His finger slid over the tender, slick skin, the rough touch rocketing through her like a flame burning up a fuse. His lips moved from her mouth to her throat, from her throat to her breasts, his tongue flicking and swirling over her skin while his finger slid inside her and out again, and she decided to let him be the boss, just for a little while, because being naked and willing and helpless and *his* just felt so good, so dirty and slutty and deliciously, fantastically right.

She closed her eyes and heard the chair skid across the floor as he dropped into it and pulled close, letting her rest her feet on the arms while he focused on the business of pleasing her, his fingers opening and exploring while his tongue licked and probed. She could feel tension rising inside her, spiraling up and up, making her clench her muscles tighter, tighter, impossibly tight—and then he raised one hand to her breast and squeezed. She came in a sudden explosion that made her lift her hips off the desktop and cry out, her hands clutching his hair to pull him away before the spiral spun into space. One more touch of his tongue and she'd die, right there, of pleasure and passion and need.

She opened her eyes to see him watching her, his gaze skimming her body before his eyes met hers. He held her with his gaze, pinning her down without touching her while he stripped off his clothes with the quickness and efficiency of an athlete. He had the body of an athlete too, long and lean and muscled, the ridges of his ribs relaxing into the rippled muscles of his stomach. He bent over her, putting his hands on either side of her while she lifted her hips to meet him. He slid inside her, just a bit, and his gaze sharpened with a question, waiting for her to nod ever so slightly before he did it again.

This was the part where Trent would close his eyes and lose himself in some internal world, while she'd stare up at the ceiling and wait for him to take his pleasure, but Chase's eyes never left hers, cautious and questioning until she nodded hard, twice, and he didn't stop watching her until she came again. Then he tilted his head back and closed his eyes, and she sensed the fireworks inside him, the snapping and popping of flame hitting powder as he strained into her and groaned.

She didn't realize she'd closed her own eyes until she opened them and saw him looking down at her. The shield was still down, but what it revealed now wasn't need—it was tenderness. He eased his hands behind her shoulders and helped her sit up, holding her to him while their breath slowed and their hearts stuttered and started again. She could feel his heart thumping steadily against her cheek, and she knew that beat had held steady and strong for all the years she'd been gone and it always would.

She prayed he wouldn't speak and break the fragile silence in the room. She couldn't put words to what had happened, couldn't define her feelings in conscious thought. Their relationship had changed, but only for her, and only because she had a new sense of the importance of it. Whatever she did, wherever she went, a part of Chase would go with her from now on. And maybe he'd been there all along.

She remembered the decision she'd made before she stepped out of the hotel room into the rainy night and dashed over here and knew she'd be leaving soon. She had to.

She wondered how much she'd miss the part of her heart she'd leave with him.

CHAPTER 22

WHEN CHASE STEPPED INSIDE THE TRAILER THE NEXT morning, the air was still alive with Lacey's presence, shimmering with the promise of the night before. They hadn't spoken when they parted. They'd barely spoken the whole time they'd been alone together. He stared out at the street, wondering if she'd tossed and turned and relived every moment of their union the way he had.

But the way she'd held him for a heartbeat before she stepped out the door had felt somehow final, as if she'd made up her mind to leave. He knew he couldn't stop her; he wouldn't want to if he could. What he and Lacey had wasn't something either of them could control. It was just *there*, and it always would be. She was free to go, but wherever she went, a part of him would be with her.

The phone rang, shattering the silence, and he stepped over and picked it up, hoping it was her. Dropping the receiver, he bobbled it twice before he managed to jam it under his jawline.

"Hey." Casual, yet welcoming. Warm, but not so warm that it made rash assumptions. "Hey" wouldn't scare her away.

He hoped.

But the voice on the line wasn't Lacey. It was a man—a man with a gravelly voice and a distinct Southern twang he was clearly trying to cover up with some kind of fake English accent.

"Hello. Could I speak to Lacey, please?"

Lacey?

"Uh, no. She's—not here."

"Can you tell me when she'll be in?"

Chase wished he knew the answer to that himself.

"No, I, uh…" Damn. He sounded like a true professional.

"She works there, right?"

Chase pulled the phone away from his ear and looked at it. Had Lacey been so sure of her reception from Chase that she'd told someone she had a job here? She must have known he'd jump through hoops for her in the end, just like he had when he was a kid, and she'd been right. It might have taken him a while to come around, but at this point, she could set the hoop on fire and hang it from the ceiling. He'd get through it somehow.

"No." He tried to hide the note of regret in his voice. "She doesn't work here."

"But you know her, right?"

Chase felt a sudden surge of dread. He was pretty sure Lacey hadn't told anyone she was coming to Grady. That had been the whole point, after all—that nobody would look for her here.

But someone was. And he'd almost given her away.

"Who were you looking for again?" he asked.

"Lacey Bradford," the voice said. "Pretty lady, brown hair, nice tits?"

Chase resisted the impulse to respond to the coarse description. That wasn't how he'd describe Lacey. Her smile, that's what he always noticed. Her eyes. Although…

He set his mind back on track and spoke into the phone. Maybe if he played his part well enough, he could convince the caller he hadn't known who he was talking about.

"Nice tits, huh? I'd remember that." He huffed out a coarse laugh. "Haven't seen her. Wish I had, buddy."

"She might be calling herself Lacey Keene. You sure she doesn't work there? This is the address I—the address she gave me. Maybe you just didn't meet her yet. She would have started in the last week or so."

"Nobody works here by that name," Chase said. "I'd know. I'm the owner."

"*Caldwell?*"

He knew that voice. Was it Trent? He'd thought the guy had more class than to talk about a woman's breasts, but maybe he was playing a part. He clenched the phone in his fist as if he could strangle the caller via long distance.

"Do I know you?" he asked.

"No." The denial was a little too loud. Chase *did* know this guy. He strained to catch the nuances of the voice and find something familiar.

"This is her—her boyfriend," the caller said. "She left her husband, and I just want to find her and take care of her."

The caller was trying to sound compassionate, but what kind of boyfriend talks about his girlfriend's breasts to strangers? And was it Chase's imagination, or did the phrase "take care of her" have ominous undertones?

He suddenly realized who he must be talking to.

"Don't know her," he said. "And I'd have noticed if a new set rolled into town. Be glad to call you if I see her, though." He glanced up at the old-fashioned phone hanging on the wall. He'd been meaning to get Caller ID to help him get back to customers who called with questions about cars. Now he wished he'd gotten around to it. "You want to give me your number?"

There was a click, and the line went dead. Chase set the receiver gently in the cradle. Somebody was looking for Lacey. Somebody knew she was here.

And he was pretty sure it was Wade Simpson.

Grabbing his keys from the counter, he slammed the door behind him without locking it and sprinted across the street, taking the steps to the motel balcony two at a time.

———————————

Lacey was brushing her hair when someone knocked on the motel room door. The sound was soft, slow, and eerily reminiscent of Wade tapping on her door back home. She'd woken with light swirling inside her from the night before, but now dread closed in like darkness.

"Lacey." She knew that voice. "Lacey, I need to talk to you."

She almost laughed. It was Chase. He couldn't wait to see her. Setting down the brush, she trotted to the door and popped up on her tiptoes to look through the peephole. He was standing with his hat in his hand, shifting from one foot to the other like a kid on his first date, but his expression was somber.

"It's important, Lacey. I got a phone call. For you."

"But nobody knows I'm here." She swallowed a bolt of panic and opened the door, glancing left and right, the sweet warmth of the night before chilling to a feeling of being hunted. "Come in."

"You'd better sit down," he said, taking her elbow and guiding her toward the bed.

Bad idea. Her head and heart were already humming

with just the awareness of where they were: a motel room. With a bed. Just one small step, one moment of weakness…

"Tell me about the phone call," she said, sitting down on the bed.

"It was a man, asking for you."

"A man?"

"He wouldn't say who he was. But he asked for Lacey Bradford. I think it was Wade."

She bit her lip, looking up into his eyes. She was sure he was telling the truth. But how could Wade know she was here?

"He thought you worked for me. He didn't seem to believe me when I said you didn't. He said you'd given him my address."

"I didn't give anyone…oh. Shit."

Chase's eyes widened, and Lacey realized she'd sworn. She normally tried not to, because her English teacher in eighth grade had said it indicated a lack of imagination. He said there were always better ways to express yourself than using four-letter words.

"Shit-fuck-damn," she said. That had twelve letters.

Chase's eyes widened more. "What, Lacey? What's wrong?"

"I *did* give somebody that address."

"My address? Who?"

"I don't know who." She sighed. "I got a credit card. I signed up for it from a mailing that came to my house. It's in my name only—not Trent's, not Mrs. Lacey Bradford. Just Lacey Bradford. I never told Trent about it, and I figured nobody would know about it to trace it."

"Lacey, all he had to do was get your credit report."

"What's a credit report?" She felt hot tears stinging at the back of her eyes. She was so stupid. She didn't know anything. She'd figured that as long as they didn't know she had an account with MagiCard, Trent's former pals wouldn't be able to trace it.

"A credit report tells what money you owe, and whether you're current on your bills."

"But I am current on it. The bill won't even come for two weeks." She looked down at the ground. "One week now. And I didn't charge anything. I wasn't going to leave the bill for you to pay or anything. I figured I'd have a place to live by then."

"It doesn't matter if you're current or not. Your credit report tells what lines of credit you've opened. What cards you've applied for."

"So just anybody can get this report and find out my private financial information?"

"Not anybody, but almost. A landlord. A bank. A car dealer."

"A cop?"

He shrugged. "Apparently."

"Shoot." She collapsed on the bed, covering her face with her hands. She had no car, no money, no place to go, and she couldn't stay in Grady. She could only run like a rabbit, off across the plains, but there was no hidey-hole out there for her. If Wade didn't find her, she'd die of sheer nervousness worrying that he might. "What am I going to do?"

"Well, you can't stay in Grady."

She was surprised at the anger, despair, and hopelessness she felt at the truth of that statement. She'd been in Grady less than a week, but she'd miss it more than she missed home. She had friends here—a place in the world. And she was Aunt Lacey.

"But I can't just leave," she said. "There's Annie. And Pam." *And you*, she thought. *You most of all.*

"Lacey, I know." He sat down beside her, and she leaned into him, wondering if he really did know. If he understood the words she'd left unspoken. "But you have to get out of town." She felt the mattress shift as he settled beside her and his arm wrapped around her shoulder.

She knew she should shrug him off, start standing on her own, but she needed him, just for a minute. She let herself tilt sideways, her head resting on the hollow below his shoulder. He turned his head so that his lips were inches from her hair. As he spoke, she could feel the warmth of his breath, the stirring of her hair as he said the words.

"Come home with me."

She felt a surge of relief wash over her like a wave. She could go home with Chase. She could hide there, and he'd take care of her, and she wouldn't have to worry about a thing. She could just depend on Mr. Dependable, like she'd planned on in the first place.

Fighting the undertow, she floundered to the surface and shook off the urge. Going home with Chase wasn't a solution. For one thing, they'd find her. They had the car lot address—it would only take them a quick hop, skip, and jump to find his house. And more important, she'd be breaking her promise to herself—the promise she'd made when Chase himself pointed out that she'd always depended on a man. Surely she could do better than that.

They had the address from the credit card, so it wouldn't hurt to charge on it now, as long as she was leaving. She could get a cash advance and take off, head to Denver, get another cheap motel room, and find a job. She could disappear into the city. They'd never find her.

If only she had a way to get there. She glanced across the street at her Mustang, still parked in front of Chase's trailer.

"Did Jeb ever look at my car?"

"Not yet." Chase gave her a wry smile. "I think he was too busy screwing my sales associate."

She sighed.

"Lacey, running isn't the answer anyway. Where would you go? Come stay with me."

"They'll find your address."

"The ranch doesn't have an address. The deed's not even registered to me."

"I thought it was your ranch."

"It is. But I registered it in the name of my corporation."

"Which is?"

He flushed. "Princess LLC."

"You named your corporation after your *goat*?"

"Hey, Princess meant a lot to me. You wouldn't laugh if I named it after my dog."

"No, I wouldn't." She giggled.

"But it's not something anyone else would connect with me."

She scanned him from head to foot—the tousled hair, the square cheekbones and strong jaw, the virile, neatly-trimmed beard—and she had to agree.

"No, you've got a point." She couldn't help smiling. "You're definitely no princess."

CHAPTER 23

"LOOK, YOU CAN EARN YOUR KEEP IF YOU WANT." CHASE held up both palms in a "stop" gesture before she could protest. "I don't mean like that. You could actually work for me. I could give you a job. I fired Krystal, so I don't have anyone to watch the lot anymore."

"I can't do that. That's right where…"

"I know. But you don't have to work at the lot. I can do that, but I'm already away from the ranch too much. If you stay out there and do some chores for me, it would actually help a lot. I'll pay you what I paid Krystal, but you can work there instead of in town."

She shook her head. "Chase, I don't know anything about ranching."

"It's not rocket science," he said. "You're smart, Lacey. You'll catch on fast."

She blinked. That comment meant way too much to her. She almost asked him to repeat it. That was pitiful. She'd been confident once, so sure of herself. The top of the pyramid.

What had Trent done to her?

Chase sat beside her and set one hand on her thigh. Did he realize he was touching her? Did he know what that did to her? The warmth of his touch crept across her skin, moving upward from the spot where his hand lay.

"It's hard work, but you might like it. You like horses?"

She shrugged. "I guess. I used to go to the racetrack with my dad."

"Then you'll be fine. And being alone at the ranch would beat being all alone on the road, with no money and a broken-down car."

She realized he was right. Being alone didn't scare her. At least when she was alone, she was with someone she could trust. But being broke was a problem, especially with her automotive issues.

She'd sworn she wouldn't trust a man again, and she'd made that vow in a moment of clear rationality. A moment when Chase wasn't sitting right beside her, the warm spot on her leg lingering after the touch of his hand. Her impulse was to trust him. Her impulse was to lean toward him, let him touch her again—but that would be surrender. She wondered if he could follow the complicated ribbon of her thoughts, unspooling and tangling, snarling into knots.

"I shouldn't," she finally said. "I can get a cash advance and get out of town before they track me. I'll go to Denver."

He went to the window, staring out at the parking lot. "Lacey, if you go, I won't know where you are. I won't know if you're alive or dead, if you're safe or if they found you. I have to do more than that for you."

"That's for me to decide."

"Look, a week ago you *begged* me for a place to stay," he said. "I don't get it. You would have jumped at the chance then."

"I never begged for anything. And that was before I got to know you."

"You always knew me."

"No." She shook her head. This was one thing she was sure of. "I knew the old Chase," she said. "That sweet, awkward kid back in high school."

"I'm still that kid," he said. "Still awkward."

She looked him up and down. He was wrong. He was no kid, and there was nothing awkward about the way he stood, feet planted, arms crossed over his chest. She scanned his jaw, hidden under the lumberjack beard, and the way his arms swelled from the sleeves of his T-shirt. His jeans, the worn denim at the fly emphasizing the decidedly un-kid-like developments that had taken place since high school. Suddenly, the room seemed smaller and hotter, and she realized she was staring at his crotch. She flicked her gaze to his face and felt a blush warming her chest and cheeks.

This was a whole new kind of awkward.

He sat down beside her and put one arm around her shoulders. Next thing she knew, his hand was on her thigh again and his face was close to hers.

"You need help, Lacey. There's no shame in that."

She stiffened at his touch, sitting rigid against him, but he just pulled her closer and rocked slightly from side to side in a soothing, rhythmic motion. She couldn't help laying her head on his shoulder and closing her eyes. "Don't worry, Lace. Trust me. Let me help."

"I'm not worried." She relaxed just the slightest bit as he patted her shoulder. "I'm just sad. I don't want to leave. Pam and I are making friends. I haven't had a girlfriend since school." She pressed her cheek against his chest. "You must think I'm pathetic. That I never had a girlfriend before when I had all that money."

"Money isn't everything." He brushed his lips against the top of her head. "I don't think you had a chance."

"I had one." She put her arms around his waist and gave in to his embrace. "Everybody does. I just didn't take it."

"*This* is a chance, Lacey. Take it. Come to the ranch."

She didn't want to depend on him—but maybe she really could help. He was a man living alone. It would be nice for him to have someone to cook and clean, someone to come home to. She'd make herself useful, just like she had for Trent—cooking, cleaning, being supportive. She'd even do some ranch work. It would be fun.

And as long as she stayed out of his bedroom, she wouldn't be selling herself for safety.

"All right. I'll go." She pulled away. "But only as an employee. No hanky-panky with the boss." She took his hand and set it firmly in his own lap. "Chase, last night was—well, it was good."

He met her eyes with a smile. "Good?"

"Better than good. But if I go stay with you, and we keep—you know." She waved her hand in a gesture that joined his body to hers. "If we keep doing that, I'll end up falling into another relationship. Depending on you."

"I don't mind," he said.

"But I do. If we're ever going to have a chance, I have to be on my own for a while. You know, I've never had my own place. My own job. My own life. I need to do that." She sighed. "I'll stay for a few days. But let's cool it, okay?"

Chase nodded his agreement, but somehow the atmosphere in the room didn't feel the slightest bit cool. It felt warm—warm with promises of tomorrow, with memories of the night before, and with his presence right there, right now.

Chase squelched a series of inappropriate reactions to the idea of Lacey coming to the ranch. He ran through elation, excitement, and anticipation, settling on urgency as an appropriate response. He was just keeping her safe. Even if Wade had found her in Grady, he wasn't likely to find the ranch. Looking north from town, all you could see were miles and miles of vacant ground. The only relief from the interminable isolation was an occasional rock and a faint line of blue mountains bordering the horizon in the distance.

And anyone coming to the ranch had to pass Galt's place first, which meant crossing acres of scrub and near-desert on dusty dirt roads. Galt's land was so bleak and worn-out, most people would be clinically depressed by the time they made it to Chase's.

But lonesome was how he liked it. In fact, if it had been anyone but Lacey, he would have regretted having to share his solitude. Krystal had proven that a woman would just be in the way.

But Lacey? That was different. A thousand unlikely scenarios leaped to mind. She'd fall in love with the place. She'd fall into his bed. She'd fall in love with him and stay forever.

That would make him happy. Really happy, for the first time in years.

Or would it?

They could only rehash the old days for so long, and once that was done, they'd have nothing in common. She wouldn't want to talk about crops and cattle, and he wouldn't want to talk about clothes and whatever else women like Lacey were interested in.

The thought rebounded, bouncing back to what he

wanted to believe. They didn't really need to talk, did they? They hadn't talked last night, and they'd communicated just fine.

She startled him out of his thoughts by jerking to her feet. "I need to pack. I'll be ready in a minute." She opened a drawer, pulling out a pink flowered shirt and a pair of jeans.

Good. She had jeans. Appropriate ranch wear. Her cotton pants looked nice, but the jeans would skim her curves and stretch when she moved. They'd be harder to get off, though.

He closed his eyes tight, just for a moment, trying to change his way of thinking. Lacey wanted him to cool it, and he needed to respect that.

She bent to lift her suitcase, which was propped open on the floor. Chase shook off the urge to stare and went to help her.

"I'll get that."

The two of them almost knocked heads as he bent down and grabbed the handle. She looked up, startled, and for a moment, her wide eyes met his. A bolt of attraction and lust rocketed straight to his groin, and he stepped back, almost knocking her down as he lifted the suitcase. It tilted and dumped its contents onto the floor.

"Sorry." He knelt to gather the spilled clothes, grabbing a handful of silky undergarments that slipped through his fingers as he tried to set them on the bed. They slid to the floor in a flowered, polka-dotted, lace-bedecked mass.

"I'll get those."

He backed away, unwilling to let her kneel at his feet. Standing awkwardly against the wall, he tried to concentrate on the splotchy painting of a Spanish matador that hung over the bed. The guy was flailing around with a red cape and wore a desperate expression on his mustachioed face.

Chase could identify with the guy. Trying to control his own libido in Lacey's presence was like trying to control a charging bull with nothing but a pair of red silk panties.

CHAPTER 24

Shutting the suitcase, Lacey stared at it a moment, then flicked the clasps open again and frowned down at the contents.

"I forgot. I have to get some stuff from the bathroom."

She stepped toward Chase, and he realized he was blocking her in, trapping her between the bed and the cheaply paneled wall.

"Sorry." He backed up and shoved his hands in his pockets, looking away from her so she wouldn't feel threatened.

She stepped into the bathroom and swung the door almost closed. He could hear her in there, rattling stuff around, and his gaze fell on the suitcase. He focused on a scrap of silk that flowed out of the side like water and pooled on the bed. It looked like a slip, or maybe a nightgown. He took a step toward the bed, wondering what it would look like draping softly from Lacey's breasts, what it would feel like between his fingers.

He sat down on the end of the bed and glanced at the bathroom door again. He could still hear her rattling around, apparently pitching toiletries into a bag or something. He shifted slightly, moving closer to the suitcase, and put out his hand to touch the puddle of silk.

Soft. He pinched a fold between his thumb and forefinger. There was something so feminine about the feel of silk. He grabbed a handful of the material and closed his eyes.

"What are you doing?"

His eyes flew open to see her standing in front of him, arms folded. Looking down at his lap, he realized he was getting pretty excited about the nightgown. He'd pulled the thing out of the suitcase and held it in his lap.

Good thing too.

"Nothing." He stood and shoved it back into the suitcase. "I just—nothing. I just—it was falling out of the suitcase, and I went to put it back in and it just—just wound up in my lap somehow." He flushed, realizing how stupid that sounded.

"Chase." She packed the last of her supplies, then whipped the nightgown out of his hands and stuffed it inside. Pressing down on the top, she skimmed the zipper around the edges and stood, setting the suitcase on the floor. "Don't. I can't…"

He lifted his hand and put a finger to her lips, stopping her words. She widened her eyes, and time stopped.

Just stopped.

People said time slowed down when you were hurt, when you were in danger. They said everything ran in slow motion when fear chilled your blood. For her, time slowed down when Chase touched her, and chilling wasn't the word for it. She felt her blood warm, heating her chest, her cheeks, but especially her lips. They felt hot and swollen where his finger rested, and she felt the rasp of his calloused finger against the pillowy cushion of her mouth. She took a breath to speak, but that would have meant moving her lips and intensifying the sensation, so she simply stared.

Big mistake. There it was again, the heart of him glowing in those eyes.

She blinked, and time ground slowly back into motion.

Chase lowered his hand and set it on her waist. She stared down at it, barely able to hear him over an ominous rushing in her ears. Closing her eyes, she felt all the steel in her spine go soft as she reached up, pulled him close, and kissed him.

Oh, she hadn't meant to do this, but it felt so *good*. His mouth was hard and firm as he tensed in surprise, but then she felt his arm sweep around her, and they were rolling, falling onto the bed in a surrender that felt mutual. They rolled over until he was the one prostrate on the mattress and she was on top, in control, straddling his hips and kissing his lips, his chin, the angle of his jaw that had hardened and defined itself in the years they'd been apart. She flicked her tongue in his ear and moved up to kiss his eyebrows, his eyelids, and then back to his lips. He let out a quick breath as she ran one hand over his chest, pausing when she hit the flat circle of his nipple and stroking down his ribs to lay a palm on the flat of his stomach. His hips pulsed, but she tensed and tightened her thighs, holding him down. He'd have what she wanted to give—nothing more.

This was *not* surrender.

Chase flexed his muscles and felt Lacey's thighs tighten against him. He could easily throw her off, push her down, master her, but that wasn't what he wanted.

What he wanted was to see what she'd do next. She was holding him down, her palms pressing into his shoulders, her lips moving back up to his as her hand gripped his T-shirt and gathered the cloth in her fist.

Lacey had always been all dimples and sweetness, her

flirty smiles hinting that a man could have whatever he wanted from her, but this wasn't the old Lacey. This was a new woman. A stronger one. He'd have thought fear would make her tremble, make her needier and softer, but instead it seemed to have given her the courage to ask for what she wanted.

She thrust her tongue in his mouth and jerked his T-shirt up to expose his chest. Hell, she wasn't asking for anything. She was taking it.

And he was giving. He didn't mind surrendering to her demands, as long as those demands involved licking and sucking and thrusting in a kiss that echoed what they'd shared the night before. He flexed his hips and felt her thighs spread to let him press against her, and the next thing he knew, she was tearing at his belt and the snap of his jeans, fumbling with his zipper. Tugging his Wranglers down his hips, she hauled them off and tossed them on the floor.

Oh, God, if she didn't touch him, he'd come right now. Her hand rose to his chest and she held him down while her lips slid from his mouth to the column of his throat to his chest. She kissed her way from one side to the other, her tongue flipping over one flat nipple, then the other, then licking its way down the faint trail of hair that flecked his abs and led closer...closer...*oh, please. Closer.*

When she flicked her tongue and closed her lips around him, he bucked hard against her, clenching his teeth to keep from bucking them both off the bed. He tried to think of something that would keep him from losing it before she even started. Reaching down, he plowed his fingers into her hair, sweeping the hanging curtain up so he could see her lashes lying dark against her pale cheeks. She took him deeper and opened her eyes, and he gasped and tried to pull away. The sensation was one thing; the frank intimacy of her gaze another. He couldn't hold himself back another moment if she watched him, but she wasn't giving in. Her gaze met his with a challenge, a demand, and he didn't have any choice but to submit.

Damn. He'd known she was sweet. He'd known she was sexy. But he'd never really thought of Lacey as someone who was as willing to take as she was to give. He tilted his chin up and stared at the ceiling, clenching his jaw to keep from losing it.

"Lacey," he said. "Please."

He felt suddenly cold as her lips let him go. "What?"

Well, he might as well ask.

"Take your clothes off."

She went still, and he opened his eyes. Had he ruined the moment by telling her what to do?

She was watching him, considering.

"Please," he said again.

She relaxed, and a slow smile spread across her face.

"Okay. But don't move." She touched him with one cautious finger, and he almost lost it. "Not one move."

She scrambled off him and shucked off her shirt, then flicked open the clasp of her bra, letting her breasts spill out. The nipples were swollen and peaked, and his fingers clenched at the thought of reaching up and letting her flesh fill his palms. But Lacey was in charge and he had the feeling she needed to stay that way. What was happening here went way beyond sex in a motel room. Lacey was redefining herself.

"Stay right there," she whispered, flicking open the button at her waist.

He went perfectly still, not moving a muscle as she peeled off her pants and stood before him in a scrap of lace that almost passed for panties. Tugging down one side, she bit her lower lip and looked down at him, her eyes flicking downward as she took in her obviously appreciative audience. The next thing he knew, she was naked on top of him, straddling him again, her breasts brushing his chest. He started to reach for them, but she sat up, clenching her thighs around his and covering her nipples with her hands.

"No touching," she said.

He nodded, knowing if he opened his mouth, he'd let out some embarrassing masculine grunt of need and frustration.

She moved her hands down to cup her breasts and squeezed them together like an offering. He couldn't help flexing his hands, but he kept them at his sides and watched as she swept her hands up and pinched the rosy tips between her fingers, letting her lashes drift almost shut while she squeezed and tugged and watched him lick his lips in frustration as her fingers did everything he wanted to do—pinching, squeezing, stroking. He couldn't control himself another second. Letting out the desperate groan he'd been holding back, he lifted his hands, then remembered her words and clenched his fists, dropping them to his sides again. He closed his eyes. He had to, so he could resist reaching up to touch her while his pelvis tensed and ached with need.

"Please, Lacey. Please. Just—please."

Rising up to her knees, she reached down and gripped him in one hand while she knelt above him, her damp curls inches away. He watched, mesmerized, as she lowered herself onto him, the moist bead at the tip of his cock meeting the slick wet heart of her for just a heartbeat before she tensed her thighs and lifted herself away. Slowly, she lowered herself again and let him slip just inside her before she pulled away again. He knew she was watching his face while he watched her slide onto him, over and over, further each time until he was deep inside her.

He felt her muscles tense and flex, and he grabbed her hips, helping her rise when she wanted to but letting her slide onto him at her own pace, feeling her warmth slip around him like a slick, hot sheath that tightened and tensed before she fell forward onto his chest and let out a shuddering, heaving breath of relief and satisfaction and everything, everything but surrender.

CHAPTER 25

LACEY BLINKED, FEELING HER LASHES BRUSH THE softness of Chase's beard. Her head was nestled in the curve between his shoulder and neck, and his arm held her curled against him. His palm cupped the crest of her hip, and his fingers splayed across the soft skin that dipped toward her stomach.

She drew in a long breath, savoring the scent of him, and he tightened his grip, then released it.

"You all right?"

She pondered the question. She *felt* all right—more than all right—but was she? She'd just shared the ultimate intimacy with a man she'd sworn not to fall for—again. And she was about to go home with him, which had to be the worst idea ever for a woman who was trying to strike out on her own.

"I don't know." She reached out a hand to push herself up to a sitting position and grazed his warm skin. Ignoring the faint electric flicker that sparked from the touch, she turned her back and reached for her panties. She could feel him watching her as she snugged them over her hips and shimmied into her T-shirt.

"You just going to lie there?" she asked. She tried for a teasing tone, but her impatience sharpened her voice to an edge.

"No." He swung his legs off the bed and reached for the jeans she'd left crumpled at the bottom of the bed. "I'm going to get dressed, and then I'm going to take you home."

She yanked her pants on, tugging the waistband closed and jerking up the zipper. It was like closing the barn door after the horse had fled, but for now, it was the best she could do.

"I shouldn't be doing this."

"Why not?"

"Because…because we can't…" She flailed helplessly at the rumpled sheets. "We can't keep doing this."

"We won't, then. You'll have your own room, and I'll be gone all day. Hell, you don't even have to do anything if you don't want to. I'm just trying to give you a safe place to stay."

"But every time we get together, you—we…"

"That was your choice, Lacey," he said. "If you want to lay down a hands-off policy, I'll abide by it."

"But…" She was suddenly appalled at herself. He was right. That last encounter had been entirely her idea. She'd forced him down on the bed, straddled him, held him down…

"You could have told me no," she said.

He gave her an incredulous stare. "You do know I'm a man, right?"

She blushed. "I'm just saying, I didn't *make* you do it. And besides, you *told* me to take my clothes off."

"I know. You've got to get over this compunction to do everything a man tells you to do. Unless the man is me." He grinned. "Hey, take your clothes off again."

"No." She crossed her arms over her chest.

"See? You do what you want."

She heard the hum of an engine and the crunching of gravel as a car cruised down the street outside the hotel, and she felt alarm spiraling in her chest, reminding her that whatever the merits of Chase's ranch versus the motel, she definitely wasn't safe where she was.

"I told you, I need somebody to help out," he said. "It might as well be you."

"You'll show me what to do?"

He grinned, and she flashed him what she hoped was a quelling look.

"In the *barn*."

He grinned wider, and she pictured the two of them literally rolling in the hay. She could feel herself blushing. "Stop it."

"Okay. I'll show you how to do ranch work. And I won't touch you." He narrowed his eyes. "But don't expect me to control myself if you jump me again."

"I didn't jump you!" She winced. "Well, I guess I did. Kind of. But I won't do it again."

"Your choice," he said, raising his palms in that "no hands" gesture.

"All right. I'll go with you. We'll try it for tonight, okay?"

Lacey expected Chase to look happy, maybe triumphant. But his expression was serious, his mouth drawn into a thin line, his eyes on hers, and she realized too late that she'd done it again—met his eyes and made that connection that drew them into a partnership. She'd worried about kissing him, but that was nothing compared to this.

She bit her lip and looked away. "I'm going to earn my keep, though." Actually, she was going to do more than that. She was going to work her ass off. Pam had asked her to help her brother, and this was one way she could do it without breaking her promise to herself. If she helped him with the ranch, really helped him, maybe the guilt would leave her alone. It wouldn't be quite what Pam had in mind, but it was the best she could do. Maybe then they'd be even. And then…

And then she had no idea what would happen. Somehow, she'd build herself a new life. One where she didn't need to rely on anyone but herself. Maybe she'd let Chase visit. Yeah, that would work.

He hoisted the suitcase in one hand and grabbed her backpack with the other. "You got all the baggage you need here?"

"Oh, yeah, I've got plenty," she said. "I've got more than enough baggage for both of us."

The ranch house was hardly the kind of place that shouted home to Lacey. The gray, weathered two-story house stood alone on a vacant stretch of flat plain graced by one solitary tree that looked like it would fall down any minute. And when the tree fell, it would probably land on the low addition that had obviously been tacked on fairly recently. She wondered if Chase had built it himself. She wondered if he'd taken his shirt off when he did it.

She smacked her inner slut and returned her attention to the house.

"You'll be sleeping in the addition," Chase said. "I built it for a family room, because the rooms in the main house are so small. I felt kind of boxed in, you know? Couldn't relax. So I put in a couple of guest bedrooms while I was at it. They're on the far side, so you'll have plenty of privacy."

She remembered his parents' sprawling old southern house, with a wide screened-in porch where palm leaf fans spun slowly through the hot summer days. No wonder he felt boxed in here.

"I'd have to cross the whole house to get to you," he said, taking her silence for nerves.

She looked up at the tree, wondering not if, but when it would fall. It was bound to happen.

Maybe falling for Chase was as inevitable as the eventual breaking of the branch. Maybe the pull between them was as strong as the gravity that was bowing the old tree toward the ground.

Not if, but when.

No. She could do better than that. She was strong. She *felt* strong tonight.

Of course, she felt strong because she'd totally mastered Chase back in the motel room, but that wasn't quite the kind of strength she needed now. She didn't need Xena the warrior princess; she needed Scarlett, canny and tough and tightly laced, keeping her feelings hidden with a flash of flirty eyes and a fiddle-dee-dee smile.

She tossed that look at Chase as he pulled the truck to a stop, flinging open the door and stepping out so she didn't have to spend another moment beside him in the close confinement of the truck cab. Just being in the pickup had reminded her of that day by the creek. Of course, that hadn't been in this truck. It had been in the Dodge. But trucks plus Chase equaled trouble.

"How many acres do you have?"

"'Bout six hundred, plus five hundred leased."

More than he'd had back home. Something fluttered in her heart, and she wondered if it was a tiny shred of her guilt flying away.

She hung back, not wanting to stand by the door while Chase fished for his keys. This was the moment the boy kissed you good night. She stood poised on her toes, ready to retreat if he turned and faced her, but he simply swung open the door. It wasn't even locked.

She attributed the sinking feeling in her chest to worry. "You always leave it open?"

"Usually. Nobody comes out here," he said.

So they were alone.

She followed him inside. The house was old-fashioned, with uneven plaster walls and a narrow staircase that led to the second floor on their right. Opposite the stairs was a wide doorway leading to what was apparently a living room or parlor with a fireplace against one wall. A brown leather sofa stood in front of the hearth with its back to them, flanked by two matching chairs. The furniture was masculine and old-fashioned, with brass tacks along the edges, but it looked fairly new, almost unused.

As she followed Chase past the staircase and took a left turn through a door beneath it, she saw why. Dropping down two steps, they entered what had to be the new family room. It was a long, open space with unfinished wooden beams spanning the ceiling. Another fireplace, built of rough rock, angled across one corner. A pool table stood to one side, balls racked and ready, and the furniture was upholstered in dark brown tweed fabric and scattered with needlepoint pillows featuring deer, bears, and flying ducks. The room was carpeted in a warm brown Berber, and the walls were painted a deep chocolate brown that made her feel like she was safe inside a cave.

A man-cave.

Beyond the pool table was a foosball table, its armless players dangling above the fake green field, their torsos skewered by shiny metal poles.

"Where's the big-screen TV?" she asked.

He nodded toward the fireplace, and she realized a three-foot screen was mounted on the wall above it, flanked by two sets of mounted antlers. The room was all man, but something about it felt strangely domesticated. Maybe it was the fact that all the textures and patterns meshed so well. The decorating had been put together by someone who cared.

"Who did the decorating?"

"Decorating?" He looked amused. "Nobody. I just bought some stuff and stuck it in here."

They passed through the room and into a narrow hallway, then into a small guest bedroom neatly appointed with a dresser and a bed heaped with plump, inviting pillows. Lacey looked over at Chase, then back at the pillows.

"Well."

"I'll let you get settled in."

She watched him leave with long strides, tossing a casual "good night" over his shoulder. She'd been prepared for a kiss or an attempted seduction, but Chase didn't seem to have any problem turning and walking away. She should have felt relieved, but for some reason, the sparkle of the night had dissipated and she felt a little flat.

She'd been expecting a fight, she told herself. She wasn't disappointed—she was just a little let down. That was all.

Just a little let down.

CHAPTER 26

"Sleep okay?"

Chase drank in the sight of Lacey leaning against his kitchen counter, her glossy hair lit by the morning sun slanting through the window above the sink. His eyes drifted down the body he'd dreamed about all night. She wore a short, white terry cloth bathrobe that covered everything but a swath of cleavage and her long, lean-muscled legs. As she watched her Eggo brown in the toaster oven, she folded her arms across her chest. She was probably trying to hide her assets, but the result was to press them together and amplify the cleavage.

"Syrup?" He held up the bottle, half-full now that he'd slathered his own waffle with butter and doused it in syrup. He'd already been out on his horse Captain, checking the herd, and he was starving.

"Nope. Thanks."

She shifted her wary gaze to the window. Yesterday, she'd been all confidence and spunk. Today she looked lost, like a kid someone had dumped out of their car on the highway. It was obvious she'd only accepted his hospitality as a last resort, and she'd probably spent a restless night worrying about her next move.

He wanted to tell her she didn't have to make a move. That she could stay as long as she needed to. He hadn't slept either, but it wasn't because he'd regretted his invitation. It was because he couldn't stop reliving that crazy hour they'd spent at the motel. He couldn't erase the image of her naked body from his mind, couldn't forget how she'd looked down at him through her lashes and mocked him, tempted him, trusted him.

Trust was the best part of it. When Lacey gave herself, she didn't hold back, and in the motel she'd shown more of her true personality than he'd ever seen. Hell, he doubted anyone had ever seen that side of Lacey.

He hoped not. He wanted it to be his, only his.

He'd tossed and turned the night away, wondering what would happen if he crossed the family room and tapped on her door. He was still thinking about it, but he needed to stop. Needed to focus.

"Well, I'd better get started." He brushed his hands on the thighs of his jeans. "Lots to do today."

"Hold on." Lacey snatched the waffle out of the toaster and bit into it like a giant cookie, holding up a finger while she chewed and swallowed. "I'll be right there. You mind if I, um, freshen up first?"

He shrugged. "No problem. But the horses and cows don't care what you look like."

She snorted a very unladylike snort. "I'm not prettying up. At this point, I think it's clear I don't care what I look like either." She ran a hand through her tousled hair. Obviously, she didn't realize that her just-out-of-bed look was far more of a turn-on for him than anything she could do with brushes and makeup.

"I'll wait." He let his hip slant against the counter as he fished the next waffle out of the toaster. "Take your time."

When she emerged from the powder room off the kitchen, her face was pink and fresh from a splash of cold water and she'd finger combed her hair into a knot at the nape of her neck. She was right—she wasn't Little Miss Perfect anymore. She was something far more real. He'd always admired Lacey for her shiny hair and perfect clothes, but surprisingly, he liked this new incarnation even better. There was something earthy about her—something feminine but strong.

Maybe ranch work would suit her better than she realized.

"You can't wear those shoes," Chase said, pointing down at Lacey's running shoes.

"It's okay. I don't mind if they get dirty."

"I bet you mind if a horse steps on your foot and breaks your toe."

She paled. "I'm going to be that close?"

She realized she was being stupid the minute the words came out. Of course she was going to be close to the horses. She was working on a ranch.

"I thought you said you liked horses."

"I do. I think they're pretty. But I've never been close to one."

He gulped, clearly swallowing a curse. Maybe this wasn't going to be a dream come true after all.

"I'll learn, Chase."

"Let's hope."

His tone made her stiffen. She'd show him. She'd be fine. She'd probably be good with the horses. How hard could it be? She liked animals. And horses were just like big dogs. Really big dogs, with huge, heavy feet that could break your toe right through your running shoes.

She closed her eyes and willed herself to stop thinking about their feet. She pictured Black Beauty. Seabiscuit. Misty of Chincoteague. Horses were wonderful. Magical. Like unicorns without the big pointy horn. She'd be fine.

Chase led her into the tack room, where a pair of scuffed brown cowboy boots were sitting next to a bale of hay. "Put these on. They're Pam's. She won't mind."

She sat down and toed off her shoes, taking the boots from him and sliding her feet inside. Wow. Pam was cute and all, but she didn't have feet; she had flippers. Tugging at the back of the boot, she slid her foot home and wiggled it from side to side, then slid on the other boot and stood up. Her feet were swimming in them, but she didn't complain as she scuffled down the aisle after him. Hopefully she wouldn't trip.

Trip and fall and land under a horse. And get her head crushed and die.

She squared her shoulders and tried to channel Scarlett O'Hara, remembering how her role model had driven a frightened team of carriage horses through the burning streets of Atlanta. You could do anything if you had to. It just took courage and determination.

They headed down a long, straw-strewn aisle. Ahead, horse's heads protruded over the stall doors, watching their approach. The first one, a gray, lifted his head and let out a shrill whinny, and Lacey started. It was such a jarring noise, high and desperate. Like a battle cry.

"We're coming, bud," Chase said in a soothing tone. "That's Captain," he told Lacey. "He's always hungry. Likes a lot of attention."

"He does that when he's hungry?"

"Yup." Chase stepped up to the horse, who was leaning

against his stall door and blowing through his nose. "He's like a two-year-old—a spoiled two-year-old."

Lacey looked up at Captain. He seemed all black nostrils and bulging eyes, with veins standing out beneath his black-flecked silver pelt. Nodding his head, he rolled his eyes, showing the whites as he kicked the stall with one foot. The noise ricocheted around the barn, echoing in her ears.

She took a step back, but the horse stretched his neck and sniffed the air in front of her face with his nostrils distended. His breath seemed to roar like a dragon's. Stumbling on the uneven floor, she fell against the stall door across the way, causing another smaller horse to snort and retreat into the stall with a shrill whinny.

She hadn't expected them to be so big. So wild. So freaking scary. She'd figured handling horses would be hard, with lots to learn and remember, but she hadn't expected this immediate, instinctive gut reaction. Her heart was pounding so fast and hard, she could barely catch her breath, and she felt chilled and sweaty all at the same time.

She was having a damn panic attack.

She leaned against the rough wood with one hand on her chest and struggled to catch her breath. It rasped as if someone had fastened a steel corset around her ribs and was tightening the straps more every second. She bent double and put the other hand to her forehead, closing her eyes and willing herself to *calm down, calm down, calm down*. The fear spiraled and expanded in her chest, leaving room for nothing but panic and the faint fluttering pulse of her heart.

Chase was looking at her with more confusion than concern. "You okay?"

She closed her eyes tight for a second. Horses. Beautiful horses. Black Beauty, Seabiscuit, Misty. She recited the childhood icons like a mantra and sucked in a long breath, letting the oxygen flood her chest and surge up into her brain. It washed out the fear and pulled in courage. A stammering, stuttering, Cowardly Lion kind of courage, but courage nonetheless.

She straightened, ignoring the ache in her ribs and the dizziness that made her grab for the stall door behind her.

"Fine. Sorry. Got wobbly for a minute." She forced a smile. "Guess I've been kind of stressed lately."

He was staring at her, his eyes narrowed. "You going to be able to do this?"

"Of course I am." She resisted the urge to wipe the clammy sweat from her forehead and hoped she didn't look as weak and pale as she felt. "I'll be fine."

CHAPTER 27

Chase swore to himself. This was a disaster. The woman was afraid of horses. Deathly afraid.

She was trying to cover it up, but Chase had seen her struggling for breath. She wasn't just a little hesitant—she was terrified. Didn't rich girls ride horses? How come her dad hadn't bought her a pony? He'd bought her everything else.

This was hardly the scenario he'd pictured the night before, where he and Lacey had mounted up and galloped into the sunset. He'd thought today might start a new life, a better life for both of them. Instead, it was going to be an ordeal.

She watched him, wide-eyed, as he clipped a lead to Captain's halter and led the horse past her to the hitching post outside the barn. Jimbo was already there, tacked up and ready to go.

He tied Captain with quick, vicious gestures. The rope lashed in his angry hands and almost hit the horse. Damn. This was getting to him. He was never careless with the animals.

This was more than disappointment; it was anger. He always felt this way when his careful plans were foiled, when the future he'd counted on went astray.

Maybe Lacey wasn't the spoiled one. Maybe it was him. He took a deep breath, clenching his fists, then unclenching them, calling up his calmer, better self. This wasn't Lacey's fault. Her fear of the horses was clearly visceral—not a conscious reaction, but something from deep inside.

He swore under his breath. He'd treasured the dream of them riding together. He'd expected it to come true today. And he wasn't going to give it up.

Lacey wouldn't want to stay if she couldn't be useful, and she wouldn't be useful if she couldn't handle the horses. It wasn't like there was anything else for her to do. There wasn't enough housework to keep a child busy; it was just him in the big house, and he did okay cleaning up after himself. The cattle took care of themselves most days, and yard work wasn't an option either. He glanced out the barn door at the brown, crumpled grass surrounding the house. Landscaping was hardly a priority in this dry country. You didn't have to mow grass that wouldn't grow.

"*I can do it. I can do it.*" He didn't know if she was talking to him or trying to convince herself. She gripped the stall door behind her, her fingers white on the rough wood like she was holding herself up by sheer will. Her face was still pale, with a sheen of nervous sweat glossing her forehead.

"I'll be fine." Her eyes flickered toward Captain, wary and fearful, but her jaw was clenched in a rigid line he'd learned to interpret as her stubborn streak. "He just...surprised me."

At least she wasn't running away. Maybe there was hope—but it wasn't going to be easy. Having a tense, fearful person around would be hard on the horses. They were sensitive to the mood of their handler, picking up on tension as if they could see into your mind. You could fake it all you wanted; horses knew what you were feeling. Lacey wasn't going to be able to coast through this on courage; she needed to really conquer her fear.

Captain shifted and whinnied again. Lacey jumped, then shook her head and smoothed her hands down her thighs. Chase suspected her palms were sweating.

"Okay. Come here." He took her hand and led her over to a spot just outside the tack room door where he'd lined up a few bales of straw against the wall. "Sit down."

She lowered herself onto the straw and tried to pull her hand away, but he tightened his grip and forced her to face him. "Let's talk about this."

"It's okay." She tried to pull her hand away again. "I can do it."

"You can't fake this, Lacey. Horses are sensitive. They can feel what you're thinking. You're going to make them nervous, and then they really *are* dangerous. So let's talk it through."

She bit her lip and looked doubtfully over his shoulder toward the horses, who were watching them curiously from their stalls. Captain seemed to sense something was wrong; he'd gone quiet, but his ears were pricked and alert.

"What is it that scares you?"

She rolled her eyes. "Horses, apparently."

"But what is it about them?"

"They're so—so *big*. And they seem—I don't know— nervous." She shrugged, her eyes tearing up. "It's stupid. People deal with them every day. *You* deal with them every day. I know there's nothing to be afraid of. It's just—it's *in* me. I'm afraid of the stupidest things, Chase. Men sometimes, like Wade, and being alone."

"That's not stupid," he said. "You should be afraid of Wade. He's a psycho."

"I guess." She looked down at her hands. "But I'm

afraid of everything. Cocktail party crowds. Subway trains. Flashing lights." She sighed. "Horses are just the latest thing on the list."

"What are you afraid is going to happen with the horses?" He edged closer to her. "What's the worst-case scenario?"

She looked down at her hands, both of them now held in his. "I guess I'm afraid they're going to hurt me. Kick me or bite me or something."

"Okay. Come on." He led her over to Captain, but as they neared the hitching post, she stepped back and stumbled, her hand to her throat. Chase could tell she was trying to control her breathing, and he suspected her heart was galloping like the horses she was so afraid of. But she caught herself and closed her eyes for a moment. When she opened them again, she seemed to have regained some control.

Chase had never had a panic attack in his life. Maybe he was too dumb to be scared of stuff—he'd had enough close calls to prove that theory. But he could sense how hard Lacey was trying.

"Look." He lifted the animal's upper lip, displaying a yellowed row of square, straight teeth. "He's not made for biting. Some horses nip, but it's a vice—something you can train them out of. I can guarantee my horses won't bite you. That's a promise."

He walked around the horse in a circle, setting his hand on the animal's rump as he passed his hindquarters. "He won't kick you either, as long as you don't surprise him. And if you stand close, he can't get any power behind a kick anyway. You just have to be careful he knows where you are, that's all. Just talk to him."

"But..." She shook her head.

"But what? Tell me."

"I know it's stupid, but if you're that close, he might step on you."

Chase leaned into Captain's shoulder, and the horse stepped aside. "He's easy to move. They move away from pressure, so all you have to do is give him a push if he's clumsy enough to step on you. Come on. Get to know him a little. Pet him. Honest, he won't hurt you."

Lacey took a tentative step toward the horse, then another. "Go on," he urged.

She lifted a hand to stroke the horse's long muzzle. She was shaking slightly, and the horse blew out a nervous raspberry, making her jerk her hand away.

"Sorry," she said.

"It's okay. What you have to remember is that horses are flight animals. Their instinct is to run from what they fear."

"Hey, we have a lot in common." Lacey's smile trembled at the edges, but at least she was smiling. "I'm a flight animal too."

She reached up and stroked the back of one finger over the smooth velvet pelt. Chase had the feeling that she saw herself as a fairy-tale princess taming a fire-breathing dragon, when really old Captain could be trusted with toddlers.

He stepped up behind her and lifted her arm, smoothing her palm down the length of the horse's muzzle. Despite the realization that she might never be the cowgirl he wanted and needed, he couldn't keep himself from responding to her nearness. Guiding her hand meant he was snugged behind her, her back flush against his chest, and his body was enjoying the experience even as his brain struggled to resist. A surge of arousal threatened to hijack his good sense, and he almost stepped back, but he didn't want to make a sudden move and scare the horse. Or Lacey.

She brushed against him as she hiked herself up on tiptoe to reach the crest of Captain's neck, just behind his ears. She really was a small woman. Maybe it was a little scary when the horse dwarfed you like that. He drew in a slow breath, willing himself to be patient.

"Good boy," Lacey said again. She moved her hand slowly down Captain's neck, her forehead furrowed in concentration, her lower lip trapped between her teeth. She glanced back at Chase. "How am I doing?"

"Fine." He thought a moment. The only fear he could remember was fear of water when he was practically a baby. Wading, splashing around in shallow water, and easing his way in hadn't helped; his fear had remained until his dad tossed him in the deep end. Maybe that's what he needed to do for Lacey. He stepped into the barn and hefted a saddle from a sawhorse just inside the door. "You ready to go for a ride?"

CHAPTER 28

"A ride?" Lacey blanched. "On a horse?"

"Well, yeah." Chase chuckled. "Captain won't be able to kick you, step on you, or bite you when you're on his back. Besides, maybe you need to see the fun part first. You like fast cars, right? And when you were a cheerleader, you never minded being thrown up in the air and stuff."

She remembered how much she'd loved the high-flying cheer stunts—the feeling of giddy freedom as her teammates tossed her into the air, and the feeling of trust as she crashed down into their waiting arms.

Then she remembered getting dropped.

It had hurt, but she'd survived. Spent a few days on the bench nursing a bruise, and then gotten right back on the pyramid. The worst-case scenario was never as bad as your fear made it out to be.

"It's not like you're not brave, Lacey."

"No, I guess not. Actually, being so scared of Captain kind of surprised me. I've had the opposite surprise so many times since I left home. I like being alone. I like being on the road at night, going fast. I even like Grady. I like making a life for myself, and when I first left, I wasn't sure I could even do it."

"I could have told you that."

"But you knew me 'when.'" She sighed. "I changed later on. I spent so much time playing second fiddle to Trent that I didn't do anything for myself. I was just there to support him. Heck, I didn't even support him. I just decorated his life."

"That was a shame. A waste," he said.

She cocked her head, wondering if he was joking. Clearly, he wasn't. And he was right. She'd wasted the woman she used to be. She'd given her life to other people—her father, her husband—and failed to use all the advantages of being popular and pretty and lucky and rich. She'd lived a life that didn't matter—not to herself and not to anyone else.

She remembered hosting a cocktail party for Trent's investors, wearing an elegant, expensive new dress. She'd felt every eye upon her, the men covetous, the women envious as she tossed her head back and laughed a perfect, tinkling laugh. She was the ultimate treasure, the shining diamond in the luxurious setting of Trent's enormous house. They'd all watched her. Envied her.

But when she'd caught a glimpse of a woman with flawless makeup and perfect hair reflected in the window, she'd wondered who it was for a moment before she realized she was looking at herself.

That had been her first panic attack. She'd wound up on the back deck, struggling to breathe, praying no one would see her sweating, gasping, being so much less than perfect. She'd wanted to run away, fast and far, and never go back.

She'd told herself to suck it up, to be brave and stick it out. It wasn't until total disaster demolished her life that she'd packed up and run.

As it turned out, she should have done it sooner. She'd been proud she'd overcome her fear that night, but it would have been smarter—and braver—to run.

"Once I almost ran away from home in the middle of a

party," she said. "I had this crazy urge to rip off my dress and kick off my heels and take off."

"I like the dress part." Chase's slow Tennessee drawl tasted each word as he probed her eyes with his own. "But you can leave the heels on if you want."

"Hey," she protested. "I'm your employee now. That's sexual harassment."

"You're the one who started talking about ripping your clothes off." He grinned unapologetically and hoisted the saddle onto Captain's back. She watched his shoulders and the muscles in his arms flex as he set it in place and suppressed the urge to tell him she'd rather ride him than the horse.

But that wasn't what she was here for. She was here to work, to prove her worth—not only to Chase but to herself. She squeezed her legs together to quell the rush of warmth let loose by the brief lapse into flirtation and did her best to wipe the thought of Chase's muscles from her mind.

"Don't you have to go to work?"

"I don't know." He scuffed one booted toe in the dusty barn aisle. "I thought I'd stick around today and make sure you were okay. You need to learn to ride, and I'd feel a lot better if you mastered Old Bess too, so you can defend yourself. I don't think Wade will find the ranch, but you never know, and then there's Galt."

"Galt?"

"The guy who shot my cow. But don't worry—Old Bess'll send him running for the hills."

"Who's Bess?" She wasn't sure she wanted the answer. It sounded like a cow's name, and she was having enough trouble dealing with horses. Chase didn't think she was going to ride out and rope the suckers, did he?

But he'd said Bess would help her defend herself. Did they have guard cows?

"Bess is my shotgun. She was my dad's."

Lacey heaved a sigh of relief. It wasn't a cow. She'd forgotten how men were always naming things. Cars. Trucks. Guns.

Wait a minute. *Guns?*

"Chase, I don't want to meet Old Bess. I really don't. I'm…" She let her voice trail off. She'd been about to say she was scared of guns, but at this rate, he'd think she was scared of mice too.

Okay, she was. But she wasn't a scaredy type of person. It was just horses and guns and mice. And maybe cows. She hadn't had much to do with cows, but judging from her reaction to the horses, she was probably afraid of them.

"So do you want to shoot first and ride later?"

She didn't want to do either one. Maybe he should just shoot *her.* She struggled to quell the fear building in her chest and wished she was anywhere but there. She should have left town. Stolen a car if she had to.

Maybe she still could. She scanned the cluster of ranch buildings, her eye lighting on a huge green tractor standing behind the barn, her desperation making her create wild, reckless scenarios in her head. Maybe she could steal the tractor and take off for Colorado. Nobody would expect to find Lacey Bradford on a tractor. She'd stick on a straw hat and poke along the rural roads. Drivers would curse her, shake their fists, beep their horns—but they'd have no idea they were dealing with an escaped trophy wife.

But taking the tractor would be stealing from Chase, and she wasn't taking anything from him—not even the things he offered. She was here to earn her keep, so she was going to have to find a way to deal with the horses.

It shouldn't be so hard. People rode horses every day, and she trusted Chase. She always had.

She'd certainly trusted him back in the motel room. She'd opened herself to him in a way she'd never done before with a man. And despite the occasional hot, hungry look, he hadn't touched her. He'd proved worthy of her trust.

She'd have to trust him about the horses too. "No," she said, "let's ride first."

She recited her litany of storybook horses as she watched Chase fasten buckles and tug on leather straps until Captain was all decked out like Trigger.

"Stand beside his shoulder, facing his rear." Chase handed her the reins and showed her how to bunch them in her left hand and hang onto the saddle horn at the same time. He put one hand on the back of the saddle and turned the stirrup slightly. "Left foot," he said.

She tamped down her fear for the umpteenth time and tucked her toe into the stirrup. Chase was right—once she was on top of the horse, he couldn't kick her or bite her.

He could throw her, though.

She shoved that thought out of her mind and launched herself toward the saddle—and slammed into the side of the horse. Fortunately, old Captain stood firm, simply swishing his tail once in annoyance. For a flight animal, he was dealing with scary stuff pretty well.

Sliding to the ground, she tried to act casual, as if she hadn't hit her mouth on the saddle and bruised her left boob.

"You might want to bounce a couple times. It uses muscles that don't get much exercise in everyday life," Chase said.

"No kidding. It feels like my thigh's on fire, and I'm not even on yet."

"You want a leg up?"

She did, but she wasn't about to say so. What she wanted and what she needed to do were two different things. She looked up at the saddle, grabbed the horn, and bounced three times on her right foot before she pitched herself upward. She thought she was going to fall again until Chase grabbed the inside of her thigh and more or less tossed her into the saddle.

"Thanks." She fished for the opposite stirrup and grabbed the reins, holding them tightly in her fist. Captain stood patiently through the whole ordeal, but once she was on board, he took a couple steps backward.

"Whoa." She grabbed the saddle horn.

"Loosen the reins."

"Won't he run away?"

"Nope. Hold 'em like this." He mounted Jimbo in one fluid motion and held up his hand to show her. "Lay 'em over the right side of his neck to turn him left, the other side to turn him right." Spinning the gelding in a dizzying demonstration that smacked slightly of showboating, he settled deep in the saddle and the horse stopped short.

Captain shifted his weight, eager to follow, and she let out a little squeal. Chase's lips thinned, but he was obviously doing his best to be patient.

"You won't have to do much. These guys stick together, so Captain will follow Jimbo." He gave her a critical once-over. "Keep your heels down, toes out. And hold the reins lower. You look like you're scared to death."

"I *am* scared to death."

"Oh yeah. Sorry. Just remember, you're on top now, so there's nothing to worry about." He grinned and gave Jimbo a click. Lacey clutched the saddle horn as Captain turned and followed. She tried to look straight ahead, because if she looked down, she'd remember how far she had to fall.

"Where are we going?"

"Just to those trees." Chase pointed toward a green smudge near the distant horizon.

The stupid trees had to be five miles away, but at least Captain was cooperating. He plodded after Jimbo at a sedate, rhythmic pace, his head held low. Lacey rocked with the easy motion and did her best to relax.

"So." Lacey could tell Chase was hunting for a topic to distract her from her fear. He'd never been the best conversationalist in the world, but it was nice of him to try. "Once you settle down, what kind of job are you looking for? I take it ranch work isn't your first choice."

Lacey stared down at the horse's ears. "Real estate," she mumbled.

He grimaced, and she rushed to clarify herself. "Not like Trent. I want to find people homes. Find homes that need families, families that need homes...help people build a life." She stared down at the horse's ears. "Believe it or not, I wanted to help Conway. Be a part of things, you know?" She sighed. "Trent said I didn't have the instinct for it."

"I think you'd be good at it."

Lacey jerked her head up to see if he was joking. Captain perked up too, quickening his steps. She pulled back on the reins, and he settled back into a slow walk. "You think?"

"You'd be good at lots of things, Lacey," he said. "You always were."

"Cheerleading," she said. "And dating."

"Motivating people. Leadership," he countered. "Personal relationships."

She warmed inside at the compliment, but Chase didn't know that most of those personal relationships involved fighting off teenage hormone attacks.

"I never really thought about it that way." She gazed at the horizon and suddenly realized she wasn't thinking about falling anymore. The steady rhythm of Captain's body shifting under the saddle was almost soothing. "This is nice," she said, surprised. "He's a good horse, isn't he?"

"He is."

She looked past Captain's ears across the prairie. The horses were following a shallow dirt trail that snaked through the grasses and meandered into some rocks scattered on a hillside up ahead. It seemed like Chase's horse was following the trail on its own; he sat easily, relaxed in the saddle, holding the reins loosely while he scanned his surroundings.

He looked good on a horse. At home. She studied his posture and tried to imitate it, relaxing her shoulders, holding the reins a little lower and slacker.

They started up the shallow hill, winding between rocks that were shaped and stacked as if some giant had left suddenly while at play. One huge boulder sat atop another smaller stone, balanced like the oversized head of a top-heavy snowman. At the top of the hill, a slice of red rock was exposed, standing out against the green grass like the slash of a knife. They followed the gash down into a ravine, Lacey imitating Chase as he leaned back and let his horse navigate a weed-choked two-track.

When they emerged from the ravine, the land opened up in front of them. Miles of green prairie spread beyond the hillside, cut by barbed wire fences supported by gray posts that leaned one way, then another. The placement of the fences seemed totally random, but the grass and brush that had grown up around them made them appear to be as much a part of the landscape as the rocks and trees.

A short distance away, a small building stood beside a shallow, winding stream. It was obviously abandoned.

"Was that a homestead?"

Chase nodded. "I think it was originally the Galt family place. That stream's the border between our properties."

"Guess we won't check it out, then," she said.

He nodded agreement, then tilted his chin toward a few coal-black cattle that were grazing placidly nearby.

"I need to check that calf. The one Galt shot."

"He shot one of the *babies*?"

Chase nodded. "Sit tight. I need to rope her and check her out." He spun his horse and grinned. "This is the cowboy part."

He fed out a loop from a coil of rope that hung on his saddle and prodded his horse with his heels, whirling a wide loop in the air before settling it over the calf's head.

As he wrapped the rope around the saddle horn, his horse backed rapidly and pulled the lariat taut. The heifer bawled as Chase slid down from the saddle and grabbed her, hefting her into the air and laying her down on her side. Quickly and smoothly, he bound her legs together. She struggled once to rise, then gave up, laying her head on the ground.

Lacey decided she'd better behave herself. The guy was downright dangerous with a rope.

The thought gave her the shivers.

"She looks good." He leaned over the calf, oblivious to the fantasies floating through Lacey's mind. "There'll be scars, but not bad ones. No redness or swelling." He tugged a small spray bottle from his back pocket and gave the animal a few well-placed squirts. "Fly spray." Giving the knot a pull, he set the heifer free. She struggled to her feet and stared at him a moment with a bemused expression in her long-lashed eyes before trotting away.

Lacey tensed and leaned forward to watch her go. As her legs tightened on the horse, she felt his muscles gather beneath her. He'd been restless the moment the rope came out, but now his head came up, his ears tilted forward, and he was suddenly prancing, his front legs dancing in place. She grabbed the saddle horn just as he took off like a stone flung from a slingshot, hurtling toward the herd.

For a moment, Lacey felt like she was suspended in the air, still seated, her hand still poised in front of her like she was holding the horn, but there was no saddle beneath her. No horse, either. With a heavy *whump* she hit the ground, her seat-bones taking the impact and sending pain rocketing up her spine.

Chase was beside her in a heartbeat, his face anxious.

"Sorry. He's usually so good. Damn." He punched his fist into his thigh. "You must have cued him somehow."

She tried to give him a smile, but it was a weak, watery one. She couldn't seem to catch her breath. Maybe she'd collapsed a lung. She brought her fist to her chest and sucked in the fresh prairie air, once, twice, three times.

"Oh, lord." He rolled his eyes. "Now you'll be even more scared of horses."

She felt her heartbeat slow and something moved in to replace the fear. *Anger.* A much healthier emotion, and more useful. It fed her lungs and heart, giving her strength to sit up and glare at him. "I *fell*, Chase. Your horse *threw* me."

"He didn't throw you. He bolted. You just—you just didn't bolt with him."

Dammit, he was suppressing a smile. She could see the telltale twitch at the corner of his lip, the amusement in his eyes.

"Whatever." She felt the anger rise, swamping the pain and the fear, heating her up inside and threatening to spill out and set the grass on fire.

Chase squinted to watch Captain, who had settled down a few feet away to crop the grass as if nothing had happened. "He's an old rodeo roping horse. He's gentle and well-trained, but when he sees action, he goes a little nuts."

"A little," she said. "Just a little. How did he do that? It's like he shot out from under me." She struggled to her feet, trying to ignore the pain in her tailbone.

Chase grinned. "That's what it feels like, doesn't it?" His smile faded as she grabbed her back and winced. "Sorry, Lacey. I guess that wasn't the greatest introduction to riding." He looked back the way they'd come. "Do you think you can walk?"

She pictured herself staggering home, defeated, trailing behind Chase and the horses.

L is for loser. Might as well brand it on my forehead.

"No," she said decisively. "I'll ride."

"Really?"

"Sure. Don't they say you should get right back on the bucking bronco when it throws you off?"

"That's what they say."

"Then that's what I'll do." She walked over to the horse, trying not to show how much each step hurt, and grabbed the strap of his bridle. "Come on, bud," she said. "Let's try that again."

CHAPTER 29

CHASE WATCHED, SURPRISED, AS LACEY LIFTED HER foot toward the stirrup. Sucking in a quick breath, she clutched at the saddle, then set her jaw and started to try again.

"Hold on." He took Captain's reins and led the horse over to one of the big rocks that littered the hillside. "Can you climb up there? It'll be easier to get on."

"Sure."

He could tell she was gritting her teeth against the pain as she scrambled up onto the rock, but she managed to ease a leg over the saddle as he held the horse steady. He handed her the reins and couldn't help admiring her courage when she straightened up and turned the horse toward home. It was too bad she was so scared of horses. That kind of determination could make a good ranch wife.

Wife? Now he was getting way ahead of himself. And way ahead of Lacey. After getting dumped in the dirt by the horse he'd promised would never hurt her, she'd probably run as far and fast as she could once she got away from the ranch.

He rode home slowly in deference to Lacey's sore seat, and they barely spoke the whole way. She didn't have much to say once they got home, either, but she was hungry enough to follow him into the kitchen and help him slap heaping helpings of turkey and ham onto slabs of wheat bread.

He tilted his head for her to follow and carried his lunch

onto the wide front porch, plopping into one of the mismatched side chairs that lined the wall. Lacey stood at the
railing.

"You want to sit down?" he asked.

"Not really."

"How bad are you hurt?"

"Not bad." She hunched over her tailbone like she didn't
want to put any weight on it. "I'm fine."

"Fine enough to do a little shooting after lunch?"

"I don't know, Chase. I hate to tell you this, but I'm kind
of scared of guns too." She stared out at the road, probably
wishing she were home. Her house back in Conway was
high on a hill, looking out over miles of green grass waving
in the warm Tennessee breeze. Actually, now it probably
looked out over a checkerboard of cropped green lawns
speckled with brand-new double-wides. His, on the other
hand, looked out over a long dusty driveway and a corral
bordered by twisted, sunbaked fence rails.

A dust cloud kicked up in the distance, growing as it
neared the ranch. Not many cars passed the place; you had
to turn three times onto dirt roads to find it, and there was
no indication to the casual traveler that anyone lived out
here. Once in a while a lost tourist passed by, or a hunter,
but that was about it. Chase squinted, trying to see what
kind of car it was. Or was it a truck?

He glanced over at Lacey. She'd seen it too, and she'd
shrunk into the shadow in the corner of the porch.

"You don't think…"

"I don't know. People don't come out here often. It's not
an easy road."

Lacey was white, her hand shaking as she set down the

last bite of her sandwich. As the truck bounced up the drive, she set the plate on the railing and headed inside the house.

"I'm going out back."

Chase remembered the guns he'd left on the picnic table in preparation for their shooting lesson. "Wait. Don't touch those." He looked back at the approaching dust cloud. As he watched, the blurred shape resolved itself into Cody's Jeep, with its tattered canvas top fluttering from the roll bar. There were two silhouettes behind the windshield.

"It's Cody," he said. "Cody and Pam. It's all right."

"Good," Lacey's voice called from the back porch. "They can help teach me how to shoot."

"I thought you were afraid of guns."

"I am, but I just realized I'm more afraid of Wade Simpson."

Lacey hoisted Old Bess to her shoulder, waiting for her heart to speed up, wondering if her chest would tighten with panic, but she felt fine. Strong, even, like Scarlett drawing a bead on a no-good Yankee marauder.

"Step your left foot forward, but put your weight on your back leg," Chase said, pointing to Lacey's still-booted foot.

"Just make sure you shove the stock into your shoulder," Pam said from her perch at the picnic table. "Lessens the kick."

"You can shoot?" Lacey couldn't picture her good-natured friend squinting through the sights of a shotgun. Actually, it was weird to see Pam in jeans instead of her ever-present apron. She fit into the warm, homey atmosphere of the café like a native species in its natural habitat. *It must be nice to find the place you belong,* Lacey thought. She felt like an imposter everywhere she went, like she was pretending to be someone she wasn't.

"Of course I can shoot. Don't sound so surprised," Pam said. "Cody taught me. I hit a tree once."

"It wasn't the one you were aiming for," Cody said.

She made a face, and Cody slung an arm around her shoulders. "You have other talents. And really, you don't need accuracy for self-defense. 'Specially with a shotgun. So here, Lacey. Here's how you stand. This way your body absorbs the kick."

He demonstrated the stance with a beat-up shotgun he'd dragged from the backseat of the Jeep. It had a short muzzle, way shorter than Bess's. Lacey wondered if it was what they called a sawed-off shotgun. Weren't those illegal? The thought gave her a shiver of dread, but at least it was Cody's gun, and Cody was one of the good guys. Having a guy with a sawed-off shotgun on your side probably wasn't a bad thing.

Lacey did as she was told, but if she ever used the gun for real, she doubted she'd be thinking about her stance. Hell, she wouldn't even be standing still. She'd be running away, praying she wouldn't have to shoot anybody.

"So who's this guy you're worried about, Lacey?"

"Wade Simpson." She shuddered. "He was a friend of my ex-husband's. I think they did some business together, and now Wade—he wants to stop my ex from testifying about it."

"By hurting you."

"I don't know what he wants to do," Lacey said. "I'm not

sure *he* does. But he said he'd follow me, and now Chase got a phone call from him looking for me."

"At work," Chase said. "He knows she was in Grady."

"Better get on with the lesson, then." Cody adjusted Lacey's hold on the gun.

"Let your breath out, all the way, then squeeze the trigger once you're steady," Chase said.

"You don't hold your breath?"

"Nope. Let it out."

"Holding your breath makes you shake," Pam added. "When you let it out, you get steady."

Lacey let her breath out and felt the world spin to a stop. Focusing on the shotgun's metal sights, she stared through them at the target the way she'd stared through Captain's pricked ears while she rode.

At least you couldn't fall off a gun.

"Squeeze the trigger. Slow." Chase crooked his index finger to demonstrate. "Don't pull it. Squeeze."

She squeezed. Nothing—nothing—nothing—*blam*! The gun roared, the stock slammed into her shoulder, and a gash opened near the center of the target—all in a half-second of stopped time. Pam whooped and hopped up and down, clapping her hands.

"Hey," Chase said. "That was good."

Lacey put the gun down and grinned, admiring her first-ever bullet hole. The shotgun had ripped a nasty gash through the red band bordering the bull's-eye. It was probably beginner's luck, and her shoulder was killing her, but there was something satisfying about making a good shot.

"Try again."

She lifted the gun, holding it like he'd shown her.

"Press it hard against your shoulder. That'll keep the kick from hurting so much."

She snugged the stock into the soft flesh below the hollow of her shoulder, fitting it right over the bruise from the previous shot and trying not to think about what it would look like when she took her clothes off that night.

It wasn't like anyone would see it. She was keeping her body to herself.

Yeah, right. Maybe she should take the shotgun to bed— not for Chase, because he seemed to have the self-control necessary to maintain the employer/employee relationship. No, she'd need it for herself, so she could shoot herself in the foot if she was tempted to sneak down the hall to his room.

"You gonna shoot or just look cute?" Cody demanded.

She pulled the trigger again, but this time, she jerked the barrel up and missed the target by a mile.

Damn. That first shot really was beginner's luck.

"Squeeze, don't pull," Chase said, reloading the gun and handing it to her. "That way, the shot'll surprise you, and you won't anticipate it. Try again."

She did, and to her surprise, another gash opened in the target right beside the first one. Pam whooped again.

"Man, she's good," Cody said.

"Good job." Chase grinned. "Want to try the revolver, Annie Oakley?"

She laid Old Bess back on the table, carefully keeping the muzzle pointed toward the bleak, empty fields beyond the house. Beside it was an evil-looking black pistol that seemed square and modern and cruel, and an old-fashioned six-gun, the kind Clint Eastwood carried in those old spaghetti Westerns.

"Revolver?" she asked.

Chase picked up the six-gun and showed her how to tip out the cylinder and load bullets into the chambers.

"Two hands." He slapped it closed and raised it toward the target to demonstrate. "Pretty much the same deal. Let your breath out, squeeze."

He showed her how to cock it and she shot low and wide, barely hitting the target.

"Keep your wrists stiff," Cody said. "You're letting the muzzle drop."

She tried again and gave a vintage cheerleader hop, kick, and handclap after a bullet tore into the bull's-eye.

"I feel like Clint Eastwood."

"You don't look much like him. But here, this'll help." Chase grabbed a leather belt from the bench. It had slots for cartridges along the back and a leather holster. He came up behind her and wrapped it around her hips, trying to clasp the buckle slightly off-center, his hands fumbling at the sensitive spot where her hip bone dipped and swelled into the curve of her belly. She could feel his breath warm on her neck and she tilted her head back to press her cheek to his. He froze, his arms around her, his body pressed against her back.

"Chase doesn't think you feel like Clint Eastwood at all," Cody said.

Damn, she'd forgotten they had guests.

Apparently Chase had too. He stepped back so quickly, he would have dropped the belt in the dirt if Lacey hadn't grabbed it. She slipped the tongue into the buckle, feeling embarrassment heat her face, but Chase recovered quickly, grinning.

"No," he said. "She doesn't feel like Clint. He's kind of bony."

The four of them laughed, and the air moved again, the tree by the deck rustling in the breeze. She felt like the world had paused, maybe even spun a little bit backward, and then resumed its trip through space again, spinning like always, with no one but herself and Chase knowing it had stopped.

Although Cody seemed to know. He cast a teasing glance her way, and she felt her face flush. She might as well be wearing the handprint of shame again. Looking down, she pretended to adjust the belt. It was a little big and hung low on her hips.

"Now you're tough," Chase said.

"Wonder Woman." Cody grinned. "The Wild West version."

She laughed. Something about the other couple relaxed her. They got along so well, their camaraderie so easy and real, it was almost contagious. They seemed to help Chase relax too; his lips were tilted into a slight smile, and he didn't seem so stiff and distant. It made her realize how serious he was, how rarely he smiled.

"Try again." He gestured toward the target.

She shoved the gun in the holster and stepped forward, savoring the slight swagger the gun belt put in her walk. Having a gun on her hip really did make her feel tough. All she needed was a half-smoked cigar and a serape.

Channeling Clint, she jerked the gun from the holster and shot, and while she would have lost the draw to a genuine high-noon opponent, the tree with the target on it didn't stand a chance. One more bullet hole joined the tight grouping around the bull's-eye, and she shot again, and again, and again, emptying the six cylinders and feeling a rush of triumph and power and strength. The target was her old life. Her old habits. Her fear and her neediness and her paralyzing weakness.

"Whoa," Cody said as the dust cleared. "Don't mess with Lacey."

"That's right." She shoved the gun back in the holster and wished she had a cowboy hat to tilt down over one eye. "Don't mess with Wild West Wonder Woman."

CHAPTER 30

AN HOUR LATER LACEY STARED INTO THE OPEN refrigerator, wondering what the hell cowboys ate. She wanted to do something for Chase in return for the shooting lessons, but making a nice dinner with nothing but beer and stale bread was going to be a challenge. There was something toward the back, a foil-covered tray, but that was probably leftovers. She wanted to make something good.

She swung open the freezer. So that was where he kept the real food. She carefully peeled back the aluminum foil on two disposable trays, revealing something that looked suspiciously like homemade lasagna. Tupperware containers appeared to contain beef stew, macaroni and cheese, and some kind of noodle casserole—probably tuna.

She flicked on the oven and pulled out one of the lasagna trays. That would hit the spot—homey and satisfying. Trent had liked it when she made glamorous food—chicken piccata, prime steaks rubbed with pepper and spices, elaborate pasta dishes with artichoke hearts and exotic cheese—but she'd never really cared about that stuff. Making it took up the long dull middle of her idle days, but everything had tasted the same when she ate it across the table from Trent.

The door opened behind her, and she whirled, one hand hovering near her hip.

"Whoa," Chase said. "Easy there."

She flushed. She'd changed back into her pink pants and

flowered t-shirt, and traded Pam's boots for sandals—but she'd kept the gun belt. And the gun.

"Sorry. I was—I was cooking dinner."

"What are you going to do, shoot a rabbit to eat?"

"No." She flushed. "It's not loaded. I just—it feels good to wear it." She looked down at the lasagna. "I thought I'd heat this up. Who made you all this stuff? Pam?"

"No. I did." He was indignant. "What, you think men can't cook? I can do it, Lace. You're a guest." He shoved the tray back into the freezer, then bent to take out the one she'd seen in the fridge. "This one's already thawed."

"Oh." She tried to picture Trent in the kitchen, whipping up a meal. She couldn't even picture him opening a beer. She'd always done that for him. "I'm not a guest, though. I told you, I'm earning my keep."

"I can take care of myself." He unhooked a length of cloth from the pegs behind the door and ducked his head into what turned out to be an apron, knotting it around his waist. It was red-and-white checked and made him look like a denim-clad, muscular picnic table. She turned away and hoped he wouldn't notice her shoulders shaking as she suppressed a giggle.

"And Galt," he said, oblivious to the picture he presented. "We need to bring him some of this."

"Galt?"

"Old guy next door."

"Oh. The one you wanted Pam to look after."

"Yeah, somehow she turned that around."

The oven beeped, and he shoved the pan inside, setting the timer for thirty minutes. "We'll take the cover off for the last half," he said.

She stood against the counter feeling useless. He had all this under control. He didn't need an employee. Didn't need a cook or a housewife.

House*keeper*. He probably did need a wife, but he needed one who could work on the range as well as in the kitchen. She'd gone a long way toward conquering her fear of the horses, but she was no cowgirl and probably never would be.

"It was nice to see Pam and Cody," she said.

Chase nodded. He had a stack of mail in his hand and was sorting through the envelopes, tossing most of them onto the table. Two or three that looked like bills remained in his lap.

"Cody seems like a nice guy. Funny."

"Yeah. Sometimes he's a little too funny." He gave her a wry smile. "I'm never going to live down that episode in the creek."

"*You* aren't? I was the one with the handprint on my— well, you know. You're probably Cody's hero for that, and I've probably got a reputation now."

"No, Cody'd never say anything. He's a friend."

They sat side by side on the picnic bench facing the fields, resting their elbows on the table behind them. Lacey stretched her legs out and crossed her feet at the ankles, downing a swig of beer as the wind kicked up and made the long grass shimmer in the fading sunlight. She felt oddly comfortable despite the alien setting. She was used to decks with elegant, cushioned patio furniture, with fire pits burning sweet-scented logs of cherry or apple as glasses clinked and conversation hummed. Instead, the place was silent except for a chorus of crickets and the whisper of the wind.

The silence seemed to draw Chase out, overcoming his usual reticence. "When I came here to Grady, I figured it was Pam and me against the world. But then Cody came to town. He's a good guy, and he takes good care of Pam."

"What did he do before he moved here?"

"Cooked somewhere. He doesn't talk much about it. I think he's had a hard life."

"He looks like it, with the tattoos and stuff. I'm surprised Pam trusts him around Annie."

"Looks can be deceiving. He's done a lot for Pam. She had a tough time as a single mom, and he's really there for her. I think he has a rescue complex. He's always helping strangers, doing things for people. I mean, you saw how fast he came out and helped us with the truck. I'd trust that guy with my life."

"Yeah?"

"Yeah. It might sound corny, but he kind of restored my faith in human nature. After what happened back home, I figured everybody had an agenda, but he's just...just good."

"This is what they call a *bromance*, isn't it?"

Chase flushed. "No, I just—he's a good friend, that's all." He stood abruptly. He obviously wasn't comfortable talking about his feelings, and the mention of *bromance* had put a halt to his confessional mood. "We need to get some dinner over to Galt."

Lacey wasn't sure she dared step into Galt's trailer. For one thing, the place looked like it was about to fall down. For another, the man looked anything but welcoming. He swung the door open, gave them a beady-eyed glare, and turned away to stomp into the kitchen. Lowering himself into a chair at the head of an old-fashioned Formica dinette table, he squinted at Lacey.

"Who's this?"

He sounded so hostile she wanted to drop the Tupperware salad bowl she was carrying and hightail it out of there, but she didn't want Chase to think she was scared of grumpy old men along with everything else. She stepped up and put out her hand. "Lacey Br—Keene."

She needed to start using her maiden name. Forging a new identity.

"I'm helping Chase with the ranch. Nice to meet you."

Galt continued to give her the stink eye. He didn't make a move to shake her hand, but she refused to back down.

"Nice to meet you," she repeated.

He reluctantly slid his dry, papery hand into hers and shook, giving her a skeptical up-and-down assessment. "Lacey Brruh-keene, huh? You don't look much like a ranch hand."

"And I'm not a very good one," Lacey said. "But I'm trying."

Galt was hauling stuff out of the grocery bag. Chase had wrapped the hot pan in towels and set it on the bottom, topping it with a Ziploc bag of dinner rolls from the café along with paper plates and plastic flatware. It was like a very elaborate picnic. Too bad he'd taken off the apron.

Once everything was on the table, their less-than-gracious host made a vague gesture toward the food. "Eat."

He tucked into the food like he was starving, shoveling alternating forkfuls of pasta and salad into his mouth.

Chase followed suit, eating in a barely more civilized fashion. Lacey looked from one to the other, then shrugged and served herself some dinner.

"So," she said brightly. "You sold Chase his land."

Galt scowled. "Bastard."

Maybe that wasn't the best topic of conversation. Maybe something less personal would be better. She cleared her throat. "Nice weather we're having."

"Need rain."

"I suppose we do."

It wasn't until Lacey started to clear the table that she managed to lure Galt into conversation. "That's a handsome kid." She nodded toward a picture on the wall. It was a typical school photo of a dark-haired boy grinning self-consciously against a blue background.

"My son," Galt said. "He died."

"Oh, I'm sorry." Lacey wondered why Chase wasn't making any effort to rescue her from her disastrous conversations with his neighbor. He was worse than Galt, scraping plates into the sink and tossing them into the garbage can without a word.

"He should've had this place," Galt said. "Caldwell's place too."

"I'm sorry. You must miss him."

Chase tugged the nearly full garbage bag out of the plastic trash bin and carried it to the door, tying the top as he went and stepping out into the darkening day, presumably to take it to the trash.

"Hard to miss him when he was never around," Galt said. "Liked fast cars better than farming. That's what kilt him." He snorted. Lacey wasn't sure if it was a snort of disdain or an effort to keep tears at bay. "Was a job, getting him to do any chores around this place. He hated it."

"Oh. Chase loves farming. He appreciates the land, I can tell you that."

"Bob would've appreciated it after a while," Galt said. "He would've come around if he hadn't died. Wanted to be a mechanic, though. Wanted to go to school for it. I couldn't spare him. No time for fancy educatin' when you got a farm to keep."

Lacey felt a sudden ache in her heart for the lonely old man. No doubt he'd been a difficult father. Some of his taciturn manner might be from losing his son, but the hard-set lines of his face told her his negativity was a long-standing habit. Still, the moisture in his eyes proved he'd loved the boy he lost.

"I'm sorry for your loss."

"I'm over it." Galt hobbled into the living room and lowered himself into a worn recliner, picking up a remote. "It's time for my show." He snorted again, and this time it was obvious he was holding back emotion. "You done talkin' now?"

Lacey reached out and touched his arm, just a quick pat. She wondered how long it had been since the old man had touched anyone, or had anyone touch him. He seemed so alone, living on this isolated patch of ground with nothing but his grief to keep him company.

"I'm done," she said. "But maybe I'll see you again."

CHAPTER 31

CHASE DIDN'T HAVE MUCH TO SAY ON THE BRIEF RIDE back to the ranch, and he headed out to the barn as soon as they got home, muttering something about feeding the horses and waving Lacey away when she offered to help.

"Maybe I'll go for a walk." She slumped her shoulders and headed for the house, walking straight through to the back door. She felt like an intruder, useless and defeated, but when she stepped out onto the back deck twilight had just started to settle over the landscape. There wasn't a light in sight—just acres of empty prairie as far as she could see. After the upheaval of the past week, it looked peaceful and serene—a good place to think and plan.

She stood at the edge of the deck, unsure which way to turn. How did you take a walk over a landscape so feature-less? To just start walking seemed foolish—like taking off across a trackless desert without a destination in mind.

There were a few trees in the distance, silhouetted against the silver sky. They weren't as far as the ones she and Chase had tried and failed to reach on horseback, and there were only a few—so it wasn't likely they'd harbor any bears or wolves or Wild West outlaws.

She paced away from the house, swinging her arms reso-lutely. She'd tried the suburban sport of walking for exercise once, getting together with her sometime lunch partners to cruise through the neighborhood with exaggerated strides and swinging arms. Speed walking was supposed to keep your figure trim and your cardiovascular numbers in the "healthy" range, but she'd come to the conclusion that it also made you look and feel like an idiot.

She lengthened her stride, figuring no one was looking and she might as well get some exercise, but it didn't take long to figure out that kind of walking didn't work here. The prairie was dotted with sagebrush and yucca, making it impossible to walk in a straight line. The only way to get anywhere was to mosey, tracing a crooked, meandering path through the spiky flora.

As she left the golden light from the house behind, the world seemed to grow even more hushed. Looking up, she saw the sky speckled with stars, some hard and bright, some faint and far away. She'd seen the same stars from Tennessee, but they'd been lost in the lights from town, a dim constant she'd taken for granted. Here in the darkness of the high plains, they demanded attention, creating a landscape of their own in the limitless night sky.

Craning her neck, she stumbled backward and arched her back, almost tipping over in her effort to take in the entire display. She wanted to see the whole sky, to savor the sense of being surrounded with nothing and everything, time and timelessness.

These stars had shined on the world long before she was born. They'd shine after she was gone, too, distant and unchanging, unaffected by her life or anyone else's. She felt a lightness, as if a burden had been lifted. She may have wasted her life, but what good could she have done? She could make things better for those around her—she *should* do that—but in the long run, her petty problems made no difference. She lowered herself to the ground, crossing her legs yoga-style, her eyes never leaving the sky. She just wanted to enjoy the show.

Chase headed for the barn with a purposeful stride. This was his favorite time of day—when the sun sank below the horizon and he could wrap up his day with the animals, settling them in their stalls, feeding them, making sure everything was finished, ready to start again in the morning.

Catching the horses in the evening wasn't a problem. Captain and Sheba practically ran for the barn, knowing their daily ration of sweet feed was coming. Jimbo was slower, trusting in the routine, knowing hurry wouldn't help things move any faster.

After measuring out the feed, Chase clipped the wire from a fresh bale of hay and shook the rich alfalfa into the feeding troughs. He sat back, enjoying the sounds and scents of everyday life—the rhythmic munching of the horses, the rustle of their big bodies shifting in their stalls, the clean, crisp smell of hay mixed with the musk of animals. Feeding time always gave him a sense of plenty, a feeling that he had what he needed in life.

If only he could carry that satisfaction over into the rest of his day. Most of the time, he felt impatient and rushed, as if there was something he needed to do that he couldn't quite grasp, some essential element that was missing in his life.

It seemed like he always wanted to be somewhere other than where he was. When he was at the car lot, he wanted to be at the ranch. When he was at the ranch, he wanted to be in Tennessee, back at the farm where his future had seemed so assured. Even now, on this perfect quiet evening, he wanted to be somewhere else.

He wanted to be with Lacey.

He wondered if she'd really gone for a walk. She was hardly a country girl, and the plains at night were wide and lonesome—hardly the place for a suburban socialite. She probably wasn't much better suited for hiking than she was for horseback riding.

But she'd said she was going for a walk, and she'd probably gone, even if the dark open prairie scared her. He was starting to realize there was more to Lacey than he'd expected—a core of steel at the heart of her soft beauty. She'd ridden, even though it was obvious that the horses scared her half to death. She'd even climbed back on Captain after he'd confirmed all her fears by dumping her in the dirt. It had obviously hurt her to climb back in the saddle, but she'd done it.

He stroked Captain's mane as the horse bent over the feed trough. He needed to stop thinking about Lacey. Maybe it would help if he thought about the woman he really needed, the woman he hadn't met yet. The one who would be an equal partner. Who would love ranch life and work with him, side by side, every day.

He'd pictured her a dozen times, a dozen ways, but she changed all the time. Maybe she'd be blonde, maybe brown-haired. She'd be sturdy but not heavy, muscular yet feminine. She'd come with all the qualities he wanted in a wife: a love of animals, some ranching know-how, and a steady, rock-solid disposition. She'd also have an insatiable appetite for sex.

Hey, ranching wasn't everything.

Thinking of sex took him back to the motel, back to the moment Lacey had taken charge. He remembered how she'd pushed him back on the bed, straddled him with her hips, set her hands on his shoulders, and gripped him with her thighs like a barrel racer in a tight turn. He remembered her face, upturned in ecstasy, the yellow light casting faint shadows on her cheeks from her shuttered lashes, her lips pink and swollen from his kisses.

He pictured her breasts, the soft flesh cupped in her hands as she rode him. Her total lack of self-consciousness as she took her pleasure, and the way she'd blinked in surprise when she finished the long, shuddering arc of her orgasm. She'd looked down at him as if she'd forgotten where she was, and then light had dawned in her eyes as if she was recognizing him for the first time.

He shook his head, trying to shatter the image. He needed to focus on the attributes Lacey *didn't* have. She liked animals, but he doubted she wanted to dedicate her life to them, and she didn't know a dang thing about ranching. As for her disposition, it was anything but steady. She seemed to swing from passion to fear to anger to elation in quick succession, her feelings always at the surface, her passion always threatening to boil over and burn somebody. He'd be better off with someone more solid. Placid. Even-tempered.

Boring.

What was he going to do, marry a cow? With passion came strength, and at least he always knew what Lacey was thinking. She wasn't devious like Krystal, who was always nursing an ulterior motive like a little demon hidden in her heart. Lacey he could trust. In that way, she was steady as a rock.

He kicked at a clump of straw on the floor, scattering it over the worn boards. He was rationalizing. He was trying to make Lacey over into the woman he needed.

But maybe he could do that. Hell, you could learn about ranching. You could grow to trust animals, and once you trusted them, you could love them. Even in the short time she'd spent with Captain, she'd managed through sheer force of will to move from hesitant fear to a cautious affection.

And if she was willing, Lacey could do anything. Even back in high school, she'd been full of that indefinable quality cowboys call "try." Try meant you made the effort to take on challenges. It meant you were willing to change and grow. It meant you confronted the things that scared you, and took them on every day.

"Try" meant you could take what life threw at you and make the best of it, and that was the single most important thing when it came to ranching. Nothing in nature stayed the same. One year might be prosperous, the next a disaster. One day might bring sunshine, the next a blinding snowstorm. Surviving the challenges was one thing; continuing the fight was another. Sticking with this life took courage and stamina and the determination to get back on the horse after it bucked you off.

And Lacey had all those things.

It might be handy to find a woman who had all the qualities he wanted—but how likely was it that he'd ever find another woman who inspired him with the feelings he had for Lacey?

Suddenly, he needed to see her. He knew she felt trapped

here, hunted by strangers, stuck with nowhere to run. He knew she felt trapped by her feelings, too, stuck in a situation where her determination to stay independent was endangered by their enforced togetherness.

He knew she didn't want a relationship right now—maybe not ever. Her marriage had been difficult, and she was as reluctant to love again as she had been to ride—but he knew she had the courage to try.

All she needed was for someone to offer the challenge.

CHAPTER 32

SOMETHING MOVED AT THE EDGE OF LACEY'S VISION, a bright slash in the sky. She turned, but she'd missed it—and as she turned, something streaked across the patch of sky she'd turned away from.

"Meteors," said a deep voice behind her. Chase's boots crunched on the dry earth.

She wanted to turn and look at him, but another gleam of light sped across the sky, and she felt riveted, her eyes searching for the next streaking comet. What seemed so permanent was changing minute by minute on a scale she couldn't even imagine.

"Falling stars," Chase said, as if she didn't know what a meteor was.

"Falling?" she asked. "Or flying?"

"Flying, maybe." He settled down beside her, bringing his knees to his chest and clasping them in his arms as he tipped his head back to share the view. "I never thought of it that way."

"Falling would mean they're failing." She spotted another and traced its path with one finger. "Flying means they're moving, changing, going somewhere."

"Like you?"

"Not right now." She'd been flying as she sped across the country, the Mustang's bald tires eating up the highway. But she wasn't flying now. The urge that had struck her at Trent's party—the urge to simply run fast and far, wherever her feet could take her—had struck her over and over, but she had nowhere to go.

"You're still flying, Lacey. Still changing."

She was scanning the sky, concentrating on something outside herself, so she almost didn't notice when his hand stole into hers. When she focused on it, she felt everything keenly—his skin rough and warm, the faint pressure as he squeezed her hand.

"I mean, look where you started with the horses this morning, and look where you are now. Even a seasoned rider might not have gotten back on Captain after getting tossed like that." She could hear a smile lightening his tone. "I mean, your butt had to hurt on the way home."

"It still hurts."

He reached up with his other hand and rubbed her back between her shoulder blades in slow, gentle circles. It was nowhere near her injury, but somehow it made the ache in her tailbone feel better. She tilted toward him. The fathomless depth of the sky, the wide expanse of the land, the sounds of crickets and calm breezes going about their business without her, had made her feel alone and insignificant, but Chase's touch reminded her she was real. She wanted to feel his warmth, savor the feeling of closeness to another human being. *It wasn't Chase*, she told herself. She just didn't want to be alone.

Another star traced a shining path across the sky, and he paused, resting his hand on her shoulder. They sat and watched the slow, distant fireworks of the universe in silence for a long while, her hand still clasped in his, his arm around her back, sitting in the dirt by a clump of sagebrush in a world she didn't know and had never expected to find.

For some strange reason, she'd never felt so at home.

Chase stared resolutely at the stars, knowing that if he looked at Lacey, he'd kiss her. She'd looked so alone when he'd walked up. So forlorn, seated Indian-style like a toddler in front of the ultimate big-screen TV—but what she was watching was the whole world, spinning around her without a thought for a woman alone and struggling.

Everyone needed somebody. Lacey might not want to trust a man again, but she had to trust someone. And he wanted it to be him.

But he'd promised. He shouldn't even be holding her hand. He was her boss now, and any sexual shenanigans were out of the question.

She sighed and uncrossed her legs, tilting toward him as she bent her knees and tucked them sideways. Her hand was in his, his arm around her shoulder. He could hear her breath soft beside him, the one human sound in the quiet Wyoming night.

Maybe he could fire her just for tonight. Then they could do what they wanted. Because he had a feeling she wanted the same thing he did.

She rested her head on his shoulder, and they watched another star streak through the night. He knew the stars were falling, not flying. Nothing was constant, and there wasn't a single thing in the universe you could depend on—not a sky, not a star, and certainly not the future. He'd worked out a perfect plan for the ranch—one that included finding the right partner so he'd have children to pass it on to. He wanted to pass on all his father had taught him—but now here was Lacey, the last person he'd expected to see in

Grady, throwing a cosmic wrench into his carefully planned life like a new star spinning into his orbit and throwing him off course.

"Calamity Lacey," he said.

"What?"

"Like Calamity Jane. She came out here and shook up everybody in the West. That's what you're doing to me."

"I'm sorry."

"I'm not." He turned, brushing her forehead with his lips. "You're fired."

She tucked her head under his chin. "Thanks."

She tilted her face up to his so his next kiss fell on her lips. That was all the signal he needed. Moving his hand up from her shoulder to her nape, sliding his fingers into the silky mass of her hair, he let her hand loose and swept his fingers over her face. Tracing the curve of her smooth cheek with his fingertips, he kissed her temple, her cheekbone, the hollow beneath it, and finally her lips.

Suddenly the night sky wasn't black and cold and bottomless; it was deep velvet, soft and nurturing, a shroud to hide and protect them. Lacey paused when his lips brushed hers, and for a heartbeat, he thought she might push him away, but then her lips parted and let him in.

He lost all sense of where they were and focused only on the feel of her skin and the touch of her lips. Drawing her close, he let himself fall, the sky swelling over them as she let him pull her with him onto the ground. A pebble dug into his shoulder blade and a stick poked his ribs, but he didn't care. He didn't care how prickly or hard or unyielding the world was as long as he could be the one to bear it. Him, not Lacey. Pulling her on top of him, he steadied her as she caught her balance and settled on top of him.

"You'll hurt yourself," she murmured, scattering soft kisses down his jawline. "The rocks..."

"I don't care." He brought his hands up to frame her face and scanned her face. "I don't care, as long as nothing hurts you."

Her eyes closed while she drew in a breath. He knew she'd retreated inside herself to decide on her own whether she'd let him in or not. She was choosing what power she'd give him and what she'd keep for herself.

When she opened her eyes again, her gaze was soft as the night sky and her lips curved into a smile.

"Let's go home," she said. "I don't want anything to hurt you either."

Lacey tugged Chase to his feet and they walked back to the house hand in hand, helping each other as they stumbled over rocks in the dark. Staring at the stars had made her night-blind, and he wasn't doing much better at navigating the uneven ground.

She'd vowed to steer clear of Chase and decide her own future. But she'd known ever since she'd seen him sitting behind the counter at the dealership that he'd be part of it. She could fight it, or she could face it.

If she faced it, maybe she could be the one to determine just how far this craziness would go.

It wasn't like Chase took anything away from her when he touched her. Having sex with her husband had felt like handing over more than her body, but having sex with Chase felt like she was setting herself free.

She paused inside the back door, glancing from the hallway on the left that led to his room to the new rooms on the right where she'd been sleeping. They'd go to her room, not his.

Of course all the rooms were his. It was his house. But she'd put out her things that day, stacking a few paperback novels on the nightstand, tucking her clothes into an empty dresser drawer, arranging a bottle of perfume and some lotions on the dresser. She'd done her best to make it her own small space in the world, and she wanted to share it with Chase—not intrude on his world, but welcome him into what little she had that was her own.

She'd been grateful for the soft mattress the night before, when her back had ached from her fall, and she was even more grateful now to feel it give beneath her as she fell into it with Chase. There was no time for preparation, for plumping pillows or turning back the quilt. Chase fell with her, propping himself on his hands and knees at the last moment so he wouldn't crush her while they resumed their kiss.

His mouth met hers again, and he let his hips fall, laying the length of his body against hers. She could feel his arousal between them, impossibly urgent, as she wrapped her legs around his waist and pressed him closer with her. Everything in her body warmed and softened. She felt nothing but elation, pure joy, and she wondered if the stars minded falling, because she was falling, falling fast and hot, and she didn't care. She'd let her emotions burn high tonight, and if it was the last time—well, she had a feeling it was going to be worth it.

Chase slid his hips against hers and she reached up to pull at his collar, a rush of giddy joy bubbling up when it gave in her grip. Snaps, not buttons. They popped open one after the other, top to bottom, and she watched her hands slide over his skin. She took in the square shadows that defined his chest and the muscles below it, memorizing the dark trail that narrowed and dipped below his belt buckle and flowed like a river through the muscular topography of his body. Running her fingertips over square hills and subtle valleys, she followed her fingers with her gaze. She'd seen it all before, but now they had time, and she wasn't going to miss a single detail.

He kissed her again, and she focused every ounce of her consciousness on the feeling of his lips brushing hers—the taste of his tongue, the slight hint of mint on his breath, and the sweet scent of grass and pine and straw that might be some manly aftershave, or more likely the scent of a man who led his life outdoors. She tucked her face into the angle under his jaw and breathed him in as she rubbed her cheek into the softness of his beard. Slipping the shirt off his shoulders, she stroked her hands over the muscles of his back.

She could feel his hands running over her too, exploring with the same fervor. He was watching her with the same intent determination to see everything, to miss nothing, to savor every second. They were both living wholly inside the moment, relishing every detail of touch, taste, and scent.

She was determined not to miss a thing, and she hadn't—except for the one, inconsequential detail of how she'd ended up naked so fast. She'd been so lost in tracing the contours of his body that she hadn't realized he'd uncovered hers, and her T-shirt and bra, the jeans and her sandals, were scattered on the floor like debris from a bomb blast.

She laughed, tilting her head back, but the laugh turned to a gasp as his hands swept down her belly and cupped the warmth between her legs. His fingers stroked while his kiss deepened. She was slick, so wet and ready, and his touch made her lose her sense of how perfect *now* was. She arched up to meet the next moment, the one where he'd be inside her, where the heat would build and she'd explode like one of those falling stars slamming to the earth and sending up a fountain of sparks and flame.

"Easy," he whispered. "We have time."

She knew he was right, but she wanted that release so badly. Struggling to slow her heartbeat, she clenched her fists and pressed her cheek into his shoulder, closing her eyes and letting her body move with the feelings building inside her as his fingers dipped and stroked. Twice she thought she was lost, and twice he drew back, kissing her back to the present. Then he kissed her breasts, her belly, the curve of her hip, and suddenly his mouth was there, right *there*, and she could feel warmth rising inside her.

She rose on the wave, the warmth cresting and breaking until it washed away and left her lying limp on the bed. When she swam back to reality, he was propped on one elbow, watching her with all the wonder she'd felt watching the stars. She felt like what they'd discovered in each other was as big as the universe and just as deep, just as far-reaching, and just as eternal.

Reaching up, she stroked her hand down his chest, starting at his shoulder and trailing her hand down the hollows and swells. She traced his muscles with the back of her fingers, then swept her hand back up to wrap around the back of his neck and pull him down for a kiss.

She might not be on top, but she was in charge. She sipped and tasted, stroked and soothed, dipped and licked, then flexed her hips against him. Tugging at the waistband of his jeans, she twisted the button undone and tugged the zipper down, trailing her fingers down the hard length of him.

Things were moving fast—too fast. Chase wanted to take it slow this time, make sure Lacey knew this was about love, not sex.

"Wait," he whispered. "Wait."

"What, are you scared?" She looked up at him, all glimmering eyes and teasing smile, and waiting got even harder.

"No. Yes. Maybe," he said. Then he said something unintelligible, a cross between a moan and a shiver as she stroked him, then moved her finger in a slow, teasing circle. She tugged at his jeans, spreading the fly open and hauling them halfway down his hips before pulling away the elastic band of his boxers to reveal one very clear indication of how he felt about her.

But that wasn't the feeling he wanted to concentrate on tonight. They'd had sex in the office and in the motel, but he wasn't sure they'd really made love either time. They'd been too caught up in their physical needs to think about their feelings.

And tonight, she wouldn't meet his eyes. Whenever he

met her gaze, she shied like a scared filly. It was as if she didn't want to acknowledge who he was; as if she wanted to pretend that it was his body she wanted and not *him*, his love and his faith, his willing and inevitable surrender.

"Lacey, wait." He sat up, pulling her with him. "Wait."

"I don't want to wait. I..."

He kissed her again, slow and tender. She almost pulled away, but then she relented and moved her tongue and lips in a sweet, sexy mambo while her hands nested in his hair. The feeling was almost too much for him, especially since he was busy with his own hands, stroking that fair, smooth skin in its softest places: the sides of her breasts, the hollow of her shoulder, the curve of her waist. He ran the tips of his fingers down the slope of her hip bone and she moaned, pulling him down on top of her.

She was fighting him now, fighting his determination to take this slow. It wasn't much of a contest, and her first salvo won the battle when she pulled at his jeans and wrapped her small hand around his cock. He reared back, closing his eyes and letting out a groan of love and frustration and need.

"My sentiments exactly," she said. "Please, Chase, do it *now*. I *need* you."

He wasn't sure he could deny her anything, and he damn sure couldn't say no to that. Floundering his way out of his jeans, he propped himself up on his elbows and looked down at the beautiful, willing woman in his bed.

"Now." She parted her legs and lifted her hips so that he brushed her with the tip of his cock, and it felt so good, he did it again, and then he was inside her, easing in slow, savoring the warmth and the slick, hot wetness of her. He forgot he was supposed to be going slow as whatever rational thoughts he'd had about this whole thing flew out of his head and vanished into the dark. The world became him, her, and the magic between them. He forgot about their past, the complicated waltz they'd danced half their lives—the one where he stepped forward and she stepped back, where he reached out and she spun away, where Trent Bradford cut in and took her away before he even realized the dance had begun. There was only *now*, and *now* was perfect.

He matched his body to hers, bone for bone, flesh for flesh, filling all her dips and hollows. The two of them together became something far bigger than they'd ever been apart. When he came, he knew the world he'd constructed so carefully had fallen to bits in the explosion—but the pieces of his life, tossed by the storm of their union, had fallen into a new pattern, an unexpected, unexplored perfection that would define his life from now on.

No matter what happened—whether she stayed with him or left forever—nothing would ever be the same. This experience would color his whole life, and even if the colors were the faded blues and browns of regret, his life would be richer and deeper for it.

Holding her close, breathing in her scent, and savoring her soft skin, he fell into the deep, sated sleep of completion.

CHAPTER 33

CHASE WOKE TO DARKNESS AND WATCHED THE windowpanes take on a silvery glow as dawn crept into the day. Lacey lay beside him, her cheeks pink with the night's exertion, her lips slightly swollen from kisses. She'd flung one hand up onto the pillow to curl in her tangled hair, and her throat bore a rough spot just below her jaw. Was that from his beard scraping her skin? Had he done that?

He couldn't help feeling a little proud of himself, because whatever he'd lost, Trent Bradford had lost more. Chase could imagine a life with Lacey—seeing her like this every morning, seeing her like *that* every night—but he couldn't imagine having it and then losing it. Wherever Trent was, part of his punishment must be regret for the life he'd toyed with and squandered.

And Chase would have to bear the same punishment if he screwed up this day.

It was Sunday. He couldn't have planned better if he'd tried. The car lot was closed, so he could spend the whole day at home convincing Lacey she ought to stay.

He rose and slipped quickly into his jeans, then tugged a T-shirt over his head and grabbed his boots. He'd get the chores done while she was sleeping, then run the few errands he had to do in town. After that, he'd have the rest of the day to show her the high side of ranch life. He'd tried to show her the day before until Captain had acted up and ruined everything.

Well, not really. If Captain hadn't tossed Lacey, Chase wouldn't have seen her climb back on that horse despite the pain, and he would have kept on underestimating her. He wouldn't have seen how she rose to challenges, adapted to change, and conquered her fears.

He wouldn't have seen past her champagne-and-hors-d'oeuvres veneer to the real person underneath.

He whistled softly while he worked, getting the horses pastured in record time. Tossing their leavings in the wheelbarrow with quick strokes, he headed back to the house before the glowing disc of the sun had burned through the gray shroud of morning mist and risen above the horizon. Lacey wandered into the kitchen just as he breezed in the door, her feet bare on the hardwood floor. Her eyes were still slightly swollen from sleep, and she blinked at him as though she'd forgotten who he was.

"Chase." She glanced at the window. "You did all the morning chores, didn't you? And you didn't wake me up."

"Didn't need to." He stepped in close. "But I'll wake you up now if you want."

He'd intended to kiss her awake, but she shrugged him off. Undaunted, he gave the tie on her bathrobe a teasing tug. She scowled, yanking it tighter.

Well, you really learned about a person when you lived with them. Evidently Lacey was grouchy in the morning. You'd think he'd tried to pull the robe open, but he was just teasing. Although he wouldn't have minded if it had come undone. Come undone and fallen to the floor in a pool at her feet, revealing...

"Is there anything left to do?"

She obviously wasn't in the mood to reveal anything.

The girl was all business. He swallowed his disappointment and turned away, opening the cupboard over the toaster and getting out two boxes of cereal.

"Nope." He held up the boxes. "Corn Flakes or Raisin Bran?"

"Corn Flakes. But I'll get it." She moved to the counter and opened one cupboard, then another, finally finding the cereal bowls in the third one she tried.

"If you ask for help, I'll tell you where things are," he said.

"I'm here to help *you*. I'll figure it out."

"Okay."

He busied himself getting the milk and sugar while she opened the box. The crispy flakes chimed into the bowl— one of those homey morning sounds that reminded him of his childhood. If he closed his eyes, he could imagine his mother standing at the counter pouring something sugary and sweet like Fruit Loops or Captain Crunch.

"You're almost out of cereal." She took the milk from him and hefted it in her hand. "Milk too."

"I'll go into town and pick up some stuff."

He didn't want to go. He didn't want to leave her— partly because after last night, he wanted to be with her every minute, and partly because he felt the urge to protect her even more keenly than before. That phone caller, with his coarse voice, had talked about her in a way that would have made Chase punch the guy in the jaw if he'd been there in person.

But he didn't just need cereal and milk; he needed sweet feed and supplements for the horses too. He could make do, but the animals always got what they needed.

"I wish I could go with you."

"Me too." He glanced up at her face, expecting to share a smile, and realized she didn't mean she wanted to be with him. She meant she wanted to go to town. To go anywhere, probably. She was still feeling trapped.

She sat down across from him and stirred her cereal thoughtfully, pressing down the flakes and watching them float up again. Finally she lifted a spoonful to her mouth, and he watched her lick a drop of milk from the underside of the spoon with the tip of her tongue like a kitten lapping cream. She looked at him over the spoon and then flushed, putting it down without eating.

"Sorry," he said.

"Yeah." She looked down at the cereal, playing with it again. The whole meal would be mush before she got around to eating it. Something was bothering her. "I'm sorry too."

"Sorry for what?"

"Well, last night…"

"I'm not sorry about last night."

"Me neither. But this morning…"

She lifted her eyes to his, and they looked troubled. Haunted.

Sorry.

"This morning you're acting like we're a couple. And we're not. I'm not ready for a real relationship, Chase."

"Okay. That's fine."

She looked a little shocked that he'd acquiesced that easily. Shocked, and maybe a little hurt. He hadn't meant to be so abrupt, but he wasn't comfortable talking about relationships. He'd hoped for a good day, a day where they'd share an easy rapport after last night's intimacy. But evidently Lacey was going to make it complicated, and now he'd hurt her feelings.

"Lacey, I want what you want. I want you to be happy." He smiled, trying to lighten the mood. "You seemed pretty happy last night."

"I was. And I know it felt like…" She flushed, struggling to go on, and he couldn't help smiling. He wanted her to say how it felt. He knew, but he wanted to hear it. "It felt like we were good together. Like we fit."

There. Now they were getting somewhere.

"But I need to get my own life together, Chase. I'm not ready for *together* together. Just because the sex was good…"

"Lacey, the sex doesn't have anything to do with it."

She looked stunned. "What?"

"I mean, that was important. It was good, really good, but you know what really meant something to me? It was when we were sitting out there on the ground, looking up at the stars, just the two of us. That was the part where I really felt like we fit. I felt like I was sure of my place in the universe for the first time ever. The rest of it was good, but that…"

He set down his spoon and leaned forward, willing her to understand. "I used to look up at the sky and wonder how it looked from Tennessee. I used to think that was the one thing that hadn't changed—that I was looking at the same stars, but I just wasn't looking at them from quite the right place. But last night, I knew I was right where I belonged."

"You do belong here, Chase. Wyoming fits you."

"Wyoming's not where I belong, Lacey. It doesn't matter where I am." He reached out and took her hand. "I belong with you. I always knew that."

"Chase, don't," she said.

"Don't what? Don't tell you how I feel? I thought girls liked that." He tried to smile, like he'd been joking, but he had a feeling it came off as a cockeyed, phony grin.

"Don't ruin it. I'm stuck here, remember? I have to stay. And if you try to make it into something more..."

He shoved his chair back, letting the legs screech on the linoleum floor. "It's not anything more than it's always been, Lacey. I always felt that way, and I never did a damn thing about it. If you want, I never will. I just thought you ought to know how I feel." He carried his bowl to the sink so he wouldn't have to look at her. "Would you rather I lie about it? Pretend that was just a fling?"

She bit her lip and looked away. "Maybe."

"I don't do flings." He turned the water on full blast. That way she could pretend she didn't hear what he was about to say and spare both of them the awkwardness of the aftermath. "I love you. I always have. I always will. You go on and live that life you want, and if you get tired of it or you change your mind, just come on back. I'll still be here, and I'll still love you however long it takes."

He scrubbed hard at the bowl even though it didn't need scrubbing, and almost dropped it when he felt her hand steal around his waist. She rested her head against his back and held him close, just for a moment, before she pulled away.

"I know, Chase. And I might love you too. I think I do. But I can't just let myself fall."

"Okay." He rested his hands on the counter and stared out the window. "I know. You have to fly. Just fly back here when you're done, okay? I've lived long enough without you."

CHAPTER 34

CHASE WAS ALMOST GLAD TO CLIMB IN THE TRUCK AND drive away. He wanted to think about what Lacey had said, turn it over in his mind and figure out what it meant—and he couldn't do that with her in the same room. When she was with him, all he could think about was touching her, kissing her, holding her.

Taking her clothes off.

All right, so his love wasn't always entirely pure. But it was real, and it sounded like she felt the same way.

So what should he do now? Lacey was going to have to stay at the ranch for a while. Would they spend every night together like they had last night? Now that she'd told him she loved him too, the nights would be even better.

But she'd also told him she needed to be alone—to be herself, not half of a couple. Did that mean he should let her be?

He needed advice. He needed to talk to Pam.

He picked up milk and cereal at the mini-mart, even though it was more expensive there, and rushed through the feed store like the place was on fire. Finally he headed for the café. He was so eager to talk to his sister that he jerked open the door and practically slammed it behind him, making the string of bells that hung on it jangle almost as much as his nerves.

Normally, Pam would appear in her pink dress and apron the minute a customer walked in, but there was no response. The only people in the place were Cody and some lady Chase had never seen before. The two of them were sharing a booth, and they were so engrossed in their conversation they didn't even look up at the sound of the bells.

"Hey." Chase strode toward the table. "Pam around?"

Cody about jumped out of his skin, and Chase took a better look at the woman he was sitting with. She had red hair like Pam, but there the resemblance ended. While Pam's eyes were warm and brown and her whole being exuded friendliness, this woman had cold blue eyes and didn't even acknowledge his presence. In fact, she gave him a chilling look, tilted her chin up, and turned her head away from him, gazing out the plate glass window as if he was beneath her notice.

"No. Um, Pam's out. You want somethin' to eat?" Cody practically ran toward the kitchen, as if he couldn't wait to distance himself from the woman he'd been so engrossed in conversation with a moment before. He hit the swinging door with the flat of his hand and reappeared at the pass-through window. "What do you want?"

He seemed nervous. Really nervous. Shit. Was he having an affair? That would break Pam's heart. Chase stepped behind the counter.

"No. I was looking for Pam. You know, your girlfriend." He spoke loudly and emphasized the last word for the benefit of Cody's new friend.

"She's—she took a break. Had some errands to run. I think she'll be back in an hour or so."

"Okay." Chase glanced at the woman again, then back at Cody. "So you playing waiter?"

"Yeah." Cody nodded. "Waiter. Waiting tables."

"You always sit at the table when you take an order?"

"No, man." Cody leaned through the window, resting on his forearms, and lowered his voice. "She's somebody— somebody who knows me." He flailed a hand in the air, feigning carelessness. "Nobody important. Just somebody from—before."

Before? Nobody had known Cody "before." Chase had half a mind to sit down and ask the woman a few questions.

No. *You trust him*, he reminded himself. Cody was his friend, and he didn't need to justify himself. Sure, nobody seemed to know much about him, and he had a couple of tattoos that made Chase suspect he'd had a colorful past. One was a snake that wound up his left arm, and the other was a knife dripping blood on his chest. But he'd made Pam happy, and she claimed he'd told her everything she needed to know. Pam was super-protective of her daughter, so Chase had assumed she had reason to trust Cody or she wouldn't have let him anywhere near Annie.

But the appearance of this woman and Cody's obvious nervousness made him wonder.

"You want to introduce me?" he asked, just to see what Cody would say.

"No." Cody glanced over at the table. The woman was perusing the menu and didn't seem to be paying attention to them.

"I didn't know her very well," he said. "And frankly, I didn't really like her."

———————

Pam breezed into the café then, a paper sack of groceries cradled in each arm. The woman left the minute Pam walked in, confirming Chase's suspicions that there was something going on between her and Cody, who grabbed the groceries and disappeared into the kitchen. Annie was right behind her mother, chattering like usual.

"And then Tracy said—oh, hi, Uncle Chase." She grinned, tilting her face up to the light.

Damn, he loved this kid. He'd been so upset when Pam got pregnant her senior year. She'd been planning to go to college, figuring she'd major in business and come back to keep the books for the farm. Having a baby had put a hold on those dreams, and the loss of the farm had put them forever out of reach—but Annie was worth it. She was smart, she was sweet, and Chase couldn't imagine his life without her.

Pam lowered her voice as Annie headed for the stairs. "How's Lacey?"

Annie turned and brightened. "Aunt Lacey? Where is she? Sinclair misses her."

Chase smiled. "Sinclair does, huh?"

"Well, me too. She's, like, my best friend. And don't you think she's beautiful?"

Chase choked.

"Yes, he does," Pam said. "Uncle Chase definitely appreciates how beautiful Aunt Lacey is. Now go upstairs and change out of your school clothes."

Chase leaned back against the counter, shifting his weight uncomfortably. "Lacey's doing fine. But hey, Cody was sitting with some woman earlier. He said she was someone he knew."

"Yeah, I saw her. She came in and asked for him."

"Who is she?"

"I don't know. Actually, he said he needed to talk to me about it."

"Damn, Pam, if he…"

"He didn't do anything wrong," Pam said. "Don't assume the worst." She started unloading the grocery bags. Evidently, the café needed milk too, because she'd bought four gallons, half skim and half whole. "Actually, I was wondering if you and Lacey could maybe take Annie for the afternoon. Give me and Cody a chance to be alone."

Chase was reluctant to give up his day alone with Lacey, but she'd seemed a little down that morning, and Annie could cheer up a grave digger. "Okay." He grabbed a gallon of milk in each hand. "I'll put these away. Go tell Annie to put on her boots." He lowered his voice. "Don't mention Lacey though, okay? We don't need it spread all over that she's at the ranch." He grinned. "I'm not sure your daughter can keep a secret with that motor-mouth of hers."

CHAPTER 35

"SINCLAIR IS THE BEST DOG, AUNT LACEY." ANNIE HAD been talking nonstop since she'd arrived. "He lets me put hats on him and everything. Yesterday I even got him to wear booties, but it didn't look right because I only had two and he has four feet. I guess the front ones are hands, though. Do you think I should get him mittens?"

Lacey looked down at the dog's grim expression and smiled.

"Definitely. Sinclair would love mittens."

"Yeah, I think so too. I'm so glad you gave him to me, Aunt Lacey. I'll never, ever forget the day you did that. It was the best day *ever.*"

Lacey felt her eyes tear up. At least she'd made a difference to someone in her life. Two someones, really—the dog and the child. It was nice to know she'd always be in Annie's memory as Aunt Lacey.

"Come on, let's go." Annie was mounted on a pony Chase had led from the barn. She trotted the animal in a tight circle, her posture perfect and her face aglow with happiness. The jolting gait hardly affected her seat at all, while Lacey felt like she bounced a mile into the air and crashed back into the saddle, over and over, whenever Captain broke into anything more than a gentle walk.

"You're going to have to teach me to ride better," she told Annie.

But when she gathered up the reins and turned the

horse toward Chase, she felt surprisingly competent and confident. She'd been reluctant to ride again, but the crash course she'd taken the day before—and it had literally been a *crash course*—had worked. Now that she'd been bucked off, there wasn't anything left to be afraid of.

Captain followed the other horses without any direction from Lacey as they trailed along the line of the pasture fence. Chase would occasionally lean out and tap the top strand of barbed wire with a stick he was carrying, and once he got down and tightened a sagging wire. She started to get down and help, but Annie vaulted off her horse before she could even gather up the reins. It was just as well; staying on board saved Lacey the embarrassment of clambering clumsily onto the horse again.

She took in the gray-green sagebrush and the yucca spikes, the ruddy rocks in the distance and the blue-tinted mountains beyond them. A herd of antelope trotted away, then turned to stare, making a sharp spitting noise that was apparently supposed to be a threat but just sounded absurd. She slipped one hand around the saddle horn, worried Captain might get it into his head that he ought to run into the herd so she could rope a 'lope, but he stayed calm and placid.

In fact, everything was calm and placid. With the cool, blue-sky weather and Annie's cheerful prattling, Lacey was starting to enjoy ranch life so much that she almost wished Captain would kick up his heels and buck her off again, just to jolt her back to reality. She didn't belong on a ranch—not with Chase, not with anybody. She was scared of horses—other than Captain, anyway—and she didn't like dirt and she didn't know a damn thing about cattle. She belonged on horseback like a nun belonged in a strip joint.

She was jerked out of her reverie when Annie kicked her heels into the pony's flanks and took off toward the cabin they'd passed the day before. The basic structure was hewn logs, but over the years scrap lumber, old fence posts, and rusting slabs of corrugated metal had been added to the roof and sides. A chipped cement pad lined with cracks from decades of freezing and thawing served as a front doorstep.

"Annie, get back here." Chase's command was loud enough to make Captain toss his head. Lacey grabbed the saddle horn, but the horse settled down.

Annie kept her seat effortlessly while Sheba seemed to flow in a graceful arc over the narrow stream. "What? I want to explore." Annie pulled up the horse and turned pleading eyes on Chase. "Look how cool this is. People must have lived here."

"That's Mr. Galt's land. I've told you before never to cross that stream."

"Oh." Annie slouched in the saddle, turning the horse and splashing back through the stream. "I forgot."

"You can't go forgetting that. Mr. Galt's—well, he's mean. You know that."

"He's not mean. He's sad," Lacey said. "Poor guy."

"Yeah, well, that poor guy shot my calf. Pardon me if I don't join the pity party."

"He *shot* your *cow*?" Annie looked outraged. "Why? What did he do that for?"

"It was on his land." Chase nodded toward the cabin. "Kind of like you."

"Oh. Well, that doesn't mean he has a right to shoot it."

"I know that. Unfortunately, Mr. Galt doesn't, so it's very, very dangerous for you to go over there."

"Sorry." Annie seemed genuinely contrite, but she recovered fast, bouncing in the saddle and pointing to a cluster of trees in the distance. "Are we going to the woods? That's on your land, right?" He nodded, and she bounced higher. "You'll love it, Aunt Lacey. It's got a little waterfall and everything, and once I found mushrooms there."

Chase glanced at Lacey. "Your seat gonna be okay with that much riding?"

"I think so." She settled her feet deeper into the stirrups. "Not sure about my thigh muscles, though."

"We'll get off and stretch halfway home."

She forgot about her thigh muscles once they entered the woods. The heat of the afternoon sun cooled in the green dappled shadows of the trees, and the trail turned from pale dust and trampled grass to cool dirt sprinkled with a layer of last year's fallen leaves. Shafts of sunlight slanted through the foliage, casting spotlights on random features of the forest: a tiny pine tree, a tortured root, a fallen log covered with moss. The pasture was flat and featureless and harshly lit, but in the woods there was a sense of hidden magic and possibilities that even made Annie hush with reverence. The unknown lurked beneath the leaves, behind the trees, under the roots. The ranch was the real world; this was an enchanted kingdom where anything could happen. If Chase had told her tiny fairies in cowboy hats herded ants in secret glades, she'd have believed him.

She ducked to avoid a low-hanging branch, then tilted her head back to look up through the interlaced branches to study the jigsaw patterns of yellow and green leaves, blue sky, and pine boughs. She'd felt uneasy on the wide plains, vulnerable and exposed, but this was homey. She could imagine curling up in the roots of an old tree and spending the night like a fairy princess.

Chase evidently felt good here too. He'd been whistling softly since they entered the woods, some song she didn't recognize.

"This is beautiful," she said. "I feel so safe here, compared to out there."

"Out there?"

"Where it's so open."

Chase snorted.

"What?"

"Nothing. It's just that a lot of other things feel safe here too. Bears. Mountain lions. Stuff like that."

She glanced around, searching for hulking, furry shapes in the shadows. "Bears?"

"Yeah, although they're not that much of a threat as long as you don't surprise them. That's why I've been whistling. Probably the horses make enough noise, but you can't be too careful."

"And mountain lions?"

"Whistling won't help much with them. They've been known to attack humans for no reason. I have a friend who has a scar clear across his skull from when he was a kid and one jumped him on a family hike."

"Yikes."

But nothing could spoil Lacey's good mood. Sitting astride an animal that had induced a panic attack two days ago and steering it through unknown territory made her feel so brave she figured she could conquer anything. She pictured herself in a suit of armor, a woman warrior riding into battle.

She snapped out of her reverie when Captain stumbled, almost pitching her off as he tripped over a root and nearly fell to his knees. He caught himself, holding one hoof off the ground, and let out a whinny. Chase and Annie stopped and turned, then dismounted when they saw what had happened.

"Captain tripped." Lacey climbed down and stroked the horse's neck. "I think he hurt himself."

Captain was agitated, his eyes rolling. Lacey stepped back as he nodded his head and took a few steps backward as if he was afraid of the rock he'd tripped on. Chase's eyes grew serious as he ran his hand down the horse's leg.

"It's not broken, is it?" Lacey had seen movies where they shot horses with broken legs. She was sure veterinary science had advanced since the days of John Wayne, but it still showed how serious an injury could be.

"No. But he might have pulled a tendon, or torn it." He tugged on the horse's reins, but the animal just tossed his head up and refused to move.

Chase glanced back the way they'd come. "We're going to have to go back for the trailer."

"And leave him here?" She put one hand on the horse's neck. "I'll stay with him."

"He'll be fine," Chase said. "He's not going anywhere."

"But you said there were bears and mountain lions."

"Which would see Captain as the main course and you as a tasty dessert. I'm only going to be gone an hour or so."

"Then I'll be fine."

He sighed. "Okay. Thanks, I guess."

She sensed relief in the slump of his shoulders. Finally, she was actually helping. Doing something right.

Annie stood beside her horse. "I want to stay with Aunt Lacey."

"No, you'd better stick with me," he said. "It's not safe, hon."

"Okay. But Sinclair's staying." She pointed a finger at the dog and gave him a stern, no-nonsense glare. "*Stay*. He'll protect you, Aunt Lacey."

The dog shot his new mistress a rebellious glare, then looked over at Lacey. She could swear his lip curled in disgust, but he lowered his skinny butt to the ground and stayed.

"You'd better be nice to me," she said to the dog as Annie and Chase rode out of sight. "Or I'll feed you to the bears."

CHAPTER 36

CHASE URGED JIMBO INTO A GALLOP AS HE EMERGED from the woods into the bright, flat spread of the pasture. Annie followed suit, her hair flying behind her, riding like she was part of the horse. The kid was going to make a great cowgirl. She'd been running barrels since she was six, and she could already beat a lot of older riders' times.

They could get back to the ranch in twenty minutes, but hauling the trailer over the uneven ground was going to take a while. Lacey would be worried if he took too long.

As he neared the ranch, something unfamiliar caught the light and reflected it back like a mirror. Had to be a car, parked in the turnout. Maybe Cody had come to pick up Annie. It was too early, but sometimes Pam got to missing her daughter and shortened her dates down to nothing. Cody seemed to take it in stride.

But it couldn't be the Jeep; the Jeep didn't shine. There was no chrome on the bumpers—just dull cast steel, and generally even that was coated with mud. If Pam was out here in her own car, it meant she and Cody had had a fight.

Chase swore. He'd had a bad feeling ever since he'd seen Cody with that woman at the diner. If his friend broke his sister's heart, he'd kill the guy.

He rose in the stirrups, keeping his body tilted forward so his center of balance was just ahead of the horse's. Jimbo's natural instinct kept him running fast, striving for balance. Behind him, Annie whooped and urged Sheba into a lope.

As they came to the corner of the fence line, he saw the car clearly. It wasn't Pam's Escort. It was a big car, some kind of sedan, black with a vinyl top.

Nobody he knew.

He slowed Jimbo and eased him to a stop, shading his eyes with his hand and squinting. He couldn't tell if anyone was in the car. It might just be a lost tourist or something—but since he hadn't had a lost tourist show up in the past two years, that didn't seem likely.

And the fact that a strange vehicle had turned up three days after the phone call, three days after Lacey moved in—that just didn't seem a likely coincidence.

"Who is that, Uncle Chase?"

"I don't know. Let's go home a different way, though."

"And sneak up on them?"

"Kind of."

He turned his horse to the right and jogged to the curve of the dirt road that passed his place and petered out somewhere to the east. If Wade Simpson was driving that car, he didn't want to show up riding straight from the location where they'd left Lacey. He'd arrive by road, and hopefully it wouldn't occur to anyone to follow the old cattle trail that led to the wooded glade.

Once they were on the road, the house and barn blocked his view of the car. He slowed Jimbo to a walk, signaling Annie to do the same. As they rounded the curve and descended the slight slope down the hollow that held the ranch, Chase could barely make out two silhouettes behind the sedan's tinted windshield. The driver was clearly a man, with a Marines-style haircut and ears that protruded like the handles of a jug. The woman beside him had what he supposed was a stylish hairstyle, one that made her head look impossibly large and round in silhouette. It was the one who had been at the café talking to Cody.

"You go put Sheba away," he said to Annie. "And groom her. Take your time and do a real good job, okay?"

She must have sensed his tension because she didn't protest—just rode straight to the barn, dismounted, and led the horse inside.

"Howdy." He led Jimbo to the corral and swung down from the saddle, draping his reins over the fence and loosening the cinch. Unfastening the buckle, he hauled off the saddle and set it on the top rail. "I'll be with you folks in a moment."

"Oh, that's all right." The woman stepped out of the car. "We'll wait."

Up close, she was attractive, though not as attractive as Lacey. She had high cheekbones, red hair streaked with blonde, and crystal blue eyes that slanted like a cat's. Her smile was sweet, but she leaned against the car with a stance that was schoolteacher-strict, with her arms crossed over her chest and her feet crossed at the ankles. He suddenly wondered if he'd done something wrong—thrown a spitball, maybe, or flunked a math test.

He led Jimbo into the corral and lifted off his bridle, giving the horse a slight slap on the butt to get him through the gate. The woman had started toward the corral, but she seemed clumsy, like she couldn't navigate the packed dirt driveway. Looking down at her feet, he saw why. She was wearing the weirdest shoes he had ever seen.

They were tiny and pointed—impossibly pointed. He didn't see how a human being could cram a full set of toes into the tips. Maybe the woman had cloven hooves. The shoes were shiny red leather for the most part, with black snakeskin tips and black laces that crisscrossed over the top of her foot and continued halfway up her shin, ending in an elaborate multilooped bow at the back of her calves. The heels were high, forcing her to stand on her toes. Maybe she had Barbie feet, like the plastic dolls his sister had played with.

Come to think of it, this woman had probably played with Barbie dolls too. Only the unrealistic expectations of Barbie World could make anyone believe it was a good idea to wear shoes like that. Still, even Barbie wore cowboy boots sometimes. Chase knew this because Pam had forced him to speak for Ken when they were kids. He'd had to congratulate the plastic princess whenever she won the gold cup at the Barbie Horse Show, which had occurred daily the year Pam turned six.

The woman teetered dangerously and started to tip sideways. Chase darted in and grabbed her arm, but she shook him off and made her own way back to the sedan. What the hell was wrong with the guy behind the wheel? Why didn't he get out and help his wife, or whoever it was? Chase believed in women's liberation as much as the next guy, but those shoes made the poor girl a virtual cripple. Woman or not, she needed help. This guy would probably make his own grandma fetch her own firewood in her wheelchair.

Which was where this woman was going to end up if she wasn't careful. Chase almost held his breath as she approached the car, running on her toes the last few steps and almost falling against it.

She turned to face him casually, as if she hadn't just had a near-wreck worthy of the rodeo, and crossed her arms over her chest again. Her blue eyes narrowed. They were cold and calculating, and he had the uneasy feeling he was being sized up by an assassin, or maybe a Ninja.

"Chase Caldwell," she said. "How nice to meet you." She put out a perfectly manicured hand in greeting, but when he went to shake it she pulled away so he was left holding her fingertips. Did she want him to kiss it or something? He gave it a squeeze and dropped it as quickly as he could.

"Likewise," he said. "But I don't recall having the pleasure."

"Oh, you don't know me." She tossed her hair and pursed her lips, staring off across the landscape like she was looking for something. Her hair was almost as pretty as Lacey's. Maybe she had a rich husband too. The color was nice, but once you saw it in the sun, you realized no normal woman had blonde streaks like that.

But this wasn't a normal woman.

Lacey stroked Captain's neck, trying not to relay her own nervousness. She wasn't afraid of horses anymore—not Captain, anyway—but she was a lot more comfortable when she was sitting on top, holding the reins. Then she felt like she was in charge. Now, all she could think about was Captain's heavy hooves. He was still keeping one foot cocked, as if he didn't want to put weight on it, so it wasn't likely he'd step on her foot. It didn't seem likely he'd kick her either. She stroked him again, moving closer, and he dipped his head and nuzzled her arm.

"Good boy. You're a nice buddy, aren't you? You're…"

She broke off as a high-pitched noise broke the silence. It sounded like a cross between a suburban catfight and the screaming banshees she'd read about in fairy tales. It was angry, almost desperate—and eerie enough to send a chill rippling up her spine.

Sinclair growled, the sparse hair on his back rising, and took a few stiff-legged steps toward the sound. His bravado would have been more convincing if his tail hadn't been tucked between his legs.

Captain snorted and tossed his head, turning to face home and almost falling when he tried to put his weight on the bad leg. She knew she should comfort the frightened animals, but how did you comfort someone when you knew the danger was real?

"It's okay, Captain." She swallowed. Her voice was so high-pitched and shaky she sounded like Justin Timberlake. "It's okay."

The horse lowered his head and limped a few steps down the trail, glancing back as if wondering why she didn't follow.

"No, Captain. Come on." She lifted the reins over his head. "Stay."

The noise cut through the forest again, louder this time. Closer. Captain lifted his head and tugged against the reins. When they didn't give, he jerked harder, almost dragging her off her feet.

Maybe she should take him over to the corral behind the abandoned house, but then he wouldn't be able to get away. He'd be bait for whatever was screaming in the forest. Of course, that meant it wouldn't attack *her*. She looked down at the dog. "You'd make better bait."

He moved closer to her, and she noticed his tufted ears were trembling. Bending down, she stroked his back. He was shaking all over. "I'm kidding. Sorry."

She looped Captain's reins over a low tree branch and settled herself on the ground under the tree. "Stay," she repeated. "And don't kick me." The dog snuggled beside her, uncharacteristically affectionate. Maybe he was grateful she'd found him such a good home. Or maybe he was just glad she wasn't making him wear bonnets and booties.

More likely he was terrified of whatever was lurking in the forest.

CHAPTER 37

"What can I do for you?" Chase wanted to be polite, but he wasn't about to ask the woman into the house. She made him uneasy with her Wicked Witch shoes and cold stare.

"I'm a friend of Lacey's," she said. "I heard she was here."

Chase bit back a swear. Cody must have told her. There was no other way she'd know.

"She's not here." He edged to one side, trying to get a look inside the car at her jug-headed companion.

"What's your name?"

"Janice."

Chase didn't remember Lacey mentioning that name. "Where are you from?"

"Conway." Her eyes narrowed, as if she was daring him to contradict her.

She wasn't being friendly, so he didn't bother either. "I went to school there. I don't remember you."

The door to the sedan clicked open, and the driver emerged. He was jug-headed, all right, and he barely had a neck at all—just massive, muscle-bound shoulders that blended into his head. His face was pockmarked, his lips fleshy and purple. He had pale blue eyes that should have been attractive or at least striking, but they were just scary.

Maybe because Chase knew the guy.

"Wade Simpson," he said. "Fancy meeting you here."

Wade stepped away from his car and shoved his hands in his pockets, looking left, then right with exaggerated ease. "Nice spread."

"I like it."

"Guess you did all right after Trent Bradford stole your land. Not as pretty as Tennessee, though, is it?"

"Suits me fine. And yeah, I'm over it."

As he said it, he realized he really was. He'd been coming to terms with his new life gradually, but today, enjoying the ride with Lacey and Annie, he'd appreciated the ranch in a new way. He was proud to show it to Lacey, proud of what he'd accomplished. Proud of his new life, of being a real cowboy instead of a goat farmer.

"You doing okay with the way your dad died too?"

All Chase's newfound contentment whooshed out in a single, pained breath. He couldn't help knotting his fists up and stiffening at the memory.

"Shame, that was, the way your dad killed himself. You must wish you could get ahold of Bradford, choke him with your bare hands."

Chase looked down at the ground and collected himself, letting his fists relax and consciously easing the tension in his shoulders.

"No," he said. "I told you, I'm over it."

Wade laughed—the same nasty, knowing laugh Chase had heard over the phone days before. "Yeah, I guess you are. Amazing what fucking a guy's wife'll do for you, huh? I guess you got your revenge." He leered. "Guess that would work for me too. She any good?"

The woman, who had been standing silently by the car, cleared her throat and cast a killing glance toward Wade, giving Chase time to take a deep breath and swallow the urge to shove his fist into Wade's face.

"Well, it would if I didn't have Janice here," Wade said, looking nervous. "Sorry about that, honey." He turned to Chase. "Janice here was Lacey's best friend. She's so worried about her that she made me drive all the way out here to check on her."

"Really."

"Uh-huh."

"So you and Janice are..."

"We're friends," Janice said. "Acquaintances, really." She shot Wade a murderous glare. "So where's our Lacey?" She simpered, which was kind of scary. She wasn't an unattractive woman, but the expression was so at odds with her personality that Chase would have been more inclined to help her if she'd scowled.

"Lacey?" He'd been developing a strategy since the phone call to deal with this very moment—but he'd expected the moment to occur at the car lot. He'd never expected Wade to find the ranch.

"Lacey left," he said. "Skipped town." He did his best to look brokenhearted.

"What'd she do? Walk?"

"No. I gave her a car from the dealership."

"Well, I guess she's still a whore, then," Wade said. "Guess you were worth fucking."

Chase stepped up to him as Janice stepped away. She seemed to be making room for him to swing a fist. Apparently she didn't like Wade any more than he did.

Wade himself grinned like a jack-o'-lantern, the expression creasing his flabby cheeks. Unfortunately, that was the only part of him that was flabby. His muscles were swollen and laced with tortuous blue veins as if he'd spent most of his life since high school in the gym and the rest of it popping steroids. He stood in a fighting stance, fists clenched, legs apart, waiting for Chase to swing. His skin had taken on an unnatural flush, as if all the blood was flowing into his corded arms and clenched fists.

Chase suspected he could win a fight. Wade might be bulky with muscle, but Chase was taller. Ranch work didn't build a lot of visible muscle, but he was strong. And he was angry.

Really angry.

The realization made him take a step back and struggle for composure. Anger was liable to make him do something stupid, something that would get him in trouble and wouldn't do a damn thing for Lacey.

Wade sneered with such venom, he might as well have called Chase a coward, but Chase reminded himself he really didn't give a damn about Wade's opinion and turned to Janice.

"So is there anything else I can do for you?"

"You can tell me what kind of car Lacey's driving." She tried to look concerned, but the expression didn't fit her any better than the simper. "I really need to find her. She's just not equipped for life on her own."

"She's fine," Chase said.

"No she's not. She's helpless." She blinked in an effort to look sympathetic, but the predatory gleam in her eyes ruined the effect. "So what kind of car is it?"

Wade stepped forward and reached for his back pocket like he was going for a gun. Adrenaline surged into Chase's brain, but despite the sudden euphoria, he knew he'd never dodge a gunshot. When Wade whipped out a wallet, he felt like a popped balloon, stretched to the breaking point and then suddenly limp.

Flipping the wallet open like a TV cop, Wade held up a polished brass badge. "I'll need the make and model," he said. "That woman's a fugitive from justice. You're harboring a criminal."

"Oh, Wade, for God's sake," Janice said.

"Yeah, for God's sake," Chase echoed mockingly. "You're not a federal agent, Wade. Being a Conway flatfoot isn't going to do you any good here."

Wade started to swell up again. If he'd been a little taller and greener, it might have reminded Chase of the Incredible Hulk. As it was, all he could think of was an angry toad he'd found in the garden one summer.

"Go home, Wade," he said. "I'm not telling you a damn thing about her."

"I'm not going home until I find her," Wade said. "You've really fallen for her lies?" He leaned against the car, affecting a relaxed posture, but a telltale vein still twitched in his neck. "She pretends to be so fuckin' helpless, so fuckin' sweet. Don't you believe it. She was as much a part of that whole thing as her husband."

He cleared his throat and turned to spit a gob of phlegm into the dirt. "Always had to have more money for her fancy clothes. I worked with Trent on some projects, and I know he was desperate to keep her. She drove him to it."

"Lacey doesn't care about money."

"No, but she cared about tennis at the club and tanning memberships and pricey clothes. That stuff added up, and

Trent was chasin' his tail to keep her happy. She used to flaunt it, too, always struttin' down the street like she owned the place. She used to brag about how Trent had taken your farm and was gonna plow the whole thing under. How everybody would be better off when they got rid of those dirty goats and stuff."

Chase folded his arms over his chest. A week ago, he might have believed that, but he knew Lacey now. She might not be a big fan of goats, but she wasn't cruel and she wasn't selfish. "You done yet?"

"She laughed when your dad died. Said he was a loser anyway."

Chase lunged forward. "Lacey wouldn't say that. But you just did."

Anger buzzed in his brain and power surged in his body as he hauled the man toward the car. He couldn't close his hand around Wade's massive biceps, but he managed to tilt him off-balance and shove him through the open door, savoring a rush of satisfaction when the back of the man's head thumped the edge of the roof as he fell inside.

"Get lost, Wade," he said. "You ever set one damn foot on this property again, I'll call the folks who *do* have juris-diction over this place. Better yet, I'll shoot you and bury you out back. It's not like anybody's watching."

Actually, someone was. He'd seen Annie's face appear at the window to one side of the barn door. Hopefully she couldn't hear him. He turned to Janice, who was already get-ting in the car.

"You too," he said. "You're no friend of Lacey's. Don't let me see you back here again."

CHAPTER 38

CHASE WATCHED THE DARK SEDAN KICK UP DUST AS Janice sped down the driveway, taking Wade with her. He tried to feel a sense of victory from chasing them away, or at least satisfaction, but all he felt was foreboding.

Annie ran out of the barn, her eyes wide. "Uncle Chase, who was that? Why was that lady dressed so scary? How did she walk with those shoes on? Was that guy from the WWE? He looked like one of the bad guys. Is that why you didn't want me to come out?"

"Yeah." He ruffled her hair. "Thanks for being a smart kid and staying in the barn."

"You're welcome. But you said a bad word."

Shoot. So she *had* been listening. Pam had always cautioned him that Annie was the ultimate big-eared little pitcher, and it looked like she was right. Dang, the kid would probably tell on him too, and Pam would give him a lecture. He cast around for a change of subject that would make her forget what he'd said.

"Are you really going to bury him in the yard?" she asked. "Because I think you should bury him farther from the house. On *Law & Order*, there was a guy who buried his wife in the yard and the cops found her right away."

"How 'bout ice cream, honey?"

"No, I'd rather help you plan this out. What about Aunt Lacey?"

He didn't want to go back to the woods too soon after

Wade had left, but he didn't want to tell Annie that and scare her more than he had to.

"She won't mind waiting," he said.

"No, I mean do you think she could help? That guy said some really mean things about her. I bet she'd help you dig the hole. But you'd better not leave yet. Then those people will see which way you go. And then you'd have to kill that guy without having time to think this through. Do you think we could hide the body in the barn until we get the hole dug?"

"Annie, I'm not going to kill anybody."

"Oh. Okay." She sounded disappointed.

He wished he had something in the freezer besides low-fat vanilla. Now that the subject had turned to detectives and police work, it would take Super Calorie Chocolate Fudge Chip Chunk Ripple Delight to make Annie forget what they were talking about.

Sure enough, she chattered about murder methods and burial plans the entire time he dished out the ice cream. By the time he settled her at the table, she'd come to the conclusion that they should chop Wade up into manageable pieces, melt his flesh off in an acid bath, and haul him into the woods—where, conveniently, Lacey was waiting to help dig the hole.

He assured her again that he wasn't going to kill anyone and left her dejected over her bowl of plain-Jane vanilla while he went out and hooked up the horse trailer. He'd just gotten it hitched to the pickup when she came running out of the house, heels and hair flying.

"I went upstairs and looked out the window and I saw those people. They didn't leave. They parked on that hill across the road, and I think they have binoculars."

Maybe Annie's obsession wasn't such a bad thing. He'd been just about to lead Wade and Janice straight to Lacey. Apparently, he wasn't smarter than a second grader.

"Let me see."

Annie led him back to the house and up the stairs to the second-floor hallway, which looked out over the front of the house. She brought the binoculars to her eyes and gazed down the driveway, then nodded and handed them to him.

"Yup. Still there," she said.

Chase peered through the glasses and saw the car parked on a hill not far from the house. It wasn't an easy place to get to in a four-wheel-drive truck, so Chase couldn't imagine how Wade had managed to get the sedan up the rocky, little-used cow path.

He focused in on the car and made out the figures of Wade and Janice standing nearby. Something caught the light of the setting sun and reflected it back. Annie was right. Wade had some kind of lens trained on the house. But it might not be binoculars.

It might be a rifle sight.

He refocused the binoculars, but the two figures were in silhouette and whatever Wade had was pointed his way, so he couldn't tell if it was a gun, binoculars, or a camera. But it was definitely aimed at the house.

They must be watching for him to go to Lacey. Then they'd follow him, and then—then who knew what they'd do? The only thing he knew was that he had to get Annie out of there. Lacey would understand.

But meanwhile, she was probably wondering where he was. And she was probably scared—with good reason. He hadn't been kidding about the bears and the mountain lions. It wasn't likely that either one would find her, but it wasn't impossible. He'd heard there had been a big cat in the area. Someone had lost a couple of stray lambs, and another neighbor had found scat that didn't look like it came from a coyote.

"You keep an eye on them," he said to Annie. Watching them would keep her busy and give him time to think.

"Okay." She grabbed the binoculars and refocused them, then swung them briefly toward the corral where she'd turned out her pony. "Look at poor little Sheba. She's just running up and down the fence, up and down. She misses Captain."

"She does, doesn't she?" Chase watched the horse a moment. She was nervous and agitated, tossing her head and prancing. As he watched, she let out a shrill whinny. If Wade and Janice noticed her, they'd realize she was pointing the way toward Captain and Lacey.

But they probably wouldn't figure it out. Wade didn't know a thing about animals, and judging from her footwear, Janice wasn't exactly the horsey type.

He went downstairs and got out his vet kit. Staring down at the supplies neatly slotted into the canvas, he pulled out a plastic splint and a roll of self-stick vet tape for Captain's leg. The splint came with instructions, and he unfolded them to make sure they were clear enough for Lacey to follow.

Grabbing a pen from the counter, he thought a moment, then wrote his own set of instructions. Folding it carefully, he laid it on the splint, then tore off a piece of vet tape and bound the rest of the roll with the instructions and the splint.

"Annie? They still there?" he called up the stairs.

"Yup. They haven't moved," she said.

"Stay and watch them, okay? I'm going to go put the horses out."

She appeared at the top of the steps, her forehead creased with confusion. "But it's almost nighttime. You usually put them in the barn now."

"Not tonight," he said. "You'd better watch. If those people leave, I need to know which way they go."

"Sorry!" Forgetting all about the horses, she ran back to her station at the window.

Out in the barn, Chase spread Sheba's cool-out blanket on the floor. He carefully bound the medical supplies and instructions into a bundle, then taped them to the inside of the blanket, placing them just behind the horse's shoulder. They wouldn't bother her too much there. He muttered softly to Sheba as he settled a blanket on her back and turned her out into the paddock.

While Sheba stamped her foot, shook herself, and gradually gave in to the odd sensation of the splint tickling her side, he blanketed Jimbo. The gelding turned his head and looked at Chase curiously, then poked him with his nose, obviously wondering why he was getting all dressed up so late in the afternoon.

"I know, buddy, it's kind of weird." It wasn't a cool night by any means. Hopefully Janice and Wade wouldn't realize how odd it was to put horses out to pasture on a warm summer night dressed like they were headed for a fall horse show.

He wondered how Lacey was doing. He'd been gone almost three hours now, so she had to know something was wrong. Maybe she was halfway home already, leaving

Captain alone in the woods. Or maybe she was still sitting under the tree where he'd left her. If she was still in the woods, was she scared? Or was she angry, cursing him for leaving her? Would she need comforting when he finally got back to her, or placating?

He didn't have any idea. He didn't know a damn thing about women.

But he did know horses, and he knew Sheba would run straight to Captain if he gave her the chance.

He led the mare out to the corral, where she started up her nervous pacing again. Jimbo followed, snorting and stamping, picking up her nerves and getting agitated. When Chase opened the gate, both horses stormed out like wild mustangs being released from a holding pen and thundered off into the deepening twilight. He saw Sheba's dark, draped form leading the way as the horses headed straight for Captain—and for Lacey.

Lacey sat with her back to the tree trunk, watching the sun sink in the sky. She might not have a watch, and she might not be any kind of woods-woman, but she knew Chase had been gone well over the hour he'd promised. Captain had resigned himself to his pain and stood beside the tree with his head drooping low, but Sinclair was still hypervigilant, his ears perked as he stared into the forest. Occasionally a shudder rippled down his back.

"You're making me nervous, boy," Lacey ran her hand down the dog's back and kneaded his bony shoulders. "Why did I have to find a sissy dog at the gas station? Why couldn't you be a mastiff, or a Doberman? Something that would protect me?"

Tilting his nose in the air, Sinclair closed his eyes in an expression of doggie bliss. "I'm surprised you didn't insist on following your new mistress. Maybe you like me a little after all."

She scanned the woods as she petted the dog, watching for movement. As the sun sank and the light began to dim, it was getting harder and harder to see what lay beyond the nearest trees. Twice now she'd thought she'd seen a shadow, large and lithe, moving through the darkness under the pines. Both times, Sinclair had growled. She'd thought at first his reaction confirmed her fears, but maybe he was just responding to her own tension.

She wanted to go to the edge of the woods to see if she could see Chase heading her way, but that would mean leaving Captain, and if she really had seen something stalking them from the shadows, they'd be safer together.

She scanned the sky. The sun was almost to the horizon, and the clear, watery blue of day was giving way to the deeper tones of sunset. The shadowy depths of the woods were growing darker by the minute.

"Can't you be more like Lassie?" she asked Sinclair. "Go home, boy, and bark at that man until he comes and gets me." She made a shooing motion. "Go on. Tell him Timmy's in the well."

The dog trotted a few steps down the trail, then turned and gave her an aggrieved look.

"Go," she said, flicking her fingers. "Go."

He walked back to her, sighed, and lay down beside her, resting his head on his paws.

"Damn dog," she said. But she was secretly pleased.

She rested her head against the tree, stroking the dog and letting her eyes close. She was tired from the week's stress, and the day's fresh air and exercise had added to her exhaustion. The clatter and cheep of birds settling themselves for the night faded in and out of her consciousness.

At some point, she must have fallen asleep because she woke with a start, gazing around her in confusion. It was almost dark. Where was she? The forest gradually slid into focus as she took in the horse, the dog, and the scattered leaves. But what had woken her up? Sinclair was awake too, standing with one foot lifted like a pointer, his ears and tail trembling, his body rigid.

A hoarse, high-pitched scream tore through the night. Sinclair took a step forward and growled. She grabbed him and clutched him to her chest.

"Forget everything I said about Lassie," she whispered into the dog's fur. "Whatever that was, it's way bigger than you. You don't have a chance."

Neither did she. Neither did Captain. That had to be a mountain lion, and it sounded close. Her instinct told her to run for the cabin, but she had no idea what direction the cry had come from. It had surrounded her, filling the air.

She scanned the woods all around, looking for the gleam of predatory eyes, the glide of a shadowy form through the dense undergrowth. Listening for the snapping of a twig that would indicate stealthy footsteps.

The silence that surrounded her was almost more unnerving. The thing could be anywhere—two yards away or twenty. She'd seen a house cat stalking a bird once, all stealth and steely eyes. A mountain lion would probably move just as quietly and pounce just as fast. She held the dog tighter and waited for the rustle of approaching doom.

But when the sound came, it was no mere snapping of twigs. It was an explosion of noise, as if something was crashing through the underbrush just down the path from where she sat. It didn't sound like a mountain lion; it sounded like an elephant. Or maybe a whole herd of elephants. How big was the damn thing? Maybe there was more than one.

Sinclair jumped to his feet and let out a sharp bark as Captain reared up on his hind legs, jerking away from the tree. He took off down the trail as fast as his injury would allow, reins trailing behind him, stirrups flapping at his sides. He was headed toward home—toward home, and toward whatever was crashing through the trees.

"Wrong way! Oh, you stupid horse, *no!*"

Lacey dropped to her knees and grabbed the dog, clutching him to her chest. There was nobody to save her now.

She'd wanted to be on her own, and now she truly was.

CHAPTER 39

Sɪɴᴄʟᴀɪʀ ʜᴜᴅᴅʟᴇᴅ ᴄʟᴏsᴇʀ ᴛᴏ Lᴀᴄᴇʏ ᴀɴᴅ ʟᴇᴛ ᴏᴜᴛ ᴀ
pitiful whine that was hardly the Call of the Wild. She
watched Captain stumble and fall with a shrill whinny,
landing hard on the shoulder opposite his injured leg. He
lifted his head and neighed again, sounding as desperate
and hopeless as she felt.

She ran over to the horse. His hooves cut through the air
as he thrashed and struggled to rise, and she moved to the
other side to soothe him. She stroked his shoulder and her
hand came away sticky with warm blood. The noise grew
louder, the ground seeming to shake with the pounding of...

Hooves?

Lacey stood stock-still as the bushes parted to reveal
two horses, both dressed to kill in multicolored blankets.
She recognized Jimbo in an Indian pattern and Sheba in a
shocking pink number that had Annie written all over it.
They looked like they were headed to an equine prom.

Captain managed to struggle to his feet and stretched
his neck to greet Sheba. Their muzzles came together in
gentle greeting, and she felt tears stinging her eyelids. She
couldn't believe how happy she was to see the animals she'd
been so scared of only a few days before.

Maybe it was the clothes. That had to be Annie's work.
They were lucky the baby clothes didn't fit.

But where was Chase? Had he been thrown or something? "Sheba, where is he?" She stroked the horse's shoulder

through the fabric. Her hand hit a lump, and the animal stepped aside.

"Hey, wait." She stepped toward the horse, who snorted and moved away again.

"Oh, no. I'm not dancing with you." She turned her back and folded her arms over her chest. It wasn't more than a minute before she felt a soft nose blowing the hair at the back of her neck.

"Hey. I'm learning, aren't I?" She patted the horse's neck and slipped her hand under the blanket. Something was fastened to the underside. Flipping it up, she tore off a strangely shaped sheet of plastic and a roll of tape.

Maybe she shouldn't have pulled it off. Maybe it was part of the blanket or something. She looked critically at Jimbo. His blanket draped gracefully, with nothing interrupting the fall of fabric.

She pulled at the tape that held it together and a piece of paper fluttered to the ground. *Instructions for Adjust-a-Splint*. It was folded tightly with another piece, a handwritten note she unfolded with shaking hands.

Lacey: Wade was here.

She shivered. The sun had fallen behind the distant mountains, but its heat still lingered. It was the thought of Wade that made her cold. Suddenly, the mountain lion seemed like the least of her problems.

He left, but he's watching. I sent Sheba to bring you this note. She also has a splint for Captain. Don't worry, he's good about his feet.

Actually, Captain's feet were the least of her worries.

> I'll come and get you as soon as I can, but as
> long as Wade's watching I can't. Don't worry
> about the bears and mountain lions. I was kind
> of exaggerating.

Lacey remembered the cry she'd heard and almost crumpled up the note. Chase was just trying to make her feel better. It had to be a mountain lion. She looked down and read the last lines.

> Stay safe, and Do Not Come Home.
>
> —Chase

Chase headed inside to get Annie. He'd done all he could for Lacey. Now it was time to deal with Wade.

"Come on, kid," he said. "I better take you home."

"I thought I was spending the night."

"Change of plans. Sorry." He hated to see her disappointed, but seeing Wade and his new lady friend had left a knot in the pit of his stomach and a nervous twitch pulsing in his temple. They were dangerous, and Lacey would understand that the first priority was to get Annie someplace safe.

"But Aunt Lacey…"

"I'll go get Aunt Lacey when I get back. I sent her a note with Sheba."

"What about Sinclair?"

"Can he stay with Lacey tonight? I think she needs him."

"I don't know. I don't think Aunt Lacey's going to be too happy if you leave her out there in the woods."

He had no doubt Annie was right—but at least Lacey would be alive. God knew what she'd be if Wade found her. Kidnapped, probably. Dead, if something went wrong. Even after all these years, he could sense rage simmering under the man's bulging muscles.

But as long as Chase didn't lead Wade to Lacey, the Conway cop would never find her. Nobody who'd seen her dressed in designer duds sipping margaritas at the country club pool would ever look for her camping in the woods.

Annie thrust out her lower lip in a world-class pout, but she climbed into the pickup without another word. Pam always wondered how he got the kid to do stuff without arguing. He'd told her the answer: he didn't argue. But somehow, it didn't work the same for Pam. Or for Cody. Annie ran roughshod over them both.

And they both enjoyed it.

Or at least they used to. He flashed back to the sight of Cody sitting at the table with that woman and smothered a feeling of doom. Cody had given Lacey up. That was the only possible explanation. And that was unforgiveable.

He felt terrible for Pam, for Annie—even for Cody himself. Everybody's life was about to change, and not for the better.

Pulling out of the ranch gate, he glanced over at the hill that hid Wade's car. He was tempted to go over and have a little chat, but not with Annie along. He didn't want her anywhere near the guy.

Annie chattered endlessly about Sinclair as they

followed the winding county road into town. The ugly dog Lacey had given his niece was apparently the next best thing to Rin Tin Tin, brave and loyal and true—at least in his mistress's loving eyes.

When they reached the café, the lights were on in the kitchen. Giving Annie's ponytail a farewell tug as she took off for the stairs, he walked into the kitchen.

"See you, Uncle Chase," Annie called over her shoulder. "Go get Aunt Lacey now, okay? She might be scared in the woods by herself, even with Sinclair there."

Cody was chopping a pile of poached chicken breasts while a soup pot simmered on the stove. He looked up with his standard crooked grin. "Hey, bro."

"Hey." Chase leaned against the huge stainless steel refrigerator and watched Cody wield a butcher knife with *Iron Chef* expertise. "Who was that lady I saw you with?"

Cody stiffened, and his fist clenched on the knife, shifting it just enough to graze his thumb. "Damn." He dodged over to the sink, cranking on the cold water and grimacing as he held the thumb in the stream.

"Who was she?"

"I don't know. Hold on, I cut myself." He turned away from Chase, hunching his shoulders.

"You know her?"

"Can you hang on? I'm fucking bleeding here." Cody snatched a paper towel from the dispenser over the sink and dried off his hand.

"Who is she, Cody?"

"Look, I'm not cheating on your sister." Cody returned to the chicken breasts, bending his head over his work.

"Don't you need a Band-Aid?"

"No. I'm fine." Cody refused to meet Chase's eyes, acting as if the chicken would run away if he stopped his fierce concentration on its destruction.

Chase eased sideways, trying to steal a glimpse of Cody's thumb. It looked fine. He hadn't cut it; he'd just wanted an excuse to turn around. To hide his expression? To think of a lie to cover his guilt?

"Who was she?"

"She was—a friend, okay? She knew some people I knew, and we got to talking. That's all." He chopped a length of chicken with quick, vicious strokes. "Don't you have someplace you have to be?"

"Yes, I do." Chase stepped up to Cody. "I need to be with Lacey. She's out…" He caught himself before he gave away Lacey's location. "She's out somewhere, and your lady friend is parked by my house, watching me to see if I'll lead her to Lacey. How did she know Lacey was at my house, Cody? Huh? How did she know?"

"Whoa, bro. I didn't tell her."

"No? Then who did? And what were you doing sitting with her?" He clenched his fist. "I trusted you, *bro*. I trusted you with my sister, with my niece, and with Lacey's secrets. Guess I made a big mistake."

Cody paled. "Where's Lacey then? She's not out there alone, is she? Because those people are dangerous."

"Interesting that you would know that. I'm not telling you a damned thing." Chase turned and headed for the door. "And stay the hell away from my sister."

He was almost out the front door when Pam called down from upstairs. "Chase, come here."

"I'm in a hurry," he hollered back.

"It's about Lacey. Where is she?"

He let go of the doorknob and bounded up the steps. He wasn't about to tell her in front of Cody, and Annie was liable to holler out the answer any second. He shut the door behind him and faced his sister. "She's waiting for me, that's where she is."

"Look."

She was sitting at the kitchen table with a cup of tea and a copy of the *Conway Times* laid out in front of her. He knew she'd subscribed to the Tennessee paper since they'd left, but he'd never paid much attention to the news she relayed from it. That part of his life was over.

Once she'd tried to show him a picture of Lacey at some charity thing. He'd refused to look and stormed out, but a week later he'd noticed it at the top of the recycling bin and spent about ten minutes staring at it before he caught himself and tossed it aside in disgust.

"Lacey's husband testified."

"Ex-husband," he said, and then the news registered. "What?"

"He testified. Gave up all his associates in exchange for a light sentence." She folded the paper over and handed him the front of the local section. What appeared to be a mug shot of Wade Simpson stared out at him in black and gray and white, the man's light-colored eyes looking nearly as threatening in newsprint as they had in person. "That's Wade Simpson, isn't it?"

Chase nodded, swallowing. If the cops were looking for Wade, he had backup. He could call the police, let them know he had reason to believe a fugitive was in the area, and Rick Platt or someone else would come out and get him.

"I'll call," she said. "You have to go tell her. She's free."

Chase put a hand to his forehead and leaned against the counter behind him. He could bring Lacey good news. He could let her know the nightmare was over. She'd be happy. She'd smile. Maybe she'd put her arms around him and kiss him.

"And then you have to tell her how you feel about her." Pam was in bossy big sister mode. "You have to, or she'll leave."

She was right. Lacey was free to go now. *Not again,* he told himself. *I'm not going to lose her again.*

Tossing the paper on the counter, he headed for the door.

"Take the paper with you so you can show her," his sister said. "And tell Cody to take you. He can get there faster than you. He's down in the kitchen."

Chase wasn't about to tell Cody anything. According to the article, Wade Simpson was a wanted man now. A desperate man. He couldn't stop Trent now, but he might not know that. And even if he did, he might still hurt Lacey for some kind of twisted revenge.

He galloped down the stairs, glancing through the kitchen door as he passed.

The room was empty. Cody was gone.

Cody, who was evidently friends with Janice, who was here with Wade Simpson, who was looking for Lacey.

Cody, who might have heard Annie's comment about Lacey being in the woods.

Chase swore. There weren't a whole lot of trees in this part of the world, and there was nothing within a twenty-mile radius of Grady that could be called a woods other than the little copse of trees on his land. If Cody had heard Annie, then he knew where Lacey was.

Slamming out the door, Chase hiked himself up into his truck and squealed out of his parking space. He'd just have to hope his truck could catch up to Cody's Jeep before the guy could get to Lacey.

CHAPTER 40

LACEY STOOD BACK AND GAVE CAPTAIN A CRITICAL look. She'd fitted the splint to his leg and wrapped the tape around it, being careful to keep it smooth and wrinkle-free so it wouldn't irritate his skin. The big horse had stood patiently through the entire process, seeming to sense that she was trying to help him. The only problem was Sheba, who had insisted on observing the process closely—so closely that she nearly got her curious muzzle taped to Captain's leg along with the splint.

"Git," Lacey protested as the pony crowded against her. She'd overcome her panic, but annoyance at Sheba's antics had quickly taken its place. "I'm almost done." She smoothed the tape one last time, then patted Captain's shoulder. "Good boy. You're a great introduction to horses for newbies, aren't you? Unlike your little friend here." She gave Sheba a playful swat, and the horse backed away, snorting.

"Let's see if you can walk." She took the reins just below the bit like Chase had shown her and led Captain a few yards down the trail. He was slow, but he seemed to be in less pain than before.

Maybe she should start toward the ranch. Chase had told her not to, but he'd also told her she was safer out on the plains than in the forest. And it would feel good to do something other than sit and wait for an unknown fate.

She clicked to the other horses, but it wasn't like she

needed to tell them to follow; Captain was evidently the leader of the pack. Sinclair brought up the rear, his plumed tail waving. She felt like the grand marshal of a rodeo parade. All she needed was a sparkly hat and a whistle to clear the way.

But it was a very slow-moving parade. By the time they cleared the edge of the woods, Captain was obviously in pain. He hobbled gamely on, but his head was held low and his steps were slow.

"You're not going to make it, are you, buddy?"

They were out of the woods, but once again the vast space of the plains made her feel vulnerable and exposed. A faded moon was rising, casting a feeble glow that felt more spooky than safe, and a faint breeze rattled the dry grass, making a sound like skeletons dancing in a Halloween graveyard.

"Oh, for God's sake," she muttered to herself. "Get a grip."

She cast a covetous glance toward Galt's off-limits cabin. It loomed in the darkness, pale and dim, the only feature on the stark, barren plains. It was almost full night now, and there wasn't a single light in sight. Galt's trailer was apparently over a rise, or behind a rock. He'd never know she'd trespassed.

"And even if he did, what's he going to do?" she murmured to Captain. "Shoot me? Grump me to death?"

He might shoot the horses. He'd shot a cow, after all. But it seemed to her there was a pretty good chance he'd never know they were there. Tugging at Captain's bridle, she urged him across the shallow stream. The other horses followed, their progress making faint splashing sounds, then a series of irregular thumps as they mounted the bank and headed toward the cabin. Captain had trouble climbing the shallow grade, and she felt cruel tugging at his head, but instinct told her the horses would be safer in the shadows of the cabin, and she knew she'd feel safer inside.

When they got to the cabin, the horses milled around in the yard, stamping and shaking, their blankets slapping against their sides. Lacey sighed. She wasn't done fighting dragons yet.

"You guys want to take those off, don't you?"

Fortunately, the blankets had Velcro closures and slipped easily off the horses' backs. She tossed them on the step and walked into the cabin, figuring she'd better learn her way around before the last moments of daylight slid into darkness. The place had two rooms: a big, main one and a little lean-to on the side that seemed to have served as a kitchen. The big room had a bed in one corner and a rusty wood-burning stove in the other. Sinclair had already found the bed and curled up in a ball at the foot of it, as if he were waiting for her to join him. It was a metal frame with a blue-ticked mattress on it. The thing was lumpy and looked like it was stuffed with straw. It probably had mice inside. And bugs.

The kitchen had a tin sink, a few wooden cabinets with the paint peeling off, and a rickety, handmade table. There had evidently been wallpaper once, but now it hung in strips and tatters from the wall, making the place look like it had a bad case of mange.

She cranked the faucet.

Nothing.

She wondered who had lived here. Was it just a line

shack where cowboys stayed when they were watching their cattle? Or was it someone's home? She looked at the window above the sink. The tattered remnant of a lace curtain hung in one corner, and there was a colored glass bottle on the windowsill—a touch of prettiness in this starkly practical building.

A woman must have lived here once. Lived here, and tried to make it a home—probably for the sake of a man. Surely no woman would choose to live in such an isolated, barren spot.

Opening a cabinet over the sink, she found a few cans of tomato soup and baked beans. A drawer held spoons but no can opener, and there was a ripped-out hole where the stove should have been, so the food wouldn't do her much good. Not that she was hungry. Her stomach was so roiled up with fear and worry, she couldn't even think about food.

But there was a light—a sort of camping lantern thing. She flicked the switch, and a bright LED bulb lit up the cabin. Nice.

She took it out and set it on the woodstove. Somehow, just having the place lit up made it look more like a house and less like a deserted shed. Mice didn't like lights, did they? Neither did bugs. Sinclair looked up and thumped his tail.

"Annie's spoiling you, isn't she? You want attention all the time now." She patted his head, then went back outside, where the horses stood in a loose semicircle around the cabin.

"Shoo." She flicked her fingers. "Go home."

They trotted off a ways, all but Captain, who stood gazing at her expectantly. Or was it adoringly? She'd fixed his leg. Maybe he was grateful, like that lion in the Aesop fable. That would make her the mouse, which was pretty damn appropriate. She was like a mouse, skittering around, scared of everything.

Then again, maybe he just wanted her to take the saddle off. How could you tell what a horse was thinking? They seemed to have two expressions—this one, stoic and unblinking; and the one where they freaked out and pulled their lips back, making all the veins stand out in their faces.

"You want that off, boy?" She moved to his side and stared at the saddle, trying to remember how Chase had put it on. Flipping up the stirrup leather, she found a metal ring with a strip of leather wrapped around it. The cinch, he'd called it. Remembering how he'd tugged at it, she picked at the knot until she managed to undo it, then lifted the saddle off and set it on the cabin's front step.

She unbuckled the bridle and let the bit drop from Captain's mouth. What she ought to do was put it on one of the other horses and ride back to the ranch, but what if she put it on wrong? Riding was hazardous enough without the saddle falling off or the horse balking at a poorly-fit bit. Besides, that would mean leaving Captain alone and defenseless. Even with the splint, he couldn't move very fast.

She scooped up the horse blankets she'd tossed on the porch and paused, listening. A breeze rattled the dry branches of the lilac bush by the door and ruffled the prairie grass. The only other sound was Captain's soft breath. No mountain lion. No engine noise. It was as quiet as it had been that night under the stars with Chase.

She looked up. The stars were barely visible, the sky not

yet dark enough to put them in high relief. She could see the moon rising, a pale disc just over the horizon, and a bright star next to it. She wondered if Chase was looking up too.

Clutching the blankets to her chest, she brought them inside, tossing them on the bed. Sinclair immediately climbed on the pile and nosed himself a cozy nest.

"Hey, I'm using those," she said. "Move over."

She snuggled next to the dog, grateful for the company. Even the musky horse scent rising from the blankets seemed comforting, a reminder of Chase. The lantern cast its cold white light over the interior of the cabin, making spooky shadows where the peeling strips of wallpaper swayed in the slight breeze.

That was when she heard the engine approaching, distant but distinct in the quiet night.

Chase. Finally.

She stepped out on the porch and started to wave at the approaching vehicle. He probably couldn't see her yet, but she was so glad to see him, she couldn't contain herself.

The headlights rocked as the vehicle plowed over rocks and ruts.

Wait a minute. He'd said he'd bring the trailer. There was no trailer.

She remembered the note. *Wade was here. He left, but he's been watching.*

Watching. And she'd been fool enough to light the lantern, letting it beam from the cabin like a beacon announcing her location.

Stay safe, the note had said. She had a feeling it was too late for that, but better late than never. She ran inside and flicked off the lantern, plunging the cabin into darkness.

CHAPTER 41

CHASE FLICKED OFF THE RADIO AND TAPPED HIS FINGERS meditatively on the steering wheel, barely registering the scenes from his everyday commute as the truck ate up the miles. He was surprised he hadn't caught up to Cody yet. Maybe his friend—his former friend—hadn't gone looking for Lacey.

But he didn't trust Cody anymore. The guy was hiding something. Chase had always known that. He'd had reservations about his sister dating Cody, but Pam had insisted the cook was a good guy and there had never been any evidence that the guy was anything but a straight shooter until the thing with Janice. Chase didn't know who the woman was, but she was with Wade Simpson—and that meant she was definitely trouble.

Meanwhile, it was getting dark, and Lacey was still in the woods. He wondered if she'd gotten the note. If she'd splinted poor Captain's leg. He was tempted to turn off the ranch road and take a shortcut through the pasture. Hell, he'd been tempted to drive overland, taking a shortcut across Galt's ranch, but the old guy hated four-wheelers with a passion. Chase had flicked his headlights on ten minutes ago, and if Galt saw a vehicle on his land, he was liable to come running with a shotgun. Besides, if Wade and Janice were still watching, he'd be lighting a trail straight to Lacey.

Instead, he passed the turnoff to the house and drove

another hundred yards, then hung a left and drove toward the hill where he'd seen her pursuers last. There was an old two-track that was barely visible in the near dark, but he managed to navigate far enough to see the side of the hill where Annie had spotted the sedan an hour earlier.

There was nothing there but tire tracks. They must have given up for the night. Revving the pickup over stones and through a shallow stretch of alkali, he swung around the far side of the hill and sped up the ranch road.

They were gone. He could finally rescue Lacey.

He hoped she was okay. He really shouldn't have scared her with all that talk about bears and mountain lions. He just couldn't believe she'd thought the wooded area was safer than the plains.

The plains were far more safe. You could see what was coming from miles away, and they never changed. Winter might toss a blanket of snow over the dry grass, and spring might turn the yellow hills to green velvet for a week or two, but you could always count on the unchanging landscape. Since he'd moved to Wyoming, their permanence had been a comfort and a touchstone—a promise that he could depend on the land forever.

But maybe change wasn't such a bad thing. Spring would come, and with it a new year. New flowers would bloom, and new calves would be born.

He wondered if Lacey would be there to see it.

Lacey glanced around the cabin, wondering if she should hide under the bed, run into the kitchen, or jump out the window. The first two options would leave her trapped inside the cabin; the third would put her out on the plains with no place to hide.

She heard footsteps crunching on the dirt of the cabin's parched yard and waited for the familiar hitch in her breathing, the dizziness, the helpless thudding of her heart. If ever there was a reason for her to panic, this was it—but to her surprise, her lungs continued to function, her heart kept its normal beat, and she didn't feel dizzy in the least. In fact, her mind felt oddly alert.

The interior of the cabin was lit by a slash of light where the headlights of her unexpected guest shone through the window. Everything in the light seemed unnaturally clear— the dry floorboards with their grain raised by a century of summer heat and winter cold, the chipped white paint on the iron bedstead, the torn shreds of wallpaper dripping from the walls. Metal scraped on metal as the rusty doorknob turned, and she dodged behind the door and pressed her back against the wall.

The door flew open and gave her a full-frontal smackdown, skinning her toes to slam against her body and knock her head into the wall behind her. She blinked away the stars and planets whirling inside her head and saw a hunched figure stomp into the room raising a shotgun to his shoulder. He was backlit into a silhouette against the gleam of the headlights.

She screamed without thinking, loud and long. Why did her lungs have to work now? If the panic was going to steal her breath, why couldn't it happen when she needed to be sneaky?

The sheer volume of the scream made her gun-wielding

assailant stagger backward. Sinclair let out a high-pitched bark and the man swung the gun toward the dog. Lacey dove to the floor and grabbed the intruder's ankles, knocking him off-balance so he fell backward. Later, she wasn't sure if she'd been heroically protecting her dog or just trying to avoid being shot, but the net effect was to make the man tighten his finger on the trigger. He blasted both barrels at the cabin's peeling ceiling, sending a shower of plaster and paint chips onto the floor.

Sinclair let out another bark and ran outside, his tail plastered between his legs. Lacey scrambled up on her hands and knees. Grabbing the barrel of the gun, she pushed it away and looked down into the face of Fletcher Galt. The old man looked shocked for just an instant before his sagging, wrinkled face hardened and twisted. His eyes squinted up at her with a malevolent glare.

"What the hell are you doing in my house?"

"Oh, this is *your* house?" She'd play dumb—it was her only hope. She tried to look confused and helpless while still stiff-arming the gun. "I thought it was Chase's."

The man clenched his face like a fist, wrinkling his nose, scowling, and lowering his brows so that all his features squinched into the center of his face. "This is *my* house. Caldwell might think he owns the whole county, but he don't own this. It's *mine*. Should have been my boy's by now."

Great. Mentioning Chase was probably the worst thing she could have done. "Oh," she said. "Sorry."

"Bastard stole my land, you know. Stole it."

"He did?" Lacey was so surprised, she let the gun go and sat up on her heels, letting the old man scramble to his feet.

"Came in here and took advantage when I was grieving," the old man said.

"You're kidding. Chase did that?" She knew she should feel disillusioned and disappointed, but the idea that Chase might not be the blameless, morally perfect model of a man he seemed to be was strangely gratifying. Wait until she saw him again. Just wait. "I'm so sorry. That must have been terrible. I had no idea Chase would do a thing like that."

The man still clutched the gun, but his features were starting to relax. Instead of looking ornery, he just looked craggy and tired. She gave him her best flirty smile, but he was apparently immune to her charm because suspicion crept back into his eyes again as if he'd realized he'd let down his guard. "So what are you doing in my house?"

"Hiding."

"What, is he beating you? That bastard. I'll…"

"No. He's—he's actually trying to protect me."

The man snorted.

"Seriously. And he was doing a pretty good job. This guy who's looking for me—he's at the ranch, and I guess he's watching, and we came out here and the horse got hurt and now he can't come get me because they might see, and…"

"Whoa, honey, whoa. I can't follow all that. Who's…"

He paused and grabbed her arm as headlights swept across the far wall of the cabin. "Git down," he hissed, pulling her to the ground. "If somebody's huntin' you, we're rats in a hole." He grabbed the gun and scuttled over to the window, jerking his head for her to follow. Lacey crouched beside him as he levered himself up and out of the window with surprising agility. The rough wooden sill scraped her already bruised body as she scrambled after him and fell to the ground.

Galt stood to one side of the window, his back pressed against the cabin wall. He brought his finger to his lips to signal silence as a new set of headlights cast a fan of light on either side of the cabin. She was out in the open now, barely hidden by the shadow of the house, but she had Galt and he had a gun.

A cloud of dust drifted into the darkness as the car skidded to a stop. A door slammed.

"She's here somewhere."

She knew that voice. It sent a shudder rippling up her spine and pooled dread in her belly. Wade Simpson.

He'd found her.

She'd known he was coming. Chase warned her in the note, and once Galt had found her, she knew the light in the cabin had doomed her to discovery.

But still, the sound of his voice scraped up her spine like icy fingers, leaving her almost dizzy. When a low growl rumbled from the darkness, she felt the night get a little darker.

"Look. It's a fuckin' dog."

Oh, God. What would she do if Wade hurt Sinclair? He was just a mutt she'd rescued from a service station on the highway, but he was Annie's dog now, and she couldn't let anything happen to him.

"Come on, boy." Wade's voice slid up to a higher register, taking on a sweet, insipid tone that made Lacey's flesh crawl even more than his usual rasp. "Where is she, buddy? Go get her. Go get her."

Sinclair growled again, then let out a high, questioning bark as if he was trying to determine if Wade was a new friend. Was he going to lead her stalker straight to her? She glanced over at Galt, who was still pressed against the side of the house, the shotgun across his chest. One hand was on the barrel, the other wrapped around the stock with his index finger just above the trigger. His thin lips were drawn into a tight line. If you replaced his John Deere cap with an army-green helmet, he'd look like an old *Life* photo from Vietnam.

Sinclair growled again, louder and higher this time, and then yipped in pain. Wade must have kicked him. She heard the dog scrabble over the dirt and saw his shadow as he ran off into the night. At least he didn't come straight to her. She felt a little disappointed that he would abandon her, but it was for the best.

It wasn't like she could help him survive.

Wade flicked on the lantern and she winced as the bright light shafted across the plains. How could she have been so stupid? She might as well have put up a blinking neon arrow pointing to her location. She felt her heart speed up as her chest constricted. Closing her eyes, she chanted to herself. *Calm, calm, calm.* She sucked in a breath, then let it out. *Calm.*

She was getting better at this. Her heartbeat was slowing, the ache in her chest easing. Maybe it helped to have a grumpy old man on your side. She stayed flat against the wall as a second pair of feet hit the cabin floor and clicked across the room. They sounded crisp, authoritative, feminine—like teacher shoes clicking down the hallways at school. Sure enough, the shadow that appeared was distinctly feminine. And it was growing—getting closer and closer to the window.

"So help me, Wade, if you led me on a wild goose chase, I'll sue you for new shocks." The voice was high—definitely a woman—and it rose in volume as she neared the window. "That car's no redneck four-wheeler. That's my dad's fifty-thousand-dollar Lincoln."

"Well, your dad's not gonna have much use for it if he ends up in jail, is he?"

Her dad. Who could her dad be?

"And if we don't find that bitch and use her to shut up Bradford, the only chamber your daddy's gonna be looking at is the inside of a jail cell."

Chamber. Chamber of Commerce? Senate chamber?

That was it. The woman had to be Senator Carrol's daughter. Lacey had seen her standing behind her daddy at press conferences. Evidently, Wade had talked her into some scheme to save her father's reputation by keeping Trent from talking.

Beckoning to Lacey, Galt dropped down and duck-walked sideways to squat under the opening. She followed his orders without thinking, and the two of them crouched together like soldiers in a foxhole. If the woman looked out, she wouldn't see them, even if she looked both ways. Long as she didn't look down, they were safe. But how likely was that?

"Should have shot the dog," Wade said in a casual, conversational tone. "It'll probably run back to the house, and then he'll know something's wrong."

"Who, the cowboy? He's not there."

"He'll get back eventually."

Chase wasn't *there*? He *left* her? She felt a rush of hopelessness, then anger at the thought that he'd abandoned her. Then she remembered Annie and prayed he'd taken her home. If Wade got anywhere near Annie, she'd shoot him.

She longed to yank the shotgun from Galt's grip, but judging from his determined expression, he'd probably shoot the first person who crossed him even if it was her.

It was just as well. The man seemed a little crazy, and you probably had to be nuts to actually shoot another human being. She might want to in theory, but who knew if she'd be able to actually pull the trigger?

She realized she was closing her eyes, as if that would keep them from seeing her. She forced herself to open them and saw Wade step around the corner of the house. The light streaming from the windows and doors illuminated the whole area, so she could see him clearly. He stood in a fighter's stance, feet apart, hands hanging loose like a gunslinger's, and surveyed the prairie. She felt totally exposed as his glare swung her way, but his eyes weren't accustomed to the dark and they flicked right past her.

"You idiot, she's right *there*," said a voice from behind her.

The beam of the flashlight slashed across her face, and she sprang to her feet and bolted. There was nowhere to go, nowhere to hide. She sprinted across the flat ground, but she wasn't much of a runner.

Shoot. She aimed her thoughts at Galt. *Shoot.*

Apparently he got the message. A shot split the quiet night, but when she glanced back, the old man lay on the ground and Wade was gaining on her, a pistol in his hand. Putting on a sudden burst of speed, she pitched forward as he hit her legs in a flying tackle.

When she struck the ground, Galt's shotgun roared from somewhere behind her, but the shot scattered harmlessly out over the empty pasture. She pictured the pellets speeding across the open ground, heading for the quiet woods where the mountain lion lurked.

Then there was a sickening thud like someone dropping a melon, a grunt from Galt, and silence. She looked back to see the woman standing over his prone body holding the shotgun like a baseball bat. The stock was shiny with blood.

"Galt," Lacey whispered, her stomach lurching. Her heart leapt into her throat. "Not Galt."

CHAPTER 42

CHASE GRITTED HIS TEETH AND CLUTCHED THE WHEEL as the pickup bounced over the prairie, the trailer bouncing behind it like a heavy ball and chain. It swung first to one side, then the other, constantly foiling his efforts to keep clear of rocks and clumps of sagebrush. His eyes were fixed on the ground in front of the headlights, so he was startled when a movement to one side caught his attention, and he turned to see two horses galloping past.

Sheba and Jimbo, headed home. Lacey must have spooked them somehow. At least she'd managed to get the blankets off their backs. He hoped she'd found the note. She must have. Otherwise surely he'd have passed her by now, because she wouldn't realize she was walking into danger. He clutched the wheel and sped up.

He hadn't gone far when Galt's old claim cabin appeared in the distance, lit up like a church on Christmas. Dang. The old man spent most nights sitting on his porch, that damn shotgun on his lap, guarding what was left of his land and his life from intrusion—even well meaning intrusion. He was more crazy than mean, but crazy could kill.

If it was Lacey that lit up the cabin, Galt would probably head out there and shoot her without even knowing who she was. Chase cursed himself for not taking the gun. Hopefully the old man would look before he pulled the trigger, and Lacey would have a chance to charm her way to survival. Even Fletcher Galt could probably be swayed by one of her luminous smiles and the glow of those green eyes.

He wondered if she'd had one of her panic attacks. He was pretty sure she'd almost had one when she fell off the horse the other day, and again when Captain stumbled, but she'd managed to get herself under control. He shouldn't have left her alone, though. Should have left the horse, taken her with him. But she'd been stubborn, determined to protect the horse, and that kindness had kept her from walking right into Wade Simpson.

He squinted as he neared the cabin. The light didn't look right. The windows and doors were lit, as if someone had turned on a light inside. But the whole place was lit up, bright against the dark night sky. Lit from the outside.

By headlights.

They found her. He reflexively pressed the accelerator to the floor, then realized he needed to think and jammed on the brakes, shutting off his own headlights. Cruising in there with the horse trailer rattling and banging behind him was hardly a stealth strategy. He couldn't rescue Lacey if Wade and Janice knew he was there. He'd have to drive down the narrow two-track into the ravine and get as close as he could, then walk the rest of the way.

Hopping out of the truck, he disconnected the trailer, then got behind the wheel and headed for the ravine Peering through the windshield into the darkness, he steered the truck down the narrow path through a dense tangle of brush. He kept the pickup in low gear and moved slow, but between the hum of the engine and the snapping and cracking of sticks as he eased through the undergrowth, he felt like he was being about as subtle as a brontosaurus.

When he hit the stream, he had to stop. He'd just end up stuck again if he tried to navigate the mud, sand, and boulders.

Reaching under the seat, he pulled out a lockbox and keyed in a combination to reveal his emergency gun—a sleek, black Wilson nine-millimeter. He flicked off the dome light, then shoved the pistol into his waistband and slid out of the truck. He eased the door almost shut, knowing the click of the latch would sound like a shot in the quiet night.

He thrashed through the brush in the dark, running upright when he could and scrambling on all fours in the rougher patches. He didn't see the Jeep until he'd practically run into it. It was parked behind the rocks a short distance from the cabin, and it was empty.

Cody was out here somewhere.

Chase remembered Annie's words as she ran up the steps to the apartment. *I think Lacey might be scared in the woods alone.* Cody must have heard her. But how could he have gotten here so fast? He must have braved the wrath of Fletcher Galt and crossed the sacred ground of the old man's ranch. Chase cursed himself and moved on. He should have done that himself. Why did he always follow the rules, even when so much was at stake?

Cody would tell Wade's lady friend everything: that Lacey was here, that Chase was on his way. A cold fist of fear squeezed Chase's heart. Worry for Lacey, pain for his sister. Disappointment in Cody, and in himself.

I'd trust that guy with my life. That's what he'd told Lacey. That made him an idiot—a stupid, trusting fool. Outside of family, Cody was the first person he'd trusted since the farm got taken away. He'd forgotten all the lessons he'd learned back in Conway: that everything you depended on could turn on you, that nothing in life was fair, and that people were predators just waiting for you to make a mistake. They lulled you into a state of Pollyanna positivity and then snatched everything you had right out from under your nose.

He'd started to believe different in Grady. Started to make friends, to open up his life. Watching the way Cody took care of Pam, he'd actually begun to believe he could count on someone other than himself.

He'd been wrong.

Lacey twisted, flinging out an elbow as Wade's heavy body fell on top of her. The scent of rage, sweat, and hate filled her consciousness, giving way to the smell of gunpowder and metal as he jammed the cold muzzle of a gun against the angle of her jaw.

"Get her into the car," the woman said.

Lacey felt the gun twitch against her neck as Wade cocked it. "Why bother?" he said between gritted teeth.

"What do you mean, why bother? That's the plan. I told you, I have a line to Bradford. He hears we have his wife, he'll forget everything he ever knew about those deals. My dad'll be in the clear, and you'll keep your job."

Wade was breathing hard making the gun shake. It felt like every artificially pumped muscle in his body was tensed. "I already lost my job. I don't give a shit if Trent talks."

"*What?* We had a plan, Simpson. And shutting up Bradford is all I care about. You want to kill her later, you can do it on your own."

"I just want Bradford to feel the pain." Wade jabbed the gun harder into Lacey's jaw. "I was never good enough to invite to his fancy parties, but I was good enough to do his dirty work. Good enough to use. I shut up Caldwell's dad for him, you know. It's time I got paid." He was straddling her, one hand holding the gun, the other working at his belt. She could feel him trembling—maybe with rage, maybe excitement. Maybe those were the same things to Wade.

"Get over yourself, Simpson. Caldwell committed suicide. You didn't have a damn thing to do with it."

"That's what you think. That's what everybody thinks." He switched the gun to his left hand and Lacey bucked hard, thinking she might have a chance to get loose, but his right hand grabbed the back of her neck and slammed her head onto the ground. She felt his fingers snaking around to the front, pressing painfully hard on her throat. Her pulse throbbed against the pressure, then began to flutter and fade. Darkness welled up in her mind—not the dark of the night, but a darkness from deep inside her that flooded her mind and made the real world fade away. "Thirty seconds like this, and she'll be real easy to handle. Put the gun in her hand, pull the trigger, and boom. Too bad, so sad. She just couldn't live with what her husband did."

"Quit it." The woman shoved at Wade and his grip loosened. Lacey struggled against the darkness, trying to see, trying to hear, trying to find a way to live. She opened her eyes and saw the woman's feet inches away from her face. She must be brain damaged already, because the shoes were like something out of a nightmare.

"You're killing her," the woman said.

"You bet. But not yet." Wade let go of her neck, but he

was fumbling with his pants again. "First I'm gonna show her what it's like to be used. What do you think of that?"

"I think it's not what I signed on for," the woman said. "Get off her."

The cold metal left Lacey's skin as Wade swung to point the gun at the other woman. "Shut up, or you're next. Sad how you tried to prevent your father's disgrace. You killed her, and then you killed yourself. That's what everybody will think, and I'll be long gone."

"You're crazy. Crazy." The woman backed away. "I'm clearing out. You do what you want."

Lacey heard the woman's footsteps running away as Wade shoved the gun back under her chin. Even with the gun away from her neck, Lacey couldn't move. She tried to twist against Wade's weight, but he was too strong.

Maybe the woman would come back with a gun, or club Wade with the shotgun like she had Galt. Maybe...

An engine started on the other side of the house, and the beam from the sedan's headlights swung sideways and disappeared. Lacey heard the tires crunching across the ground as the car drove away.

Her only possible protector was gone.

She closed her eyes tight. *Calm, calm,* she told herself. *Calmcalmcalm.* But the fear wouldn't go away this time. She'd die afraid, but she wouldn't die without a struggle. She drew in one more desperate breath and arched her back, twisting away from Wade. He slipped to one side and cursed, then grabbed her hair and pulled her toward him.

"Too bad we don't have some of those nice girlie drinks you liked so much back in high school," he said. "That would make this better for you."

Lacey's stomach turned over and she felt her lunch surging hot at the back of her throat. She was still dizzy, her throat hurt, and Wade was going to kill her once he got done with her—but at this point, she felt like she'd die anyway if he did as he planned.

She turned her head away to avoid his sour breath on her face and saw Galt lying a few feet away. His face was twisted with pain now, not anger. A gash on his forehead had streaked half his face with blood, but he blinked as she watched, then pointed his gaze downward.

He had the shotgun. Janice must have dropped it after she hit him. He was trying to get a grip on it, but he couldn't seem to close his hand properly. He blinked again, his eyes glassy and desperate.

Dammit, Janice had almost killed him. An old man. Killed him to save her father's golden reputation. Suddenly, what Trent had done didn't seem so bad. He'd just wanted money. It was terrible, but it wasn't murder.

Wade was the root of all of it. He was the hate at the heart of her hometown, the festering sore that never healed. He'd hounded her, and hated her, and now he was going to kill her.

She felt her chest constricting with panic, her old enemy stealing her breath. She'd learned to fight the attacks by being rational—by taking in the reality of the situation, seeing a way out. But right now, reality was the last thing she wanted to face. There was no way out of this situation. The gun…

The gun. It wasn't pressed against her head anymore. She didn't know where it was—maybe an inch from her temple, maybe lying forgotten in the dirt. There was a chance Wade didn't really know where it was either; he was too intent on his other goals. He'd loosened his hold on her to grapple with his clothing.

She had nowhere to run, no way to defend herself—but she had to get away from Wade. His breath, the smell of his skin—she felt like she was going to be sick. She took a deep breath and felt her brain kick back into gear. Looking to one side, she saw only the wall of the cabin and a vast expanse of plains beyond it. There was nowhere to hide. Nowhere to run.

But on the other side was Galt—and Galt's shotgun. If Lacey could just get out from under Wade and grab it, she'd have a way to defend herself.

Lunging sideways, she tore her hair out of his grip and skittered out from under him, scrambling sideways to grab the gun. Her fingers slipped on the bloody stock, but she managed to grab it and bring it up to her shoulder. She grabbed the stock to pump it.

Nothing. It wouldn't move. There wasn't a damn thing in the chamber. She'd hoped Wade was too crazed by anger and lust to know that, but without the click and thump of the pump action, the shotgun wasn't much of a threat.

But Chase had pumped his own gun for her, and it had been empty. There had to be a way. She pressed and squeezed and floundered for what seemed like a small eternity and finally felt something give way—a button in front of the trigger guard. Her other hand shoved the pump forward, and the satisfying clunk changed everything. Now she was the one with the power.

She watched Wade's face as he took in his new situation. Malice was replaced by fear, and she suddenly felt powerful and in command for the first time since—well, since the day she'd left home for Grady, before she realized how hard it was to make it on your own.

Wade's eyes were wide, his mouth stretched into a grimace of fear. Obviously, he didn't know there was no load in the gun. He'd never been the brightest bulb on the Christmas tree, and right now, he was looking at her like he thought she might be the last sight he'd ever see. His hands lifted from his belt buckle, rising in the air.

Maybe she could somehow bluff her way out of this. She surged to her feet and poked him in the chest with the muzzle of the gun, pushing him toward the cabin and away from the small black pistol that lay in the dirt.

She could grab the pistol, but that would mean looking away from Wade. And while he looked scared, he still looked attentive, as if he was just waiting for her to blink. She glanced down at the pistol on the ground, then back to Wade, then back to the pistol.

"Don't move." Her voice was so thin and shaky, she was worried he'd figure out she had nothing to fight with. "Stay right there."

The light from the cabin lit up Wade's face, making the sweat on his brow almost sparkle and throwing deep purple shadows under his eyes and cheekbones. His eyes were crafty, his gaze flicking from her to the pistol and back again. Suddenly he dropped to the ground and rolled, scooping up the pistol and rising to his knees to aim it straight at Lacey's heart.

She might die, but she would not faint. She'd go down fighting. Her hands trembled, but she kept the shotgun aimed at Wade's chest. If he thought it was loaded, he'd think this was a Mexican standoff, each of them armed. She fixed her eyes on his trigger finger, waiting for it to twitch, wondering if she could dodge a speeding bullet.

CHAPTER 43

CHASE CLIMBED THE WALL OF THE RAVINE, PLACING HIS feet carefully, praying he wouldn't miss a foothold and slide to the bottom. As he neared the top, a faint shout rose up, and then the roar of a shotgun split the night and chased away any possibility of sensible thought.

He set off for the cabin at a run.

He could see the cabin. There was the sedan parked outside it with its headlights on, and he could hear voices first talking, then shouting. He put on a burst of speed, concentrating on his feet, willing them to slap the ground harder, faster, willing himself to fly, fly to Lacey.

He was closing in on the cabin when the sedan pulled a quick K-turn and headed straight toward him, almost blinding him with its lights. It swerved and passed him, going way too fast.

Somebody was running away. Maybe Lacey had managed to protect herself after all.

He kept on running, his breath burning in his chest, his thigh muscles aching. He was probably too late, but he couldn't slow down. Couldn't stop and take a chance that he'd fail Lacey. He dodged a clump of sagebrush and concentrated on his feet. A fall would mean a delay, and a delay could mean death. He stared at the ground as he ran, barely able to see his feet in the darkness. The stars that had lit the world the night before were dim behind a cover of clouds that cloaked the prairie in darkness so deep he could barely see his own feet.

He slowed to a stealthier pace as he approached the cabin, trying to move quickly but quietly while he took in the sounds coming from the other side of the small building. Footsteps, curses, and heavy breathing had given way to an ominous silence, but at least there hadn't been any more gunshots. He pulled the revolver out and clutched it in his fist as he carefully shifted his weight from one foot to the other.

As he approached, the windowless side of the cabin was in shadow while the rest of the landscape was lit with fans of light that spread from the windows and door. He caught a hint of movement against the dark wall and paused, squinting as if that would help his eyes probe the darkness.

Someone was there, standing against the cabin wall. A man, his back against the wall by the corner. One hand was at his side; the other was raised and held a pistol at the ready. He was moving slowly, preparing to edge around the corner.

Somewhere beyond that corner was Lacey.

He heard the ominous pump of a shotgun in the distance, but it was Lacey's voice that followed.

"Don't move," she said. "Stay right there."

His heart surged with joy at the knowledge that she was alive, then squeezed tight, wincing at the thin, frightened sound of her voice. But if she was telling someone not to move, she must have some way to enforce the command. She couldn't have a gun; everything but the pistol in his hand had been locked up safely before Annie arrived.

He edged sideways, steering clear of the beams of light streaming from the windows, and Lacey came into view around the backside of the house. She was standing next to something on the ground, a hump in the darkness that might be a body or might be a rock. She had a shotgun snugged against her shoulder, aimed at a man who was standing behind the cabin.

Chase wondered where she'd gotten the gun. He'd heard a blast from it earlier, so there was a good chance it was empty unless she'd somehow managed to reload. He took a few steps closer and peered at the figure at her feet. She took a step away from it and light fell across it. It was Galt, lying on his back and staring sightless at the sky. The pain that pierced Chase's heart at the thought of his old neighbor dying surprised him. Somehow, delivering the old man's dinner had linked them together, made Chase responsible for him. Pam had been right—you had to help somebody. If the old man was dead, there'd be a hole in Chase's life that would be surprisingly hard to fill.

But he didn't have time to think about that now. Lacey's face was white, but her little chin was jutted out in determination, and she never took her eyes off Simpson, who stood in front of her. If that gun was loaded, Chase didn't doubt she'd shoot the guy if she had to. And considering that Wade was aiming a handgun at her, she really did have to.

The fact that she hadn't pulled the trigger made him almost sure the gun was empty. So he was the one who had to shoot. But he couldn't shoot around corners, and he couldn't afford to miss. He had to get closer.

He glanced back at the figure in the shadows just in time to see it step into the light.

Cody.

Chase lifted his gun and stared through the sights at his friend's wide shoulders. Cody had been with the woman in the diner, and now he was here—with Wade. Right now the gun was at his side, but it would take only seconds for him to lift it and shoot Lacey.

Shoot Lacey? Would Cody do that?

Chase shook his head, trying to clear the cobwebs that seemed to have taken over his brain. Cody wouldn't shoot her. Would he?

In a flash, he remembered his friend sitting at the table with Janice, looking up with a guilty, hunted look. Remembered him lying about the cut finger to avoid answering questions. Remembered the way he'd disappeared, left the diner right at the time he could have overheard Chase talking to Annie and realized Lacey was alone in the woods.

Chase clenched his teeth. Cody was on the wrong side of this fight. He lifted the revolver and took aim. He'd been wrong to trust Cody. Wrong to think he could trust anybody.

But then there was the way the guy looked at Pam when he didn't realize anyone was watching. The way he tried to help Annie with her homework even though Chase doubted he had much of an education himself. The way he came running when anybody needed him.

He has a rescue complex.

That's what Chase had told Lacey, and it was true.

He kind of restored my faith in human nature… He's just… just good.

It had to be true—because if Cody turned on him, the world would turn to shit. If Cody was one of the bad guys, Chase wouldn't be able to trust anybody, least of all himself and his own instincts.

But he couldn't risk Lacey's life to blind faith, could he? He was her protector, her champion. If he made the wrong choice now, he'd fail her, sure as he'd failed her the day she'd arrived, when he'd struck out at her, afraid to trust. Afraid to let even the woman he'd loved all his life into his world.

He lowered the gun and took a few steps forward. When the dry grass crunched under his feet, Cody whirled to face him, and in an instant, Chase knew he'd chosen right. His friend's white teeth flashed in the moonlight in a relieved smile the moment their eyes met.

"Bro," he whispered. "'Bout time you got here. Come on. Let's take out this son of a bitch."

Lacey's arm was starting to shake. She didn't know if it was muscle fatigue from holding up the shotgun or fear of meeting Wade's eyes. Maybe it was tension from watching his expression for the slightest twitch that might mean he was about to pull the trigger.

All she knew was that she couldn't hold out much longer. Eventually Wade would realize she wasn't going to shoot, and he'd end the standoff with a bullet. Even worse, he might realize her gun wasn't loaded. Then he'd simply take it from her and proceed with whatever he'd had in mind when she'd managed to grab the gun.

At least she was still upright and breathing, holding panic at bay. That proved she'd beaten the fear. If she could stare down Wade Simpson without blinking, she could do anything.

Her eyes welled with tears, making the image of Wade and his gun shift and waver. Unfortunately, she'd never get the chance to do anything. Ever again. She couldn't see a way to survive this. She was as good as dead.

She'd never get to live that independent life she'd envisioned. Never get to make up for all the years she'd wasted. Never get to hold Chase, to be friends with Pam, to be Annie's favorite aunt. She'd never get the chance to help anyone, ever.

A rustle to her right startled her out of her self-pity, and she glanced over to see two figures in the shadows. Two men. Their presence had barely registered before a shot rang out and one man slammed into Wade, knocking him to the ground. The pistol flew into the darkness as a flurry of fists hit her tormentor like a hurricane. The sickening crunch of fist smacking bone sounded half a dozen times before Wade went limp.

Lacey went limp too as the world spun and her breath caught in her chest. She'd faced down death without panicking, but now that it was over, she couldn't breathe, couldn't see, couldn't stand. She dropped the shotgun and buried her face in her hands, her breath rasping painfully in her chest.

Moments later, she was lying on the ground with someone bending over her. She blinked, trying to bring the face into focus.

"Shh." It was Chase. "You're all right. There's nothing to be afraid of."

"Not now," she said. "But there was. I thought he was going to…"

She couldn't finish.

"He won't," Chase said. "He won't ever. He's going away for a long time, Lacey, and he'll never bother you again. Trent testified, hon. It was in the paper. It's over."

The rush of relief told her more about her fear than the panic attacks ever had. Without Wade out there, stalking her, the world suddenly seemed safe. Especially right here, right now, with Chase bending over her and Cody behind him, knotting the barely conscious Wade's wrists behind his back with Captain's reins.

"Galt," Lacey said, glancing over at the huddled figure of the old man. "Oh my God, Galt. I think they killed him."

"They didn't kill me." Galt sat up, putting a hand to his head and staring at it when it came away bloody. "What do you think I am, some kind of pansy? They just knocked me out, that's all. It's nothing."

The old man struggled to his feet. Blood streaked the side of his face, but his eyes were glimmering hard and mean as ever as he held out a grasping hand. "Give me my gun. I'll shoot the whole lot of you." He stomped toward the front of the cabin and pointed down at the dirt. "Look at that. All those ruts from your goddamn four-wheelers. Ruined my perfectly good land."

Chase decided now was not the time to argue the merits of Galt's played-out acreage. "Sorry, sir, but you're hurt. We need to get you to a doctor."

Galt shrugged him off. "I'm fine."

"Just let us drive you home, then. I'll get the truck."

"All right," Galt muttered. "Didn't have dinner yet. Guess we're skipping it tonight. Guess it doesn't matter to any of you if an old man starves to death."

"It's just going to be late, that's all. I'll get the truck." Cody grabbed the keys from Chase. "You stay with Lacey."

When the pickup's headlights fell across Galt's face, Chase realized how pale the man was. Wade and Janice really had almost killed him, and yet the man was worrying about dinner. Old age and grief had shriveled Galt up like a strip of rawhide, but it had toughened him too.

"I'm driving you home. Then we'll see about dinner." Chase seized Galt's arm in a no-nonsense grip that didn't allow argument. "Let's bury the hatchet for tonight, okay?"

"I'll bury the hatchet," Galt muttered. "Bury it right in your goddamn head."

Lacey laughed, and though there was an edge of hysteria to it, there was still a note of the carefree girl she'd been. She'd laughed a lot when he first knew her, but he realized now he hadn't heard her laugh in the whole time she'd been at the ranch.

The thought made him ache. She'd never learn to like it. She'd been miserable there.

She was safe, she was free, and now she could live the life she wanted. But he was pretty sure he wouldn't be around to watch.

CHAPTER 44

"I'm used to a hot dinner," Galt grumbled. Lacey had done her best with the sandwich meat Pam had stocked in his refrigerator for emergencies, but he poked at his meal like she'd served him day-old roadkill. "Don't like ham, neither."

"Well, I'm sorry we can't feed you in the style to which you've become accustomed," Chase said. "But you might remember it was me who got you accustomed to it."

"Wasn't you," Galt said. "Your sister made you do it."

Chase turned to Cody, who was slouched in a dinette chair, his eyes fixed on the TV. The guy had spent two hours closeted with the state cops. They'd spent as much time with him as they had with Lacey.

There was something going on with the guy. He'd come through tonight, but doubt had been simmering in Chase's mind for months, doubt and guilt. He shouldn't have taken Pam's word for it that the guy was trustworthy. He wasn't protecting his sister or his niece the way he should. It was obvious Cody had a past, possibly a shady one.

"Speaking of my sister, I need some answers from you," he said. "How did you know that woman, anyway?"

"I didn't." Cody shifted uncomfortably. "Not until that day in the café. I guess Wade did a background check and he, um, found out some stuff about me. She was working with Wade, 'cause her father was involved in the whole scam and she was trying to protect his reputation. He's some senator or something."

"Senator Carrol? She's his daughter?" Lacey asked.

Cody nodded. "So Wade sent her to talk to me. She threatened to tell—well, never mind. I told her no."

"Threatened to tell what?" Lacey slid into a chair beside Galt and picked up her sandwich.

Cody slumped, staring down at his meal. "I was in some—some trouble before I came to Grady. They knew about it, and they said they'd tell Pam about it if I didn't tell them where Lacey was."

"You told them?" Chase's head spun. This was exactly the answer he'd feared. If Cody had betrayed Lacey, he'd have to cut his friend out of his life—his life and his sister's. But the prospect looked a lot more difficult close-up.

"No." Cody flipped off the top piece of bread and plucked a lettuce leaf off the sandwich, setting it aside. "I didn't. I told them to fuck themselves. I don't know how they found her, but it wasn't me. I'd never do that." He replaced the bread and lifted the sandwich, but his appetite seemed to have failed him, and he set it down without taking a bite.

"So what did you do?"

"Nothing." Cody shoved his chair back from the table. "I told you, I didn't tell them. Come on, man, what do you want?"

"I want to know what you did before you came to Grady. I don't know why Pam trusts you with Annie when we don't know a damn thing about you."

"That's Pam's choice." Cody rose to his feet, and Chase was surprised to notice how he filled the small kitchen. He wasn't particularly tall, but he had an imposing presence hidden under his goofy, joking demeanor—a subtle, simmering strength Chase had never really noticed before. "I don't have to tell you anything."

"Look, I trust you," Chase said. "I'm not going to fight you over it or anything. I'd just feel better if I knew."

"Okay. Okay." Cody blew out an aggravated breath. "But it stays here, okay? I'm not supposed to tell anyone. Pam's the only one who knows, and that's 'cause she wouldn't have anything to do with me until she was sure she could trust me with Annie."

Chase nodded, and Lacey followed suit. Galt just kept on eating, ignoring Cody's stare.

"He doesn't talk to anybody anyway," Chase said, nodding toward the old man. "Shoot."

"Okay," Cody said. "I was a cop."

"A cop? Buddy, you've got a knife tattooed on your chest."

"I was undercover. Busted a branch of a cartel in Texas, and they figured out it was me who got 'em popped. Feds sent me out here so they wouldn't kill my ass." He grinned, and suddenly he was back to being the Cody Chase knew. It all made sense now. The rough exterior, the good-guy heart.

"Witness Protection loves towns like this." Cody turned to Lacey. "You made a good choice for a hiding place."

"Not good enough."

"No, but that Simpson guy would have found you wherever you went. That was one sick, determined dude. What'd you do to him, anyway?"

"I said no."

"Figured it was something like that."

"I'm surprised he never killed anybody," Chase said.

Lacey put down her sandwich. "He did." She stared down at her plate, and when she looked back up her eyes held such a heartbreaking combination of sorrow and pity that he wanted to take her in his arms and comfort her.

But then he realized the pity was for him.

"He did," she whispered. "Oh, Chase. Your dad—he didn't commit suicide."

She was looking at Chase like she expected him to yell or throw something or break down and cry, but all he felt was relief flooding into his heart and breaking down years of shame, distrust, and despair. He'd known his father would never take his own life. Everyone else figured losing the land would be enough to make his dad fall apart, but Chase had known he was stronger than that.

"He confessed," Cody said. "With a little encouragement. He's a talker, that one." A faint shadow of his usual grin crossed his face, but he sobered immediately.

"Your dad figured out Bradford was bribing government officials. What he didn't know was that some of the cops were part of it too. When he called the police, Simpson told him to meet him at the barn. And…well." His expression hardened and Chase got a glimpse of the cop under the carefree facade.

"Don't worry," Cody said. "He'll pay. He's going away for a long time."

When they finally got home, the ranch kitchen looked the same as it had when Lacey had left it hours before, but somehow it seemed warmer. Maybe it was the golden glow of the light fixture over the sink, or the contrast with the starkness of Galt's cabin. Maybe it was the fact that she'd almost fallen to whatever fate Wade had in mind for her, and she was just glad to be alive.

Or maybe it no longer felt like a prison, because Trent had testified and she was free to stay or go, whichever she chose.

She looked at the bare window and remembered the scraps of curtain dangling at the windows of Galt's cabin, the homey touches that had seemed so out of place on the wide, vacant plains. Someone had made that lonely outpost a home.

She wondered about the woman who had hung the curtains. Had she chosen a life on the land? Loved the wide-open spaces? Or had she loved a man who lived there and sacrificed her own way of living to stay with him?

She remembered Chase's words the last time they'd been in this room. *I love you. I always have. I always will.* The fact that this quiet, private man was willing to put his feelings into words—frank, honest, almost desperate words—meant he was ready to sacrifice almost anything to make their relationship work.

But she had a different sort of sacrifice to make.

It was Chase's own fault, in a way. She'd forgiven him for his harsh words on her first day in Grady, but what he'd said had sunk into her soul, scarred her heart, and twisted her bones.

Go sell yourself to someone else.

Deep down, she'd known she wasn't living an independent life—but she'd always told herself she'd climb out of the ditch Trent had stuck her in somehow, get that real estate license, and start a new life at the heart of her hometown, helping families find homes. Making a difference.

But the truth was, she'd never made an effort to make any of that happen. She'd belonged to her father first, then

Trent. And now she was having a hell of a time resisting the temptation to belong to Chase.

When he came up behind her, his voice was as honeyed and warm as sunlight. His chest brushed her shoulder blades, and his arm swept around her waist.

"Lacey."

She closed her eyes and gripped the edge of the counter as his lips swept over the hollow just behind and below her ear, stirring the fine tendrils spilling from her knotted hair and raising a chill on her skin even as she warmed from the inside.

She turned, thinking she'd press her hands to his chest and push him away, but his lips traced her jawline and found her lips and she fell into him instead, just like she'd fallen into her trophy wife life back in Conway. It would be easy to let Chase carry her away, take her to bed, take her into his life and fold love and comfort around her like a soft flannel blanket.

"Chase," she said. "Wait. We need to talk."

His lips brushed hers. "Not after that kiss. We need to finish what we started."

He turned her away from the window, waltzing her backward across the kitchen floor while he kissed the corner of her mouth, the swell of her cheekbone, the soft spot at her temple. They were halfway down the hallway before resistance crossed her mind, and they hit the bed before the thought fully formed.

"We can talk tomorrow, Lacey. We can do whatever you want. Just give me this—give *us* this—for now." He hiked himself up on his elbows and looked down at her. "I thought I'd lost you. I thought he might have…" He shuddered. "I can't imagine the world without you in it."

She smiled. "You lived without me all that time. You'll be fine."

He shook his head slowly, emphatically. "No. Not without you. Even back before you came to Grady, I knew you were there in Conway, and that was all I needed. I never thought..." He bent and kissed her cheek, brushing her hair away from her face. "I never thought I'd have you here. But I don't ever want to live in a world without you in it. You don't have to be with me. You just have to *be*."

She wondered for a half-second how she'd wound up sprawled on the bed beneath him, but she loved the way he was looking at her, and suddenly she didn't wonder anything except how she'd ever be able to leave him.

He was an honest man, and when he'd said he loved her, he meant he loved her forever. *I don't do flings*. That statement defined him, his serious view of the world, his loyalty, and his love. She could depend on him the rest of her life, whether she stayed or left. It was her choice.

She looked up into his eyes and felt all her resolutions wavering, fading in the light of his love.

"I'll think about it tomorrow," she said.

The quote from Scarlett somehow separated this moment from the rest of their lives. She felt like she was hovering in the space between her old self and something new, a space that didn't have anything to do with who she was or what mattered or what she could, would, or should do. This moment was about her and Chase. Nothing else.

"You're not falling, Lacey," he said. "You're flying. It's just that you're flying toward me."

She reached up and set her palm against his chest, savoring the warmth of his skin, the slow, steady beat of his unchangeable heart. "No," she said. "I'm falling. But that's okay."

He kissed her again, and she felt like she really was falling, out of the world and into love. Grady, the ranch, the horses, the horror she'd been through with Wade—it all seemed small and distant compared to the feelings for Chase that were warming her from the inside out. She closed her eyes and let go of everything but the feeling of being with him, the sensation of touching and being touched.

He pulled away from the kiss and sat up, stroking her hair once more before he set to work on her blouse. His eyes were serious as he undid the delicate buttons and pulled the thin fabric aside. Her jeans were next. As he frowned over the button fly, the touch of his fingers made her close her eyes and toss her head. He was hurried and clumsy, and she finally helped him, shimmying her hips to reveal the thin lace panties she'd put on that morning. It seemed like it had been days since morning, when she'd sorted through her suitcase, picking and choosing, passion and rebellion building low in her stomach as she thought about what to wear.

He slipped his hand under the lace just like she'd hoped he would, and her body sparked and flared, thrilling at his touch. She was ready, more than ready, but he seemed determined to take his time, tugging the panties slowly down her legs, then going to work on the clasp of her bra. She wanted to help him—hell, she wanted to rip her clothes off and jump his bones—but he seemed so mesmerized by the revelation of her bare skin that she let him do it his way.

But his way seemed to consist of removing her clothing unbearably slowly, and then staring at what he'd revealed. Running his hands over it until her skin prickled and her nipples peaked and ached, and then staring some more. She'd never felt so appreciated, but she was frustrated too.

"Please, Chase. I thought you wanted to finish what we started."

"I do. But I want to take my time." He lifted her bra away, first one cup then the other, and slid the scrap of lace off the bed and onto the floor. Running his hand down the slope of her breast, he swept his palm over the hard-budded nipple and traced the ripples of her ribs and the soft swell of her belly. She opened herself to his touch as his hand slid down into the valley between her legs, but it only brushed her curls and kept on going, stroking the muscles of her thighs, the soft spot behind her knees, the tender arch of her foot.

"I thought you wanted to finish it *today*," she said.

"I don't want to ever finish it," he murmured. He stroked the arch of her foot with one finger, and she wanted that finger everywhere, on her and inside her, especially inside her, where she was welling over with hot slick heat, anticipating what was coming.

At least it might be coming. Eventually.

Chase sat up beside her, still serious, and moved one hand over her breast, cupping it in his palm running his thumb over the nipple. Bending down, he licked the slick aureole, his tongue teasing the hard peak before he closed his lips around it and sucked gently, his tongue still swirling over her skin in a complicated dance that made nerves dance at the surface of her skin, flickering signals running from her nipples all the way down to the ache between her legs.

She arched her back and groaned. This was what she needed, what she had to have. Coming close to dying had made her want to live in a new way, experiencing every-thing, savoring every sensation. His tongue teased her nipple while his lips tugged at it, and she thought she'd explode if he didn't touch the other one. She wanted him, even more than she'd wanted him in the office, even more than she'd wanted him in the motel, and she wanted him in a new way—rough and hard and fast. She wanted him to take her, own her, but damn if he hadn't chosen this time to be tender.

Grabbing his hand, she pulled it over her breast and pressed it there, guiding his fingers until they closed around the tight bud and pinched away the unbearable ache.

"Chase, give me *more*." She cupped her breast and pushed it into his hand until it hurt, tossing her head back and arching her back, opening her body to him in full sur-render that asked for nothing and demanded everything. "Please. I need you to touch me *hard*."

He made a hoarse, helpless sound in his throat and rasped out, "I don't want to hurt you, Lacey. I can't ever hurt you." But what she'd said seemed to push a button some-where that flicked him from "on" to "high" and suddenly he was all over her, breasts to belly to between her legs, his fingers rough, his tongue and lips greedy. He took what he wanted, tasting and teasing, raking her tender skin to a hot flush.

His breath was harsh, and she could feel him trembling as he struggled to control himself. She knew he wanted what she was offering, wanted to take her fast and hard. She knew he was barely able to keep from shoving himself into her like an animal, and it was a testament to his love that he was trying to be tender. But she let out a growl and pulled his mouth down to hers, letting a deep, swirling, tugging kiss tell him what she wanted, and it seemed to flip a switch that set him loose. He pulled away just long enough to shed his clothes and toss them away, and then his hands cupped her hips and he forced her over, belly down. His teeth grazed the back of her neck as he pushed against her, his erection unbelievably hard, his touch insistent.

She hiked herself up on her knees, offering herself, and he slid against her but not into her, until she pushed back against him and wiggled her hips just right. He slid inside with a sharp intake of breath, then lost all his hard-won scruples and pumped fiercely into her, taking her with no holds barred, no filters, no rules.

She rocked forward and back, forward and back, and finally he reached up and grabbed a fistful of hair and took her like she wanted to be taken, fast and hard and almost brutal. She felt owned and mastered and realized this was the one way she could let a man dominate her—the only way. She'd offer herself this way and slake that need to give herself to a man, and then she'd walk away with all the pieces of herself intact, the need fulfilled, her satisfaction freeing her to find herself.

He tugged her head back and his breath rasped in her ear as he slid home again, his free hand guiding her hips and snugging her hard against him while he pushed himself into her over and over. He stroked her hip, then slid his hand down to stroke the heart of her, his finger slipping over the wet, slick skin until he found the spot, *the spot*, and rubbed it hard and fast while he thrust until heat spiraled from her center and plumed inside her like a typhoon wave that knocked her off her feet and tumbled her over and over in an unrelenting sea of love and need that washed away the fear and the caution and every rational thought she'd ever had, freeing her to revel in the feeling of release.

For some reason, the rough, animal joy of it made her love him so hard it hurt, and she almost cried when he stiffened and groaned with his own release.

They slumped together on the bed, exhausted and limp with no secrets possible between them. She turned over and pulled him close, nuzzling into the hollow at the base of his throat, breathing in the scent of him. She felt like she'd broken a code, unlocked a door, and freed herself from prison. Tomorrow she'd wake up to the world with a new kind of strength. She'd find her own way, but she'd always come back to Chase, maybe not right away but someday soon, because eventually the hunger for what he gave her would be too much and she'd need to do this again. And again. And again.

Later, she woke in darkness and felt his hand sliding over her body. Turning in his arms, she kissed him and they made soft, sweet love that was so tender and pure, she vowed to forget it as soon as day came, because if she remembered how sweetly he'd touched her, she'd never be able to leave.

CHAPTER 45

IN THE MORNING, SHE EASED OUT OF SLEEP SLOWLY, blinking and confused and exhausted. Chase was beside her, his hand stroking her hair, his eyes on hers and filled with love and promises that made her bolt upright and flail around for cover. She slipped on his shirt while she hunted around for her own clothes, finding her bra hanging on the bedpost, her panties on the floor. He watched her with a half smile on his lips that made her heart ache. She had to go. She had to be herself before she could be his. She tugged on her jeans and tried not to look at him, then left the room without a word.

"We need to talk," she said over breakfast.

"*You* need to talk," he said. "I'm fine."

She stared down at her cereal, determined not to meet his eyes. If she looked at him, she'd give up. She'd stay. She'd link her life with his and never make it on her own. "I don't know what to do, Chase. I-I shouldn't stay, but I can't go."

"You have to stay," he said. "I need you. You need me. We're good together, and you belong here."

"I don't belong here," she said. "I'm not good at this life. If I stay, I'll just be dependent on you. I need to make a life of my own."

"You already did."

She looked up, forgetting her resolution. His gaze was open and honest as ever.

"You don't depend on me, Lacey. Not now, not ever. Just

because we're together doesn't mean that I own you." A grin flashed over his face. "Well, except when we—you know."

She thought of the night before and flushed.

"This *is* a life of your own, Lacey. You barged in and made it your own, because God knows, you own every inch of me. You're not giving up. You're taking over." He shook his head in wonder. "Look at my life since you got here. I had to fire my only employee. My horse is lame. My house is suddenly way too big for just me, and that bed in there? Way too wide. I can't sleep there by myself. Not anymore."

She stared at him, thoughts tumbling in her mind. She wasn't quite awake yet. Was he accusing her of something?

She frowned. "It's not my fault you had to fire Krystal," she said. "She was the one who screwed…"

He put a firm finger to her lips, looking pained. "Don't say it. I don't want to think about it."

"But I didn't make her do that."

"Okay. I'll give you that. But the rest of it?"

"I don't know. The horse wasn't really my fault."

"Okay, maybe not. But here's what *I* know. My life was finally in order. I had my land, my house, my business— everything all arranged. Solid. And then you came in here and scrambled it all up."

"Chase, I didn't ask you to…"

"Yes, you did. You asked me to help you. And I did."

He had, she realized. He hadn't just helped her; he'd saved her. And he'd saved her from herself, making her see what she'd become—a limpet, a barnacle, dependent on others for her very survival.

She really did owe him her life. Her new life.

The one she'd made, here at the ranch.

He reached over and took her hands in his.

"You don't have to stay here, Lacey. You're free to go wherever you want. But I was thinking maybe you'd want to go to Grady."

She thought of Cody, of Pam, of Annie. Galt, too. Her new makeshift family of friends. "I do want that."

"So go. Go to Grady every day. But come home to me at the end of it."

She shook her head. "But the horses, Chase. The whole ranching thing. I'm just not cut out for that."

"And I'm not cut out for a life in town. That's what makes it so perfect."

She went back to her cereal, stirring the sodden flakes into the milk. She didn't see how leading completely incompatible lives made anything perfect.

"Lots of ranch wives work in town. And I need somebody to run the car lot." He raked a hand through his hair. "Look, I know it's not what you want for the rest of your life. But you could go to school too. Cheyenne's not that far. You can get that real estate license, and by the time you're ready to start selling houses, you'll have practiced on the cars. Everybody here will know you. Love you. You'll be the heart of the whole town. Really, Lacey, you will."

She looked up at him. The car lot. She could do that. She'd gotten so accustomed to being a prisoner at the ranch, she'd forgotten there were other options—better ones. Working at the car lot would be the kind of job she'd imagined. She'd keep things organized, make decisions, help people. She'd matter—and at the end of the day, she'd come home to Chase.

After school. She wasn't going to let that go again. She was going to make sure it happened.

But it would all still depend on Chase. On a man.

"Chase, I'm not selling myself to a man again. Not even you."

"You're not selling yourself to me. Hell, I'll sell myself to you if it'll help." He grinned. "My heart and soul, for more nights like that." He reached over and took her hand, his tone softening. "Remember that night we looked at the stars?"

She turned away, as if there was something captivating happening outside the side window. "Yes."

"Remember the next day, when I said I always used to wonder how they looked from Tennessee?"

She nodded, turning slowly to look at him.

"I lied. That wasn't what I was wondering. What I was wondering was how they looked to you. I used to think maybe you were looking up at the same stars, and feel like maybe that was a link between us. It wasn't much of a link, but it was something."

She blinked, slowly, as if she was having trouble absorbing what he was saying. "But you hated me. When you recognized me, you looked at me like I was the Antichrist."

"I was scared."

She remembered how he'd looked, tall and brawny, with his arms folded across his chest and that arrogant up-and-down stare. "Scared of what?"

"Scared you'd take away my world again."

"Chase, it wasn't me. It was my husband." She clenched her fists. "My *ex-husband*. I had nothing to do with your father losing the farm. I did *not* take away your world."

"*You* were my world. And you kissed me, and then you married someone else."

Lacey stared at him. "What do you mean, I kissed you?"

He looked away. "That night I drove you home from a party. You were drunk."

Oh, shit. That was how she'd hurt him. "I'm—oh my God. Chase, I don't even remember."

"That explains a lot. Like why you married Trent even though—it was a great kiss, Lacey. Pretty much the highlight of my life." He smiled and shook his head. "Pathetic, I know."

She wondered how a man who could speak so directly could have nursed a secret love all these years and never said a word, never tried to contact her. The fact that he'd tried to push her away when she'd walked back into his life just showed how much she'd hurt him.

"Why didn't you say something?"

"You married Trent."

"But before that..."

"I guess I'm not much for words," he said. "But I was there for you, wasn't I? When you needed me, like with Wade, didn't you ever notice I was always looking out for you? I never stopped thinking about you."

She smiled. "If you weren't such a nice guy, that would be creepy."

He laughed. "I guess it would."

She looked down at her lap. "I feel bad that I didn't know. That I didn't think about you. If I'd known..."

"But you did think about me."

"When I needed help."

"That's all I want, Lacey. I just want to be the one you turn to."

"You are," she said. "You always were. It just took me a really long time to turn."

A month later, Lacey found herself tugging awkwardly on Captain's reins, struggling to steer him around the first turn in the homemade barrel racing course Chase had put up for Annie. The horse's mild ligament injury had fully healed, but Lacey's riding hadn't improved much.

The horse veered to the left. She overcorrected, steering him too far to the right so they were reeling around the ring like a couple of drunks. Annie swallowed a giggle as the normally cooperative Captain stopped dead and laid his ears back, finally fed up with his rookie rider's conflicting signals.

"You're doing fine, Aunt Lacey," she said. "Just think, you used to be scared of horses. And now you're a barrel racer."

"Not really." Lacey straightened in the saddle and poked Captain with her heels, urging him on. He plodded toward the barrel at a slow walk. "I'm not breaking any records here."

"No, but you're doing it," Annie said. "Now rein him to the right."

Lacey slanted the left rein against the horse's neck and managed to steer him around the barrel in a reasonably tight circle.

"See? You're doing good."

Lacey poked Captain with her heels again, since he'd stopped to wait for her command. She suspected he could run the course perfectly on his own, but her riding was so bad he couldn't figure out what she wanted. He took her to the next barrel and dutifully plodded around it, then followed the standard cloverleaf pattern to circle the third. He would have done it just as well with no rider at all.

"This is the fun part! Now spur for home!" Annie crowed.

But Captain didn't need spurring. This was apparently his favorite part of the race too. Lacey felt his muscles bunch beneath the saddle, and he shot off like a cork from a popgun, stretching out and flying for the gate while she hung on to the horn. Only after they'd passed through the gate did she manage to pull him to a stop.

"You did it, Aunt Lacey! That was awesome!" Annie ran up and took the reins, leading the horse to the hitching rail. "It was fun, right? You don't even think about falling anymore."

Lacey arched her leg over the horse's rump and lowered herself to the ground. Annie was right. She'd kind of enjoyed the run at the end just like she used to enjoy cheer stunts. Falling wasn't really so bad. There was always a way to pick yourself up and start over, a way to gather the reins and take control again.

She watched Chase step out of the barn and into the sunlight, a battered hat shading his eyes. He was all cowboy now, spending all his days on the ranch and even managing a growing herd for Galt. Lacey's cowgirl learning curve was a long, hard-won slope, but the car lot was thriving under her care, especially now that she'd hired away one of Jeb's mechanics to help out in the evenings while she drove down to Cheyenne for school. Jeb had hired Krystal again, and she'd become a combination receptionist/bridezilla as they prepared for their wedding.

"Uncle Chase is going to be so proud of you." Annie hauled the saddle off the horse's back and set it on the fence rail, then lifted the big horse's hooves one by one, clutching them between her knees as she cleaned them with a pick.

"I didn't do it for Uncle Chase," Lacey said. "I did it for me."

Chase strolled over and slung an arm around her shoulder, tugging at a lock of hair that spilled out from under her rakishly tilted cowboy hat.

"I know," he said. "That's what makes me so proud."

ACKNOWLEDGMENTS

I've never been much for touchy-feely, self-absorbed, Oprah-type navel gazing. But I've surprised myself by climbing on the "gratitude journal" bandwagon lately, listing a few things I'm grateful for every morning.

Right on top of today's list is the chance to make my gratitude public by writing these acknowledgments for this rerelease of my fourth published novel.

I was fortunate enough to find the right agent and the right editor for my first published book. Through ten subsequent books, agent Elaine English and editor Deb Werksman have helped steer my career and made my books the best they can be. It's rare to find kindred souls on the first try, and I know how lucky I am!

I'm always grateful for the support of my tall, dark and handsome husband, Ken McCauley, who gives me love and support every day while providing me with inspiration for scenes that are sometimes funny, sometimes spicy, but always romantic. Even my sexy cowboys can't beat the real thing.

I have many wonderful writing friends who help me navigate the rapidly-changing world of publishing and offer advice on craft, including Mary Gillgannon and Amanda Cabot, who are my spiritual sisters, I love you both. And thank you to Janice, formerly of Barnes & Noble Thornton for being a good sport about playing the villain!

Most of all, I'm grateful to have readers who let my

cowboys into their lives and make them come alive. Thank you, from the bottom of my very grateful heart.

I can be reached through my website at JoanneKennedy Books.com, or on my Joanne Kennedy Books Facebook page. I share writing news there sometimes, as well as pictures and stories about my life on the wild edge of Wyoming. I love to hear from readers and hope to see you there!

ABOUT THE AUTHOR

After dabbling in horse training, chicken farming, and organic gardening, **Joanne Kennedy** ran away from home and ended up in Wyoming, where the unique blend of past and present inspires her to write contemporary Western romances with traditional ranch settings. She is the author of ten novels, including the RITA-nominated *One Fine Cowboy* and *How to Handle a Cowboy*, which was named one of *Booklist*'s "Best Romances of the Decade."

She lives in a secret mountain hideout on the Colorado border with three dogs, two cats, and her husband, who is an airline pilot and volunteer fireman. When not reading, writing, or loving a man in uniform, she obsesses over birds, horses, wildflowers, and squirrels.

Joanne loves to hear from readers and can be contacted through her website, joannekennedybooks.com.

COWBOY SUMMER

Fall in love with Joanne Kennedy's sweet and sexy cowboys in the brand-new Blue Sky series!

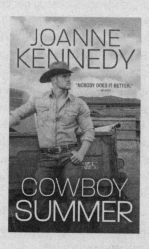

Jess Bailey left Cade Walker years ago, trading small-town simplicity for city sophistication—but she's still a cowgirl at heart. She heads home when her dad announces he's selling the ranch, and comes face to face with all she left behind. As for Cade, he's ready to win back the woman he still loves—but can she really abandon the career she worked so hard to build?

"Get set for the ride of your life."

—Fresh Fiction for *How to Wrangle a Cowboy*

A COWBOY STATE OF MIND

The good folks of Creedence, Colorado get behind Creedence Horse Rescue in a brilliant new series from Jennie Marts

Scarred and battered loner Zane Taylor has a gift with animals, particularly horses, but he's at a total loss when it comes to knowing how to handle women. Bryn Callahan has a heart for strays, but she is through trying to save damaged men. But when a chance encounter with a horse headed for slaughter brings Zane and Bryn together, they find themselves given a chance to save not just the horse, but maybe each other...

"Full of humor, heart, and hope...deliciously steamy."

—Joanne Kennedy, award-winning author, for *Wish Upon a Cowboy*

For more info about Sourcebooks's books and authors, visit:
sourcebooks.com

BIG CHANCE COWBOY

At Big Chance Dog Rescue, even
humans get a second chance

TERI ANNE STANLEY

After a disastrous mistake disbands his army unit, Adam Collins
returns home to Big Chance, Texas. He just wants to sell the
family ranch, set up his sister and grandfather with the funds, and
then ride off into the sunset. But when an old flame asks for his
help training her scruffy dog, he can't say no. As his reluctant heart
opens up, the impossible seems possible: a second chance with
the woman he's always loved in a place where he, his friends, and
the other strays who show up can heal—a place to call home...

*"A real page-turner with a sexy cowboy, a sassy
heroine, and a dog that brings them together."*

—CAROLYN BROWN, *New York Times* **bestseller**

For more info about Sourcebooks's
books and authors, visit:
sourcebooks.com

WHEN TO CALL
A COWBOY

Rekindling old flames can be dangerous, but June
Faver's Dark Horse Cowboys are up for anything

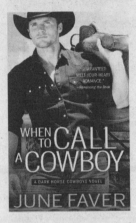

Beau Garrett may look rough around the edges, but under that
exterior beats a heart of gold—a heart that was broken when his
high school sweetheart disappeared days before graduation...

When a family emergency calls Dixie Moore back to her
hometown, she brings with her an explosive secret that could
divide them forever. But Beau's never forgotten the fiery-haired
girl who turned his world upside down, and he'll do anything to
make up for lost time and win Dixie back for good.

"Guaranteed melt-your-heart romance."

—Romancing the Book for Do or Die Cowboy

Also by Joanne Kennedy

Cowboy Trouble
One Fine Cowboy
Cowboy Fever
Tall, Dark and Cowboy
Cowboy Crazy
Cowboy Tough

Cowboys of Decker Ranch
How to Handle a Cowboy
How to Kiss a Cowboy
How to Wrangle a Cowboy

Blue Sky Cowboys
Cowboy Summer